GLASS CEDARS

GLASS CEDARS

A NOVEL

KATHERINE SAAD FEGHALI

NEW DEGREE PRESS

GLASS CEDARS
A Novel

ISBN   979-8-88926-683-9   *Paperback*
          979-8-88926-684-6   *Ebook*

Glass Cedars is historical fiction. Resemblances to any person, living or dead, is coincidental. Certain places, events, and public figures are mentioned in the context of the story.

For

Charles, who in spite of many cold nights,
never wavered in his love for and faith in me;

All of my unbelievably wonderful children;

My dear parents, family, and to the ultimate giver,
my Teta.

CONTENTS

———

PROLOGUE

BEIRUT, LEBANON
1975

Fear can conquer with a sudden strike or in small, creeping steps. Once it enters, it will never leave.

—*MAYA*

A dark figure hovered over my bed. Shards of light filtering into the room backlit her shape. I turned over. No matter if she were a dream, a hallucination, or an intruder about to murder us, after another night of intense shelling, fear had rendered me too exhausted to care. I pulled the pillow over my head. A hand snatched it away, forcing me to open my eyes.

"Maya, get up. We must leave before it's too late." Her rapid breathing alarmed me awake.

I tried to focus on her face, but I felt nauseated from lack of sleep as I sat up and rubbed my eyes. My mother tried to keep her voice steady. "We have one hour to get out."

"What?" Why? I wriggled higher, pressed my back into the headboard, and forced myself out of the final remnants of sleep. "Why do we have to leave to the mountains so quickly?"

"We're not going to the mountains. This time is different. It's much more dangerous."

Fear had seeped into my blood over the past months, and now it seemed to freeze under my skin, purging all fatigue. Sweaty on the outside, icy on the inside, the whole thing felt like a dream.

"People say it's going to be a long war," Maman continued. "Amo Fred called this morning. It's no longer safe for him to commute to work. He's going to live in his airport office until things improve. He'll take us with him. It might be our last chance to leave the country. You can bring one suitcase."

She glanced over at my sleeping sister. The fall breeze entered through the shutter slats and blew the white chiffon curtains against the open glass window panels above her bed. My mother took a step in her direction and looked back at me before she gently touched her arm.

We had barely slept the night before; in fact, we'd had little restful sleep since the Lebanese Civil War began to rage around us six months earlier. Huddled together in a back room of our first-floor apartment, we listened to gunfire and explosions all night, every night. Sometimes we sat alone and other times neighbors joined us, each declaiming their analysis of the situation.

The battery-powered radio, our only source of information and the most important object in the room, blasted. Whenever it faded to static, we nervously fiddled with its dial and antenna, desperate for any news of the events happening in the streets around us.

As the sky lightened, the clatter of gunfire outside would taper off but never entirely stop. Oddly, less frequent meant less predictable and more terrifying. At dawn my sister and I would stagger to our beds hoping for a few hours of sleep. This morning, we had gone to bed two hours before Maman woke us.

Maman's determined demeanor seemed to waver as she stepped away from Rima's bed and to the door. With a hopeful look, perhaps wishing something had changed, she flicked the light switch on and off. Nothing. We hadn't had electricity for days. She muttered something under her breath.

"Now hurry. One suitcase, one hour."

She was gone.

I slouched and my gaze darted around the semi-dark room where I had slept almost my entire life. It settled on the series of square interlocking knick-knack shelves on the wall facing my bed. My eyes flicked across each of the seventy-three treasures I had collected over my lifetime—the crystal ballerina, the Limoges miniature tea cup, the glass cedar, and all the others. I had admired and placed each one in a special place.

I turned to the framed batik I made in high school, the furry pile of stuffed animals in the large basket in the corner, the stereo with its real diamond chip needle, the LP record albums neatly stacked on the shelf beneath, the long wardrobes stuffed with the trendy clothes of college girls, and the two windows with wooden shutters closed tightly—one overlooking the main street below and the second the garden at the back of the apartment.

Glass window panes were never closed in those days for fear they would shatter inward in an explosion. I pulled my grandmother's handmade quilt up under my chin, turned my head from side to side and rubbed my face against it. Despite this slow cat-like motion, my eyes still raced around the room, trying to record everything soon to be lost to me.

My sister's crying interrupted my cold, sweaty frenzy. Rima still lay in her bed.

"Maya, I'm scared." She clutched a pillow to her chest, her eyes wide with terror. "We could be killed in the streets on our way to the airport. Lots of people are dying every day. And what's going to happen to everyone we're leaving behind? How can we leave Teta alone? She's our grandmother! How can we do this to her?" Her voice trailed off as if extinguished by the tears dripping from her face through her long auburn hair.

She put into words the fear and anxiety I had heard in my mother's voice.

My body stiffened. I realized we had no other choice. "We'll be fine, Rima. Besides you're with me, and I'm too evil to die." My attempt at humor failed, so I tried to sound confident enough for both of us. "Things will work out. Teta's in the mountains and she has everyone in the village around her. They'll take care of her. Remember her stories about the Ottoman occupation and the world wars? The mountains will protect her. She'll be sad to hear we left, but she'll be happy we're safe and out of this war."

"And how can we leave Selma?" Rima sobbed.

"She and Roger and the baby will probably go to the mountains and stay with Teta." It was the most reassuring scenario I could imagine for our cousin, who was more like an older sister. I knew Lebanese needed hard-to-come-by visas to travel, enough money to sustain an indefinite stay, and the ability to leave their work.

Other names raced through my mind. Like speed bumps in my fast-moving thoughts, they made me slow down to focus on the faces of my two best friends. I wondered how they'd feel when they learned we'd fled. I envisioned Christina and Leila comforting one another with the hope the war would soon end and I'd return.

Suddenly, a frantic but surprisingly logical part of my mind took over, and I felt the urgency of our one-hour schedule. Leaping out of bed, I grabbed all five photo albums from the bookcase at once, threw them on the floor, ripped the cellophane off each page, and snatched out every single picture I had meticulously put in over the years. I reached for one of the two suitcases Maman had placed inside the door of our room, flung it open, fell onto my knees, scooped up the stack of curled up photos, and threw them in.

I stood up, moved to my knickknacks, ready to seize them all when my hands froze. My eyes locked on the glass cedar tree—a gift from Teta when I turned sixteen. I remembered her words: *The cedar is much more than the symbol of Lebanon. It represents who we are—our past, our strengths and our hopes. It is resilient and enduring, unlike our fragile country. This is to remind you of my faith. Your generation will make Lebanon truly like the cedar.*

I slowly raised my right hand and retrieved it from the shelf. It felt cool and slippery in my clammy palm. I rubbed my fingers over its sharp points before gently closing them around it. I slid it into my pocket before I spun around and moved to the closet. I counted a week's worth of underwear and took four changes of clothes, two for cold weather and two for warm, and tossed them into the suitcase on top of the photos. I dashed down the hallway to the bathroom, grabbed my toothbrush and makeup kit. Back on my knees, I slammed the suitcase shut with shaking hands. Twenty years crammed into a small bag.

Rima still lay motionless. "I can't go," she sobbed. "We can't go."

"We have to," I snapped. "We have no choice. If we stay, we might get kidnapped or killed. Get up!"

She whimpered. "I can't move. My arms won't move. My legs won't move. Why can't this just be a bad dream?"

I knelt beside her bed and moved the damp hair from her face. I pulled the top sheet loose and wiped her perspiration. Although she continued to cry, I gently nudged her out of her bed and handed her clothes to put on.

I packed for Rima, and although she was nineteen, I placed the old stuffed monkey she had slept with as a child on top of her clothes in the bag. Our suitcases closed, the two of us stood silently at the door of our room. We dared not give voice to our thoughts. We would most likely never see this place again.

On that October morning, I understood the worthlessness of costly possessions.

Word of our decision to flee the country had spread through the building, and our apartment filled with neighbors. In spite of the crowd, it was quiet. Tears shone on faces attempting to look brave. My mother drew Rima and me away from the people and into the dining room.

Maman, looking thinner than usual, wore one of her nicest suits and black leather heels. Her coiffeur had come to our apartment the day before and her teased hair had definitely not been slept on. The red lipstick on her tightly pressed lips formed a short horizontal line above her chin.

She gave each of us our passport, a wad of one-hundred-dollar bills, a small cloth bag, and two safety pins, instructing us to hide the money in our clothes. "Just in case we get separated." But we knew what she meant—just in case the unthinkable happened, just in case we were kidnapped, or just in case Maman died.

I had never been given such a large amount of money. Almost all transactions in Lebanon were cash, and I knew my parents kept money in the house, including American dollars, but I never imagined such a large amount. Had she withdrawn additional funds from the bank because she thought they might close, given the situation? Had she anticipated our departure?

"I tried to call your father this morning, but the few times I got a dial tone, I couldn't reach an operator." Maman shook her head.

Papa, an engineer, worked in Saudi Arabia. He returned to visit us for a few days each month, and several times a year Maman visited him for four or five weeks while my grandmother looked after Rima and me.

Maman handed us each a piece of paper with three neatly written Saudi Arabian phone numbers: my father's office, his home, and the number of a friend in Riyadh. "Remember, once we make it out of Lebanon, our first priority is to call him. No matter what happens, call him immediately. Poor man, I wonder how he's managing to work when he's worried sick about us."

Before I had time to process her words, she walked away. Rima and I, too scared to cry, silently followed her as she went from room to room, sometimes pausing for a moment longer in one before closing each door as she left.

The cluster of neighbors and friends trailed us out of the apartment and into the hallway, many dabbing at their eyes. My mother locked the door and handed the key to the elderly widow who lived in the unit above ours. She and her maid would clean and remove all of the food. Neighbors still planned to spend some nights in our back bedroom, one of the safest places in the building. The old lady pulled me aside. "Maya, we're counting on you to take care of your mother and sister. Your mother's acting strong now, but she's going to feel the strain, especially after you arrive in New York."

Snippets of conversations filtered through to my ears, and I tried to take in as many as I could.

Tante Lina, our saucy upstairs neighbor said, "When evening comes and we hear shooting and explosions in the streets, I put on my best clothes, jewelry, and makeup. If they take me out dead, at least I'll leave in style."

"Are you serious?" retorted Tante Mona, Maman's best friend. "All I care about is grabbing the night guard for my teeth. I've spent too many nights stuffing a cloth in my mouth so I don't chip another tooth. What pain I have in my ears and jaw from grinding my teeth."

The two middle-aged women stepped forward to hug me as I wondered if I'd ever see them again.

Amo Fred arrived as we walked down the stairs to the building foyer. He tried to act nonchalant, but his car, parked in the middle of the street, had the engine running and the trunk open.

We rushed through the dark, cool, marble lobby and into the bright sunlight, each carrying a handbag and a suitcase. The concierge gawped, too taken aback to even think of assisting.

The morning sun warmed the ancient city. The same sun had touched the land for thousands of years. The sun of the ancient Phoenicians, the sun that had shone on the long line of their conquerors—Assyrians, Babylonians, Persians,

Macedonians, Romans, Byzantines, Arabs, Ottomans, French—the sun, the only indestructible common denominator, shined brightly.

No one spoke as the car sped through the nearly empty streets. Our tension level rose as the car accelerated when we passed groups of armed men. An armored tank belonging to the Lebanese army, which was incapable of defending its citizens, was parked on the side of the road. They were sitting ducks at the mercy of heavily armed militias—groups representing refugees, extreme ideologues, and patriots. I wanted to yell at the soldiers, to beg them to protect us and act strong, but their thin bodies and anxious looks told me they, like the majority of their countrymen, were victims of the agendas of bigger powers. Evil knew how to exploit the fault lines of our nation.

We moved quickly between two worlds: on one side buildings, cars, trees, and empty roads and on the other, the shining blue of the calm Mediterranean Sea. It felt like we traveled through the post-apocalyptic world Nevil Shute wrote about in *On the Beach*—only physical objects remained, glistening but meaningless.

Maman sat erect next to Amo Fred and neither uttered a word. She continuously scanned the landscape, as though looking for danger he might not notice. Rima sat next to me sobbing softly. I wanted to comfort her, but like my mother, I watched our surroundings.

The moment we turned onto the airport road, everyone exhaled simultaneously and the tension eased. All eyes searched for the symbol of safety, the airport building.

"Thanks be to God," Amo Fred muttered while he crossed himself twice quickly. He raised his eyes to the sky for a brief moment and pushed the gas pedal down to the floor.

Beirut International Airport had never looked this desolate. Only a few months ago, it served as a destination for families and groups of teenagers who would gather to greet a single passenger one of them knew, or better yet, make the trip just to purchase the one-of-a-kind soft serve ice cream cones.

The car stopped in front of the terminal, and two men rushed out. One took the cases from the trunk and Amo Fred threw the car keys to the second one, who jumped into the driver's seat and sped away.

"Passports," Amo Fred almost yelled at my mother. We handed them over and rushed behind him into the building, passing chaotic crowds of people trying to get on a flight to anywhere. We followed him into a small office.

"You're fortunate to have current American visas." The ticket agent spoke in heavily accented English as she handed us handwritten airline tickets. "It's a pleasure to welcome the Coury family to our *round-the-world service.*"

For a brief moment, I imagined we were in this busy international hub in a line of happy travelers with tickets to everywhere.

Maman counted out one-hundred-dollar bills. She mouthed the number twenty-four and put down the last one. Amo Fred shifted from foot to foot, anxious to escort us to the plane.

The passengers, who we later discovered had been seated for almost an hour, looked at us nervously as we boarded. Flight attendants rushed us to seats in different rows. Everyone moved quickly, but the plane started to taxi before I managed to take my place by the window.

The man in the aisle seat reached his hand out and helped steady my walk. I flopped down and snapped the seatbelt as the wheels lifted from the ground and the blue sea turned into an aquamarine carpet beneath us. A cacophony of nervous voices drowned out the engine noise. Only two hours ago, I'd been in bed.

"We voted," the man said.

My face must have shown my confusion. "We were ready to leave when an announcement came on and we were asked if we were willing to wait for a woman and her two daughters who needed to be on this flight. Although we were anxious to leave, almost everyone voted to wait."

When I spoke, my voice sounded weak. "Thank you."

"You don't have to thank me. It's our duty to help one another during difficult times. But I wonder how they knew to ask us."

I shook my head. I wasn't going to tell him my Amo Fred was the station manager. More importantly, I would never say my Teta had long ago saved Amo Fred's life.

On that October day, we were the final passengers on the last Pan American flight to leave Beirut. *Round-the-world service* came to an end.

PART I

AMERICA
1975

CHAPTER 1

——

The Atlantic does not sparkle like the Mediterranean. The ocean brushes the shores of a powerful nation while the sea licks at a small country caught in the turmoil of history.

—*MAMAN*

We disembarked in New York and searched for a pay phone and a place to get change. Rima held the bag of quarters while I dropped them one by one into the slot. I think I counted thirty clinks when the operator told me I had three minutes to talk.

"Papa," I shouted. "We're safe. We're in New York."

I handed the receiver to Maman, and she began to cry. Rima and I stepped away. About a minute later, I gently took the phone from her.

"We'll find a hotel tonight and tomorrow try to get a flight to Austin."

"Please deposit more money to continue talking," the operator interrupted.

"Don't worry, Papa. I'll call you soon. I love…" The line went dead.

I picked up both Maman's and my suitcases, and she and Rima followed me to the counter. I needed to inquire about flights and a hotel before I called Papa's cousin, Frida. We knew we'd be welcome to stay with her while we figured out what to do. Besides, we had nowhere else to go.

We had planned to visit her during the summer but at the last minute, Papa couldn't leave his work, and Maman didn't want to travel without him. I'd met Aunt Frida only once, ten years earlier, when she came to visit *the old country*. A successful business woman, she had never married. The elite shopped at her exclusive ladies and gentlemen's stores in downtown Austin.

"Frida," Maman exclaimed when we deplaned the following afternoon, "you never change. You look wonderful."

Aunt Frida had shoe-polished black hair pinned in a neat bun. Her face carried smooth foundation-filled creases and red lipstick meticulously painted beyond her thin lip-lines. A patterned silk dress elegantly sculpted the curves on her slender five-foot-six frame.

"You've been through enough," Frida said. "You need to let me take charge for now."

By the end of the week, through a contact at the American embassy in Lebanon, she obtained official university transcripts for Rima and me. By January, we were enrolled at the University of Texas with all of our credits transferred. I finished my undergraduate classes in a semester and a summer session but opted to receive my degree from the American University of Beirut to avoid having to meet different general course requirements.

Aunt Frida helped me fill out graduate school applications and was disappointed when I chose to go to California instead of remaining with her. Rima decided she didn't want to stay alone at university and took a semester off to travel to Saudi Arabia with Maman. They planned to wait out the war with Papa.

*   *   *

At the end of the summer, Maman, Rima and I flew to Dallas. An hour later, I stood at the door of the plane waiting to take them to London on their way to Riyadh.

"Maya, it's not too late. There's still time to change your mind and come with us or return to Frida's." The plea in Maman's eyes was unmistakable.

"I love you, Maman, and I'll miss you. But I have to give this a try."

She forced a smile. "I know."

Rima cried uncontrollably.

The gate agent approached to tell us all passengers needed to board. I watched them slowly walk down the jetway. They turned around to wave before they disappeared into the waiting plane. I moved to the bank of windows to watch the plane shrink into the afternoon sky. With queasy excitement and painful sadness, I turned around to look for the Los Angeles gate.

"Please extinguish all cigarettes, check to ensure your seatbelts are fastened and your seats are in the upright position. We are making our final approach into Los Angeles." Engine noise muffled the voice.

Through the airplane window, I stared at what I thought were giant parking lots filled with rows of cars. But they were houses. One after another, after another, look-alike houses running on and on. Almost a year after fleeing Lebanon, I still felt anonymous in America. In the crowd I was a faceless refugee, appreciated only by the few who knew me. Were the people in those homes random and nameless, too?

I'd had the most confusing conversation with the middle-aged man in the seat next to me. He asked where I came from and told me he had visited Lebanon when he spent two years in France doing his missionary work.

"Missionary?" I repeated.

"I'm a member of the Church of Jesus Christ of Latter-Day Saints."

"So, your mission was to find people who would later be saints?" I'd turned my whole body sideways to get a better look at him.

"No, I belong to the Church of Jesus Christ of Latter-Day Saints—the Mormon Church."

"Oh, I belong to the Maronite church. You must be part of the Catholic church?"

"No, no. The names might sound similar but they're different." He took off his glasses and rubbed between his eyebrows.

"Oh, how so?" I flipped my long chestnut hair back over my left shoulder. I realized his eyes were the same shade of deep blue as mine. I had been told many of the fair-skinned people in our region are the descendants of Crusaders.

"The prophet, Joseph Smith, established our church. The angel Moroni visited him and revealed where the golden plates were buried, and he translated them into *The Book of Mormon*."

"*The Book of Moron?* What's that?" I thought about the two required years of civilization studies I'd taken at the university in Beirut and tried to remember if Joseph Smith and *The Book of Moron* were in the curriculum. They weren't. *This must really be modern cutting-edge stuff.*

"Mormon," he corrected me. "It's another Testament of Jesus Christ—a record of great ancient-American civilizations—but we also believe in the *Bible*. Now, considering where you are from, you should find this fascinating. Did you know the Star of Bethlehem was seen in both hemispheres? People in the Americas knew when the Savior was born and he later made an appearance upon this continent. You might be interested in finding out more."

"Why would I? My ancestors saw the Star of Bethlehem over Bethlehem and Christ performed his first miracle just miles from where I was born. We were the first to know Christ."

I surprised myself by how defensive I felt, as if Jesus belonged to us, the people of the Middle East, and was somewhat resentful that others wanted to claim He had traveled around the world to walk among them. I realized I probably sounded obnoxious. "On second thought, I would like to learn more. Until now, I thought we exported Jesus to you."

"Why don't you visit our temple on Santa Monica Boulevard? It's serene, spiritual, and comforts those in turmoil." He took a notepad out of his briefcase and wrote down the address. As I reached for the paper, he pulled it back. "Let me add my home phone number. Feel free to call me or my wife, Julie. You're new to the city and you might need something."

"Prayer," I answered quickly. "Prayer for my country is what I need."

I couldn't look at him. I could barely keep my voice steady. I swallowed around the rock forming in my throat in an attempt to control the warm pressure building behind my eyes. Loved ones in Lebanon were always on my mind.

He nodded. "I will."

I felt better. I was taught the prayers of any good person could be answered. I carefully put his contact information in the zipper section of my purse. It was like tucking away an insurance policy.

Christina, a triumphant grin on her face, was the first person I saw when I stepped off the jet bridge and into the terminal at LAX. She wore a large-collared deep blue shirt, tucked into the waist of flared jeans, and her platform shoes made her almost as tall as me. Her long brown hair, parted down the middle, appeared lighter than I remembered.

Christina Karkourian and I said our friendship began the moment we were born. At a young age she called herself Chrissy, and the name stuck. Our parents had enjoyed many happy events together until 1975, when the Civil War snatched away our idyllic lifestyle. Her family fled the country shortly after mine. By then the airport had closed, so they escaped by sea. They made their way to Los Angeles where the Armenian community in Glendale helped them settle. After a few months, her father needed to get back to his job in Beirut, and her mother and high-school-aged brother returned with him. Christina stayed and found a job and an apartment.

"I can't believe you made it to LA. When you said you'd been accepted to grad school, I didn't think you'd actually come."

I smiled. "I had to go somewhere, and this is as good a place as any."

She pulled me into a fierce hug, and my mask of humor cracked. I buried my face in her hair, breathing in its scent. "Besides, you're here, Chrissy. It helps."

We wiped away our tears. Fear and hope vied for dominance in my mind as I followed her on the long walk to the luggage belt. We grinned at one another when several young men stopped and turned to get a second look at us.

"I can hardly wait to show you around. I'm glad tomorrow's Saturday. I've dedicated my whole weekend to you. Wait until you see how beautiful this place is. In many ways it's like Lebanon. In fact, when there's no news on Lebanon, I check the weather in the *LA Times* and feel closer to home. It's almost always the same temperature. And, Maya, there are mountains and water here, just like home. I only wish Leila was with us."

"Me, too. I called her last week. She's going to try and get a visa to visit."

"That would be so fun. I wish it was easier and cheaper to call. But we'll try this weekend."

It took both of us to lift the two suitcases, putting one in the trunk and stuffing the other in the back seat of her Toyota Celica. I wondered how my belongings had multiplied this much in less than a year, but I took comfort in knowing the contents of the cases were useful without having any value to me. My well-wrapped glass cedar was protected in my purse, and my photos were sorted into envelopes in my square hard-shelled, carry-on vanity case.

Christina pulled out a map to show me where we were headed: Corona del Mar. She emphasized the freeways—a way to get anywhere in no time—not factoring in traffic. I sat back and gazed out the window.

"LA looks like New York and Austin," I observed. "How come I know all these names? Are McDonald's and Pizza Hut like viruses? I flew across a continent and everything looks the same. I fly less than five hours from Beirut to Paris and everything looks and feels different. Even if I fly an hour to Jordan, everything changes. Are these states all the same?"

Christina cocked her right eyebrow. "There's stability and beauty in sameness. You'll soon learn to value the common denominator—one language, pride of country, shared goals, and the freedom to express differences in a nonviolent manner. Just think where we'd be now if we'd had more common denominators in Lebanon. People with more in common have less to fight about."

"Isn't standardized boring?"

"Maya, be serious. You know what I mean. Tribalism destroys a country."

The car rolled through the parking lot of an apartment complex and came to an abrupt stop in the number 105 spot.

"Isn't this exciting?" she asked. "We can start a new chapter. Here, we're free."

I looked away from her and out of the window at the cement column. Sadness mellowed my enthusiasm. At only twenty-one, these were supposed to be the fun, carefree years of my life, not a time when war scars were permanently imprinted within me.

I remembered not being able to look to the top of the University of Texas tower. The thought people had been killed by a sniper aiming from there made me sweat. Other students knew what had happened, but ten years earlier, they were children and the event had no emotional context. Loud noises made me jump while everyone else seemed not to notice. If something looked suspicious, I crossed the street or ducked into a building. The July 4 bicentennial celebration was the worst. Rima and I, like the whole country, could not contain our excitement. But the moment the fireworks began, we burst into tears, covered our ears, and ran for shelter.

"Maya, we're here." Her words cut through my thoughts.

We struggled to lug the suitcases up the exterior steps to the second-floor apartment. Even before we entered, I knew exactly what the place would look like—identical to the ones in Austin where my friends lived. *All this sameness. Maybe the beauty takes a while to see.*

When I opened my eyes the following morning, Christina sat at the foot of my bed. "I thought you'd never wake up. This is going to be one of the best days ever. You're going to love Disneyland, and I'm willing to bet I know your favorite attraction. Oh, Maya it's amazing. We need to get there when the park opens and stay until the Electrical Parade finishes."

An hour later, with a small booklet of multicolored tickets and a map of Disneyland in my hand, I tried to take it all in. I'd never been in such a perfect-looking place. Everything appeared organized and clean. I thought about the dusty, drab, streets I'd fled and all of the people who would never experience a Magic Kingdom. I looked ahead and noticed Christina halfway down Main Street. She must have realized I was missing because she came to an abrupt stop and turned around.

"Hurry up, we've got to beat the lines. You'll be happy to know I made a strategic observation. Usually there are two lines and one is often a lot shorter. I don't know why, but I think people are like sheep. They naturally migrate to where others are standing and don't bother to look beyond. Whatever, it works for me."

She grabbed my hand, and we headed to the shorter line of people waiting to ride the Matterhorn. She sat behind me in the bobsled and by the time we climbed out, I'd made a decision.

"Chrissy, I'm going to follow your suggestion and let go. I'm giving myself permission not to worry for a week. No past and no future. And another thing you're right about: I want to ride the Matterhorn again."

"I knew you'd love it."

For the first time I'd experienced fun fear. All I'd ever known was real fear. Spinning around in the giant Mad Tea Party cup in Fantasyland, my magic kingdom happiness mixed with sorrow remembering the people caught up in the upheavals of ancient kingdoms.

We returned to the apartment late at night. We giggled and talked about the parade while Christina rummaged through her purse for her keys. When she unlocked the door, I was surprised to see her boyfriend, my old college classmate from Lebanon, sitting on the sofa.

"Where were you?" Omar growled. He stood up. Blue hues from the TV illuminated his face and bounced off his protruding nose and ears as he took a step in our direction.

"I told you I was spending the weekend with Maya." Chrissy's voice sounded uncharacteristically meek.

As if noticing me for the first time, Omar turned my way. "Welcome to LA, Maya. It's good to have you here. Christina's missed you." He kissed me on each cheek.

"Thanks. It's hard to believe the three of us are here. It's surreal."

By the way he stared at Chrissy, I could tell he wasn't listening. I excused myself and went to the bedroom. I'd kicked off my shoes and had gathered my shower things when Christina walked in.

"Omar wants to go get something to eat and wants to know if you'd like to come?"

"No thanks. I'm tired. I'd rather make a sandwich and watch TV."

She stood for a moment with her head down. "I'm sorry, but Omar wants me to sleep at his place tonight. Do you mind?"

"No, it's fine."

"I promise I'll be back before you wake up."

The apartment door closed, and I stood alone and annoyed, not by the fact she went to his apartment for the night but because he had interrupted our planned time together. I felt disappointed she hadn't kept her promise to spend the weekend with me. I climbed into bed thinking the only two people I knew in California had left me all alone on my second night in this anonymous city. I'd never slept in any place alone in my entire life. Then I remembered the paper from my Mormon friend tucked in the safest part of my purse and drifted to sleep.

Rubbing my eyes, I took a second look at my watch. Noon. I closed my eyes again. The apartment was quiet, and I imagined Christina moving around softly, not wanting to wake me. Fighting the urge to go back to sleep, I dragged myself out of bed and opened the door. Silence. I moved slowly to her room. Empty. I entered the living area. No one. I sat on a kitchen stool.

Christina met Omar our sophomore year at the American University of Beirut. From the beginning, her father, Amo Levon, said, "It's important to be friends with everyone, but never think love will triumph over the difficulties you'll experience if you marry into a different religion." Amo Levon was an Armenian Catholic, and Omar was the only child of wealthy Syrian, Sunni Muslim parents.

Despite being her father's favorite child, Christina ignored him and made sure everyone knew she and Omar were an item. For students it wasn't an issue, but in a society where the majority of university pupils lived at home, families talked, and the more they gossiped, the more defiant Christina became.

"They're a bunch of old-fashioned idiots," Christina liked to say. "What do they know about love and happy marriages? Look at them."

Due to the deteriorating security situation in Lebanon, the university didn't open in the fall of our senior year. They announced a delayed start, but after several postponements, the semester was canceled. Between bombs and snipers, neither students nor faculty could make it safely to campus.

Omar returned to Damascus, where he applied and got accepted for second-semester admission to complete his civil engineering degree at the University of Southern California. Christina, already in Los Angeles, waited for him. When her parents found out, her father stopped speaking to her.

The ringing phone interrupted my thoughts. I answered, anticipating Christina's voice, but instead encountered an elderly lady who had dialed the wrong number. Christina returned at 4:45 p.m. I'd eaten lunch and emptied my suitcases.

"I'm sorry, I—"

"Don't worry about it. I'm fine." I didn't look up. She'd always jumped to Omar's tune. Why did I expect her to change now?

"It's a beautiful day. Let's go for a walk. You'll love the little Corona Beach across the street. We can eat sea urchins."

"Eat what?"

"Come on. You'll see, and I guarantee you'll like them. On top of that, I also guarantee you'll like the cute boys."

Chrissy slowed down as we approached the busy beach road. "Maya, always be careful when crossing this street. Lots of crazy drivers, especially those who have drunk too much beer in the sun."

For a long while we walked in silence. I focused on the waves, embossing their rhythmic sound and motion into my brain. I felt my shoulders drop and became aware my breathing was deeper and slower. The wet sand formed molded cushions around my feet. The salty breeze blew my hair back from my face, and I imagined it entering my head and taking all my thoughts and worries away as it passed through me.

"Are you ready for sea urchins?" Christina's abrupt words brought me back to attention.

We sat on rocks and ate the freshly cracked urchins bought from a man on the beach. For the first time, I turned away from the ocean and acknowledged to myself Christina was right on both counts; the sea creatures tasted creamy and rich, and the boys were definitely cute.

I looked at people relaxed around a bonfire on the beach. They seemed about the same age as us, early twenties. They laughed, sang, and casually drank beer or Coke. I stared at the fire they'd built and fantasized about running through it, being turned into ashes and rising again as they were—carefree, like the phoenix of my ancestors, the ancient Phoenicians.

Christina stood and dusted off her legs and shorts with both hands. We slowly walked along the shore.

"I called my parents this morning." Christina stopped to pick up what looked like a flawless seashell. "My mother was abrupt. No doubt, my father stood beside her. I don't understand him. He needs to come into the modern age; all he talks about is the wisdom of the past. He thinks by not speaking to me he'll make me leave Omar, but it isn't going to happen."

She turned the shell over and ran her fingers along the large crack on the reverse side.

"You know you've put him in a difficult position. You don't have to rub things in his face. You could be more discreet about your relationship with Omar. You didn't have to broadcast to everyone in Beirut the reason you stayed in LA is because he's here."

"That's you, Maya. You're the people-pleaser, not me. I know you do whatever you want, but you're diplomatic."

I remembered the Arabic proverb Teta used to ask us: *Did you come to steal grapes or kill the watchman?*

"I really don't care. It's my life, not his. He keeps trying to control me—like telling me to go to graduate school. Maybe if he didn't want me to go, I would."

"What about your mother? She's in a tough situation—torn between the two of you."

Christina raised her arm above her head and flung the cracked seashell into the waves. As she bent down to pick up another seemingly perfect one, I noticed a large purple bruise on her thigh.

"How'd you get the bruise on your leg?"

She dropped the shell and tugged down on her shorts. "It's nothing. I must have hit my leg when we rode the Matterhorn. We need to go. I have a lot of work to do before tomorrow."

She took a long wistful look at the happy people around the bonfire before turning to run up the sand to her apartment.

CHAPTER 2

———

The haste of life is like grave dirt. Each handful buries my soul deeper and deeper.

—MAYA

We walked back to the apartment in silence, no doubt both thinking about the bruise on her leg. She unlocked the door and asked if I wanted to eat. I shook my head, and she repeated she had work to do. I went to my room and soon fell asleep.

Chrissy left for work at 6:30 on Monday morning, and Omar came at noon to take me car shopping. If I hadn't known him for several years, I would've been very unnerved by his behavior toward Chrissy. I decided not to say anything and just watch closely for the time being.

"We'll go to the Toyota dealership first—where Christina bought her car. Then we'll check out other places. Any idea what you want?"

"Not really. My budget is four thousand dollars, but if I can get something for less, that'd be great."

"We'll soon find out. Christina was determined to buy an American car. She thought it the right thing to do, and it made sense. We discovered Japanese cars offer much more for the same price. Can you believe in some US cars the back seat is an option? Everything seemed to be an option? At Toyota, everything is standard."

He opened the car door, and I bent low to get into his red Corvette. I pulled down on my skirt, wiggled into a comfortable position and reached for the seat belt. The smell of leather and stale cigarette smoke lurked beneath a strong scent of musk.

Omar and I had been college classmates for almost a semester at the American University of Beirut (AUB) before I introduced him to Christina. We often hung out with a group of students in the cafeteria—*The Milk Bar*. Omar was handsome, intelligent and fun-loving but for some reason, I was never attracted to him. Christina became obsessed the moment she met him. We plotted how we'd get him to ask her out. Although only four years ago, those days seemed far away.

"Maya, remember Dan, the American guy with us in Professor Haidar's Cultural Studies class?"

I turned and examined his profile. I'd never noticed how defined his features were—a straight nose and sharp chin. His lips had a dark purple tint which complemented his olive skin tone.

"The junior-year-abroad student? How could I forget the gentle giant? I wonder what's happened to him." I focused on his long black eyelashes, accentuating dark brown eyes.

"Well, I can tell you. A couple of weeks ago, a friend and I from UCLA walked into a restaurant near campus, and he was working as a waiter. He saw me and almost dropped his tray of plates. He pulled me into a huge hug, lifted me off the ground, and yelled, 'Oh my God; oh my God, I can't believe you're alive.' Everyone in the restaurant watched us."

"Wish I'd seen that." I laughed at the vision of big, blond, six-foot-three Dan lifting skinny, five-foot-nine Omar.

"When he put me down, the manager stood next to us. Dan began a long, impassioned spiel telling everyone we'd been students together in Beirut and how he, as an American, could leave, but his friends didn't have an option. He stepped away, bowed and presented me like a ringmaster introducing the next act. Diners clapped."

"And then?"

"The manager told Dan to take a break and enjoy a complimentary lunch with us."

"That's funny. Is he doing anything else?"

"He's at UCLA finishing his degree in economics. After he left Lebanon he traveled to India because he needed to clear his head before returning home to California. Remember, he grew up in Delhi."

"I'll never forget how he squatted on the floor while we sat on chairs." We broke into laughter. "I tried it a couple of times, but it was uncomfortable. Besides, I think I looked stupid. It's one of those things I'll try again when I'm older and don't care what people think."

"I got his phone number and told him we'd get together before you start classes on Monday."

"Sounds fun." I mentally chalked up another friend in LA—four.

Omar pulled up in front of a dealership, jumped out, and hurried around to open the door and help me out. We repeated this scene five more times until Omar negotiated a deal, even better than Christina's, with the same salesman. I chose a deep blue Toyota Celica. Omar volunteered to bring me back to pick it up in two days.

"Let's get a bucket of Kentucky Fried Chicken and whatever else looks interesting. This way we'll eat as soon as Christina gets back from work," Omar said as we walked to his car. "And how about you drive?" He held the driver's door open.

"Me? I don't know the roads, and I don't feel comfortable driving your car."

"Why not? You're an excellent driver, and you'll be driving on these roads in a few days. You might as well start now."

"But not in a Corvette."

"A car's a car, and they all have insurance." Omar looked relaxed in the passenger seat.

Turning the key in the ignition was the most intimidating part. After that, everything came easy. I marveled at the sense of power I felt driving a car that responded instantly to my commands. Every time I approached a truck or a fast vehicle on the freeway, I quickly and gleefully overtook them. The cars I was accustomed to were not like this. Omar seemed amused. As far as I knew, cars like this were all he'd ever driven.

"Why did the car on the other side of the freeway flash his lights at me? Are there cops ahead?"

"Don't worry about cops. You're not speeding. There's camaraderie among Corvette drivers. We always acknowledge each other this way."

Only Corvettes? I wanted to ask. *Did all high-end car drivers have an affinity for one another?* I pressed on the accelerator. I'd entered a new world.

Back at the apartment, the three of us drank beer, ate chicken, and laughed about car shopping. Omar dramatized our experiences and imitated the salesmen.

"I'll never forget the expression on the face of a salesman when he told Christina the back seat was an option in the American car she considered buying. She said she didn't need it. She'd put a Persian carpet in and her friends could sit cross-legged smoking hookahs while she drove them around." Omar stopped eating his chicken and pretended to smoke a straw.

"Well, I couldn't take any more of *everything's an option*." Christina seemed more relaxed than she'd been over the past couple of days. I figured she was enjoying Omar's mood. It felt like old times.

"I would never have thought I'd buy a Japanese car in America," I said.

Omar proclaimed he had done his good deeds for the year, but I reminded him he couldn't make this claim until we picked up my car. He raised his Coors can. "Here's to Wednesday and the end of my mission." He took a long drink, pushed his chair back from the table and slid lower into it.

"Here's to many more missions." Christina tapped her can against his.

I finished almost the last sip. I hadn't grown accustomed to drinking out of cans and missed bottles. Liquids tasted different in metal. I found it annoying not being able to get the last drop; I could feel it move in the can and could see it, but I couldn't reach it. To make up for it, the aluminum tabs we pulled off intrigued me. People turned them into interesting, useless items like necklaces they never wore and wind chimes they couldn't hear.

When Omar left the apartment after midnight, I went to bed, but Christina removed papers and a calculator from her briefcase and sat down to work. She'd recently been promoted to a cosmetics buyer for the Broadway department stores and had endless paperwork. She never complained, but it always seemed to hang over her head. The one perk I thought made the job worth it were the full-sized samples of cosmetics and perfumes vendors gave her. She had five or six shopping bags stashed in her closet. She invited me to take what I wanted anytime. Every couple of months she'd donate them to a woman's shelter. At the beginning, it was like working in a chocolate factory. I couldn't get enough. But as time went on, I rummaged through the expensive merchandise only when I needed something.

On the third day of my allotted week of no worries, I realized how fast time passed when it wasn't consumed with anxiety. Each time a fearful war thought came into my mind, I would repeat to myself, *Don't think,* and find a distraction.

I looked forward to beginning the semester. I finally had my chance to get a Master of Science degree in Industrial Psychology—ergonomics in particular. However, when classes started, I began to feel isolated. Christina worked all day, and I left to the university in the late afternoon and finished classes at ten thirty. She also worked on weekends and spent more time at Omar's apartment.

One evening I called Dan. We'd spent a lot of time together as friends during the year he lived in Lebanon. We scheduled a day together. His driving directions to UCLA included specific trees as landmarks.

On a sunny afternoon we walked along a campus path. "I guess in many ways we were naïve." I looked up at Dan. "Things in Lebanon were happening all around us, and we were oblivious—cocooned inside our circle of friends."

He draped an arm around my shoulder. It felt comforting.

"Dan, remember how political the student council was?" I put my arm around his waist. "There were Lebanese groups, pro-Palestinian groups, pro-American groups, pro-Soviet groups, and pro-Arab groups. Remember the big fight on campus between Lebanese and Palestinian students when the university actually let the police come in and arrest students?"

"Sure, I remember. I got caught up in the middle of it. I left the library and got hit in the head by a glass bottle someone threw. Fortunately, my friend dragged me back in before the police arrived. But you're right. It was dangerous and we were oblivious. Big powers playing the game of nations."

Dan looked pensive. We walked to a bench and sat.

"Maya, it's beautiful here, but no campus is prettier than AUB. I'll never forget my first day in Beirut. I arrived with a group of students at night. When I left the dorm the following morning, I saw a banyan tree overlooking the Mediterranean, and when I turned around, I saw snow-capped mountains."

"That's Lebanon." My words were wistful. "Remember the time you were so excited to ski in the morning and swim in the afternoon? Exciting things were always happening—good and bad. We couldn't choose to live a calm life like people in America can." I unclipped my barrette, shook my hair loose. "Did I ever tell you about the cruise my family took the summer of my sophomore year?"

"No, you didn't." I loved the sound of Dan's voice, deep with an easy reassuring tone. It reminded me of when life had been safe. "Maya, you're like a magnet, always attracting interesting people and events. Can't wait to hear your story."

"My mother booked the trip. My father questioned the cheap price. She said it was a Soviet ship going to communist countries—Bulgaria and Romania."

He shrugged. "Makes sense."

"Rima and I visited the travel agent to ask if our hairdryer would work. He said luxury ships have dual voltage."

"I'm guessing it wasn't?" He jumped from the bench and assumed the squatting position, the one Omar and I joked about. I watched his body spring slightly before he settled with his bottom a few inches above the ground and his knees below his chin.

"We cleared immigration at the port and immediately realized the *luxury ship* was a Russian freighter outfitted to accommodate about a hundred passengers. For the next five days we ate black bread with sardines for breakfast and other horrible meals. We had no electrical outlets in the cabins and a ping pong table provided the only entertainment." I stopped and watched two girls walk past us. The shorter one looked like Rima—strange, since my story involved her doppelganger. "We spent most of our time talking with Soviet citizens returning home after serving their government in Egypt. Among them, a doctor who hadn't seen her two young children in three years, a dentist, two engineers and a university professor. Their personal sacrifices paled in comparison to the marvels of communism. They gave us copies of the *Communist Manifesto*."

"You didn't read Marx and Engels. Did you, Maya?" Dan bounced like a rubber band.

"Oh, I'm way off the point." I had no interest in a *Manifesto* discussion and looking at him made me feel seasick. "What I want to tell you is, a member of our student council was on the freighter. For the first couple of days, he avoided us, but we eventually came face to face. He simply offered a courteous greeting. We found out he was going to Moscow for the summer as a guest of the government."

"I'm not surprised. The superpowers see Lebanon as a chess piece. It's crazy. Here's this guy attending an American university, elected democratically to the student council and he goes to Russia for indoctrination." He looked up at me. "For me Lebanon is a beautiful memory. But for you, it's home. You can escape, but never leave." He stared off into the sunny day.

I felt an odd mix of angst and comfort from familiar memories. "Do you think it was chance I was born Lebanese and you were born American or was it predestined? Can we change our destiny?"

Dan laughed. "Maya, that's pretty deep stuff. Who knows? But I do know a great place for ice cream, and it's my treat."

During my time in LA, Dan and I rekindled our friendship but I could never have imagined the critical role he would play in my life years later.

* * *

The graduate coursework was plentiful, but not overwhelming. Fortunately, subjects like Multivariate Analysis were intrinsic for me. I became the "go-to" person and assisted classmates.

Donna was one of the students I helped with statistics and she, in turn, reviewed my term papers for grammar and spelling errors. She had raised three sons as a single mother and returned to school at the age of forty, determined to pursue her PhD. We had the same class schedule and spent most of our time on campus together. I'd drive to her house in Long Beach on some of the weekends Chrissy spent with Omar.

Donna had lived her whole life in California, but we joked she must have been Lebanese in a past life. Without my saying much, she seemed to understand my background. When I talked about my small mountain village overlooking Beirut, it felt as though she, too, had lived there. She had read about the university, the city, the people, the religions, the history, but, interestingly, knew very little about the civil war and its politics. California politics was her passion.

"Angela Davis is speaking at a campus rally tomorrow. We should go before our programming class," Donna said one evening as we were leaving campus.

"Who's she?"

"Angela Davis."

"You said that, but I don't know who she is."

"She's a political activist and a feminist. She used to be a professor at UCLA until she got fired because of her leadership in the Communist Party USA."

The following day, the civility of the Angela Davis gathering surprised me. I remembered the flying glass bottles and the flaring tempers when people presented their ideologies at Speakers Corner on the campus in Beirut.

"Donna, I don't get it. How come everyone is subdued?"

"You missed the sixties. The fire is only ashes now. I wish we could get the vigor and passion back. Even our Governor Moonbeam…"

"Who?"

"Jerry Brown. Even he doesn't arouse much excitement."

"I thought you liked him?"

"I vacillate on him. I think it's pretty neat the way he left the seminary, and the state is doing well with his fiscal policy. I kind of like the fact he is dating—but Linda Ronstadt? Just doesn't figure. As crazy as we Californians are, she isn't who I like to see influence our governor. She does too much cocaine—*nose cauterized Ronstadt*."

I knew who Linda Ronstadt was and missed home more than ever, in a beautiful sentimental kind of way, when I loudly sang *Blue Bayou* with her on the car radio. Now, Donna had made her seem like a different person than the voice I loved. I would have to find out more about her and Governor Moonbeam.

"What are you doing this weekend?"

"I don't have any plans. Chrissy will probably be with Omar." I didn't want to sound lonely, but from the way Donna looked at me, I could tell that's how I came off.

"Want to go to Catalina Island on Sunday? We can take the ferry from Newport."

I wanted to jump and shout. I had something to look forward to on the weekend.

* * *

The routine of classes and weekends became comfortable and I began to fit into the rhythm. I made a conscious effort to minimize the time I worried about Lebanon. I managed to get a call through to my parents about every two weeks and limited conversations to three minutes. At $3.15 per minute plus tax, it added up. All international calls had to be placed by operators. This made it almost impossible for them to call me because Saudi operators rarely answered.

The moment my family picked up the phone, I'd hold my breath in anticipation of bad news. As soon as I hung up, I'd leap in the air, knowing they and loved ones in Lebanon were alive. Energy drain and energy surge within moments, at the mercy of news.

I knew Maman was anxious to visit Lebanon. She wanted to check on the family and, if possible, go to the apartment we'd left in such haste. Thinking about it made my stress level rise, but I was helpless. I wished she'd go and return as quickly as possible to spare me the tortured anticipation of constant worry.

Although a tedious process, Chrissy and I tried to call Leila once a month. American operators would try to dial the Lebanese phone number three times and if it didn't connect, the transaction ended, and we had to begin all over again. If we got through, the sound quality was often poor, but we felt intoxicated knowing the war had not touched our friend.

California's beauty, weather, laid-back atmosphere, opportunities, and especially security, made me comfortable. I forced myself to relish it using rationalization. I was attaining my goal of excellent grades and a graduate degree. Regrettably, every time I felt my life was on an even keel, something happened.

One Monday, a few hours before I left to meet Donna on campus for an early dinner, I heard a radio announcer report numerous casualties from a car bomb in West Beirut. I knew Maman and Rima were there and tried to call but couldn't get through. The American operator told me their phone rang several times, but no one answered.

I could tell she felt sorry for me because after several attempts, she spoke with a Lebanese operator who told her the situation was very bad and most of the phone lines were down, but not to worry because the explosion wasn't in the area of our apartment. She reported this and tried to reassure me my family should be fine. I cried at the kindness of two strangers halfway around the world from one another, bonded by their profession and their desire to comfort a frightened girl. Despite the efforts of the two women, I couldn't focus and walked aimlessly around the apartment until time to drive to campus.

"Donna, hurry, I have to find a TV." I ran past her at our meeting place. She followed me into a large room in the Student Union building where guys drinking beer watched football. They cheered for the winning team, unfazed by the girl zigzagging through the couches and chairs to the front of the room. I reached for the channel dial and faced the thirty or forty pairs of eyes focused on me. "We need to watch the news."

Walter Cronkite immediately appeared on the CBS Evening News, and I heard him say, "Lebanon." With wide eyes, I searched the screen for a familiar landmark or face—anything to give me more information. The segment lasted a minute or two or maybe even thirty seconds, but it was more than I could get from any other source, and I had only one chance to hear and see everything. I stood inches from the large screen, oblivious to anything else. No one in the room uttered a word.

When the piece ended, I switched back to the game and moved to the side of the TV, but the mood in the room seemed somber. People looked at me, and I felt I should say something. "Thanks for letting me watch. My family's there." I tried not to cry.

I stood rooted in place. Donna edged her way to me. She put her arm around my waist, and we wound through the football fans to the door. A couple of the guys stood up as we walked past them and voiced sympathy. Another asked if he could do anything to help. Donna thanked them and, as if in a funeral procession, we slowly flowed out of the room.

Back in the food court, I didn't feel like eating and neither did Donna. We sat at a table and watched students walk past us. "I can't believe you did that," Donna finally spoke while we both stared at a guy who had probably broken a record with a foot-high salad. He'd mastered the art of vertically placing carrot sticks around the edges of a small bowl to increase its capacity. "But what I really couldn't believe was their reaction. At first, I was sure one of them was going to yell at you. But other than Uncle Walter's report, there wasn't a sound in the room. I've never seen anything like it."

"Uncle Walter? Amo Walter?"

"Oh, that's how people feel about Walter Cronkite. He's like everyone's trusted uncle. He's an amazing newsman. He's like the *god of news*." She smiled at her words, and we left for class.

* * *

"Dr. Braden, you're never going to believe what Maya just did."

The professor, accustomed to hearing tidbits of news about Lebanon from me, kept up with world affairs. When Donna told him, he put his hand on my shoulder. "Good for you. Those boys need a glimpse of the real world."

Shortly into my second semester, Dr. Braden asked to speak to me after class. I spent the next three hours worried I had done something wrong. As students drifted out of the classroom, he erased the chalkboard, and I waited anxiously. When he realized I stood there, he stopped.

"One of the companies I consult for is McDonnell Douglas—Douglas Aircraft. They're embarking on several new ergonomic projects in the engineering department and need to hire additional consultants. I thought about you. It's full-time work for the next six to eight months but could be extended or become regular employment. I told them you would fit the bill."

"Why would I have to fit Bill?"

"It's an expression." He tried to keep a straight face. "It means you meet the requirements. They're focusing on cockpit safety with new technologies. You have the skills to design, implement and analyze the projects. To give you an idea, digital technology now allows us to replace the bells and buzzers used for cockpit warnings with voice messages, but these need to be tested before installation in an airplane."

An unexpected surge of excitement gripped me. The only work I had done in my field consisted of designing airline passenger safety instruction cards for a tiny engineering firm. This was a leap.

"If you are interested, there's no need to do anything other than let me know." He had a broad smile. Part of it might have been the one he was trying to suppress regarding my question about Bill.

"I'm interested." I tried not to stammer. "I'm definitely interested."

I felt I'd been given a beautifully wrapped gift, and I was almost too scared to open it. Even happiness was tempered by the permanent worry I carried within me about the situation back home. I had worked to achieve this moment of accomplishment. I wondered if this would change the direction of my life.

* * *

"It's a consulting job in the engineering department."

Christina laughed. "I gathered."

"I'm going to work on the cockpit design of commercial aircrafts. Can you imagine that? And I start next week with no interview or anything! This is just like Lebanon—*wasta*—connections. It's who you know!"

"What's the pay?"

"Fifty dollars a day!"

"*What?* That's incredible. I'm so proud of you. You're going to work at McDonnell Douglas. You've talked about this company forever."

"And I didn't even have to ask. They came to *me*," I marveled. "What's the expression about how things happen here and not anywhere else?"

"Only in America?"

"That's it." I raised an imaginary glass. "To Only in America. Where we make things happen—where we control our destiny with hard work."

"And to Maya Coury. Who will probably be the only woman in the engineering department."

CHAPTER 3

———

Life's rampant opportunity taunts inner loneliness.

—MAYA

"Chrissy, I'm nervous. I've never had a real job. I didn't interview so I don't know anyone there. I'm worried about making a good first impression. Will they be nasty to a woman in engineering?"

She leaned forward and rested her arms on the stack of papers in front of her. "You're one of the smartest people I know. You'll figure out how to manage anyone. Why don't you meet me tomorrow night at the store to get some professional outfits. The proper clothes will give you more confidence." Her mouth twitched, and she lifted her chin in a confident pose.

I smiled. "You mean I don't look intelligent and sophisticated now?" I stood up from the dinette chair and posed—hips to the left, head to the right and lips puffed out. Then I tossed my head back and swung my hair like a pop goddess.

Christina laughed. "If I didn't have paperwork to do, I'd say we should go out for a drink but…"

"*Life ends and work doesn't end.*" I quoted the old proverb in Arabic.

"Maya, this is America."

"Are you insinuating life will not end and work will?"

"Okay, okay. Let's go to the new place by the flower shop."

For the first time in a long time, Christina and I enjoyed an evening alone. I avoided any mention of Omar.

Two hours later we made our way up the staircase to the apartment. Through the door, we heard the phone ring. My first thought was of my family. From the way Christina's hand shook as she put the key in the door, I assumed she, too, thought of home. I stayed close to her as she lifted the receiver.

"Where in the hell were you?" I heard Omar's muffled yell.

I stepped away and went to my bedroom, but I could still hear Christina speak in a small, apologetic voice. I wanted to go back and yell at her.

A few minutes later she came to find me. "I have to go see Omar. He's been calling for the two hours, and he's upset."

"We left late—after ten. Couldn't we have been asleep with the phone unplugged? What business is it of his if we go out?"

"He was worried, and I feel bad because it's my fault."

"How's it your fault? Is he your guardian? Do you need to clear every step you take with him? Chrissy, this isn't you. Since when do you let someone rule you?" I felt my face redden, and it was all I could do to hold back and not physically shake her. In my culture women were expected to be more submissive, but I'd never witnessed fear or abuse in a relationship.

"I'm sorry, but I have to go. I'll see you tomorrow evening at the store." She pushed past me and was gone.

I wasn't sure how long I sat on the bed with my head in my hands.

* * *

The vast parking lot at Douglas Aircraft in Long Beach accommodated fifteen thousand employees. I felt fortunate to park in one of the visitor spots next to the building. A guard directed me to the engineering department and into a partitioned area where the ergonomics division was located.

My boss, John Nicholson, waited for me at the entrance to the cubicles. He introduced himself, and I followed him down winding hallways to another department. A middle-aged woman with thinning brown hair presented me with a sheaf of papers to sign. John silently led me back, and we must have passed at least thirty people. He greeted no one. It was a community of strangers.

In his office, he reviewed the project I'd been hired for—work in the simulator with Douglas production and test pilots. "Cathode ray tubes, CRTs, are being put in aircraft cockpits. We need to compare pilot reaction times and errors using this new technology with traditional instrumentation."

I focused on the perfectly spaced pens and mechanical pencils aligned in John's plastic pocket protector, compulsively counting them—seven. I looked back at him.

He continued. "There are three emergency scenarios. You'll know them, but the pilots won't know what's going to happen during the flights."

"Will each set of pilots fly all three scenarios?"

"Yes, in the first phase. Then, depending on reaction time and errors, they might be modified. You'll be in a special seat slightly behind and between the pilot and copilot. All of the flight information will be recorded, but you're to log observations and go through a checklist with the pilots afterward. The hardest thing for you to get accustomed to will be the crashes."

"Crashes? Like in an airplane crash?" I immediately realized the foolishness of my question.

John didn't react. "You'll get used to it. You'll feel the quick altitude drop and see the ground approaching. Then at the very last second, everything will stop. It's nerve-racking at first. The simulator's extremely realistic."

"Sounds neat." *Couldn't you think of something cleverer to say?*

I needed to familiarize myself with the project and make sure I had a good understanding of aircraft cockpits before I began the work. My body was practically humming with excitement, and I wondered if I could wait. "This will be a DC-10 simulator, right?" My third faux-pas.

"This is Douglas Aircraft, and it's what we manufacture here," He replied in a matter-of-fact tone.

"I know, but you have a Boeing model plane on your desk."

For the first time, he smiled. "That's my motivation. Once upon a time Douglas was the leader and then Boeing came up with a plane called a jet. Leadership at Douglas thought the jet was a fad and the flying public wanted a good, sturdy, reliable propeller DC-3. After all, this aircraft revolutionized air travel. Douglas continued to build propellers and Boeing built jets. We've been playing catch-up ever since."

"Do you think you'll catch up?"

"I hope so. I keep this model as a constant reminder." He picked it up, turned it around and placed it down again. "How about we go get some lunch?"

I stood, put my purse strap on my shoulder, and followed him outside. I watched his back as he strode ahead. He seemed around six feet tall and had a medium build. His brown hair was straighter than any I'd ever seen, and I imagined his mother putting a bowl on his head to cut it.

I lifted my nose into the air. "Something smells good." We passed a food truck parked between two buildings.

John stopped and turned to face me. "Never eat from the roach coach." His voice was stern. For the first time, I noticed the unusual color of his eyes—dark green.

In the cafeteria, we joined the long food queue. I ordered at the salad station and the cafeteria lady asked me to wait. She returned from the kitchen with an enormous plastic bag stamped with a number and labeled, "LETTUCE." She cut it open with scissors and another employee helped her dump it into the serving bin. I had never seen anything like this before.

John watched me. "What's wrong?"

"Where I'm from, lettuce doesn't come chopped in labeled bags."

"It's a convenience. How else could they feed thousands of people?"

"Somehow, I suspect the roach coach is more personal."

"And the way it attacks you later is a lot more personal, too. Believe me. I know."

Over lunch he opened up. I learned he was thirty-one and divorced with a two-year-old daughter. He had his master's degree in aeronautical engineering, and he had worked at Douglas Long Beach for three years. He eventually wanted to earn a PhD but wasn't sure he could swing it with his financial responsibilities.

At three o'clock John said I could leave but to return at eight the following morning for a departmental meeting.

At the first one of these fascinating sessions, led by the department head, the discussion on the Ermenoville air disaster perturbed me. Three hundred and forty-six people lost their lives in this fatal DC-10 plane crash. The Turkish Airways flight took off from Orly Airport in Paris, and the baggage handler who latched the cargo door couldn't read the English or Turkish warnings.

"Why warnings and not directions?" I asked John, who sat next to me.

"Greed," the engineer seated next to him said.

I gave him a questioning look and he continued talking. "The door had a design flaw. We knew about this issue two years earlier when an American Airlines flight had the same problem. The Ermenoville scenario was predicted: door closed incorrectly, explosive decompression, passenger floor sucked in, severed cables, rear of plane falls off, and deadly crash."

John continued in a softer voice, "It was too expensive to redesign and replace the latch. Hence it was fixed with pins and warning signs to ensure it was closed correctly."

"Profit trumps principles," the engineer snorted.

"Some safety procedures were enacted as a result of this accident," John said. "Now safety instructions are presented pictorially instead of verbally. In this case, we realized a padlock is a universal symbol. Paralleling a picture of one open and closed with the door is something everyone can understand, regardless of language."

I perked up. "I worked part time for a company in Santa Monica designing pictorial passenger safety information cards to replace written instruction. At one point, Pan Am's safety instructions were printed in eight languages."

"You must've worked for Jim Barringer," the engineer said. "He's the best. You must've gotten some good experience."

"She did," John answered on my behalf.

After the meeting, John handed me a life jacket pack and instructed me to put it on and inflate it as quickly as possible. Instinctively I pulled it out of the plastic package and wore it. I realized I didn't know what to do next.

"Take it off and try this one." He handed me another. I took the first one off and noticed the directions were on the back.

The second one had instructions on the front. However, I couldn't read them because they were upside down. Someone facing me could easily understand what to do. When he handed me the third life jacket, I'd guessed what it looked like. The directions were written upside down on the front, allowing the wearer to lift the front flap and read them.

"We had to testify before Congress for these changes," he said. "The first one you tried on used to be industry standard."

I raised the flap and followed the directions. Poof! What a feeling. I had always wanted to inflate a life jacket.

It didn't take me long to realize John had a wealth of knowledge. It was both informative and fun to ask him questions related to human factors engineering. Over the next few weeks, I hit him with a barrage.

"When is the best time in the morning to drive from Newport Beach to Santa Monica?"

"There isn't one."

"Why are highways signs green with white lettering?"

"Because someone probably liked green."

"Don't people study these things?"

"You'd think so, but no. Traffic has no predictable pattern. Every time we think we're on to something, it changes. As to the highway signs, honestly, I haven't seen any research on why they're green."

My commuting time depended on traffic and could take half an hour or two hours each way. At work, time passed quickly. I became more comfortable and spoke to people in the hallways. On Tuesdays I brought homemade cookies to work and invited people from different departments to share. I learned names and made friends.

Many nights, after working in the simulator for several hours, I'd have trouble falling asleep. The sound of engine noise and the motion of the plane felt real in my head. When I finally conked out, I'd often wake in a cold sweat, reliving a simulated crash. The simulator would stop but, in my nightmares, a gunman held his weapon at my head.

Saturday nights, Christina went out with Omar and didn't return until Sunday. Since I had nothing to do, I often reviewed the cockpit and control tower voice recording tapes. Most were routine, but I wanted to ensure I hadn't missed anything. Once I heard someone in the control tower say, "Lebanon." I rewound the tape, and listened intently.

"Where's she from?"

"Lebanon."

"Where?"

"Lebanon. You know, the place Danny Thomas is from."

"A nice girl. Always smiling and smart as a whip. It's great to have someone like her on a project."

I listened to it again and jotted down *smart as a whip* to ask someone what it meant. I took in a deep breath and leaned back. It was an empty feeling—to be so liked yet so alone. How could this be? I made myself get up and go to bed.

* * *

Christina came home one evening, about four months after I began my job, and said we had to talk. The tone of her voice made me anxious. "I need to move in with Omar. Our relationship isn't as good as it used to be, and I think it's because we're spending too much time apart." Her words came out fast.

I immediately felt abandoned. I pulled out a dinette chair and sat.

Christina remained standing. "I feel bad leaving you. Maybe one of your grad school friends will share this place with you. I'll pay my part of the rent until you find someone, and I'll leave the furniture. Omar will help me move on Saturday. Think you'll be okay?" Her voice went up a notch higher on the last word.

"I'll be okay. I'm worried about you, though." *How dumb can you be?*

"I don't know why you keep bringing up stupid stuff. I love Omar and he loves me. Nothing is wrong. Every relationship has issues to work out. Once we're living together, everything will be fine."

"I know you want to believe that, but it's not true. Omar has a violent side, and you're not acknowledging it." I struggled to keep my voice level. "That's the problem." I looked down at the slushy orange and brown carpet.

Chrissy leaned on the wall. "Let's go out to dinner."

"Not tonight. I've got a report to read for tomorrow." I stood and walked to my room. She followed, but I pretended not to notice and pushed the door closed behind me.

She came in anyway. I lay on the bed, and she sat down on the edge. "I know you must feel cheated. I mean, part of the reason you moved to LA was to room with me. I had no intention of leaving you, but it happened. Please try to understand. Omar's the love of my life, and I want a future with him." She placed her hand on my arm.

I pulled myself up and her hand dropped away.

"Chrissy." I spoke in a slow measured voice. "I'm not upset you're moving out. Things we can't foresee happen, and we just have to deal with them."

She looked relieved. "You're not upset with me?"

"I am upset with you."

"You just said things happen we…"

"Exactly. I said things happen that we can't foresee. I didn't say everything is beyond our control. I didn't say we can't control things. We have freewill. That's why I'm upset with you. You're becoming subservient to a man who isn't treating you right. I'm not dumb. Don't you think I know what's going on? You need to leave him. He's not the right person for you. He's mentally and physically abusing you."

"I don't know what you're talking about. You know Omar is a perfect gentleman. He gets upset when people make stupid mistakes, and I seem to be making a lot lately."

"With me he's a perfect gentleman, but with you he's abusive." I looked into her eyes, and she looked straight back at me.

"You're imagining things. There's no abuse. He gets impatient sometimes, but once we're together all the time, he'll calm down. He'll change. And if he doesn't do it on his own, I know I can change him."

"You're dreaming. Have you ever seen your father treat your mother the way Omar treats you?"

"How can you even compare our relationship to my parents? Do you think they have passion? We do, and you can't isolate behavior. If we're passionate lovers, we're extreme in our emotions. This defines our relationship."

"Passion and violence are different." I could tell she wasn't listening and wished Leila was with us. Maybe together we could have gotten through to her. This time she glanced at the floor when I looked at her.

"Try to keep an open mind, and you'll see the real Omar. I know the real Omar." She smiled. "Now, how about accepting my dinner invitation?"

"I have a report to read…" Not being able to get through to her made me feel tired.

"Life ends and work…"

"Okay, okay, but someplace close."

"I'm thinking Newport Beach."

I never expected Christina to let a man treat her badly, and I never envisioned she would leave me alone in California. I dragged my heavy body up from the bed. Maybe a glass of wine and being around other people would lift my spirits.

I left the apartment early Saturday morning before Omar arrived. Donna and I were going to drive on Highway 1. We planned to stop whenever we felt like it and forget the rest of the world existed.

Sunday morning, I stayed on the phone until an operator succeeded in getting a call through to Lebanon. I needed to feel validated.

"How stupid can she be? Stupid, stupid," Leila shouted.

* * *

I'd never lived alone, and what surprised me most was how things stayed where I left them. Growing up, if I dropped something on the floor and didn't pick it up, by the time I returned home, someone else had. It was the same with a roommate; things never remained the same. Now, when

I returned home, nothing had changed. It felt strange and lonesome for someone who had spent her entire life in the company of others. Every day I was reminded no magic—no Santa Claus—human beings made these things happen.

I began to join coworkers for Friday night happy hours. Most were single or unhappily married. We talked about work projects, politics, world affairs, and sports. I was in no hurry to go home to my empty apartment.

A psychiatrist in his late thirties, a member of the happy hour group, invited me to dinner. I was excited to go out with someone, and we had an enjoyable evening at a good restaurant. I made a conscious effort to be entertaining and charmingly naïve. He laughed and shook his head as his eyes got wider when I made outrageous statements.

He walked me to the door of my apartment, stepped inside, grabbed me and pulled me close. He wasn't rough, only firm, and I pushed him back. He looked at me. "I want to make love. What do you say?"

"I say with whom?"

He put his hand out, shook mine, thanked me for a nice evening and left. I had had no intention of leading him on and felt badly he'd interpreted my behavior as such. The moment he stepped out, I leaned against the door with all my weight to shut and bolt it. Fortunately he wasn't aggressive. I should have known better. I was lonely but not that lonely.

* * *

Weekends were dedicated to finalizing my master's thesis. Mark, one of my classmates, came over on Saturday mornings, and we worked together. I found myself better able to handle lonely Friday nights when I had something to look forward to the following day. After a few study dates, he suggested we meet in the afternoons and go to dinner afterward. I loved his idea. I would only have to deal with Sunday alone.

If I described the type of man I was attracted to, Mark would not meet the criteria. He was a lanky six-foot red-head of Scottish descent. His blond bushy eyebrows formed almost a straight line above his green eyes. He seemed to know everything, which gave him an air of confidence, but he was not arrogant.

* * *

"Are you okay?" Christina inquired over the phone. "I haven't heard from you for two days, and every time I call, you're not home. I can't believe you actually answered this time. What's happening?" She sounded anxious.

"Nothing much. Work, school—mostly my master's thesis." *And Mark.*

"I miss you. Will you come to dinner tonight?"

"No, I'm tired and have to be at work early tomorrow morning to get enough done before I pick up Teri from LAX." I had told her about my friend from UT who lived between Austin and Brentwood.

"I'd like to meet her. You've talked so much about her. Any reason she's coming?"

"Her friend owns a boutique in Beverly Hills, and Teri's thinking of opening one in Austin. She's coming to learn the business." I twisted a strand of hair around my finger.

"That's a long way from her parents' oil business?"

"Yeah. Why don't you come spend some time with us?"

"How about Saturday night? Omar's playing poker."

"Sounds good. Come for dinner."

* * *

I was thrilled to have Teri with me. We sat up until dawn reminiscing.

"Remember the morning your mother put nails on your driveway because your boyfriend's car was parked there all night?" I asked.

"How could I forget? He was livid—we broke up shortly afterward. I guess it worked as far as she was concerned. But I never forgave her, and she knows it."

"I liked it when your grandmother said a girl needs at least three lovers before settling on one. She should've told her own daughter before she came up with the nail idea."

"Oh, she did, but my mother is much more prudish than her mother." She gathered her hair into a low ponytail, twisted and clipped it on top of her head. It accentuated her long neck and pointed chin. She looked even prettier than I remembered.

"I guess your dad's the most logical." I lay back against the sofa pillow and took a sip of wine from my almost empty glass.

"He's only sorry the Sexual Revolution came too late. He doesn't want his kids to miss out. But neither he nor my grandmother will ever change Mother."

I laughed. "Well, two out of three ain't bad. In my family it's zero."

"Maybe not. I get the feeling Teta might be more liberal than you think."

"No way."

"Remember the stories she told you about lovers, often married, who met in the forest?"

"It doesn't mean she condoned it." Her interpretation surprised me.

"Think deeper, Maya. Think deeper."

Teri saw things from a different perspective. Most confusing for me was the way she handled money. The following morning, she showed me her stunning new clothes from Neiman Marcus. She didn't seem to notice my admiration of her selections. Instead, she jabbered about going to the LA Fashion District for some good cheap purchases to match. She told me she had flown first class to New York to see her gynecologist and then informed me she planned to go to Texas in three weeks for her father's birthday and had bought tickets on red-eye flights. She gifted me a gold bracelet and reminded me I owed her $1.45 for letters she'd mailed on my behalf.

Saturday night, it quickly became apparent Christina and Teri didn't like each other. Christina interrupted Teri several times. She called her TT—*Teri the Texan*. Teri was not amused. She seemed totally disinterested in anything Christina had to say, especially after she heard a couple of stories about the love of her life, Omar. She rolled her eyes whenever Chrissy mentioned his name. Chrissy, in turn, made snide remarks to me in Arabic about how provincial she was for an heiress. The minute Chrissy left to be home before Omar's poker game ended, Teri commented on her bondage status. I felt comfortable with both the princess and the slave, but being with them both at the same time caused me too much stress.

I drove Teri to her home in Brentwood on Sunday night and gladly stayed to eat the meal prepared by the caretaker's wife. I promised I'd spend the following weekend with her.

I'd ask Mark to come over Friday night instead of Saturday. It felt good to have a whole weekend scheduled.

I returned home after dinner to find Christina sitting on the apartment steps. "I would've gone in, but I forgot my key at Omar's."

"What's wrong?"

"We had a fight."

I opened the door and she entered the apartment, forgetting her suitcase. I carried it inside.

"His parents are coming next week, and they're staying at his apartment. He told me to I had to leave and clear out any evidence I live there. I reminded him my parents know about our living arrangement, so why shouldn't his? He refused, and I said I wouldn't wait until next week to leave. I don't understand. I'm in my parents' bad books while he's Mr. Perfect to his parents." I noticed her left arm seemed glued to her body.

"There's no way you'd be comfortable staying there with his parents. You know that." I didn't want to stare at her arm, but couldn't help myself. Her left elbow now rested in her right hand.

"That's not the point." Her voice was loud. "What pissed me off was his attitude and his denial of my existence. Wouldn't you think he'd want me to leave little hints around? This'd give him the opportunity to bring up our relationship."

"Don't you think he's going to?"

"No." She glanced in the direction of her suitcase but walked to her old bedroom.

"You forgot your suitcase." I wanted to see what she'd do.

"I'll get it later."

"What's wrong with your arm?"

"Nothing. I fell and landed on it."

"How'd you do that?" I tried to sound matter of fact.

"I tripped after I put the suitcase in my car, but it's nothing to worry about."

"Let me see." I gently removed her hand and pushed up her sleeve. "It's very swollen. Can you move your fingers?"

"Not too well."

"How badly is it hurting?"

"More than I want to admit." She grimaced.

"Maybe we should go to the emergency room."

"I'm okay. I took Aspirin. I'll feel better soon." She flopped on the bed. I'd never seen Christina sit or lie on a bed in her clothes. She was a clean freak. Never did any clothing she wore outside the house touch her bed.

I fetched her suitcase and placed it on the desk. "Are you sure you don't want to see a doctor?"

"Yes." She closed her eyes.

Not knowing what to do, I left. I had put on my pajamas when Christina entered my room.

"I think you're right. I should go to the emergency room. The pain's getting worse." Neither of us spoke on the way to the hospital.

A middle-aged nurse examined her. "How exactly did this happen?"

"I tripped and fell on my arm." Chrissy avoided eye contact.

"How'd you trip?"

"I guess I lost my balance."

"Is this how you got the bruise on your face?"

For the first time, I noticed the faint blue mark on her cheekbone under her right eye. Chrissy didn't immediately answer, but she eventually nodded.

The nurse tipped her head and studied her. "It must've been an earlier fall."

Chrissy didn't respond, and the woman looked at me. "Perhaps you should leave the room while we examine your friend."

"No. I want her to stay with me." Chrissy sounded aggressive.

"The doctor will be in shortly." She turned abruptly and left in a huff.

"What happened?" I asked.

"I told you... I tripped."

"Twice?"

A young doctor entered. He addressed me, "Would you mind waiting outside?"

This time Chrissy didn't object, and I went to the waiting room. I knew the nurse intimidated her but she probably figured she could manipulate the doctor.

An hour later she came out with her arm in a sling. "It's sprained." She handed me a prescription. "Will you fill this for me tomorrow? They gave me enough for tonight."

As much as I tried, Chrissy wouldn't tell me anything more.

During the month and a half she stayed with me, Omar rarely called. He never invited her out, but he found time to visit two or three times a week for "quickies." When I commented, Chrissy said she was just as eager as he, and I shouldn't assume it only satisfied him. Although it sometimes seemed awkward, I tried to be in the apartment when he came. I mostly stayed in my room. As far as I could tell, things between them seemed civil.

On numerous occasions I suggested she use their time apart to see a therapist, but she would not engage in the conversation.

Teri and the ever-steady Donna filled much of my free time. I joined Teri on her Rodeo Drive shopping sprees and took long walks with Donna to collect seashells and contemplate life.

Work, although always interesting, took on a different dimension when Janice joined the secretarial pool. From the beginning, she took an inexplicable liking to me. No one in the department understood why. She would immediately tend to my reports. Her work was outstanding. She wasn't only an excellent typist. She also corrected spelling and grammar while providing the author with a critical review. Everyone wanted her to type their work, and I became the reluctant gatekeeper. Even John gave me his, instructing me to make sure Janice prioritized them.

"Girl, you're not like everyone else here. You got soul. I feel it." Janice lived in Watts and wore her hair in dreadlocks. "I've taught my five-year-old daughter to look under the car before getting in. Last year, my neighbor got killed by a man hiding under her Datsun. He grabbed her ankles and knocked her down. She hit her head. He never meant to kill her. He only wanted to steal the car."

My coworkers joked it was only a matter of time before I, too, had dreadlocks and wore Janice's colorful, sexy one-dollar shirts. This lively young woman brought me comfort. She spoke to everyone and created a sense of community. She was passionate and warm in everything she did—or refused to do. Our worlds had nothing—and at the same time everything—in common. She reminded me of home.

My projects started getting noticed. I authored two publications and gave presentations. I became confident in my work and had the ability to approach and solve problems from unique angles. More autonomy and responsibility followed. Within five months of parking in a visitor's spot, I was offered a permanent job. It was a dream come true, or so I thought.

CHAPTER 4

———

Things will work out, provided you have options.

—*DONNA*

"Do you know Laura Samuelson?" Jeff stood at the entrance of my cubical.

"I know of her," I said.

"She's joining us as a consultant to work on a project with the FAA. What do you know about her?" He entered and leaned on the edge of my desk.

"What you probably know. She's extremely competent—published and was a commissioned officer in the navy. She's now in the reserves. And it doesn't hurt that she's beautiful."

She had graduated from my program a couple of years earlier. People said Laura had it all—beauty, brains, personality, and her achievements made her seem ten years older than twenty-nine. Professors said they'd rarely encountered such a sharp mind, guys raved about her looks, and girls talked about her sweet disposition. Everyone was in awe. She had completed her MS while working full time, had numerous publications, and was a sought-after consultant to defense contractors. She was the last person I expected to add as a friend.

* * *

"You sound jealous of Laura," Donna said as we walked to the campus computer lab that night. I couldn't tell whether she was joking or serious.

"Maybe, but I'm mostly annoyed. She's starting tomorrow and sharing my office. John said it's because we're the only two women. Nobody bothered to tell me until today."

"You'll be fine. Things will work out; they always do. Provided…"

Donna's familiar words made me smile and I finished her phrase, "You have options."

"You're a quick learner."

We laughed.

We reached the door of the lab. All twenty terminals, lined up against the walls of the room, were being used. Students sat in front of screens to communicate with enormous punch-card-fed machines housed in temperature-controlled rooms, sometimes nearby and sometimes miles away. One of the three printers churned out a Snoopy calendar on the continuous-form perforated paper. Students seemed to always be printing them.

"Let's go work on the Wang. Nobody seems ready to leave."

We headed to the psychology department to use the standalone machine. I was better at BASIC and COBOL but could manage "Wanganese," the name we used for the programming language of this popular minicomputer and word processor. I sat in front of the apparatus because Donna didn't like any of this stuff.

As she pulled up a chair I asked, "What motivated you to go back to school in your forties?"

"Not having options. People treated me as if I was dumb because I didn't have a college degree. They assumed I was a stupid housewife. When my husband walked out on me, I realized I had little to fall back on."

"How old were you?" I powered up the Wang.

"Twenty-nine. I married at eighteen and had three children in five years."

"You were really young. It must've been tough." I opened my notebook to retrieve some programming notes.

"You can't imagine the feeling of barely having anything while caring for three growing boys. A box of cereal and a gallon of milk would disappear at breakfast. A loaf of bread and a jar of peanut butter wasn't enough for lunch. The alimony and child support were meager."

"What'd you do?"

"I worked as a bank secretary. Meanwhile, my ex climbed the ladder at a law firm, cashing in on the degree I worked just as hard for, supporting the family while he studied. I vowed to return to school as soon as I could. I plan to pursue my PhD. To get ahead in the game you have to have options. Remember—options."

"How about luck?"

"Luck is what pushes people to the very top, but you have to have the basics and then luck might select you over others."

* * *

John entered my office with Laura the following morning. I stood, introduced myself and welcomed her. I could tell by his body language he felt relieved. His jaw loosened, and his back relaxed slightly. I gave him a half smile, and he invited me to join them for lunch in the cafeteria.

Laura spent most of her time at her desk reading through manuals or reports and writing. She focused for long periods, but after a few days, I began to engage her in afternoon chat breaks when I returned to the office to analyze data and write findings. We took turns trekking to the vending machine for provisions—salty, sugary, and fatty snacks to share. Our conversations were mostly work centered, until the day Janice strode into our office with an irritated look on her face. Her eyes were narrow and her mouth pinched.

She faced me, her back to Laura. "Girl, tell your lady friend she's got to learn to wait her turn. I'm tired of her acting all important and telling me she needs reports typed right away. Everyone needs stuff right away."

Clearly annoyed, Laura looked up from her papers. She pushed her chair away from her desk, but I stood before she did.

"Remember the blue striped shirt you wore yesterday?" I addressed Janice. "Laura and I were talking about how pretty it is. She thinks you have good taste in clothes, and I told her you could arrange to get some stuff for her. In fact, I told her you're getting some things for me next week. She can have anything she likes. Since she's new, we need to make her feel welcome."

"Hey, I can bring extra clothes. Don't want you to lose nothin'." Her voice softened, she winked at me and opened her eyes wider.

"Laura, why don't you take a break and tell Janice the kind of stuff you like."

Laura chewed on her lower lip. She stood and looked like she might hit me, but Janice turned to face her. "I like the skirt you're wearing and your shirt." Laura spoke slowly.

"You can't wear this. You're too pale and skinny. Don't you worry. I'll pick some things that'll look good on you—make your man want you. Bring money on Wednesday because I've got to pay the dudes for the stuff." She turned to leave, but spun back around and looked Laura in the eye. "And you heard what I said about your work. Ain't nobody more important than nobody."

"Unless it's me," I said, not quite sure if I should joke with Janice.

"You're different, girl. You got soul. There's something blessed about you. Maybe it's because you come from the Lord's land and you're as close as I'll ever get in this lifetime to his first miracle." She left.

"What have you got on her?" Laura sounded somewhat shaky.

"I don't know. She liked me from day one, and I have to say, I like her, too. She's smart and competent but from a tough neighborhood. Tough like I can't envision. Despite everything I've been through, I can't imagine having to accept daily violence as a normal way of life. I ran away from a war zone, and she lives in one. Maybe that's why we've bonded."

"I'm glad you were here to protect me."

"Very funny. You're the armed forces lady." She could take on Janice in a fight, if necessary, but I had no chance against either of them.

"What are you doing after work? Would you like to come with me to my boyfriend's for dinner? He's cooking."

"Sure, I'd love to."

"I have one more Janice question. What'd she mean when she said you're as close as she'll ever get to his first miracle?"

"A few weeks ago, she invited me to Sunday service at her Baptist church and for lunch at her house. Her mother asked me questions about Lebanon because it's mentioned often in the Bible. I told her Christ performed his first miracle there at the wedding in Cana. Janice jumped up and said, 'Girl, let me touch you. You're as close as I'll ever get.'"

Laura laughed at my poor attempt to mimic Janice's accent. "Well, my miracle is you saved me from her."

On the way to dinner, we stopped at Laura's apartment in Santa Monica. She suggested I leave my car and ride with her. I had never seen a loft and found it intriguing. The spacious living room, dining room, and kitchen were on the entrance level and a winding staircase led up to the large open bedroom area. The bright, modern stylish furniture reminded me of a magazine spread.

"Make yourself comfortable. It'll only take me a minute to change." She headed up the stairs. "What kind of wine do you like?" she yelled over the half wall.

"Red—Cabernet."

"Go to the kitchen and choose a couple of bottles from the rack."

She came down, put the wine in a paper bag, and we left.

We entered the Spanish-style home through an unlocked side door. A dog barked, and Jeff yelled a greeting from the kitchen. His appearance surprised me. He was probably in his early forties, slightly taller than Laura, balding, with the beginnings of a potbelly and small spaces between his teeth. I guess I'd expected my five-nine model friend to have a companion who looked as striking as she, but when I learned he was an executive at MGM, it didn't seem like such a mismatch after all.

Our conversation launched dinner onto an amiable track. Jeff had visited Lebanon on several occasions before the 1975 war. "It was one of my favorite places. Everything about the country was spectacular—the people, the food, the historical sites, the entertainment. You name it, Lebanon had it."

It felt good to be with someone who knew my country. I could talk about things he'd understand. "I remember the first time I saw a show in Vegas, I was disappointed. Compared to the Charlie Henchis spectacle at the Casino du Liban, it seemed elementary."

"I'll never forget that show. I've yet to see anything like it anywhere in the world. And I've never seen a hotel like the Phoenicia in Beirut. I spent countless hours at the bar—what an ingenious idea to make the wall behind the bar itself the glass side of a swimming pool. Everyone loved to watch the Pan Am stewardesses swim. It was like a human aquarium featuring mermaids with the occasional hairy man."

"Don't you think it's creepy for swimmers to have people sit at the bar and watch them?" I'd always wanted to ask this question to a patron.

"I think many of them enjoyed having an audience, and sometimes they came to the bar to watch others swim." Jeff leapt out of his chair and darted out of the room.

Laura put second servings of ice cream cake on each of our plates. I had almost finished mine when Jeff came back dangling a key on a large bulky holder. "Do you recognize this?"

"No. Should I?"

"It's the key to my room at the Phoenicia. I forgot to return it on my last stay and thought I'd give it back the next time.

But there was no next time. The civil war started days later. I want to go back. But the hotel district…"

Gone. Like so much else. I tried to hide my misty eyes, but my companions noticed. Jeff offered coffee, and Laura changed the subject and told Jeff about her encounter with Janice. I shook off the sadness and carried on. It was, after all, the only thing I could do.

On the way back to Laura's apartment, she told me she and Jeff rarely spent weekday evenings together because of their work schedules. My drive home was quick, but I knew I'd be in traffic on the same freeway within a few hours on my way to work.

* * *

Mark arrived at ten sharp on Saturday morning. It was not a thesis workday. He had offered to do handyman chores, and we planned to visit a museum. He fixed the door latch on my dishwasher and tightened a loose chair leg while I prepared a Lebanese breakfast. I mixed dried thyme, sesame seeds, and sumac with olive oil and spread it on rounds of pizza dough to bake in the oven. I placed yogurt cheese, tomatoes, cucumbers, mint, and olives on top of the warm herb bread and rolled it up into sandwiches.

As we sat down, I asked, "Do you know what kind of job are you going to look for after graduation?"

"Definitely not one with a traditional company." He stopped eating. "My father worked for General Mills and invented one of their most profitable products. In return he received a plaque and an award ceremony. He became discouraged and moved to Stanford Research Institute. I'll never make his mistake and give the best years of my life to corporate America."

I stood and began to clear the table. Mark offered to drive to the Getty, and I felt glad to have a break.

"I heard the museum is in a spectacular location overlooking the Pacific in Malibu." I knew I sounded excited.

"Actually, it's in Pacific Palisades, not Malibu. That's a contentious issue. The brochure lists the address as Malibu instead of Pacific Palisades, and the city has complained."

"That's funny. With everything going on in the world, people have time to make an issue out of an address?"

He sighed. "I guess that's what happens when people live in peace and prosperity."

I'd seen pictures of the J. Paul Getty Museum and knew it would be magnificent, but I underestimated the impact it would have on me. The Roman-inspired setting took me back to the Mediterranean. I touched a column in the outer peristyle, closed my eyes, and imagined the Roman temples in Baalbek, Lebanon—some of the largest and best preserved in the world. I remembered the haunting night when, as a twelve–year-old, I watched the La MaMa Theatre of New York's production of *Medea* in ancient Greek. I didn't understand a word, but outside among the massive temple columns, it felt as though it was thousands of years ago—perception of time vanished.

In the Getty courtyard next to the long reflecting pool, the sensation felt similar. I had to drag myself away to join Mark inside. We toured the Greek and Roman antiquities, bought sandwiches at the museum café and ate lunch overlooking the Pacific. This was the most emotionally beautiful place I visited during the four years I spent in LA.

We ended the evening at a restaurant overlooking the city—accessible only by cable car. Inside the transportation capsule we waited for more people to arrive. Suddenly a whole group rushed in. Everybody fussed around a man who seemed annoyed.

Mark leaned in to whisper. "Do you know who he is?"

"No."

"Frank Sinatra"

I stood more erect to get a better look at him. The moment the cable car arrived, they rushed out. I couldn't find any evidence of Sinatra in the restaurant. I even took the long route to the restroom to search.

Mark raised his margarita and proposed a toast. "Let's drink to LA and all the interesting people here."

I lifted my glass, clinked his, and looked at the city lights below. "This could almost be home. It's like looking down at Beirut from the mountains."

"I'll drink to that." He reached across the table and put his hand on top of mine.

Never had a day reminded me this much of home. His touch made me feel safe and content. Loneliness dissipated.

Mark wanted to order a second bottle of wine, but I knew we'd already had too much and dissuaded him. He had to drive, and I certainly didn't want to be stopped and escorted home by the police. Teri had told me how humiliated she had been when this happened to her. Little did I know embarrassment was just around the corner, anyway.

I woke up the following morning when Mark entered the bedroom naked carrying a breakfast tray. Suddenly I grasped what had happened. I remembered almost ripping his shirt off as he raised my blouse. A feeling of excitement ran through me.

He placed the tray on the bed and bent over to kiss me.

"What a night. Maya, precious Maya."

"Mark." I didn't know what else to say.

"That's me. The luckiest guy in the world."

I looked down at the tray.

"Hey, Maya, why the sad look? It was a wonderful night."

"It was wonderful, but I'm embarrassed. And confused."

"Embarrassed about what? Confused, maybe." He smiled.

"You know…"

"It was beautiful and let's not make more of it than it was."

"I guess, I mean… I just wasn't prepared."

"Don't worry, I was." He showed me an empty condom wrapper. "Let's simply let things happen. Why don't you eat breakfast, and then we'll walk to the beach?"

The sand oozed between my toes as rays of sunlight penetrated my skin, the breeze and the soothing sound of water unleashing the sensation of freedom within me.

Had my phoenix fantasy happened? Had I run through the fire and risen carefree?

Sunday night, by the time Mark left, the basket next to the bed was full of wrappers. He looked at it and paused. "Thanks for an incredible weekend. I'll see you in class tomorrow."

"Remember I defend my thesis on Friday."

"It's been on my calendar for weeks. I've taken the day off from work. And after this weekend, I guess I should schedule the coming one together, too."

"Too late."

"I thought we were only beginning?"

"Seriously, Teri invited me to San Diego to celebrate my defense. She's already booked the hotel and made plans."

"Plans can change."

"Not this time. Besides, I thought you needed a weekend to visit your parents in San Francisco."

"I guess next weekend is it." He gave me a long kiss and descended the stairs in leaps.

I rushed to the phone. "Donna, you're never going to believe what happened this weekend."

* * *

The morning of my defense, a small entourage of friends and I met for breakfast on campus. I felt nervous and ate three doughnuts before I listened to the conversation.

"I can't believe you finished your thesis before me," Mark said.

"She beat us all," Donna answered. "But we'll soon follow. It's like the Arabic saying Maya once told me. *When you break a string of worry beads and the first one rolls away, the rest follow. There's no going back.*"

"Guess I'm the string," Teri said. "Not one of the beads because I'm not following you guys."

"What time is it?" I still felt anxious.

"Ten thirty-five. On a day to remember, Friday, April 6, 1979." Mark leaned over and kissed my cheek. "I'm proud of you."

Less than five minutes before my eleven o'clock defense began, Chrissy entered the conference room. I was surprised and happy to see her. Although we hadn't talked much since Omar's parents left and she moved back in with him, I knew she'd returned from a business trip to New York the night before. She looked tired and had lost weight. She introduced herself to the four professors and greeted the rest of the group with a general hello. My adviser asked me to begin.

"My hypothesis is…" I stammered and looked down at my papers.

The professor must have sensed my anxiety because before I completed the sentence, he made a comment about the importance of my research for airline passenger safety. His calm demeanor encouraged me, and I continued, ready to take on the grueling questions I'd be asked.

Over an hour later I heard the sentence I'd been waiting for. "If there are no further questions, I think congratulations are in order."

I shook hands and thanked the faculty members. My head buzzed.

Donna stepped forward to hug me. "Amazing—you did an amazing job."

"You made me want to become a *bead*," Teri said.

Mark gave me a long hug and a quick kiss.

Chrissy, still seated, wrote on a notepad. It pained me to see her this way. She had never been beautiful, but certainly was pretty, and she made the best of her features. Her air of confidence attracted people and she was easy to talk to, but something had changed. She was still attractive, but hollow. Her confidence mingled with a sorrowful demeanor. She finally said, "Congratulations, Maya. I'm glad I could be here, but I have to run. I'll call you tonight."

"I'm leaving to San Diego for the weekend."

"Okay, we'll catch up next week." She quickly left.

I knew she couldn't talk while at work, and a long-distance call from the hotel in San Diego would be expensive and useless. She'd be with Omar.

Donna, Teri, and Mark waited for me to gather my papers.

"Do you guys have time for lunch before Maya and I embark on our San Diego adventure?" Teri asked.

On our way to the Student Union building Donna told stories about my college antics.

Mark didn't know I'd changed the TV station in the middle of a football game. He laughed. "You're not serious."

"And once she brought Lebanese food to statistics class," Donna said.

"I'd never really cooked before. I called my cousin in New York for recipes. I missed eating with people. Everyone liked the hummus. No one knew what it was, but once they tasted it, they wanted more." I squeezed Mark's hand tighter and took a skip step.

"My favorite Maya story is the canary," Teri said. "I still can't believe it really happened." She pushed her sunglasses onto her forehead and looked sideways at Mark.

"What happened?" Mark seemed to enjoy hearing stories about me.

"Tell him, Maya," Teri said. "I'd like to hear it again."

"About ten years ago, we had a canary named Tweedy. When my sister received a Siamese cat as a gift, we hung the bird cage up high. But one night around midnight..." It felt as though I spoke about a distant land and another lifetime. "I went into the family room and noticed the maid had forgotten to hang Tweedy's cage back up after cleaning it. The cat had managed to open the door and nearly bite the bird's head off. It flopped down on his chest, held by a cord." *I remembered how frantically I screamed for Teta.*

We stopped walking, and they all looked at me. "Teta rushed in wearing her nightgown. She picked up the little bird and held his head back in place. She petted and spoke softly to him and told me to get Scotch tape."

"You're not going to tell me she taped the bird's head back on?" Mark asked.

"That's exactly what she did. The next morning, I got up early to check on Tweedy, and he was singing."

"You're kidding."

"I kid you not. And Tweedy lived for about three more years."

"After I first heard this story, I asked *people in the know*," Donna said. "I found out it's possible but not probable."

"Possible and probable, what luxuries. People like my grandmother had to fend for themselves. They grew up at a time when there were few doctors, no hospitals close by, and Ottoman occupiers surrounding them. They learned how to survive with few resources."

"I wish I could meet her," Mark said.

"I think we'd all like to meet her," Teri responded.

Mark put his arm around my shoulder, pulling me closer to him, and we synchronized our steps.

Can I be totally happy in Los Angeles?

CHAPTER 5

———

Never compare your inside (feelings) to another's outside (displays).

—*TERI*

"Maya, hurry. Follow me."

"Good morning to you, too, John," I said, but he ignored me.

He must have been standing at the entrance of the ergonomics department for quite a while because I noticed he had almost finished reading a thick report.

He began walking, and I tried to keep up with his pace to hear his words. "One of our big clients is being sued by a woman who applied for a job as a pilot and got rejected. She's claiming discrimination and, in all honesty, she's probably right. She has extensive military flying experience, and I doubt some of the men they hired had her credentials. We're having an emergency brainstorming session to help our customer win the lawsuit."

"That's not fair."

He stopped abruptly. He faced me with his chin almost touching my nose. "No, it isn't fair, but since when is life fair? She's one person—one family. If we lose, multiple families could be affected by layoffs. You're part of the team, and it's your responsibility to help. Remember our purpose is to sell airplanes."

We entered a conference room. Laura sat alone on one side of the table. Six other male colleagues were seated across from her and at the heads. I sat next to her, and John positioned himself in the empty chair to my right. From her facial expression, I could tell she was not happy to be there, and she and I mostly listened. Laura finally asked how many DC-10s the airline had purchased and if any were on order.

When I raised my hand to ask a follow-up question, the man across from me jumped up. Everyone stared, stunned, as he raced around the table, grabbed my wrist, and waved my hand in the air. "Look at the size of her hand."

I pulled my wrist away and moved slightly closer to Laura.

The man continued in an excited voice, "See what I'm getting at. This lady's hands are tiny. They must be in the lower two-and-a-half percentile of the female population— probably in the one percentile of the entire population." He reached for my hand again but said, "Please, Maya, may I?

I voluntarily raised it, and he continued, "Our equipment is designed for ninety-five percent of the male population. Maya, for example, would have trouble operating an air-to-air refueling tanker because she cannot wrap her hands properly around the controls in order to push the correct buttons. She would fail, not because she wasn't competent but rather because of physical limitations. I bet there's a physical reason why this lady pilot cannot fly a commercial DC-10." He beamed like he'd discovered the Holy Grail.

Everyone began to talk at once. John volunteered me to test out equipment. The meeting adjourned and shortly afterward, my hands were extensively measured by two men who politely kept commenting they'd never seen such small adult hands—in the bottom one percentile of the US population.

We later learned the airline won the lawsuit. They argued the female pilot was half an inch too short to safely fly the DC-10. If her feet were comfortable on the ground, her back was not positioned correctly in the pilot's seat, and if she sat properly in the seat, her feet didn't rest on the ground. This could cause body fatigue and a potential danger. The lawyers successfully made the case she wasn't hired for safety reasons.

This case was cited when the law changed to mandate aircraft cockpits and equipment had to be designed to accommodate ninety-five percent of the entire population, not only the male population.

"Well, at least women count, now," Laura said. "Too bad some of us had to be sacrificed to get to this point."

Although I'd realized we were treated differently as women, I'd never quite seen us as a group. I'd regarded situations from the perspective of individual fairness. This was a new viewpoint for me.

* * *

Later that afternoon, John poked his head in my office. "I apologize for being so curt this morning. I didn't even ask you about your thesis defense. How did it go?"

"Now you can put MS both before and after my name."

"Congratulations Ms. Maya Coury, MS. How'd you celebrate?"

"My friend Teri invited me to San Diego. We had a wonderful time—lots of food and wine. But the Shamu show at SeaWorld frightened me."

"SeaWorld scared you?" He looked confused.

"Something went wrong during the show. The trainer, in the water, suddenly froze at the edge of the pool. The killer whale had cornered him. We thought it was part of the act until we were asked to sit quietly and not move. Guards took up positions around the pool. It was the first time I'd seen guns drawn since I left Lebanon." I paused. "I started shaking and sweating. Maybe they were only stun guns, but...it's kind of like when I hear fireworks and it sounds like shelling."

"I'm sorry." He pursed his lips and looked down at me.

"I think it's getting better." I glanced at my hands. "Anyway, a man, another trainer, I guess, called the whale to distract him, while two others went to the trapped man. They grabbed him under the arms and yanked him out of the water. People clapped, and I cried."

"I hope your memories of violence will fade with time and things will get better for you."

"The evening felt safer. We had dinner at Anthony's Fish Grotto. While we waited at the bar for a table, a guy asked me to dance, but I declined. Terri got upset I refused, so I walked over to him and said, 'I changed my mind.' But he said, 'Now, I've changed mine.' When he saw the look on my face, he laughed, grabbed my hand, and led me into the crowd."

"I wish I'd seen that. You're getting bold. Did you go to the zoo?"

"Of course. I don't think we missed anything. I tried a corndog. Hey, I bet the roach coach sells them. It'll be my treat." I smiled and John did, too, but he shifted his weight, which I took to mean the conversation ended.

I didn't think I'd ever talked this much with John about nonwork issues. I knew he found my approach to life in America endearing and told me he often shared my comments with his friends. But he'd never engaged or showed empathy. For the first time he seemed to have stepped out of his one-dimensional self.

*　*　*

Weekdays passed quickly. They were filled with fascinating projects and problems tackled by competent and creative people. Lebanon seemed more and more like a distant dream as I integrated into the best of America.

Laura and I became recognized for the high quality of our work, and some of the men began to consult with us on their projects. Slowly, we cracked the cement dome. We still had a long way to go, and we relied heavily on one another. We rarely worked on the same assignments but stayed abreast of each other's work.

"Which can be heard more clearly over simulated engine noise—a male or a female voice?" I wanted to hear Laura's gut instinct.

"Voice warnings are used in commercial aircraft cockpits?"

"Just beginning. You know, a pilot might fly for years before hearing a buzzer or bell warning and then he has to remember what it means. Now, digital technology can be used instead of analogue." I felt weirdly proud to know something she didn't.

"That's a big change."

"Hard to imagine the days when cockpits weren't standardized—one of the reasons for many of the plane crashes in World War I. A pilot trained on one type of plane would be flying a different one when an emergency arose. Although he knew what to do, under pressure, people tend to revert to what they originally learned."

"Now, what was your question?"

I realized I'd gone on a tangent. "Male or female voice for cockpit warnings?"

"A female voice, because it's higher pitched." Laura picked up scissors and cut out strips of text from a typed report.

"Guess again."

"A male voice because it's loud." She tore a piece of tape off a roll.

"One more guess."

"What's left?" She Scotch-taped strips of text onto a blank page, reorganizing the report.

"Preconception or prejudice."

"Okay?" She tore off another piece of tape.

"We're testing voice warning systems using production and test pilots."

"And?" she asked impatiently.

"In an analysis of the preliminary results, the split is fifty-fifty. Half of the pilots made no errors when a female voice gave the warnings over simulated engine noise, but made lots of errors with a male voice. For the other half, the opposite happened. So, I decided to give the pilots a short questionnaire before they participated. One of the questions asked which voice they thought should be used and…"

"A perfect correlation exists between the voice they thought would be better and the one they heard the best." Laura finished the sentence.

"They even made fewer errors on easily confused words, like *fire engine two* and *fire APU*. Isn't it surprising how preset people are in their ideas?"

"Only those who think they know everything." Laura smirked.

We cracked up and giggled until we noticed the team medical doctor standing in our office. "It is much nicer having the two of you in the department. Laughter in the middle of the day works wonders."

Laura stood up. "Thank you, Dr. Moset. Yes, once in a while, with all of the work pressure it's nice to take a break. I guessed the results of Maya's project and her reaction made me laugh."

Laura's stiff tone and attempt to justify our behavior surprised me.

"No need to explain." He took off his glasses and positioned a chair to see us both. As one of the senior members of the department, he made it a point to reassure us we were as capable as the men. He said we only lacked confidence—not our fault because girls are raised and treated this way. If we recognized this, we could overcome it. His message was clear. "Since this morning I've been analyzing the effects toxic fumes released in an aircraft crash would have on passengers. I can use a break."

I liked it when Dr. Moset talked with us. In spite of his brilliance, he never came across as arrogant. Every time I boarded a plane and looked at the floor lights leading to the exits, I thought of him. He and his team had created them. In an aircraft emergency, especially one involving smoke, passengers crawl or look down to escape. The overhead exit signs are not sufficient. I wondered how many lives he'd saved.

When he left, I asked Laura if she'd walk to the hangar with me.

"Why do you want to go there?"

"I don't know. I feel like watching something great being built. I always find it inspirational—pieces of metal assembled into a flying machine. This is what has made my life what it is."

"Why so philosophical?"

"Just homesick, I guess."

I was glad she'd agreed to come with me. Human relationships were minimal in the rushed LA environment. I longed to sit with Teta on her front porch and talk to the people walking by. This was the beauty of Lebanon. Despite the war, every day we were supported by family, friends, or even strangers. Now I found myself seeking out personal relationships with anyone who would engage in conversation, including the clerical and cleaning staff. And to think my colleagues wondered why my papers were typed first and why no one ever forgot to empty my wastebasket.

* * *

At happy hour, in early May, the conversation focused on gas rationing. Little did we know, the following Wednesday, it would be a reality in Los Angeles.

"If this happens, you can come stay with me." Laura lived much closer to work.

"Thanks," I replied nonchalantly.

"Besides, with your odd-numbered license plate and my even one, we'll always be able to fill up our cars."

On the way home, I saw long lines at gas stations but figured I had enough and could wait until morning. I didn't realize I would spend most of Saturday in a gas line and be rationed to seven gallons. I'd read about the 1973 oil embargo but never imagined America would let it happen again. Now, a superpower stood at the mercy of the Islamic Revolution in Iran, which had caused the closure of oil fields.

Frustrated by the long wait, I got out of my car to mingle with other people in line.

"It's those damn A-rabs again," a bald, red-faced man grumbled.

"Actually, Iranians aren't Arabs." I looked at him and the man next to him.

"We should just nuke 'em and be done," the younger man said.

"Hey, they're people just like you. They don't make these decisions," I said.

"A-rabs, Iranians, what's the difference? They're all the same in my book." The overweight, bald man locked his eyes on mine. I watched his face turn a deeper red.

"Then maybe it's time to read another book."

"What are you—the morality police?" The look the younger man gave me wasn't intimidating but rather arrogantly stupid. I realized we couldn't have a civil discussion. Their minds were made up.

I got back in my car and pulled out the owner's manual. I figured it was more constructive to read it than to talk to those guys. After a few pages, I started to daydream about the type of vehicles we'd drive in ten years. This great country would never stay dependent on foreign oil. I wondered how cars would be powered in the late 1980s.

A few days later, I moved into Laura's loft. She cleared out part of her closet and insisted we share her king-sized bed. Both Jeff and Mark made fun of this arrangement. They couldn't understand how two women could share a bed and think nothing of it. Laura believed their brains were wired differently from ours and their hormones were more primal. Girls simply grow up sharing beds.

I felt at home, and she made a great effort to include me in social events with Jeff.

One night as we were getting ready for bed, she became talkative. "You know, I've been married twice."

"Twice?" I tried not to sound surprised.

"Yes, twice. The first time to my high school sweetheart. It only lasted a couple of years. We were too young. My second husband was in the military, and it was a relationship built on passion. I mean *sex*." She threw her head back and mimed a dramatic, "*Wow*."

I giggled and tossed a pillow her way.

"No other sexual partner has ever compared. Beyond the physical, we had nothing in common. He wasn't interested in finishing college, and I got bored. He had no ambition, and I had lots," she paused, as if waiting for my reaction. I'd been in LA long enough not to be surprised by the stories.

"Do you ever think of marrying Jeff?"

"All the time. You must think I'm crazy to contemplate marriage again, but I feel I need it to make my life complete. And I'd like to have a child by the time I'm thirty-two."

"In two years? Why?"

"I need a goal. My relationship with Jeff is different. He's divorced and has two children he rarely sees because they live in Arizona with his ex. He's mature and experienced. And he's the first man who can challenge me intellectually. He knows I want to get married, and I think he's close to proposing."

"Yeah, he's definitely mature and smart, and he seems madly in love with you."

"I think he is, too. I feel this is the right relationship."

The following week, Laura had to go to a conference in New Jersey and insisted I remain at her apartment. She didn't want to travel because she'd planned to go to a party with

Jeff at the home of a movie producer. She suggested I attend the event, and Jeff embraced the idea.

"And besides," Laura said. "It'll be an incredible experience for you. You'll get the chance to meet people whose names and faces you know but probably would never meet. It'll be exciting and fun. An *only in LA* experience."

"What will I wear? All I have are school and work clothes."

"I have dresses you can choose from." Laura sounded more excited than me.

She made hair and makeup appointments for me and commented on how much better her dress looked on me.

Jeff called the evening she left to ask if I needed anything, and he offered to take me to dinner the following night, per Laura's instructions to take care of me. I declined because I planned to take Friday afternoon off to prepare for the party and needed to work late Thursday.

Teri loved the Hollywood scene, and she came over the afternoon of the party to help me get ready. "I wish I could be in your shoes tonight." She selected jewelry for me from a case she'd brought.

I smiled to myself. A few months earlier, I would have thought she was asking for my shoes.

"Remember the time we were on Rodeo Drive and ran into Anthony Quinn? I stopped to talk to him and you kept on walking." She held up a necklace.

"I thought he was a friend of yours."

"I couldn't believe how nice he was and how he took the time to chat. And then I had to tell you who he was. At least you'd seen *Zorba the Greek.*" She shook her head.

"I wonder how many famous people I'll see tonight without a clue as to who they are? I am so…"

"Clueless?"

We dissolved into cackling laughter.

"I'm sure Jeff will help you out." Teri fastened the sapphire necklace she'd selected for me.

Jeff remained by my side the whole evening. He introduced me to people I'd seen in movies and to many I didn't even know existed. At dinner, I sat next to a blonde, long-legged, and very chatty twin. Her sister sat a few chairs down. Jeff was in deep conversation with a wiry director in a yellow suit. He looked like an anorexic canary, and his bright jacket reflected from the crystal and silver on the white tablecloth.

Back at the apartment, Jeff walked me to the door. "You, my dear, were charming. I'm glad Laura suggested you come."

"I had a great time. I doubt I'll ever have the chance to do something like this again. Thank you."

"The pleasure was mine. Goodnight. I'll call to check on you tomorrow."

I couldn't fall asleep. I thought about the party: the huge house, the dream-like garden, the delicious food, the fascinating people, the festive mood, and the dynamic atmosphere. Everything kept playing over and over in my head. When I finally fell asleep, I dreamed about it. The guests were split into four groups: famous, wannabes, hangers-on, and observers.

The famous sat or walked in circles on top of a barren mountain peak. I watched their faces and realized few smiled. Some turned their face away when they entered my line of vision. The wannabes desperately tried to climb the lush, steep mountainside toward the desolate top. Their faces all looked the same—bright made-up eyes and plastered smiles. The hangers-on danced naked around the base of the mountain with foolish grins on their faces. I sat on a platform with the other observers.

My alarm, which I'd forgotten to turn off, and the phone rang at the same time ending my dream. Laura wanted to know every detail of the evening. She told me she had to stay longer to testify before Congress on her analysis of a military leadership training course.

"Good morning, lovely." Jeff called immediately after Laura.

"I think you have the wrong number." My tone was flat—uneasy with the way he emphasized *lovely*.

"Oh, I very much have the right number. Maya, you were a big hit last night. *Intriguing and exotic* are the words I heard."

"I'm glad I helped you stand out, and Laura will be pleased to hear I boosted your reputation."

"Look, I'll be in Santa Monica this afternoon for a meeting until around six. I'll pick up dinner and come over. I'm following Laura's orders to take care of you."

Before I could answer, he hung up.

Jeff arrived with two large bags of food and a bottle of wine. He wore a sports jacket over well-tailored pants. When I saw the predatory look on his face, I knew I was in for trouble but didn't know how to put a stop to what I saw coming. I pulled my oversized t-shirt down, attempting to make it longer than my shorts.

He opened the wine while I emptied the bags. In spite of the pleasant smells and my curiosity, I didn't look at the food. I put the closed containers, plates and utensils on the table and sat down. Jeff placed down a crystal goblet and, with a flourish, poured a taste of wine. "Mademoiselle, I hope this vintage is to your liking?"

"C'mon, Jeff, don't act silly. You know I don't know anything about wine." He pushed the glass closer to me.

"You can always learn and…"

"Not if I'm not interested," I interrupted.

"Whatever you say, mademoiselle." He sat, unfolded his napkin, and placed it on his lap. I opened the food cartons. The contents surprised me—filet mignon, green beans, roasted potatoes, and salad with crumbled blue cheese.

"This looks good."

"Nothing's too good for you." I ignored his comment and cut into my meat.

I ate fast, my eyes focused on the plate in front of me. Jeff attempted to start several conversations, but I cut them short. As I put the last bite of food on my fork, he placed his hand on top of mine. I immediately withdrew it.

"This isn't right, Jeff. You're my friend's boyfriend. And besides, I'm dating someone."

"Maya, this is California. It's the 1970s. If it feels good, do it."

"And if it doesn't feel right, don't." I pushed my chair away from the table.

"Why are you wrapped up in old-fashioned morals? Don't you think Laura knows I have other women besides her? And Mark, he's not your type. He's just a boy you use to keep loneliness at bay."

"That's not true. I'm very happy with Mark. And I don't think Laura knows you cheat on her. Have you ever told her?" I stood, not quite sure if I should clear the table, leave the room, or engage him. I wished he'd leave.

"She knows I have too many temptations, and besides fidelity's outdated and overrated." He picked up his half-full glass and finished it in one swallow.

"She wants to marry you, damn it. She's in love with you." I took a step back.

"What does you and I having a good time tonight have to do with any of this? If it feels good and we're not hurting anyone, what's the problem?" He poured himself more wine and emptied the bottle into my glass.

"But it'll hurt others. And it doesn't feel good to me."

"Give me a try. You won't regret it. You need to try with a real man, and I know you'll want more." He stood and handed me my glass.

"I'll try. I'll try to forget this ever happened." I walked to the sink.

"Your loss. You don't know what you're missing. Call me if you need me." I heard him slurp wine from his glass. He closed the apartment door softly. He must have taken the goblet with him because I couldn't find it anywhere.

It was too late to call Teri or Donna, but I called Mark.

"Do you want me to come over?"

"No, I'm fine but unnerved. He's my friend's boyfriend." I slid my shoes off and lay on Laura's bed.

"Just forget it. It's the way it is. It doesn't mean it's right, but this is what goes on."

"Should I tell Laura?" I looked at the happy photo of her and Jeff on the dresser.

"No, what good would it do? It would ruin your friendship. She'll find a reason to blame you because she's in awe of him. Just drop it. It's probably time for you to move on. I know you and Laura are tight, but she's in a different place, and it's not where you belong."

"I guess you're right. Listen, I have to tell you about the twins at the party. They were very pretty blonde girls in their early twenties. People referred to them as *two for the price of one,* and they were typical hangers-on. One of them sat next to me at dinner, and within five minutes she dropped ten famous names. She told me she went to Vegas last week without her sister and had a strange first-time experience. She had never before slept alone with a man—*without her twin.*" I emphasized the last phrase.

"Are you sure you're okay?"

"I'm fine, just needed to vent." I yawned and realized my fatigue. "I think I'll move back to my apartment when Laura returns."

"Good idea. I'll call you in the morning. Wait, I have a better idea. Since you're in Santa Monica, why don't I come over around noon, and we'll go to the Getty?"

"Sounds like a perfect idea."

Dream about the Getty Museum. Dream about the columns. Dream about Greece. Dream about Rome. Dream about home. I closed my eyes tight and repeated the words over and over in my head. I didn't remember my dreams.

* * *

I followed Mark's advice not to mention the incident to Laura. I picked her up from the airport early Wednesday morning. She was happy to be back and anxious to see Jeff. I redirected the conversation to her trip and asked her to tell me about testifying before Congress.

"What an amazing experience, but I'm glad to be done. Now Douglas is my only client."

I knew she had finalized a military study designed to examine if successful leadership was innate or could be taught. Through factor analysis, sixteen qualities of effective leaders had been identified with a training program designed to teach these skills to potential leaders. Laura had analyzed the results.

"How did they react to your conclusion?"

"Very well—because it makes sense. Yeah, you can improve leadership skills significantly, but real leaders have a special knack that can't be taught."

"Kind of like luck. You can do things to get to the top, but the final step is beyond our control." Donna's wisdom fit the moment. After a brief pause I continued, "I'm so glad you're back and although I'll miss our time together, I think I should return to my apartment tomorrow."

I felt relieved to have spat out the words, but she remained silent. *Did she know something?*

Laura wanted to do a few things before going to work and asked me to take her home. I decided I couldn't afford to spend any more time thinking about her and Jeff. They had to figure things out. I needed to focus on my life.

Although I thought I'd slept well the night before, I yawned and rubbed my eyes. *Definitely a cup of coffee would help.*

I hopped out of the car and started across the street. Without any warning, my whole world went black.

CHAPTER 6

———

Through the drizzle I saw a clear path, but when I looked closer, it was covered in tears.

—MAYA

I'd driven by the hospital many times, but I never imagined I would go there in an ambulance. I knew people were standing around me from the smell. Each had a distinct odor, unique forms against the flat backdrop of the sterile room. Their voices meshed into a hazy background buzz my ringing ears repelled. A soggy hand came down on my cheek and I wanted to swat it away, but the arms I willed to move refused. I knew I had arms. I could sense them at my sides—or maybe I didn't. Maybe they were phantom arms. Maybe I was a phantom.

A blurry face came close, the mouth opened and shut over and over again. I only sensed the soft and gentle odor. I began to visualize the smell—cloudy and pale. I tasted the smell—smooth and bland. The smell touched me gently, and I knew I lived.

The teeth I tried to open were clenched as if welded together. My whole body shook, but my teeth didn't clatter.

They couldn't break my jaw's grip. Rubbing hands tried to calm parts of my trembling body. I felt drool at the corner of my mouth. I hoped one of the smells would wipe it away. Fuzzy figures with soft hands wrapped me like a baby. I felt safe. Nothing could harm me.

If only they could swaddle my mind and I could go back to the start of an ordinary day before the accident. If only I hadn't walked across the busy street, if only I'd heeded Chrissy's warning about crazy drivers, if only I hadn't decided to buy coffee, if only the man hadn't been driving fast, if only I'd seen him coming. If only … if only I could make my mind stop churning.

The smells grew stronger—crisper, more distinct, and fearless. They took over the room. I felt myself receding into the background, and as I withdrew, peace increased with each step back. The shaking stopped, my jaw loosened, and my body and mind let go, giving way to sleep.

When I woke in the hospital room, the accident wouldn't leave me. The flashbacks increased as the minutes passed. The more I tried to push them away, the larger and louder they loomed. The logic games I consumed myself with were useless.

I should have looked a second time before I stepped off of the sidewalk. Maybe I was distracted, unfocused, but I couldn't admit this to anyone. It would undermine my confidence and change people's perception of me. I'm smart and successful. I would not be able to own up to doing something stupid. Maybe I wasn't neglectful? I had looked both ways, and twice to the left.

Fragments of the horrible moment kept running through my mind. I planned to have the type of day dictated by the requirements of a driven young working woman on the path to success. Everything in my life was falling into place—professional achievement and personal contentment in my new life. My plan hadn't factored in the unexpected.

The car came out of nowhere, but maybe my mind was nowhere and everywhere, the sidewalk and the street, one continuous path in a world beginning to revolve around me. My mind had been focused on a bizarre reaction a production pilot had had during an emergency scenario in the simulator. I was the only one convinced he made the error on purpose, but I couldn't think of a motive. For statistical reasons, I knew I should enlarge the test pool, but I wanted to understand his reason, which made no sense. If I could figure out why, I would earn kudos.

My head hurt, and staring at the stark white hospital celling made it throb more. I closed my eyes and remembered the smells of my childhood. The warm pita bread rising in the open-flame bakery oven on a chilly spring morning; the scents of the people standing in line, each holding a bowl filled with their own special combination of dried thyme, sumac, sesame seeds, and olive oil. The baker spreading the spice mixture on flat round dough and pushing it into the oven. I caught whiffs from the bags of those rushing out to take the hot breakfast pastries home. How many hundreds of years had this been a tradition?

I opened my eyes and again began to think about the accident. I remembered the old lady who held my hand as I lay on the street, the paramedics, the doctors, and the nurses; they were never part of my blueprint. I had no place in my life for them. Who were these friendly and warm people comforting a stranger in a crisis? Where were they on my lonely days in Los Angeles?

I gazed out of the window, through the light rain, and saw her. As a child, I'd studied her every graceful curve and delicate porcelain face. I wiped my eyes, pulled my sore body more erect and leaned forward, in an attempt to focus through the drizzle. Did she turn toward me slightly or did I imagination it? I smelled the cold moist limestone of the village church, the burning incense, the fragrant roses I placed at her feet, and the sweet sweat of a child in prayer.

I stared at the statue of the Madonna in the hospital garden—a duplicate of the one next to the altar in my Lebanese mountain church. She wore a sky-blue robe and white scarf. Her head slightly tilted to her right shoulder made her open hands appear more welcoming to the frightened and the weary. She existed for anyone who chose to seek her grace. She'd answered the simple prayers of a child, and I now looked to her to solve the complex problems of a young woman. Before I could formulate any words, my mind cleared, the foggy smells blown out by a crisp breeze, and I understood her message. I had to go home.

Loud voices in the hallway invaded my pensive mind. "I can't believe the three of us showed up at the same time."

Donna entered, followed by Laura and Teri. They positioned themselves around my bed, and I managed a weak smile.

"Oh my God. How are you?" Teri asked and then blinked. "Stupid question. But—oh, thank God you're alive."

"I'm okay. Just beat up. Doctor says I have to be under observation until tomorrow. They did x-rays and stuff."

"Girl, I got a message for you," Laura imitated Janice. "You're supposed to *look* under cars, not *fall* under them."

"What?" Teri asked.

Laura ignored her. "Janice was devastated when she heard what happened. For someone who's been through as much as she has, it surprised me. She took off work early because she couldn't concentrate. She's coming to see you later this evening."

"So, you're stuck having to deal with the boring visitors first." Donna waved her hand in the direction of the other two.

"You're calling us boring? Speak for yourself. But come to think of it, maybe Teri is getting dull. Have you heard about her latest venture? She's gonna be a cast member in the Pageant of the Masters. Can you imagine posing on a stage to look like a piece of art? *Tableaux vivant*—beautiful to behold, boring to execute." Laura stood up and struck a teapot pose.

Teri turned to me. "I'm house-sitting this summer in Laguna Beach and it happens to coincide with the pageant. I figured it'd be fun. And, Miss Laura, I haven't decided if you're invited to spend a weekend with the rest of us at the house."

They all giggled. I didn't. Donna approached the bed. "Are you all right?" She stepped forward and pulled the hospital gown up over my shoulder.

"I'm fine, but my head hurts." *And I just realized what I need to do with my life.*

"I'll get the nurse," Donna said.

Laura had already pushed the call button, and a nurse entered. "I'll bring you something for the pain."

Teri stood. "I'm leaving for Austin in two days. Mother's having a big barbeque, but if you need me to stay, I will."

The nurse handed me two pills and a glass of water. The three of them watched me swallow.

"Would you like me to take you home tomorrow? I know Mark's in San Fran. Do you want me to call him? Do you have his parents' number?" Donna asked.

I shook my head. "I don't. He probably tried to call my apartment. I guess if he gets worried, he'll call one of you. Chrissy is going to drive me home and stay with me for a few days. Thanks anyway."

"Wait a minute," Teri said. "If Mark's away and doesn't know you're in the hospital, who sent you red roses?"

"John."

"John? Like work John?" Laura's voice was loud.

"He's the only John I know."

"Why would John send red roses?" Laura asked.

"Why not? I think it's nice of him to send me flowers."

"I asked why he sent red roses?"

"Roses are flowers."

"Sweetie," Donna said softly. "Here, when a man sends red roses, it signifies love and romance."

"Has he shown any signs of being interested in you?" Laura asked.

"John?"

"Yes, John."

"C'mon, you know better than that. It's John we're talking about."

"Why would he send red roses?"

"I don't know. I'll ask him when I see him."

"Gee, Maya, you're so nonchalant," Teri said.

"I think it's great," Donna said. "She'll ask him when she sees him. End of story. Considering why we're here, I think we have more important things to worry about."

"What's important is Maya's fine." Teri blew me a kiss. "I need to get going."

"Me, too." Donna squeezed my hand. "Think positive and be thankful."

The moment they left, Laura pulled a chair close to my bed. "How's your head? Is it still hurting?"

"It's better. The medication must be working."

"If you're up to it, I want to talk to you about something."

"I can't guarantee I can focus."

"No focus is needed. It's emotional stuff." She placed her right hand on the bed sheet and leaned closer to me. "Jeff told me what happened."

I didn't say anything, and she continued. "He said you're the first woman who's turned him down." She paused and looked expectantly at me, but I showed no reaction. "As he becomes more successful, he's found it easier and easier to get women and he's taken this for granted. What happened with you made him take a step back and think about things. He doesn't want to screw up our relationship."

"I'm glad he realizes how lucky he is to have you."

"He wants me to thank you. He wanted to come with me, but thought it might upset you."

"I'm glad it worked out. You're my friend, and I'd never consider doing anything with your boyfriend." I lowered my voice. "It's not acceptable."

"There's nothing I want more than to be with Jeff. He's the only man I've ever wanted a baby with. I haven't had these feelings before. I never thought I'd put a relationship ahead of my career."

My head felt heavy, and I sank deeper into the pillow. Laura stood and moved the chair back against the wall. "Call me if you need anything. And thank you. I've never had a real girlfriend."

She squeezed my hand. I missed home where a friend would've given me a hug or a kiss.

I tried to look outside, but heavy rain and darkness blocked everything. I imagined the image of the statue in the slick, moving patterns on the window. I closed my eyes, and the Madonna came to life in my sleep.

* * *

I woke to the sound of a familiar voice outside my room. I knew it was Omar's but couldn't make out his words nor those of the other person. I closed my eyes and heard footsteps.

"Maya," he gently touched my cheek. "Christina had a problem at work and couldn't leave. I've come to take you home. Your discharge papers are ready. The nurse will bring them for your signature. I know Christina brought you clothes yesterday. Do you have anything to take home?"

"No. When Chrissy came to see me late last night, she took my purse. My clothes were ruined."

"The nurse told me you spoke to the police yesterday. I wish you'd called me to come be with you."

"Thanks, but it wasn't a big deal. I told them I only remembered stepping into the street. They didn't ask much else. But the annoying ones were the two lawyers. The first one made me believe he represented the insurance company, but I soon realized he didn't. He tried to persuade me to sue, and I told him I wasn't interested. He kept talking and said it wouldn't cost me anything. When we won, he'd take a third of the money."

"What'd you tell him?"

"Told him I'd think about it. I made a mistake though. I gave him my phone number."

"Don't worry about it. He would've gotten it anyway. You're listed in the book."

The nurse entered and Omar looked over my shoulder at the papers she handed me. I signed, and she asked him to bring his car to the front entrance while she helped me dress.

"What a handsome gentleman you have." She wheeled me to the lobby and spotted him leaning on his Corvette. "And it doesn't hurt that he's rich. My husband says you can love a rich girl just as easily as you can love a poor one."

Omar opened the car door, and they helped me in. He thanked the nurse profusely. No one could match his charm.

"You gave us a scare. When the hospital called, Christina wasn't home. I claimed to be your brother so they'd speak to me. You of all people—you're always in control. How'd it happen?"

I focused on the cars we passed on the freeway. "I don't know. All I know is it made me start thinking about my life—what I'm doing, where I'm going, and what I want. I need to decide whether to build my future here or go home."

"It's hard for people like you and Christina because you have choices. I don't have a choice, nor do I want one. I'll return home. My years in LA will be a chapter in my life— one I'll cherish, but I've never ever thought of staying here. My future is waiting for me with the family business in Syria. But as you know, I'm in no hurry to graduate and return, because once I do, it will be over for good."

Omar possessed a relaxed, confident demeanor about him. I felt envious. He didn't have to make the choice.

"Don't worry too much about deciding now. You need to rest and things will eventually work out. Something will happen, and you'll know what to do." He reached down and squeezed my hand.

I thought about the Madonna.

I had the opportunity to ask him about Christina. Even though my head throbbed and I didn't feel on top of my game, I knew I might not have another chance alone with him. Their situation was sad. If they'd been born in a different place, they might have had a fair shot at a good life together, but given the circumstances, there was little hope it could ever be. But idealizing could be a mistake. He carried a dark side within him. Did circumstances perpetuate it? *Should I feel guilty thinking like this? He's always been kind to me.*

"What's going to happen with you and Christina?"

"We'll figure it out once I get closer to leaving."

"Omar, why are you being so rough on her?"

He took his eyes off the road to glare at me. "What are you talking about?"

"I...I mean I've been around when you chew her out because you forgot her schedule. And at times, I feel she's fearful of you."

"Look Maya, I love you like a sister and you're one of my dearest friends, but none of this is any of your business."

"I know she loves you, but I see her often demoralized."

"Has she said anything to you?"

"No."

"Then, like I said, this does not concern you." He raised the volume on the radio.

He escorted me into the apartment, insisted on waiting while I showered, and brought a plate of cheese and a cup of tea to me in bed. When Christina called to say she'd leave work in a few minutes, he asked me if I thought I'd be okay alone for half an hour and left.

CHAPTER 7

To understand, I do not have to believe, nor to believe do I have to understand.

—*MAYA*

"Wait... Maya... what exactly are you saying?" Christina put down her paper and looked up at me from her seat on the floor.

"I'm going back."

"Okay," Christina spoke slowly. "So, how do you mean, going back?"

"I mean I'm going back to Lebanon. I'm leaving LA."

"You mean, like, for good?" She sounded uneasy.

"I've been thinking a lot lately, and I think I need to go back for good. I mean, what are we doing here? Is this where we belong? Look at us." I glanced down at her and then at the crocheted green afghan covering me on the sofa.

"What's wrong with us?"

"I mean—I don't mean, there's something wrong with us. That's the problem. We're good. In fact, we're great. We have amazing jobs, and we're moving up fast in our careers. We're attractive and have lots of friends. And we're empty. Chrissy, we're empty. We're going nowhere." I stood, the afghan fell to the floor, and I stepped over it.

Christina watched me.

"Look around." I raised my arms. "How long did I dream of working in aerospace? How long did I dream about meeting the authors of publications? Well, I have my dream job, and I've met many of the people I wanted to meet. And everything is hollow and lonely. The glamour's a shell. Don't get me wrong. The work's amazing, and they're wonderful people. I admire them, I care for them, I respect them, but I don't want to end up like them. I thought I did, but it's not for me."

Chrissy crinkled up her forehead and chewed on her lower lip. She raised her chin in my direction and began to say something, but I cut her off. "I want to go back to where I mean something to people; where I'm special and can make a difference. Chrissy, what are we in LA? Yeah, we're great and appreciated at work, but don't think for one second we're unique. If we leave, someone else will take our place, and the huge machine will keep on going."

I took a deep breath and listened to my heartbeat. Christina's eyes never turned away from me. When she finally spoke, she was methodical. "We're here because we had to flee from there. Don't romanticize Lebanon now. The country we grew up in is gone. Peace and comfort are gone. We're the fortunate ones because we have options. We might not like the options, but at least we have them. Talk to people there and see how many wish they could leave. Call Leila and see what she tells you. We go to sleep at night and don't worry about a rocket hitting our home. We drive the streets and are not fearful of armed men kidnapping or killing us because we happen to be of the wrong religion or political party..."

She continued talking, but I stopped hearing. I knew every argument she could make. She must have realized because she put her papers in neat stacks, abruptly stood up and went to the kitchen. I heard her preparing dinner, and she returned with two plates of food. I made space for her on the sofa.

In both appearance and taste, her food reflected her practical style. I liked it when she cooked. Besides the fact it relieved me of the chore, I knew I would get no-nonsense nutrition. Tonight we had baked chicken breast, steamed broccoli, and a recent discovery of hers—something called quinoa. None of our friends had ever heard of it, but she'd found it at a health food store. She always included a large salad, seasoned with fresh lemon juice and olive oil.

"Do you want to watch *Three's Company*?" She turned on the TV, and I asked for a glass of wine. She smirked and reached for my prescription bottle. "Are you sure you wouldn't like cognac?"

We laughed. It wasn't because I'd been told not to drink with the medication but rather a memory from the summer of our college freshman year.

We had planned a shopping trip and left our summer homes on a cool mountain morning to drive down to Beirut. Half way there, Rima complained of menstrual cramps, and I gave her two painkillers.

Twenty minutes later when we parked, she still didn't feel well. We'd been looking forward to this day and weren't about to go back. We helped Rima out of the car, supported her on either side and walked down Hamra, the main shopping street. A liquor store on the corner gave me a brilliant idea. We sat Rima on a chair in the shop, opened two small cognac bottles and made her drink both. Papa swore it cured almost everything.

For two hours, we dragged her from boutique to boutique. We seated her gently in each. Back in the car, we adjusted the front passenger's seat to a complete recline. She fell asleep, and we congratulated ourselves on a successful shopping trip and on our skillful handling of a medical situation—until we got home half an hour later and tried to awaken her.

I jumped out of the car and screamed, "Teta, Teta."

My grandmother charged down the flight of steps from her front porch, leaned into the car, shook Rima and slapped her face.

People gathered on the narrow village road. Teta yelled orders. A thin middle-aged man lifted Rima's limp body and carried her up the steps to Teta's bed. We hastily followed.

"I gave her this." I pulled the bottle of pills from my purse.

"Two bottles of cognac." Christina and I spoke simultaneously.

"Cramps…"

"Very hot day."

"Bring rose water and bring…" Teta shouted at two women, dressed head to toe in black. I didn't understand the concoctions she requested.

Christina and I stood in a corner holding on to each other. Everyone else hovered around the bed.

"*Ya Adra, Ya Adra*, Oh Virgin," Christina repeated.

I was too mortified to even think of praying. I stared at the backs of the people blocking our view.

Suddenly, one of the women shrieked and beat her right fist on her chest, "Thank God. Thank God." She raised her eyes to the ceiling. Everyone stepped away from the bed in unison. Rima sat up. Christina and I cried. Teta had done it again. She always made everything right.

The theme song of the TV show blasted, but I knew both Christina and I were thinking about the faraway story. I wondered if we both remembered it the same way.

"Chrissy, I miss the people. Especially certain ones. I want someone to knock on my door and come visit. I want to walk down the street and greet people, and I want them to ask about me when they don't see me." I looked at the cold plates of food.

Chrissy sighed. "You can have a wonderful life here without the pettiness of small-minded people and live with security, never in fear for your life because of who you are or what you believe. There's no tribalism. Everyone's American first—they're united—even though they have different ideas."

"Logic tells me you're right, but emotion tells me I'm right. There's no easy answer, but if I stay here much longer, I doubt I'll ever return. And I'm not sure it's the right thing for me. I need to go home to see what's there. LA will still be here. I figure I can afford to take a couple of years to decide. Let me put it this way—two years from now, I'll know what I'm doing."

* * *

John didn't say anything, but from the way he looked at me, I knew he was upset. His eyes narrowed and he focused on a notepad on his desk. He finally spoke. "I can't say I understand where you're coming from, but I have to respect your decision. I can't even imagine the turmoil you've experienced over the past four years. I know you're confused about where you belong and your future. But despite all of this, you're one of the most positive individuals I've ever met."

"Thanks." I felt relieved. Like poking a pin in a blister, anticipation is worse than the action.

"I hate to see you leave. You know you have a great future here, and I don't only mean at Douglas. I mean in the US. And I worry about your safety in Lebanon." He slid a pen out of his plastic pocket protector and wrote something. Dr. Moset had told me an important work skill was the ability to read upside down, but his block letters all looked the same from my angle.

"You know, I really appreciate the opportunities you've given me and your support. Remember when we reviewed the simulator tapes and heard one of the control tower guys say a woman didn't belong in the cockpit? You got angry but you never told me what you said to him to make him give me such a sincere apology." My anxiety gave way to sadness.

He wrote something else down. "You know, you'll be good at anything you put your mind to. Don't ever let anyone tell you can't do it because you're a woman."

I nodded. "I'll really miss working with you. I'd like to think I've done something to change you. You now greet people in the hallways. If nothing else, I've completely destroyed your peace and quiet." I smiled at him, but he only managed a half-smile in return.

"How about you take a six month leave of absence instead of resigning? This'll keep the door open for a while—in case things don't work out. When do you plan to leave?"

"Early June."

"Well, at least it gives us a couple of months to plan."

"I'm not going to tell many people about my decision yet."

"They won't hear it from me."

"By the way, I forgot to thank you for the red roses you sent. They were beautiful."

"Red roses?"

"Yes, why?"

"I sent you red roses?"

"Yes. Thanks, again."

"I didn't mean to send them. I mean, I meant to send you flowers but not roses."

"Whatever, they were very nice."

"Janice," I heard him mutter as I turned to leave.

I walked slowly back to my office, glad Laura was traveling. I didn't have to tell anybody else. I could pretend everything remained the same—at least for a while.

I worried most about telling Mark. His father was sick, and he'd stayed an extra week in San Francisco. I'd rehearsed scenarios in my mind, but none of them seemed right. I cared for him deeply, but our relationship lacked spark. We were comfortable with each other, but I felt his attachment to me got stronger by the day.

"Something bothering you, girl? I don't like the way you been looking since you've been back from your accident. Did they go and give you something at the hospital? You're not shining no more." Janice positioned her eyes in front of mine.

"I think I'm tired." I looked down to avoid her gaze. "How about we take a walk?"

"Best idea today."

"Do you mind if we go to the hangar?"

We walked in the passageway between two buildings. My hair blew in my face, and I held it back, but loose strands continued to fly into my mouth. It felt exhilarating—like being in a wind tunnel.

We turned the corner, and I let go of my hair. "Janice, do you believe in signs?"

"You mean like street signs?"

"No. I mean like a sign that signifies something. Like if you want to know what you should do and then something happens and you interpret it as the answer."

"My grandma always told me when she reached heaven, she'd send me a sign. One day, after she became sick, I walked home from the bus stop and a woman on the street handed me a rose. No one ever gave me a flower before. I grabbed it and ran home. I burst in the door yelling, 'When did Grandma Rose die?' My mama said, 'She didn't.' We ran to her room. She lay in her bed as dead as a doornail."

I felt goosebumps and an eternal sense of comfort. Clearly, Janice would understand, but I couldn't tell her about the Madonna. She might tell others before I was ready.

"Are you looking for a sign, girl?"

"I think I saw one. I'll tell you about it later." She didn't question me.

I stopped at the Vons Supermarket on my way home. I wanted to test a challenge I had created in my mind. *If someone recognizes me, I will reconsider my decision to leave.* I had shopped at the store for over two years and often had the same checker, but she never seemed to know me. She constantly gave the same forced smile before yelling out the price of each item while entering the numbers on her cash register. When I walked past the manager's window on my way out, he recited, "Have a nice night." And he parroted the same words to anyone behind me. Not long ago, I asked him a question, and he asked if it was my first visit to the store. He said he looked forward to seeing me again. *As if he'd recognize me. No, I belong where I am significant—where I mean something to others.*

* * *

Mark's body went rigid at my news. "Are you sure about this decision?" He pushed his chair back from the dinette table.

I could barely look at him. When he returned the night before, I didn't have the heart to tell him. Moreover, he felt badly he hadn't been around to help me after my accident.

Now, this morning, I found the courage—or acted out of guilt.

"What made you decide now?" His voice quivered.

I placed my hand on his arm and looked into his eyes. "It's now or never. If I don't try to go back, I might spend my whole life regretting it."

"But why now?"

"The more I get involved with life here, the harder it's going to be." I never mentioned the Madonna. I felt he might ridicule me.

"You know I want you to be happy. But what about us?"

"I'll miss you, but you know I'll never be happy unless I go home and see if it's where I'm meant to be."

We stood. He pulled me close and I felt sad and scared but excited.

"I understand why you have to go. My hope is you'll return."

* * *

The next two months passed quickly. Everybody, including me, wanted to keep me tied to LA. Donna planned to store my furniture; Terry would drive my car to her Austin home; my mail would be forwarded to Chrissy; and my checking account would remain open. In LA everything was arranged in anticipation of my return. In Lebanon, everything was being planned in anticipation of my homecoming.

On my last Saturday night, five days before this phase of my life became history, Chrissy insisted I have dinner at Omar's. I'd wanted to go out with Mark and my friends, but everyone had a conflict. Even though I understood, it hurt the most when Mark told me he had to go to San Francisco for his father's award ceremony.

Carrying a bottle of Omar's favorite wine, I unhurriedly walked up the steps to his apartment. He and Chrissy were the only two people I'd known when I arrived. Consequently, it seemed fitting for me to bow out with them.

I rang the bell and opened the door. They only locked it when they slept. "Surprise!" My whole life in LA shouted: Chrissy, Omar, Teri, Laura, Jeff, Donna, John, Janice, Dan, and Mark. They raised their glasses.

"To options," Donna shouted.

"To Maya the unifier," Teri added. "Who else could have brought such an eclectic group of people together?"

"To the friendship we share with you and one another," Laura said.

"To courage," Omar bellowed.

"To the mystique of the East," Dan said. "I wish I could join you."

"To following your soul," Janice said.

Jeff shouted, "Speech. Speech." Others echoed his entreaty and looked at me expectantly.

The door behind me was still open, and I considered stepping back out and shutting it.

"I'll miss you guys. Thank you for the wonderful memories." I looked around the room at my friends. In the group stood two tormented souls—Christina and me. Everybody else knew where they belonged in the world.

"She what?" Mark's voice carried across the room. "Tell everyone the story." He sat next to Chrissy on the sofa.

"I was telling Mark about Omar's parents' first visit to the US. The day they arrived, he took a break from classes to meet them at the airport and bring them to his apartment. When he returned in the evening, his place was full of people."

"I thought something terrible had happened to my parents," Omar injected. "Oh, Christina, I didn't mean to interrupt. Actually, she tells the story better than me."

"His mother rushed to the door and told him she'd brought food she'd prepared in Syria. She had made a grand dinner. Neighbors in our part of the world become family. They visit, share meals, have coffee together and take care of each other. She naturally figured, since he was single, they were a significant part of his life. To show appreciation and return invitations, she knocked on all their doors."

"I couldn't believe it," Omar continued. "The apartment was full of people I had never spoken to. She thought the whole world lived like back home. I never saw any of them again."

"Well, Maya, if you had stayed here long enough, I'm sure you would have turned your whole apartment building into a social club." Donna gave me a wistful look.

* * *

The final gathering took place at LAX. I'd spent the night at Teri's, and she drove me to the airport. Chrissy, Laura, Donna, and Mark were already at the gate when we arrived. Everyone tried to be upbeat.

"I think I speak for everyone when I say our doors are always open for you." Chrissy's words caused me more doubt and sorrow. How badly I wished I could be part of both worlds—two trajectories for one life. *Am I making a mistake boarding this plane?*

"I love you." Mark held me and gave me a long kiss.

"I'll miss you." I couldn't bring myself to say more. I knew I'd never let myself fully explore if I truly loved him. If I did, I was frightened I would never return home.

Chrissy leaned close as I stepped onto the jetway. She whispered, "As a wise woman once said, two years from now we'll know what we're doing."

I boarded the DC-10 and instinctively headed for the cockpit. The seated flight crew turned when I entered.

"I just want to say hello and introduce myself. I'm Maya Coury from the engineering department at Douglas Aircraft."

"Hey, nice to meet you. I'm Captain Thomson, this is First Officer Kelly, and our fearless Flight Engineer Erickson. I was in Long Beach last week. What do you do there?"

"I'm in ergonomics. I spend a lot of time in the simulator with production and test pilots. I recently finished a joint project with Boeing and the FAA on safety procedures." I spoke like I was still employed but couldn't bring myself to say otherwise.

"Sounds interesting. Once we get this baby off the ground, we'll talk some more."

"I'll come by later—sooner, if the meal's really bad."

"Look forward to it," the captain said. The two other crew members nodded.

I made my way to my economy cabin window seat from where I would bid the city farewell.

"Ms. Coury?" The flight attendant stood in the aisle. "A seat change was requested for you. Please follow me. Do you have anything in the overhead?"

Once out of earshot of the other passengers, she said, "Captain Thomson requested you be seated in the first-class cabin."

"Thank you. I've never flown first class."

She wouldn't let me help her with my carry-on bag. "Let's make it a complete first-class experience." She smiled.

I rubbed my hand on the leather armrest and then opened my handbag to touch my treasured glass cedar. The plane lifted off the ground, and I pressed my face to the window. It was getting dark, and the smog was too heavy for my vision to penetrate.

Goodbye, City of Angels. I came to you as an anonymous refugee and through the opportunities you offered me and my own accomplishments, I leave first class. What a wonderful country. Maybe I could've been happy here. If only the cedars of Lebanon hadn't kept calling out.

PART II

BEIRUT, LEBANON 1981

CHAPTER 8

———

Things we hear as children are planted like seedlings in the fertile soil of the brain, and as they grow, their leaves reach out to brush the soul.

—*LEILA*

We neared our destination, and a lump rose in my throat. Words became more difficult to form—heavy and incomplete with pauses between. Unable to concentrate on my conversation with the elderly man next to me, I turned and rested my forehead against the plane window. After so many years, it was too overwhelming to imagine seeing and holding my family and friends again. My mind suppressed anticipation.

The blurry strip of brown coastline met the radiant Mediterranean—a calm unity deceptively diverting years of horror. The green snow-capped mountains completed the landscape of my Lebanon. Brown, blue, green, and white all masked the red of blood that had flowed from our people over the centuries.

The plane made its approach, and the chatter tapered off. I blocked out the engine noise, imagining the waves pounding the shore and the mountain breeze blowing through fragrant cedar trees. The wheels touched the ground to an explosion of passenger applause. We were home.

A young woman in a skimpy top hugged a middle-aged lady wearing a headscarf. Together they cried. From their attire, I knew they came from different sides of the religious—and, most probably the political—spectrum, divisions created by evil leaders to keep themselves in power. For the moment, similarities trumped differences, and we were all of the same people—Lebanese returning home, the victims of political and religious leaders with greedy agendas. The bulge in my throat dissolved, and I wiped my face with my sleeve.

I paused on the platform outside the aircraft door. People pushed past me, rushing down the wheeled stairs, onto the tarmac and into the terminal. Gazing at the mountains, I filled my lungs with the soft moist air before I walked down. It was warm, but a slight breeze blew inland from the sea. It had been years since I'd stood on this soil, and for the first time, I realized why the three major monotheistic religions were born in this part of the world. Passion is in this air unlike anywhere else, and if a person listens quietly, they can hear the voice of God.

I smiled at the thought of God speaking to me, took a skip, and walked hastily to the terminal and to a passport control line.

"Maya George Coury." The officer looked up from my passport.

In Lebanon, the father's first name is the child's middle name, but for a moment I expected to be asked why I had a boy's name—as often happened in the US. Instead, he said, "Welcome. Thanks be to God for your safe arrival."

He stamped my passport. As I turned to leave the low-gated area, men in Syrian army fatigues manned the exit on either side. Their military had entered Lebanon in 1976, initially to counteract the armed Palestinian guerrillas and their allies who were gaining strength and attacking Christian villages. At first, many Lebanese Muslims and Christians welcomed them, but over the years had become a tyrannical occupying force.

"Your passport," the Syrian snapped.

"Passport control already stamped it." I clutched it tightly.

"I said, give me your passport." He raised his voice.

"No. Why should I? You're not Lebanese Internal Security."

Passengers scurried past me, complying with the demands of the Syrian army personnel checking documents. Our loud voices and the confrontation seemed to make them ill at ease.

"Ugly, ignorant occupier," I mumbled to myself. I tried to take a step forward, but he blocked me with his foot.

A husky man wearing a suit with an open white shirt approached, and from the look he gave the soldier, I figured he was his superior—an undercover agent.

"What's the problem?" he addressed neither of us and focused on a woman in a tight skirt.

"She won't show me her passport."

"Why won't you?" He glared at my chest.

"Because this is Lebanon, and Lebanese authorities stamped it."

"My sister," he snorted without moving his eyes away from my breasts. "We're all one people, Syrians and Lebanese; we're brothers and sisters. We came to help you. Now, I can see you're a good woman. You can go."

I turned to leave and overheard him say, "Why did you argue with a woman? Don't you know how dumb they are? Besides we know everything about everyone who's coming and going through the airport."

I was tempted to turn back to confront him, but I knew better. I'd already pressed my luck. They could take me away in an instant, and I might never be heard from again. Fortunately, these men wouldn't lower themselves to the level of a woman. That's what gave me the confidence to take them on. My joy and nostalgia had quickly curdled into anger. I headed to the chaos surrounding the baggage carousel. A porter found me, thanked God for my safe arrival, put my two suitcases on his cart, and led me past the customs officials.

We left the building, crossed the street, and merged into the crowd. Armed men stood watch, allowing arriving passengers to exit and preventing others from entering. The airport building was now off limits to anyone with no reason to be there. It had become a structure filled with nervous passengers, stressed employees, representatives of Lebanon's barely functioning government, foreign occupiers, militias, and the occasional peacekeeper. Departing travelers bid farewell to friends and family at the entrance of the building. Arriving passengers exited into an open-air, low-fenced area, to find familiar faces among the crowd. In Lebanon, someone would always be waiting.

Although I hadn't seen Leila since I'd fled, the moment I caught a glimpse of her, time and space vanished. She stood on the other side of the barrier like a spot-lit sculpture while everything around her moved. The earth tones of her slim body and chic clothing distinguished her in a sea of color—people dressed in bright red, blue, yellow, orange and green who waved, stepped forward, jumped, bent down, talked, hugged, and kissed. Occasionally, someone in the crowd stopped to gaze at her, no doubt fascinated by her beauty and serenity.

I spotted my parents and jumped into their embrace. I don't think I really saw them. Everything felt abstract. Rima came up behind me and threw her arms around my neck. Over Maman's shoulder, I caught Leila's smile. She waited patiently and then came forward as if she stepped out of a picture frame, like the Pageant of the Masters in Laguna Beach. "Maya, oh my God." She opened her arms.

Suddenly, we became the figures in motion while the crowd surrounding us seemed stationary. We hugged and rocked back and forth—oblivious to everyone. We stopped abruptly, suddenly aware of my waiting family.

We crossed the dusty road. A black car waited at the entrance of the parking lot, and a thin man stood next to it. Leila's driver had been with her family since we were children.

"Mademoiselle Maya, thanks be to God for your safe arrival."

"Thank you, Ali. How's your health? How's the family?"

"Thanks be to God. Will you be riding with Mademoiselle Leila?"

"Ali, what kind of question is that?" Leila retorted. "Mademoiselle Maya is going home with her family. We'll meet them there." She squeezed my hand, pulled away, and slid into the back seat of the Mercedes.

With my parents on either side of me and Rima holding on to my father's arm, the four of us chatted happily and walked to our car. The airport porter trailed behind us with my suitcases on his squeaky cart.

Papa pulled the car out, and I realized how much older he looked. His thinning hair had gray streaks, and his shoulders slumped slightly forward. I sank deeper into my seat and tried not to think about all the years we'd lost together. I remembered my last fearful journey on this road with Amo Fred. I felt as though I'd slipped into a chasm.

"What do you think, Maya?" Rima turned to face me. Her lips sparkled in the light of a passing car.

"I'm sorry. What?"

"The squatters in these makeshift homes on the airport road; do you think they'll ever move?"

Once, the road to Beirut airport was a source of pride and beauty, smooth and straight with graceful umbrella pine trees and the occasional elegant building lining both sides. The airport's long and plain building had open doors and windows. People were welcome to stroll in and out. Passengers bid farewell to their family or friends at passport control. The escorts often proceeded to outdoor terraces to watch and wave as the travelers exited the lower part of the building onto the tarmac and climbed the steps to an airplane, often pausing at the top to acknowledge those watching. An airport concession sold wonderful soft serve ice cream cones, and visitors rarely passed up the opportunity to buy one. Those who did could purchase thick, dark Turkish coffee to slowly sip. But this was before the war when life was simple.

After the fighting began, the drive to the airport became a perilous and anxiety-filled journey, getting worse with each passing day. Now, the streets were accented with potholes and blocked by checkpoints manned by armed men. The few remaining umbrella pines struggled for life among refugees and shack dwellers. Thin dust covered everything like rotting spider webs. The route was a maze of traps to be negotiated. Life had become complicated.

"Where can they go?" Maman asked. "They were driven out of their homes. Without a strong government to protect them, they have no choice."

"Let's not talk about sad things," Papa said. "Today's a celebration."

"*Habibti*," Maman addressed me with a word of endearment and reached back for my hand. "We've waited a long time for this day when we're all home, together again." She squeezed tightly.

I really didn't want to see depressing things but felt compelled to look. I focused on the road, in anticipation of upcoming Syrian checkpoints. I knew if a driver failed to stop, the soldiers would shoot. I heard they were instructed to shoot out the tires to make the driver stop, but in reality, nobody actually knew of an incident where only tires were destroyed. Everyone knew of cases where the driver or a passenger was killed.

Papa stopped the car, rolled down his window and turned on the interior light. A brusque Syrian soldier examined us and, as often happened when an older man traveled with women, he waved us through. My father muttered his thanks including the traditional phrase asking God to shine blessings on him while he worked.

The instant we drove off, I vented, "Stupid animals. I can't believe we have to put up with them occupying our country. Why can't we get rid of them?" I remembered my confrontation at the airport. I'd never tell my parents about it because it would make them nervous. They'd worry about what else I might do.

Papa turned off the airport road, and we continued through the western part of the city to our apartment. I mentally retraced my last journey in reverse. Now, the Mediterranean Sea was on the left and the tall buildings, bearing witness to the atrocity of war, stood on the right. The sun had set and the moon illuminated the calm, black water as it softly lapped at the sand, nature concealing evil scars. But darkness couldn't hide the destruction wrought by man. Pockmark-patterned concrete and stone structures made the once-stylish buildings look pathetic and sickly. Healing and disease seemed to grab me, one from each side, and caught me in the web named Lebanon.

The elderly concierge rushed to greet us as the car pulled up to our building. Everything looked older and dimmer than I remembered.

"Thanks be to God for your safe arrival. Your country missed you." The old man chanted the mantra while trying to hide his struggle with the overweight luggage.

I returned his greeting. "May God shine his blessings on you. How is your health, Abou Ziad? How is the family?"

"Thanks be to God, all are well. They ask about your well-being, Miss Maya."

We left the small elevator for the old man with my suitcases and took the stairs. Before we reached the apartment landing, the door flew open. They were all there—everyone I loved and had left amid the destruction.

My cousin Selma grabbed me first, "Oh my God how I've missed you." I hugged her and cried. Roger stood beside her and when she let go of me, he kissed me. Selma immediately embraced me again.

"Where are the children?" she asked her husband.

"Running up and down the stairs. I'll get them."

I watched him climb the steps, two at a time. They were high school sweethearts and by all accounts, perfect together. They'd married after college, traveled to New York for graduate school, returned, and had a baby the year before the war began. They'd started a public relations company and despite the situation, it had grown. Rima and I always wished we'd be as lucky as Selma in love.

A boy and a girl bolted down the steps with Roger walking calmly behind.

"Remember Jad?" Selma asked.

"Oh my God. He was a baby."

"I'm seven."

"This must be Jessie." I looked at the other child.

"She's five," Jad said.

Selma nudged both children to me, and I bent down to kiss them. She then led me by the hand into the apartment, pausing each time I stopped to kiss someone.

Leila had arrived ahead of us and stood to one side in the spacious apartment foyer. A wide smile filled her oval face and despite her relaxed stance, she retained her majestic posture. She watched everything but looked at nothing.

Inside these walls we could pretend the world was perfect. I'd fantasized about this reunion for years but never expected to experience it. Family, friends, food, and wine fused together to create a moment in time I wanted to preserve forever. This was how the Lebanese survived. Everyone forgot the hell of the surrounding reality and replaced it with love, laughter, and gourmet pleasure. Similar scenes occurred in countless homes across the country.

"Maman, where's Teta?" For the first time since my arrival, I looked at my mother, thankful she had not physically changed in almost five years.

"She couldn't come. There's sniping on the Green Line and no taxi driver would bring her. It isn't a good time to cross from one side to the other."

I knew my grandmother would have taken any risk to be with us. But the Green Line had become the notorious ten-mile boundary between the majority-Christian East Beirut and majority-Muslim West Beirut. To ratchet up the level of tension and fear, snipers would shoot at people attempting to cross from one side to the other. Kidnappings also occurred along the crossing. Yet, here we were, a Christian family, all gathered in the western part of the city, like many other Christians who had lived in this area for generations.

I missed Teta more than anyone else and desperately wished for a working phone system. I knew it would be fruitless to try and call. We rarely could get a dial tone. Even when we did, it seldomly connected. Attempting a phone call resembled gambling. One always thinks the next try will succeed, hours are wasted, and superstitious habits are developed. I'd try in the morning or, better yet, go to Leila's house where there were multiple phone lines. I remembered Chrissy holding up the telephone receiver, trying to persuade me not to return.

I snuck away from the gathering and walked down the long corridor to the room I had hastily left. I closed the door and flicked the light switch. Dim incandescent light from the ceiling chandelier filled the space. I pulled the glass cedar out of my pocket, kissed it, and placed it back where it belonged, among the seventy-two other patiently waiting treasures. I could almost swear I saw the porcelain ballerina curtsey. I smiled, crossed myself, and turned to leave when Selma entered.

"Where've you been? Dinner's on the table and we're waiting for you to invite everyone into the dining room." She adjusted the collar of my shirt.

I stood by the long, food-filled table, and Selma opened the double doors leading into the room. People filtered in, and I handed each a plate from a tall stack on the sideboard.

"There you are." Amo Fred took the plate from my hand, placed it down, and gave me a hug.

"I'm glad you're here."

"So am I. It's truly a miracle for all of us to be back where we started."

Noticing the woman standing behind him, he passed a plate to her and told me he had to leave but would come again soon.

After dinner, the people with the greatest distance to travel left first, then those who resided in nearby buildings and lastly the neighbors from our building. Only Leila remained, sitting calmly on the sofa, watching the departures and the bestowing of courteous farewell kisses. When the last visitor left, my parents and Rima went to bed.

"Finally. I can't believe we had to wait this long to be alone."

I sat down. "Leila, I'm back for good. We'll have lots of time together. Isn't it late for you to still be here? Are the roads safe?"

She didn't move. "I know it's late, but don't worry. Ali knows all of the armed groups in the area. That's why my father has him as my driver."

"Sounds like you're still your father's biggest headache." I'd missed her and was glad she was still in Lebanon.

"Think of how boring it would be otherwise. But seriously, I've been counting the hours waiting for you."

"Now *that* sounds boring. I can't imagine counting the hours waiting for me."

She didn't react. "Tomorrow, I need you to come to my house as soon as you wake up. It's very important. Don't eat breakfast. We can eat together. I urgently need to talk to you."

She stood and kissed me on both cheeks. "I get up at six." She rushed out the door.

* * *

The city air was still when I awoke. The glass window panes were open, but the wooden shutters were closed and locked with a twist bar to secure the metal rod into the frame. Small rays of light filtered into the room through the slats, making familiar shapes on the walls and ceiling. From the amount of light, I guessed it was about ten o'clock.

I'd forgotten how small my twin bed was compared to the king-sized one in LA. Adjusting myself cautiously, I stared at the ceiling. Morning noises intruded: people chatting under the balcony, car horns, and planes on final approach into Beirut airport. Over the years I'd learned to judge distance and location from sound. Before the war I did it for amusement, but once the fighting began, it became a survival tool.

I looked at Rima's empty bed. We'd shared this room since we were small children until the day we'd fled. I turned back and watched the moving patterns on the ceiling, blurring the divide between past and present. *Is reality here or did I leave it in Los Angeles?*

"Leila!" I shouted out loud. I jumped up, dug through my open suitcase on the floor and pulled out jeans and a tee shirt. I rushed down the hallway to the bathroom.

"Good morning, Miss Maya. I hope you slept well." Maria, the Filipino maid, smiled.

"Yes. Thank you. Where's everyone?"

"Sir left to work. Madame will return around two o'clock, and Rima's at the university. Can I prepare your breakfast?"

"No thanks. I'm going to Leila's. Please tell my mother I'll be back before dark."

"Miss Maya, would you like me to empty your suitcases?"

"Yes, please. One case is only dirty clothes."

"I've already finished today's laundry. Can it wait until tomorrow or would you like me to wash it now?"

"Tomorrow's fine." I relished the thought of sundried, ironed clothes. In fact, the thought of clean clothes I didn't have to wash, fold, or iron myself excited me.

Maria opened the front door of the apartment and watched me leap down the stairs.

"Good morning, Abou Ziad," I greeted the concierge.

"God be with you, Miss Maya."

Bright cleansing rays of sunlight magnified dust on the broken sidewalks and the dirty streets, but it all looked beautiful to me as I focused on familiar faces and returned the greetings of the cobbler, the storekeeper, and the baker. They welcomed me with sincere pleasure in their tired, gritty voices. These were the working poor with no place to escape to during the dark days of death. They found comfort in seeing someone who had a choice to come back. I knew my homecoming and cheerful attitude would be the topic of discussion during the day and in the evening when they sat with their families. They would say if the people who left chose to return, there was hope—meaning life in Lebanon was certainly better than abroad. Maybe my reappearance signaled a brighter future.

Leila opened the door with a nervous laugh and said she had not allowed any of the servants to touch it all morning. She'd greeted her father's lawyer, a lady from an employment agency, the grocery delivery boy, an electrician, and a neighbor coming for coffee with her mother. "Thank God, you're finally here." She kissed my cheeks.

I followed her through three magnificent living rooms filled with Persian carpets, Louis XIV-style furniture, seventeenth-century French paintings, and gold-legged coffee tables topped with crystal and silver, all guarded by the heavy satin curtains, blocking the sunlight. When we reached the last room, through an adjoining door on the left, I spotted Amo Mohammad seated at his desk. His face strained as he read through documents, quickly scribbling his signature on the lines pointed out to him by a man who stood beside him. Sensing our presence, he looked up.

"Maya, my daughter, the world is lit up!"

He came out to greet me, leaving the hard lines of his face and the rigid marks of the pen behind. He kissed my cheeks and stepped back to look at me.

Amo Mohammad was very disciplined and looked after himself. He was physically fit and always immaculately dressed—usually in a tailored suit and shirt with an elegant designer tie.

"You look well, my daughter. Thanks be to God. This is a blessed day. Will I see the two of you later?"

"Yes, Baba. Maya will be here all day."

Leila's bedroom suite had everything I'd always wanted as a young girl. Rose-colored curtains covered the three windows and the door leading to her private balcony. The canopy bed had matching sheets, covers, and pillows. Even the custom-ordered carpets and wall coverings had the same pattern and colors. I used to think if I were a princess, this would be my room, but now it seemed like overkill.

"Sit," Leila commanded, waving her arms toward two small sofas to the left of the bed. "Have you had breakfast? Would you like something to eat?"

"No, I'm fine, thanks." I felt too excited to be hungry.

"Okay, we'll wait until lunch. Guess what I told the cook to prepare for you?" A rhetorical question because everybody knew my favorite dish—small zucchini stuffed with meat and rice, cooked in tomato sauce. I knew I'd eat it at least once a day for the next couple of weeks. Despite the spread of food the night before, it was all I ate.

"You don't know how happy I am to have you back. I wish Christina would return and the three of us could be together, like before this horrible war."

"That'd be nice, but…"

"Maya," she interrupted me. "I'm glad we're finally alone. I have to tell you something important. I've waited for months for us to be together."

I straightened myself up from my slouch among the cushions on the pink sofa. A cold snake of anticipation slithered from the base of my skull down the small of my back. I knew Leila couldn't keep secrets, so why had she kept this one?

She turned her face away from me and gazed out the window at the green-blue Mediterranean.

"You're not going to believe what I've done."

CHAPTER 9

———

Once words escape, they grow wings and take on a life of their own, never to be recaptured.

—*LEILA*

"I have to face it, Maya. I can't wait any longer. I'm beginning to show. I have to tell them. I don't have a choice. Do I?"

"No, I guess not. How're you going to do it?"

"It's all I've been thinking about." Leila looked down at her fingers interlaced under her slightly protruding belly.

I shifted on the soft sofa and looked around the room, stopping at her bed. Once she told her parents she was married, I wondered if they'd allow her to sleep in it with Alex.

"I think I'll tell my father first. I know he's going to be upset, but at least he won't raise his voice and scream like my mother will. Maya, I feel scared and guilty. I've let Baba down. I wish you could be with me when I tell him, but this is between my family and me. However, I'm thinking you could come over for Sunday lunch and stay in my room while I talk to him after his nap. This way I'll have you for support. And the afternoon visitors won't start coming over until around six. When he wakes up, he goes to his study, and my mother stays in their bedroom getting herself ready for company. His assistants don't come on Sundays, and my brothers are traveling. This will give me about an hour. What do you think?"

"What do I think? How can I think? One of my two best friends meets a guy I don't even know, tells me nothing, and then throws at me she's secretly married and pregnant."

"You don't know how badly I wanted to tell you but couldn't. It would have been too difficult over the phone, we have no mail service, and I didn't trust asking someone to mail a letter from another country."

I knew she was right and softened my tone, addressing the issue at hand. "I guess your plan is as good as any. I wonder how your father will react. I'm sure it will be a relief for you no matter what happens."

Leila rubbed her hands across her belly. She didn't need to say more; I knew exactly what she was thinking.

* * *

Ten of us sat down to lunch on Sunday. The cook and one of the maids served the meal. I'd never mastered the art of using a spoon and a fork in the same hand to move food from platter to plate. The maid patiently held the serving dish while I took the fork in one hand and the spoon in the other. I preferred being waited on by the cook because he held the platter with one hand and used the other to serve the guests. Leila always held both serving pieces in one hand and effortlessly maneuvered the food.

Once I noticed she and her mother were the only two capable of serving themselves in this manner, I wasn't self-conscious. Amo Mohammad even told the maid in a loud voice to hold the serving fork while he used the large spoon to serve himself.

He sat at one end of the table, and Tante Samia, Leila's mother, at the other. Her short, smoothly teased black hair looked like an upside-down tea cup. Blue eyeshadow filled the space between her eyebrows and eyelashes. Kohl, Egyptian eyeliner, accentuated her eyes, and deep red lipstick covered her lips. She wore a thick gold and diamond necklace with a linen dress.

Leila and I sat to her right. The three other women at the table—all wives of three brothers, cousins of the family— dominated the conversation. The trio of husbands appeared quite content to focus on the food without expending energy on small talk. Tante Samia occasionally offered her uninformed opinion, and Amo Mohammad looked pleasantly at whomever spoke. I took a deep breath and smiled, glad Leila and I were not in the spotlight.

The dull conversation blurred as my mind wandered back to the first time I'd gone out alone for Sunday lunch in Los Angeles. This is never done in Lebanon, and I heard my barely audible voice asking the hostess for a table for one. I felt somewhat ashamed, but it didn't faze her. I'd never imagined doing such a thing, but as I later realized, she probably heard this request often.

"Maya," Tante Samia snapped me back to Beirut. "Have some more *mahshi kousa*. You have to make up for all those years in America."

One of the cousins' wives watched as I piled six or seven of the miniature, light green, stuffed zucchini on my plate. Fortunately, I remained thin despite the amount of food I consumed, but the look she gave me made me feel like a glutton. Tante Samia was already focused on the chatter of another cousin's wife, but Amo Mohammad looked at me endearingly.

The black forest cake, the fruit tart, the honey-dipped sweets, and the seasonal fruits were all my favorite desserts. I enjoyed them even more when I realized the same woman still appeared astonished by how much I ate. Perhaps nervousness about what lay in wait increased my appetite even more. The lunch guests continued the conversation until I finished eating, and we moved into a living room for the traditional small cups of Turkish coffee.

The three cousins' wives sat in a row on a golden velvet sofa. Each placed her stiff black patent leather handbag on the carpet next to her right foot. Leila noticed me looking at their almost identical purses, shoes, navy suits and short, teased hair.

She leaned close and whispered, "I think they get a bulk discount. Who would believe these are some of the wealthiest women in Beirut?"

After the chocolates and candied chestnuts were served, Amo Mohammad stood up and excused himself for his afternoon nap. Everyone knew this habit and did not take offense although he would occasionally skip it when he had more formal or foreign visitors.

The cousins and wives stood to leave. Tante Samia insisted they stay, but they maintained they had to go. Thus, the elaborate Lebanese departure ritual played out. The majority prevailed over the hostess, and Leila and I quietly slipped back into her room while Tante Samia called for the maid to bring the rug comb to straighten the fringes on the Persian carpets.

Leila flopped onto the bed, and I sat next to her.

"Look, it's good you're going to get it over with. You have to tell them about your marriage and especially the pregnancy. It's too bad it has to be this way, but it is what it is."

"I know. I just never imagined my life like this. Remember when we were little how we used to talk about getting married? And when we were older, we used to imagine our wedding night. It was all a beautiful fantasy with the most gorgeous white dress in the world, happy faces, a wonderful party and the fancy hotel room where we'd lose our virginity. Did we ever think about the type of man we were going to marry? Or was he only a supporting character in the dream? How did it go wrong?" She looked up at me.

"Maybe it didn't go wrong. We were romanticizing. We didn't understand the complexity of our world or our desires as humans."

"And love has to be this painful?" It sounded more like a statement.

"Did you ever think you'd fall in love with a Christian, and your love would be considered bad for this reason? But you're not the first nor the last to marry someone from a different religion. Think of all the couples we know. Relax. I think your father will understand."

She cried quietly, and I stroked her hair. We were now in a state of silent anxiety, beyond words as we waited for the next hour to pass. A few minutes before we thought her father would enter his study, Leila slowly rose from the bed and walked into her bathroom. She emerged with her face washed, makeup reapplied and her long black hair combed back. Only her reddened eyes betrayed her elegant confidence.

"You don't know how glad I am you're here for me. I can't imagine having to do this alone. Thank God you came home."

She hugged me for a long while and left, quietly closing the door behind her.

A few minutes later, I opened the door and half expected to hear loud voices, but the large apartment remained silent. I stood at the window and looked at the empty street below. The apartment occupied the entire fifth floor of the building. It was bigger than most houses I'd seen in America, probably seven thousand square feet without the servants' quarters above the kitchen. Yet, when I told people we lived in apartments, they wondered how we managed in a small space.

The door opened, and I turned to see Leila. Her eyes were glossy with tears, but the corners of her mouth curled softly upward.

"It's done." She stepped up to the window and gazed out. By the faraway look in her eyes, I could tell she wasn't seeing anything.

"What happened?"

"I think he expected it because he remained calm. I started by reminding him Alex was a good high school friend of my brother's. Of course, he needed little reminding because Alex and Hani spent all of their time together before drifting apart in university."

"And?"

"He listened—didn't say a word. I told him I'd gone with my mother to the Red Cross in February to help roll bandages and she introduced me to Alex's mother. I asked about Alex, and ironically, he was coming to pick her up. We talked, and he invited me to a party. We had a good time remembering some of the crazy things he and Hani did and how they wouldn't let me hang around them. In college he studied electrical engineering. He couldn't find a job in his field, so he worked as a project manager for the UN." She turned away from the window and began pacing the room.

"And then?"

"My father just listened, but suddenly I wanted to get it over with and began to talk really fast and blurted out, 'Alex and I went to Cyprus five months ago, got married, and I'm pregnant.' Then I stopped. He sat in his chair, and I don't know if he was looking at me or beyond me. I've never seen an expression of sorrow and pain like I saw in his eyes. My crying became uncontrollable."

I didn't know anyone kinder than Amo Mohammad and hearing her describe his reaction upset me. I could only imagine the strength it took for him to deal with the situation, his feelings and the social implications. His only daughter had let him down.

"Eventually he stood up," she continued. "I stepped forward, and he opened his arms. I sobbed too loudly to hear anything he said. When I got myself together, he told me to go wash my face, spend some time with you, and prepare for the evening, when he and I would break the news to my mother."

Leila stood on her tiptoes, slid a leather cassette holder off the highest closet shelf, removed a blue colored tape and put it into a player. She sat down on her satin sofa while the music blared. I wondered if Billy Joel ever imagined all the complicated, hopeless places around the world where his words and music provided a moment of empathetic strength.

"How I need music," Leila said. "It supports us individually yet joins us all together. It reminds me that we are all more similar than different."

I nodded and stood to go home, but Leila grabbed my arm. "Please don't leave. I need you. Please wait while Baba and I tell my mother."

When she left the room the second time, I knew I had to stay put because there would be no calm corner in the apartment. I picked up a magazine, put it down, picked up another and another until I heard shouting coming from the sitting room. Someone ran in the corridor. I opened the door and saw the cook hurrying to the bedroom.

"Miss Maya, please come quickly." I followed him to a living room.

Tante Samia sat in a golden Louis XIV armchair, her face dark and her eyes red like bulging marbles. Leila and her father stood a few feet away from her in front of a sofa. The cook stepped aside for me to enter the room.

"Maya," Tante Samia bellowed, "what do you know about this?"

Before I could answer, Leila jumped in. "She knew nothing. She wasn't even in the country."

Tante Samia hit her forehead with the palm of her hand and threw herself back into the chair. She banged her head against it and ranted. "Why's God punishing me? My only daughter has betrayed me. What did I do to deserve this? Mohammad, I demand you undo this marriage. Call your lawyer in Cyprus tomorrow and tell him what needs to be done. This can't be allowed. What will people say?" She let out a loud cry, and I turned and saw all the household staff standing in the doorway. Not knowing what to do or say, I took a step back in their direction.

Tante Samia's old nanny, who had been with her since her birth, pushed through and rushed to the chair. Tante Samia stood up, pounded her chest, pulled on her expensive dress and stared at the ceiling, her face contorted.

Though still sobbing, Leila pulled her shoulders back and raised her head. I could tell she had moved from sorrow and apprehension to anger and strength.

Amo Mohammad stepped forward. "What are you talking about?" he demanded. "Why are you acting like a child? Is it all about you? Here is your daughter who needs your help, and all you can think about is what people will say? Maybe if you'd paid more attention to her needs and were not so self-centered, she would've come to you earlier to tell you. But no, all you're concerned about is your clothes, your hair, your social status, your jewelry and being envied. This is your daughter. Look at her and for once see her needs as more important than your own. She has found love. Is that something you even understand?"

Tante Samia collapsed back into the chair and closed her eyes. The old nanny started screaming and, finding fire in her ancient bowed legs, she dashed out of the apartment yelling for a doctor. The cook ran to the kitchen and returned with smelling salts, but Tante Samia slapped his hand away when he tried to hold the ammonium carbonate to her nose.

She stood again. "We are descendants of the Prophet Mohammad, peace be upon him. I'm of a most sacred and pure lineage, but now my own daughter has corrupted it. How has this curse come upon our family?"

Amo Mohammad's face glowed red, and he shook with rage. I'd never seen him like this and could never have imagined it. He was a remarkably composed man who could make anyone regret their actions with a few well-chosen, non-insulting words.

My throat tightened, and my stomach hurt. I wished my Teta was in the room. She would know what to do.

"Do you really believe God thinks we're better than anyone else?" he bellowed. "How do you know the best person on this earth isn't a Christian, or a Jew, or a Buddhist, or a nonbeliever? Do you honestly believe God will judge you by the book you followed or do you think he'll ask how you treated your fellow human beings?"

I hadn't noticed the doctor arriving, but he seemed to materialize in the center of the room. From the expression on his face, I think he was trying to decide who needed him more—the hysterical woman banging her head on the back of the chair or the red-faced man who looked as though he was about to have a stroke.

He placed his bag on a coffee table, took out a small bottle of pills, handed it to the cook, and instructed him to make sure Tante Samia took one immediately. Then he gently put his arm around Amo Mohammad's shoulder and walked him out of the room.

Nanny sat on the arm of the chair cradling Tante Samia's head. The cook opened the bottle, and a maid produced a glass of water. Nanny gently placed a pill in Tante Samia's mouth and held the glass to her lips. Once she'd swallowed, Nanny signaled the maids to assist her in escorting Tante Samia to her bedroom.

Everyone seemed to have forgotten about Leila and me as we stood alone in the room. For a while neither of us uttered a word.

"I'm relieved it's over. Now all I want is Alex. I want him to hold me and tell me we're meant for each other. He makes everything seem right. I can't believe all we have to go through just to be together. Why couldn't we have been born in America where we wouldn't be bound by stupid old religions? But I guess this is our fate. Oh, Maya, thank God you're here with me."

"I've got to leave. It's almost eleven, and I have a job interview in the morning. Remember the one Christina's father arranged for me at Middle East Airlines?"

"Oh yes, I'd forgotten. Ali will drive you home."

Drained, I couldn't wait to get to bed.

She kissed my cheeks, held me tightly and only let go when Ali entered the room.

* * *

I thought I was dreaming when I heard Leila's voice softly call my name. She shook my shoulder, and I jumped straight up.

"What are you doing here?"

"Please get up; I need to talk to you," she whispered.

"What time is it? I have an interview at eight o'clock."

"I know, and I promise you'll be on time. It's five. We have three hours."

"I have to catch the company bus at seven. I can't be late."

"You won't be late. Ali's with me, and it'll only take twenty minutes to get you to your appointment. Get dressed. I'll wait for you in the entrance hall."

I disliked getting up early, and in LA had perfected the art of preparing myself for a day at the office in less than fifteen minutes. This paid off in Beirut because I couldn't count on a morning shower without a reliable water supply. They were precarious because even when we had water, it might not be hot, could turn cold instantly, or stop flowing altogether. It took time to heat a pan of water for a sponge bath. Getting clean every day felt like an accomplishment better attempted in the evening for those who had to be somewhere in the morning.

I brushed my teeth, splashed cold water on my face, and applied mascara and blush. I put on my suit and slipped into pointed high heels to accentuate the skirt. I had a good figure with especially shapely legs and dressed to show them off. I knew I had the skills and background to make a good first impression, but looking chic could be an asset. No doubt more sleep would have also helped. *I love my friend, but how much can I handle?*

Leila saw me coming out of the bathroom and proceeded to the door of the apartment.

"Maria, please tell madame I've gone to my new job." The sleepy maid had been awakened when Leila rang the doorbell. I wasn't sure if she knew the word "interview," but I didn't feel like explaining.

"Ali, take us to Chez Francoise." Leila put on her designer shades despite the sunless hour.

Beirut in the morning might be the only reason I could learn to appreciate the early hours. The quiet streets slowly came to life with the occasional crowing of a rooster. The butchers, bakers, and vendors, began their work. They greeted and invited those walking by to join them for morning coffee or a treat. In these moments everyone seemed to have forgotten the tragedies of the previous day, and the new one received a hopeful welcome.

The car moved quickly through the city and stopped in front of a coffee shop overlooking the Mediterranean. The café had not opened, but we saw a light on in the back and knocked on the glass door. A bald, middle-aged man in a flour-coated apron answered.

"Good morning, ladies. Can I help you?"

"We are here for breakfast," Leila said.

"We don't open for another hour, but never mind. Since you're here we'll take care of you. I'm not a waiter, but I make the best hot chocolate and can bring whatever pastries are ready."

He turned on the lights, and we selected a round table in the corner with a good view of Pigeon Rocks—two gigantic limestone formations protruding from the sea a few feet off this rocky stretch of coast. Visitors to Lebanon often admired the massiveness and beauty of these natural wonders, but to locals they're known as the "Suicide Rocks" because of the number of desperate people who have climbed them to take their final leap.

The baker returned with steaming drinks and crescent rolls filled with a mixture of thyme, sesame seeds, and olive oil. I reached for a warm pastry, savoring the aroma as much as the taste, and dipped it in my drink.

Leila didn't seem to notice anything on the table. She leaned forward, as if the room was full of people who could hear, and spoke in a low, hoarse voice, "Maya, nobody ever told my mother I'm pregnant."

The soft, warm roll became hard and cold against my lips. "What?"

"Yes, think about it. She only yelled about the marriage. Before you came into the room, my father began the conversation by telling her I had some news to share, and although it would be shocking, it was good news. The moment I mentioned Alex's name, her face darkened. When I told her we'd gone to Cyprus five months ago, she became rigid and shrieked, 'I hope you weren't stupid enough to marry him.' That's when I became angry and shouted, I am not stupid.

The whole drama centered on the marriage. We never got around to anything else."

"Did you see your father again last night?"

"No. After you left, I went to my room. I felt nervous and couldn't sit or lie down. I kept walking back and forth, and then it occurred to me. We hadn't told her about my pregnancy. I felt like hitting or ripping something apart and couldn't be alone. When everybody in the house went to sleep, I snuck out to find Alex at the small bar where he spends most evenings. The bartender told me he'd left with a group of guys and he'd overheard them saying they were going to a meeting."

"Are you crazy? You know how dangerous the streets are at night." I'd raised my voice and was glad we were the only customers.

"I know it was a stupid thing to do, but I couldn't stand being alone. I needed him."

"You're pregnant. You've got to be responsible. I'm sure Alex wouldn't want you roaming around alone at night."

"I know, but you don't realize when I'm with Alex, everything bad seems to dissipate. He sees the world differently with a future independent of the past. We'll never think of religion of birth but instead religion of choice—one where people find wisdom and comfort. People will be individuals and not as members of religious clans blindly following ignorant leaders who don't want to relinquish power. He represents the life I want to live. I think I fell in love with his ideas before I fell in love with him."

I put the croissant down on my plate. I knew she wouldn't register anything I had to say.

"After we take you to your interview, Ali will drive me to Alex's home. Together, we'll figure out what to do next."

I looked at the Pigeon Rocks rising majestically from the Mediterranean. To the ancient Greeks, they were the remains of a sea monster killed by Perseus. To tourists they are an iconic sight. To locals they represent suicides.

How differently people see the same thing.

CHAPTER 10

———

The edge of enchantment, so beautiful, so fleeting.

—MAYA

It took almost a week before I could break away from the city and its distractions, namely Leila, to spend two days in the mountains with my beloved grandmother. I knew Leila's situation needed time to resolve. Her mother eventually had to deal with reality.

I maneuvered the big black Buick through the narrow city alleys without thinking. The car came within centimeters of people, cars, and a multitude of other objects pushing into a limited space. Dwelling on it would make me a wreck, and I'd most likely run into something.

I slammed on the brakes and glared at a vegetable cart wheeled into the road a fraction of a second before I was to be in its spot. The bewildered vendor froze and gazed at me through the windshield.

"Crazy man," I yelled and jumped out of the car. "Why don't you look where you're going?" My heart pounded, and I shouted out my fear. "I could've killed you."

He didn't answer but lowered his head and maneuvered the cart across the alley, keeping body and cart pressed as close as possible to the hovering buildings. I glowered at him, in his dirt-stained baggy pants and oversized t-shirt, as he turned the corner onto a wider street. I took a deep breath in an attempt to slow down my heartbeat.

An elderly gentleman standing nearby said, "It's all right, miss. Thanks be to God nothing happened, and perhaps he will pay more attention next time although I doubt it."

I got back into my car, annoyed by the honking of the drivers behind me. I rolled down the window, pressed the tips of my five fingers together into a tent shape, put my arm out and raised and lowered my wrist slowly in the universal Arab gesture to ask those behind me to calm down.

Ten minutes after leaving our apartment, I crossed the narrow strip of land linking the coast to the base of the mountain. The car hugged the bumpy road, swiveling around the twists and turns. I began the ascent, and my hands gripped the steering wheel especially tightly as I negotiated the lane on the outside edge of the road, not daring to look at the valley below. I felt secure enough to take in the view only when in the inside lane. Like I did as a child, I wanted to gaze down into the deep green valley to spot the Roman aqueduct, but I dared not while driving.

The umbrella pine trees covering the mountains lived up to their name with long skinny trunks supported big green canopies. Their heads met and touched but never invaded one another's space. They rose from the dry mountain soil in large forest patches, but sometimes they became whimsical orphans scattered among the concrete structures sprouted among them.

The car climbed, and the air felt lighter. I took a deep breath, smiled, and immediately smiled again at the thought I was smiling to myself. I rounded a turn, looked down at the shrunken city far below and my body relaxed. I had returned home to Lebanon to recharge my soul but instead felt drained and stuck in the middle of Leila's drama. I needed to get away to focus on myself and contemplate my next steps—thankfully, the snipers, a few days earlier, had stopped their activity. Being with Teta would clear my mind.

Less than thirty minutes after leaving the city, I reached an altitude of twenty-five hundred feet and entered our village. As I got closer, my heart beat faster in every part of my body. I drove slowly past the five small food stores built close to the waterspout flowing with fresh cold water from melted snow at a higher altitude. I passed familiar people, but barely paid attention. I focused on the three-story limestone building visible beyond the slight turn in the road ahead.

I pulled up in front of the structure in time to see my grandmother fly down the outdoor steps leading to the street.

"Maya, my soul, my eyes, my life." She hugged me and buried her head into the highest part of my body she could reach—my chest. "God is generous. God is kind. I didn't think I'd ever see you again." Her warm tears soaked through my thin tight t-shirt onto my skin.

My own tears ran through her short gray hair. "I missed you, Teta." I barely recognized my own weak voice.

She clung to my hand and led me up the fifteen outdoor steps to the second level of the building. We stood on the wide open-air landing between the door of her apartment and her neighbor's. The area served as an al fresco living room shared by both dwellings for eight months of the year. The space had two parallel walls, one from each building, and community steps on the other two sides. These public stairways and the "social" landings on them allowed the inhabitants to live in homes scattered in mountains, many with no access to roads. The intricate flights of steps and landings wove from mountain village to village, connecting the people as they walked through on their way to and from shopping, church, or visiting friends. Sometimes they stopped to take a rest and chat but other times it was a destination.

"Maya. Maya." Teta's elderly neighbor struggled to stand when she saw me. "What a beautiful, blessed day this is."

I bent down, touched her shoulder to prevent her from rising, and kissed her. The sunlight glistened on her toothless gums.

I sat down beside her on the wide makeshift couch by her front door and gazed across at Teta's almost identical one. Mattresses placed on wooden support structures were covered in flowered slipcovers to make them inviting.

As a child, I'd spent endless summer hours on this landing. In the mornings, after Teta watered the garden and picked fruits and vegetables, she and her neighbor met here. They helped each other prepare the labor-intensive Lebanese meals. They collected parsley, onions, tomatoes, and mint. They snapped green beans, cored zucchini, rolled grape leaves, and stuffed pastries with spinach, meat and yogurt. Each woman had her own menu, but they worked together to prepare both.

After lunch everyone rested—sometimes on the outdoor couches because the breeze blew best between the two buildings.

Afternoons were for other work. Pine nuts were shelled or yogurt was mixed with cracked wheat and taken to the roof to sun dry for potage, revived on cold winter mornings with bits of fatty meat and garlic.

Wine making and arak making days were my favorite. Teta hired young boys to stomp the grapes picked from the gardens. Sometimes, after I washed my feet, I climbed into the barrel, but I didn't stay long because the stiff vines hurt, especially the soft skin between my toes.

Snails were gathered after the first rains and placed in burlap bags for weeks to cleanse before cooking. The women individually wrapped apples and pears, placed them in boxes and sent them to cold storage for winter use. I helped make the apricots they picked into jams and mulberries into a sweet syrup. Figs became dry winter snacks or gooey preserves. We held stones tightly in the palms of our hands to crack pine nuts and then spread the meaty nut inside on Teta's flat roof under the brilliant sun. Teta spent long working days performing satisfying tasks to create succulent meals and feed us well.

Knitting, sewing, crocheting, and needlework were late-afternoon activities. Visitors brought their own projects and worked while they chatted. People always listened and cared.

"Maya, where's better—America or here?" An old man interrupted my reminiscences.

I sank deeper into the well-padded couch. "Each has good and bad things. We have the best human warmth but no civic sense. America has remarkable civic sense but little time for extensive human relationships."

The neighbor's middle-aged daughter bustled through her mother's door onto the landing and carried more chairs. She then brought out a tray of cold homemade mulberry drinks.

In a rare moment of inactivity, Teta sat next to me and did nothing other than hold my hand and look at me. When the last visitor left, I told her I wanted to walk around the village. She gave me a hug and went to the kitchen to prepare dinner.

I crossed the street and jumped down about three feet from the road onto a terraced landing with a grove of umbrella pines. I leaned on a tree at the edge of the forest and surveyed the city of Beirut below. Although I knew better, I felt as though I could take a big springing leap and land in the miniature metropolis, or in the gentle Mediterranean.

To my right was a limestone, box-like structure—once Teta Louisa's house. The rotted, wooden shutters were closed. Through the holes the fading sunlight showed years of dust.

I remembered as a little girl, looking in through the metal window bars at Louisa sitting on the edge of her bed holding rosary beads. One late afternoon, I tightened my grip on the warm pot I carried, quickly turned the corner and entered her one-room house through the open door. The absence of color soothed me. Everything in sight was one of two colors: off-white walls, sink, bed coverings, nightgown, hair, and skin, or the brownish table, chairs, floor, and beads. An unlit lightbulb dangled from the center of the ceiling. Dim rays from the setting sun filled the room.

Smiling, I placed the aluminum pot in the center of the cracked wooden table and washed a bowl and spoon in the sink while watching the old woman slowly make her way to one of the two chairs. The corners of her mouth moved upward, revealing dark pink gums. "No one cooks like your Teta." She lifted the lid off the pot and bent over to smell the contents.

"Maya, when will you be eleven?"

"In August, Teta Louisa."

"I was eleven during the famine. Mothers would cry in the night, and in the morning their babies would be dead. People ate cats, dogs, foxes, bugs, even rats."

"Yes, I know. My Teta told me about the Ottoman food blockade."

"Maya, you know my son in America is a good boy, and he will send me money as soon as he can."

"Yes, I know." I knew Tony left over twenty years ago, lived in Cleveland and owned a successful restaurant. Louisa's only child had left her destitute with nothing other than her house and the small piece of land it stood on. The people in the village took care of her, but I still said, "One day I am sure he'll send you lots of money."

Louisa watched me with contented eyes as I placed bread on the table and dished the contents of the pot into the bowl.

"I will see you tomorrow, Teta Louisa."

"May you always be blessed, my child."

Before closing the door behind me, I switched on the light bulb. In the darkness outside, I held the cold, empty pot close to me and turned back to peer through the window bars. Two new points of color shone in the room—the yellow light bulb and the yellow chicken foot Louisa held in her hand. She gently sucked on one of the four finger-like prongs. I always wondered if she ate or spat out the long sharp talons.

Now, my body shook at the memory, and I looked up at the sky and waved to Louisa. I walked deeper into the forest. Dried pine needles crunched under my feet, and the aroma of pine cones roasting in a bonfire nearby wafted toward me. We used to pull the cones out of the fire, retrieve the little hard shells from each compartment, crack them open on rocks and eat the warm soft nut. My mouth watered as

I moved down the mountainside toward the city, watching the sun sink closer to the sea.

A distant church bell sounded, and I felt the excited pride of a little girl jumping, holding tightly onto the bell rope. Higher and higher she rose, and faster and faster I walked, leaping down from one terrace to the next, my eyes focused on the city below.

Suddenly I stopped. The air smelled heavier, and I realized how far I'd gone. Like my mountain-dwelling ancestors, I'd been trained to use my senses when wandering through the forest. The scent of the air, the sound of a howling wolf, the motion of a slithering snake, the taste of the wild grapes—all senses had to be engaged to avoid danger.

I walked away from the forest trees to the cultivated terraced plots. Each landing was carved from the sloping mountains, neatly supported by small stones, and planted with vegetables, herbs, and fruit trees.

I took one last look at the city and its sea with the setting sun melting into the water. I turned around and ran up the mountainside, making my way back to Teta's waiting feast.

CHAPTER 11

Sometimes I'm scared savoring joy will cause my luck to change.

—MAYA

"You mean you're going from *Teta's* serene world to Monique's crazy one in less than twenty-four hours?" Rima smirked.

"Why don't you come with me?" I looked away from her toward Maman as she placed two small pottery frying pans on the gas stove, poured in Teta's homemade olive oil and cracked eggs I had brought with me from the mountains. She sprinkled sumac on top. The air filled with a soothing, familiar scent.

"Go with you to see Monique's band of artsy-craftsy wanderers? No thanks." Rima scraped off a crunchy piece of egg white from the edge of the glazed clay pan Mama had placed in front of her. She wrapped it in pita bread and dipped it into the runny yoke.

We ate in silence. *Mark likes eggs. I tried to describe this flavor to him but now realize my words did little justice to this combination. Maybe he would come to Lebanon one day and eat them.*

"Are you joining Papa and me for lunch at Selma and Roger's?" Maman hadn't heard a word we'd said.

"No," Rima and I answered in unison.

Maman shrugged. She knew it was a waste of time to try and convince us to go. We weren't interested in hanging out with older people.

"I'm meeting some classmates at the library," Rima said. "We can walk together since it's on your way to Monique's." Her tone sounded consolatory.

It took us less than three minutes to walk from our apartment to the sixty-one-acre campus of the American University of Beirut (AUB). Surrounded by a stone wall and built on a gently sloping hill overlooking the Mediterranean Sea, it was a haven in a chaotic city. The property ended at the *Corniche*, a sea road with a wide waterfront sidewalk. A tunnel to the university's private beach ran from the campus under the boulevard and walkway. This American missionary-founded, secular university had educated regional and world leaders since 1866.

Rima and I entered through the medical gate. The guards knew us and didn't ask for a university ID. We walked through the landscaped grounds, renowned for its collection of trees and shrubs.

"You sure you won't change your mind and come with me?"

"No, but come to think of it, compared to what I have to do, artsy-craftsy doesn't sound bad." She laughed, waved goodbye, and walked into the library, one of the oldest buildings on campus.

As if seeing them for the first time, I admired the plaza stones in front of the structure and then stepped back onto the pavement and bumped into a man who came from the opposite direction. I recoiled.

"I'm sorry. I wasn't paying attention." I looked straight up at his face and noticed his long eyelashes. *Why is it always the men?*

"No problem. I wasn't paying attention, either. Aren't you Maya Coury?"

"Yes." I didn't think I knew him.

"It's probably been ten years and a war ago since I've seen you." He must have noticed my confused look. "I'm Joe Kassir."

"Oh, yes." I wanted to sound like I remembered him, but I didn't.

"We were both members of the drama club in school but, of course, you were much younger. You were probably thirteen or fourteen the year I graduated. Remember *Much Ado about Nothing,* Ursula?"

"Of course, I do, Conrad." I looked at his face. *How did a chubby, easily forgettable boy metamorphose into such a good-looking man?* I tried to think of something interesting to say. *If only I had an object to drop for him to pick up and hand to me to buy me time to think.*

He relieved me. "What'd you do after high school?"

"I came here." I opened my arms slightly, to indicate the campus. "But didn't graduate because of the war. I finished my degree in the States, stayed for graduate school, and worked in LA for a few years. I returned two weeks ago." I spoke faster than normal, and my voice seemed higher pitched. "What about you?"

"I graduated from here." He opened his arms as I had done. "In '74, before the war started, I went to Boston and came back two months ago."

"Small world." I stared at the corners of his lips. They were turned up in a pre-smile. "What did you study?"

"I finished med school here and my internship and residency in Boston. Nice to run into you." He took a step forward.

I ignored his last sentence and bent down pretending something was wrong with my beaded sandal. I couldn't think of another delay tactic.

"Are you okay?"

I took the sandal off and hopped on the other foot to a low wall. He followed me and sat down. *Success.*

"I'm fine. I just need to adjust the strap." I fiddled with the buckle and gazed up at him with an impish look.

"Do you have plans tonight? Would you like to go out for a drink and catch up?"

"Sure." I might have answered too quickly.

"I can pick you up at eight thirty. Just tell me where."

"I live on Rue John Kennedy, down the street from the medical gate. Do you know the furnished apartment building?"

"Yes."

"It's the building across the street. There's a pharmacy on the ground level. We're on the first floor—the apartment on the left." I wondered what someone in LA would have done with such directions.

I smiled and gave him a flirty wave, and just like that, a mundane Sunday had turned promising.

Once he was out of sight, I took a big skip, bounded into a quick pace, crossed the campus, exited from the faculty gate by the sea and continued two blocks to Monique's apartment.

I walked on the *Corniche*, alongside the water, preoccupied with thoughts about Joe. *He must be about six feet tall and, judging from Mark, probably weighs around a hundred and eighty pounds. Oh my God, Mark. Maria told me he'd called, and I completely forgot. I feel bad. I'll try to call him tomorrow.*

Monique answered the door. Light brown curls framed her heart-shaped face, accentuating large eyes and full lips. As always, she only used black mascara and bright red lipstick. Although not plump, her body was curvy.

She took my hand and pulled me inside. "I'm glad you came." She kissed me on both cheeks. "Last night, on the phone, you sounded uncertain. I couldn't believe it when Leila told me you'd returned. If you hadn't come today, I would've been at your house first thing tomorrow morning."

Monique turned to her guests and proclaimed, "Everyone, meet Maya." The people scattered in the two living rooms and adjoining dining room looked my way and shouted, "Hi, Maya."

These get-togethers were how I envisioned Gertrude Stein's *Lost Generation* expatriate gatherings in 1920s Paris. Monique's company might not be of the stature of Fitzgerald, Hemmingway, or Joyce, but it didn't matter, because that creative, free-spirited, and rebellious essence existed in her salon.

Monique lived in an exquisitely furnished four-bedroom apartment overlooking the sea. It belonged to her brother and sister-in-law. They'd bought it only months before the war began. Their office temporarily relocated to Athens, and they'd moved their family to wait out the fighting. Monique lived in their home to ward off displaced persons who often, with the help of the militias, occupied empty dwellings. They gave her upkeep money—both for the residence and for herself. She proclaimed herself a poet and a lover.

Monique directed me into the kitchen. "I want a few quiet moments to catch up."

I gave her a summary of the past years but omitted the encounter on the way to her house. She would have asked too many questions.

"How about you? How's your poetry writing?" Her unique lifestyle intrigued me.

"It's what you see." She gestured to the people in the adjacent rooms. "This is the life I love. And now it's even better since I've met Burk."

"Burk?"

"He's German, works at the embassy, and he's an amateur photographer. These are his friends here today. You're going to love him, but he's in Frankfurt this week. I'm taking intensive German classes at the Goethe Institute and photography classes with one of his friends."

"Someone actually has that much influence on you?"

She shrugged, and a faint smile ran across her face. "I've put my poetry on hold to focus on German and photography. Come, let me introduce you to our friends."

I spent the afternoon chatting with the themed guests—mostly American or European photographers, who brought pieces for critique.

Later, Monique pulled me back into the kitchen to ask if I fancied any of the men present. I told her the handsome one I'd been speaking with was married. She gave me a questioning look and informed me it didn't matter as long as the wives weren't in the country.

"If you're going to live in Lebanon, you need to take advantage of every opportunity to enjoy yourself. For all you know, on your way home this afternoon you could be hit by a sniper or blown up by a car bomb."

Her words unnerved me, and I looked through the window, realizing the sun would soon set. I decided to leave. I didn't dare take the elevator because one of the frequent electric power cuts could leave me stranded. Monique called after me as I descended the stairway. "I'll come visit you this week."

As the sun touched the sea, I hastened my speed. I wanted to arrive before darkness turned the streets desolate. I couldn't stop thinking about Joe—the wave in his dark -brown hair, the hazel flashes in his light-brown eyes, and his well-defined jawline. What possessed successful people like us to leave the peaceful, organized, systematic West to return to the chaotic passion of the turbulent East? Was it a sense of duty, a need for friendship and family, a search for relevance or were we fulfilling our destiny?

Maria opened the door to our apartment, and I asked if there was hot water.

"No, miss. But I'm heating water for you on the stove because I figured you'd be home before dark."

Maria arranged the special containers and utensils I needed for my bath. The jerry-rigged powdered milk can with a metal wire handle was filled with boiling water and placed inside the bathtub. Next to it stood an empty plastic bucket and a pot shaped plastic container with a long hand-grip. I undressed and stood in the tub.

I filled half of the bucket with cold water from the faucet, removed the makeshift circular metal disk covering the can of hot water and ladled some into the cold water, until it reached bathing temperature. I dipped my loofah in and rubbed the olive oil soap into a lather. I scooped water out with the plastic container and poured it on my body. I repeated this twice and dried off with the warm towel placed next to the portable gas heater.

I put on a wool robe and rushed down the chilly corridor. Maria had rolled another heater into the bedroom, and when I entered, I stopped shivering.

By the time I finished dressing, a stack of rejected outfits lay on my bed. Thankfully, I wasn't in LA where they would wait for me to return. I made a mental note to buy Maria a small gift the next time I went shopping.

My parents watched the news on TV. I entered the family room and Maman glanced up at me with a questioning look.

"I'm going out with a friend."

The doorbell rang, and I rushed to open the door. I looked through the peephole, but the lack of electricity revealed a dark landing. The generator on our balcony only powered a few appliances and lights inside our apartment.

I shouted through the door. "Who is it?"

"Joe."

The dim light from the foyer spread into the space outside the door, and I excitedly took a quick look at him. He wore dark pants and a light-colored dress shirt, with the top two buttons undone.

"Come in." I stepped aside. "Let me introduce you to my parents before we leave." It hit me how far away I was from LA. Even if I lived with my parents there, I doubt I would have introduced them to a first date.

Papa and Maman both stood when Joe entered the room. They shook hands, exchanged formalities, and wished us a good evening.

"Your parents are nice." We walked down the steps and out of the building, guided by the light of the lantern Maria held for us.

Joe turned on his flashlight. "I thought we'd go to Makhoul Street for dinner at a pub. Is that okay?"

"I haven't been to Makhoul in years." The narrow alleyway ran parallel to a larger street, Rue Bliss, that bordered the main gate side of the AUB campus.

I wondered if the art of charming a man was something a woman learned or if it was innate. Joe's relaxed demeanor provided a fertile setting for me to fluctuate between smart and ditzy. He seemed interested in getting to know me, and I basked in the attention of this intelligent man.

While Joe ordered a third round of drinks, I looked at the people in the room and recognized a reporter from *Time Magazine*. Next to him sat a group of doctors, whom I assumed were on call because of their white coats and the beepers on their belts. One was a very attractive woman, and I briefly wondered how different my life would be if I'd studied medicine.

When I turned back, Joe was no longer talking with the waiter but to a friend seated at the table next to ours. He introduced us, and we chatted briefly before I looked at my watch. "I just realized it's almost one."

"Do you want me to cancel the drinks?"

"No, it's fine. We can drink fast. I have another job interview at eight thirty tomorrow. I mean today."

"Another?"

"Yes, I expect to hear from MEA this week, but I'm ninety-nine percent sure I got the position."

"Great. So, one down. Where's today's interview?"

"It's at AUB. There's an opening for a psychology instructor."

"Which job do you prefer?"

"I don't think I have to choose. The airline has modified their work schedule to allow employees to get home before dark. Instead of working five days a week, they work six—from seven thirty until two thirty. I figure I can teach in the afternoons since I only live a couple of minutes from campus."

I leaned back in the chair and took a sip of my whiskey sour.

"I'm impressed. It won't be easy, but it sounds exciting."

The pub was still full when we stepped out of the noise and relative protection of the building into the dark and silent tension of the streets. Alert eyes and ears replaced our lively conversation. The sound of our footsteps echoed as we canvassed the area for lurking gunmen and listened for the sound of a car or Jeep with armed men.

We walked quickly through the deserted city. He reached for my hand, now damp with sweat, and squeezed tightly as we increased our pace. The few minutes it took to walk to my apartment distorted time.

I unlocked the large wrought-iron-and-glass lobby door, and we stepped inside. A dim single light bulb dangled from a wire next to an elegant chandelier. This meant there was no electricity from the government-owned electrical company.

The relief of stepping into a covered space washed through my body. "Thanks for a nice evening."

"I enjoyed reconnecting after all these years." He took a step toward me but then turned to leave. He pulled the heavy door closed behind him.

Through the opaque glass I watched him descend the steps and walk back into the dangerous night.

I pushed the timed light switch and quickly climbed the steps. I knew he would call the next day.

CHAPTER 12

Care enough to reach into the voids of others' lives. Help fill them, and you will experience true happiness.

—JOE

"Maya. Maya," Rima yelled from the hallway next to our bedroom. "Phone call."

"Who is it?" I reached for the receiver.

"Don't know. Some guy."

"Maya, this is Joe."

"Hi. How are you?" I tried not to sound excited.

"I'm fine. How'd the interview go?"

"I think it went well. My old professor, who's now chairman of the department, interviewed me. Fortunately, I got a good grade in his class but, unfortunately, he remembered I fell asleep during his final."

"You *what?*"

"I finished the exam quickly and had a lot more time so I decided to take a rest before I checked over my answers. I put my head on the desk. I didn't expect to fall asleep."

"How about telling me the whole story over lunch?"

I collapsed into one of the velvet chairs arranged at each end of the long hallway table. I took a deep breath and swung my legs over the chair arm and leaned back until my head rested on the side of the high table. I pressed the phone receiver closer to my ear. "Sure. When?" *Nonchalant enough?*

"In an hour."

"You mean today?"

He remained quiet for a moment. *Why do I always say stupid things?*

"Can you make it? We can meet at Murten House. That is, if you like Swiss food?"

"Yes and yes." My voice sounded too shrill. I tried to quietly clear my throat.

"Great, I'll see you soon."

"I'll meet you in front of the restaurant."

Rima stood in the doorway of our bedroom smirking, and I knew she had listened to the conversation. "Who were you talking to in such a sweet voice?"

"No one."

"What do you mean no one? It was a guy... *Hello, is Maya there, please?*" she mimicked a male voice.

"Okay, it's the guy I went out with last night."

"The doctor?"

"How do you know he's a doctor?"

"When I got home, I asked Papa where you were and he told me."

"What else did he tell you?"

"The guy seemed soooooo nice." She swayed side to side like a hula dancer. "What's his name and what kind of doctor is he?"

"Joe Kassir, and he's a surgeon. He invited me to lunch."

"I figured that. Is he cute?" She grinned like a cat.

"Yes. I knew him in high school. You probably don't remember him." I walked into the bedroom and wondered why I told her anything when she acted so immature.

She waltzed past me to the middle of the room. "*Tell me more. Tell me everything. And more. Sounds like love at first sight.*" Rima danced around belting out her sing-song words.

"C'mon, Rima. Stop acting stupid."

"Me, acting stupid? How about Miss Flutter Eyes?" She cocked her head to one side and batted her eyelashes. "Oh, okay. I guess this is no way to get information. So, what color is his hair? His eyes? Does he have big ears?"

"What difference does it make?" I found her childishness infuriating.

"A lot—tell me."

"Rima, I don't have time for this. I need to get dressed."

"Okay. I'll help you." She danced to the closet.

Rima had much better taste in clothes than me—a point I had long ago conceded. She took out a tight gray skirt, a pink print shirt, and a flowered belt. I would never have thought of wearing them together. She opened a drawer and pulled out sheer gray stockings. She rummaged through our jewelry box for a silver necklace and earrings. She placed a pair of pointed-toe high heels on the floor in front of the items laid out on the chair. "Classy but fun and young." She was obviously pleased with herself.

"Now, how about telling me more about him." Rima lay down on her bed and placed her hands behind her head.

"His eyes are light brown. He has dark brown hair and his ears are normal."

"Wow! He sounds too cute to be true. And he doesn't have a girlfriend?" She sat up and reached for a bottle of bright pink nail polish.

"I don't think he does. He recently returned from Boston." I fastened my skirt and turned the zipper to the back. I checked in the mirror to ensure it and the slit were centered.

"I can't wait to check him out." She rolled the bottle between her hands and opened it.

"I'm not sure I want to scare him away quite yet."

"Very funny. You know, I could walk with you to meet him. Since he's waiting in front of the restaurant, I could say I'm going to visit a friend in the building next door." Rima tightened the lid of the polish bottle and placed it back on her bedside table.

"No, not this time. Let me get to know him better."

"You're missing a great opportunity for an expert opinion." She reached for the polish again and began to paint her fingernails. She ignored me.

* * *

Murten House was less than a ten-minute walk, and despite the poor condition of the city sidewalks, I still liked to wear high heels as they accentuated my good legs. I turned the last corner and saw Joe. He walked to me. "I'm glad this worked out at the last minute."

"Me, too." I tried to stifle my smile and wished I could control my heart rate.

He moved aside and gestured for me to walk ahead on the narrow pathway to the restaurant entrance. I had barely taken a step when we heard a woman scream. People ran in the direction of the sound.

"Go inside." Joe hurried toward the commotion.

I rushed to the restaurant door but didn't enter. I craned my neck and stood on my tiptoes, trying to see what was happening. A few people appeared on balconies and others clustered around a prone figure on the side of the road. I saw Joe kneel down, but almost immediately the crowd swelled and blocked my view.

Suddenly a teenage boy darted out from the gathering and ran at an astonishing pace. *Was he the perpetrator of some despicable act, which had caused the woman to scream?* My heart beat faster, and sweat filled my clenched hands. Not a sound came from the crowd. Moments later, a man walked away from the group, and I stepped out of the doorway to ask him what had happened. "An old man and woman were walking down the street when he collapsed. Someone yelled, and a doctor came out of nowhere and saved him. He ordered a young boy to run to the hospital to have an ambulance dispatched. This is not his time to die."

"Not his time to die?"

"It wasn't written he die today. People only die when it's their time—when their oil runs out." He nodded seeming to agree with the old Arabic wisdom and saying.

The crowd thinned, and I looked back at Joe who was on his knees. I heard the ambulance siren as I crossed the street. People moved aside. Two men with a stretcher jumped out. Joe stood to allow them access to the man. The elderly woman sobbed, and Joe put his arm around her. "He's okay, Tante. He'll be fine."

She raised her hand, lowered it on top of his, and turned to face him. She reached for his other hand and bent down and kissed each one. "May God protect you, my son. May he protect your family. May he preserve your hands."

I wiped my eyes with my forearm.

"Tante, Tante," yelled one of the young men who had put the stretcher into the ambulance. "Are you coming with us?"

She rushed to him, and he gently helped her into the back of the vehicle. "May God protect all the young men of our country," she said as the man slammed the door shut.

"Maya, I'm really sorry, but I don't think I have enough time to go to Murten House. We can get shawarma sandwiches, and I promise I'll make this up to you."

"So I get two for one?" I tried to be witty.

"Sounds good to me. How about lunch at the same time and place tomorrow?"

"You've got a deal—or maybe I should say, I got a deal." I smiled.

"I think it works both ways." He smiled back.

The few people who lingered watched us. "Doctor, thank those hands," one man cried as we walked past.

Joe muttered a few words about it being his duty to help. I straightened my back and made myself a little taller as an exhilarating sense of pride overcame me.

We hurried to the small storefront restaurant where slices of meat were artfully stacked on a big vertical spit rotating around a flame. I watched the man cut thin slices from the edges, placed them on warm pita bread, and covered them with chopped tomatoes, parsley, onions, turnip pickles and tahini. He rolled the first one up and handed it to me.

I went to claim the only empty table and sat on a white plastic chair. An adolescent boy who worked in the shop approached. "The doctor wants to know if you want *Bebsi* or if I should go to the shop next door and bring fresh juice?"

"What's he having?" It had been a while since I had heard words pronounced without the letter "P." It didn't exist in Arabic. I grew up going to *barties* and playing *bing-bong*.

"He said to bring two of whatever you order, but I know he prefers carrot juice mixed with apple juice."

"How do you know?"

"Everyone knows what Dr. Joe likes, miss. He's the best of them all. No one cares for poor people like Dr. Joe."

I saw Joe walking to the table and told the boy to hurry back with the juice.

The pride I experienced a few minutes earlier turned to admiration. A warm sensation ran through me. I had never met anyone like him. *Was this meant to be? Was he the reason I was lured back home?*

CHAPTER 13

———

Empty streets create the deafening noise of fear, and teeming bistros provide the quiet of perceived safety.

—MAYA

I couldn't believe how fast things were moving: two job offers, Leila's marriage and pregnancy, old friendships rekindled, and a man I couldn't get out of my mind. All in less than a month. LA shrank into the recesses of my memory. The warmth of caring people surpassed the ugly events in the country. People listened, cared and helped one another. From friends to random taxi drivers, everyone was willing to hear complaints about politics, occupiers or a bad day. I felt like I'd moved from standing alone on a mountaintop to swimming in a sea of fish.

While I got ready for my fourth date with Joe, I mentally reviewed the other three—the evening of the day we met, the shawarma shop, and lunch the next day at Murten House. My body tingled in anticipation of this one.

I was on my hands and knees fishing my sandals out from under my bed when the doorbell rang. I met Maria in the hallway and told her I would answer. I paused, slipped on my footwear, took a deep breath and swung the door open.

"Hi. I'm ready. You'll never believe what happened today."

Before I could step out, he'd stepped inside. From the corner of my eye, I saw Maria still in the corridor.

"You look nice. Green suits you." He kissed me on both cheeks.

"Thanks for the compliment."

"It's not a compliment." He tipped his head. "It's the truth."

"Would you like to come in?" A stupid question since he had already entered. I quickly added, "And say hello to my family."

Papa jumped out of his reclining chair to greet him, and Maman stood up from the sofa. Rima, still seated, surveyed him up and down. She focused on his face as she rose and extended her hand. "I'm Rima."

"Joe."

"I figured. It's nice to finally meet you. You've been dating my sister almost every day for the past week, and this is the first time I get to see you."

"Maya's told me a lot about you."

Rima glared at me. "I'm sure it was all good."

"I can vouch for that."

"Why don't you tell her the truth?" I joked.

"She's your biggest fan," Joe pretended to ignore me. "We're meeting friends for dinner. Would you like to come?"

Please say no. He's just showing good manners. Certainty none of my LA dates would have met my family, much less invited them to join us.

"No thanks. It's my TV night, and *Dallas* starts soon. I've only missed one episode the whole season. But thanks for the invitation."

"Where are you going?" Papa relaxed his posture.

"The Swiss Chalet."

"It brings back lots of memories," Maman said.

On her fiftieth birthday, Papa had thrown a surprise party for her at the popular restaurant.

"Perhaps then you'll come with us?"

"Thank you, but these days, we spend few evenings in restaurants. Not to say I don't like good food, especially at my age. There isn't much left for me to enjoy."

Joe looked kindly at Papa. "You're still young, Amo."

"Only at heart, my son. Now you should get going. You don't want to walk home too late." Papa patted Joe on the back. I could tell he liked him.

We stepped out of the building onto the wide marble steps and walked down to the narrow sidewalk. To my delight, Joe took my hand, and we walked briskly. We stayed alert to our surroundings and hardly spoke. About halfway to our destination, I abruptly stopped and pulled my arm straight to my side. This sudden movement caused Joe to pivot slightly in my direction. He followed my gaze. The three Jeeps of armed men headed toward us. Entrance doors to the apartment and office buildings on the street were locked for the evening. I didn't see an alley we could duck into. We had one option.

"Keep walking." Joe tugged my hand.

My legs felt like water, but I willed them into motion to the oncoming vehicles. The militia men riding in them held M16s. The lead driver looked at us and slowed down, but the one behind honked and he increased his speed. Some of the armed men gawked at us and one raised his weapon and smirked.

Our pace increased. We almost flew once the restaurant came into sight. Joe opened the door and laughter flowed onto the street. We stepped into the dimly lit, smoke-filled room. My whole body shook, and Joe held me close until my breathing stabilized. We made our way to a table in the corner where his friends waited.

A thin man with glasses stood, and his brow tightened with concern. "Are you okay?"

"We're fine, Sammy." Joe touched his shoulder. "We met up with a few armed men in Jeeps, but they drove by. Guess we weren't interesting enough."

"Maya, I'm sorry you had such an experience, but let's make sure this evening ends with good memories."

Sammy handed us glasses of wine. I swallowed a big gulp before we sat down. Joe put his arm around my shoulder, and I inched a little closer to him.

"*Moules marinieres* is on the menu tonight. Does this sound good to you, Maya?" Sammy asked.

I nodded and finished my second glass of wine.

"And then we will have fondue." Sammy voiced the standard fare of the restaurant.

"Now the important things are settled, let's get to introductions." Joe poured more wine.

"You heard I'm Sammy."

"Sammy's an ob-gyn." Joe still held the wine bottle.

"He definitely gets the best-looking patients. I'm David. It's a pleasure to meet you. Joe's talked a lot about you."

"I guess David is the one who sees things clearly," Sammy said. "He's an ophthalmologist. That's why he notices what my patients look like."

"And, if you want to know anything about Joe, I'm the one to consult." The slightly balding man added, "I'm George. Joe and I've been friends since elementary school."

"And, he's a psychiatrist," David said. "So, he has real insight into Joe." He chuckled and raised his glass.

The waiter put two serving bowls of steaming mussels and a basket of thickly sliced baguette on the table. I craved the comfort of bread soaked in the warm sauce.

We ate and drank in silence, but the loud restaurant chatter made our quietness irrelevant. I felt comfortable with Joe's friends. I felt welcome, and they seemed fun.

I dipped into the last shell in my bowl. Food, drink and friendship made my fear subside. I turned to George. "What can you tell me about Joe?"

"He was a troublemaker but the teachers' favorite. They never believed he could do any wrong."

"You're one to talk," Joe interrupted. "I seem to remember you enjoyed a lot of favoritism."

"Only from your mother."

"I can't understand what she sees in you."

"Ah, now the jealousy shows." George looked at me. "Do you know his mother?"

"No."

"She's a wonderful woman. She's from Amsterdam, you know."

"You didn't tell me that." I turned to face Joe.

"It hasn't come up."

"She's lived in Lebanon for over thirty years," George continued. "And says she's more Lebanese than Dutch."

"You'll meet her soon," Joe said.

"Tell us about yourself, Maya," Sammy asked. "We know you recently returned from LA. What are your plans?"

"I'm glad you asked. I've wanted to tell Joe ever since he picked me up tonight, but I haven't had the chance."

Joe looked at me with a self-deprecating smile. "I'm sorry, I forgot to ask. I remember when you opened the door you mentioned something about what happened today."

"I guess Jeeps full of armed men make you forget other things."

He squeezed my shoulder. It felt like an apology.

"I accepted two jobs," I said.

"How will you manage that?" George asked.

"I told you she's amazing." Joe's eyes lit up, and my heart somersaulted.

"I got offered a management position at Middle East Airlines. They work six days a week, from seven thirty until two thirty." I speared a piece of meat with my long fork and put it into the pot of hot oil. The men waited for me to continue.

"The second job is a psychology instructor at AUB. I'll teach afternoon classes. One on Monday, Wednesday, and Friday from three thirty to four thirty and the second on Tuesday and Thursday from three thirty to five."

"A psychology instructor?" Sammy asked.

"My master's degree is in industrial psychology. I'm well-qualified to teach introductory psychology."

"You'll be a busy lady. Can you manage?" David asked.

"I think I can. They're both great opportunities—MEA's the biggest employer in the country, and having the chance to teach at AUB is extraordinary."

"Will you drive to the airport offices?" David asked.

"No. That's another great thing. The company provides bus transportation."

The people at the neighboring table began to sing, and others joined in. A man stood up and pretended to conduct. These were the evenings I cherished—friends, food, and singing strangers.

I grew pensive. We used to venture everywhere with no fear. Sometimes we'd spend all night driving along the shoreline doing *rodage*—all new cars needed to be driven on flat land to break in the engine before they could climb up the mountains. When we drove north, we'd stop in the village of Batroun for lemonade and in the city of Tripoli for baklava and sweets. We always returned to Al-Ajami Restaurant in the Beirut souk for breakfast since it never closed.

"Maya, are you okay?" Joe asked, concerned.

"Oh, yes, just remembering how things used to be."

We left the Swiss Chalet after midnight. Our loud voices competed with the echoes of our footsteps in the empty city streets. I felt more secure walking with a group.

The men waited patiently while I unlocked the building lobby gate. Joe kissed me on both cheeks. I felt better knowing he wasn't walking home alone.

"He's cute." Rima startled me in the dark bedroom.

"I think so, too"

"Real cute." Soon I heard her snoring softly.

I lay in bed thinking about Joe. *Am I blessed as one of the fortunate people who've found the perfect mate? Am I falling in love for the first time?*

* * *

"We haven't been to the beach yet," Leila shouted across a scratchy phone line. "We have to go before you start work on Monday."

"How about today?"

"Great, I'll pick you up in fifteen minutes."

I looked through the beach items stored in the hall closet. I selected a straw bag with a striped lining and a towel with "TWA—This Seat Is Occupied" written across it.

Ali rang the doorbell and told Maria to let me know Miss Leila was waiting in the car.

"I hear the Summerland Resort is beautiful." I slid into the backseat beside Leila. "My family's going to the lunch buffet on Sunday."

The streets were frightening but safe, and lovely places existed where luxuries could be enjoyed. This kept many people going during difficult times.

A uniformed valet opened the car door for us at the recently built opulent beach hotel.

"Let me show you around before we go downstairs to change," Leila said. "It's so pretty and the spa is like Paris."

Leila introduced me to Mr. Louis, the spa manager. "This is my best friend, Maya. She recently returned from LA."

"My cousin lives in LA. Maybe you know her?"

Know someone in LA? Does he think it's like Lebanon? Before I had the chance to tell him how many people live in LA, he said, "Her name's Aida Thibiant, and she owns a day spa in Beverly Hills."

"I know her," I practically shouted at the ridiculousness of it.

"I thought you would," he said nonchalantly.

"Well, I only kind of know her. I've had facials there, and I've spoken to her. She's famous. All of the movie stars go to her. I didn't know she's Lebanese."

"Yes, of Armenian origin. Now you must have a facial here to see which is better. I'll tell Aida, depending on how you vote."

"It sounds like you want to get me into trouble." I grinned at him.

"Let's schedule a complimentary facial for both of you. Remember, you can't sit in the sun afterward."

"Can we come this afternoon?" I asked.

"We have two appointments at four," the receptionist spoke in French.

We left and went to Leila's cabin to change. People rented the compartments for the season. Each had a dressing area and a shower with endless hot water.

We exited and walked to the beach. Two swimming pools with a waterfall had been built on terraces above the sea. A short man scurried before us. He arranged reclining chairs and an umbrella for us. Below, children watched by Filipino and African nannies played in the sand. Their bikini clad mothers stretched out on long chairs padded with thick towels.

"One beer and a glass of lemonade," Leila told the waiter, without consulting me. "And squeeze lemon juice on the carrot sticks." She turned to me, "Let's forget everything serious and enjoy the day like we used to. I hope you still drink beer."

"I do, and I like your idea." I needed a day devoid of drama.

The drinks were served with a bowl of roasted nuts and a plate of vegetable sticks. I reached for my beach bag, but Leila put her hand on the clasp. "It's already on Baba's account."

The cold beer slid easily down my throat. I lay back and closed my eyes. In my mind I saw the beach bonfire in Corona del Mar and heard the guitar and the voices of the young, carefree Californians. The sun seeped into my body as my tension melted away through the reclining chair and into the earth below.

"Maya," Leila shook my shoulder. "You've been asleep for over two hours. We only have half an hour before our facials. Aren't you hungry?"

"How can I be hungry? I was asleep."

"The hamburgers are great, and they come with fries and salad. I'm having one. Shall I order one for you?"

I nodded. I knew it would be a gourmet burger.

* * *

"What would you like to drink?" Mr. Louis greeted us. "After time in the sun, you need to hydrate. Perhaps fresh lemonade?"

Maybe the movie stars got this treatment in LA, but I certainly didn't. I'd already decided which facial I liked better.

The drive home took fifteen minutes, and Leila instructed Ali to carry my belongings to the apartment. I protested, but he was already gone.

"Don't forget about our date night tomorrow," she said.

"I'm looking forward to meeting Alex and introducing you to Joe."

"I'll pick you up at eight."

Maria greeted me at the open front door. "Miss Maya, you have a telephone call." She'd laid the receiver on the hall table.

"Did you enjoy the beach, beautiful lady?" I shivered with delight at the sound of Joe's voice.

"How'd you know where I was?"

"I can't reveal my sources."

"Well, there are ways I can make you talk, but I have to be with you for them to work." I surprised myself with my response.

"Unfortunately, it'll have to wait. My mother's not feeling well. I'm going to see her tonight."

"Oh, I'm sorry. What's wrong with her?"

"Nothing serious. She has a bad cold, but I won't have another chance to visit her for a couple of weeks."

East Beirut, where she lived, was less than ten minutes away, but to get there he had to cross the treacherous Green Line before dark.

"I'll be back in the morning. What time should I pick you up for dinner?"

"I'm going with Leila. We'll meet you at Le Commodore at nine."

"Sounds good," he shouted into the phone. The line crackled.

"See ..." The phone connection cut.

I found Papa and Maria in the kitchen preparing supper—a mezza spread of small dishes, to enjoy in the family room while watching TV. We ate lunch, our main meal, in the dining room around two in the afternoon.

After breakfast, Maman put an enormous round wicker tray on the kitchen table and throughout the day, small dishes of nonperishable food like olives, pickles, sliced tomato, roasted garlic, and miniature cucumbers were placed on it. Closer to evening, cheeses, sliced fruit, and boiled eggs were added. The meats were always the last items plated.

Papa often bought specialty foods on his walk home from his office. Tonight, he artistically sliced Egyptian *batarekh* into thin pieces. The fish roe delicacy was dried and pressed into slabs resembling oblong sausages. Once Teta mistook them for hotdogs and fed one to the cat. Papa arranged them on a platter, placed a sliver of fresh garlic on each, and drizzled olive oil over his masterpiece. When I entered the kitchen, he tore off a piece of pita bread and scooped up a slice of *batarekh* with garlic, dipped it in oil, and handed it to me.

"Why don't you shower and put your night clothes on before we eat?" he asked.

"I showered at Summerland, but I'll go change quickly. Tonight's mezza is too enticing."

Papa winked at me. He seemed exceptionally happy, and I knew it had something to do with me and Joe.

CHAPTER 14

———

Every friend added to the circle increases risk.

—*MAYA*

"He's a famous parrot." I couldn't tell if Leila was being sar-castic or trying to be funny. "He warns of incoming rocket attacks. He's been featured in news stories around the world. Foreign correspondents hang out at this hotel."

"Well, I guess that makes him more acclaimed than we'll ever be." I stood and watched the bizarre interaction between Leila and the caged bird. She spoke, the parrot responded, and I understood nothing. I shifted my weight and looked around. A blond man seated at the bar smiled at me and moved his head to indicate empty stools next to him. I shook my head and poked Leila. She reluctantly left the bird, and we made our way to the far end of the large Commodore Hotel bar.

"It's good to be out of the house. The tension is unbearable. My mother refuses to speak to me, my parents are constantly fighting, and the servants are jittery."

The bartender took our drink orders, and she continued, "Alex is living with his friend, Fares."

"Why doesn't he live with his parents?"

"They're in East Beirut, and it would be too difficult for him to cross the Green Line every day. He has no money to rent a place, and my mother refuses to let him enter our home."

"Why don't you pay for an apartment?"

"Baba's renovating one for us in a building he owns. It'll be ready next month."

The blond man still looked at us.

"It's hell. My mother wants me to get a divorce and, above all, an abortion. She knows a doctor someone's daughter used. I finally yelled at her in front of her best friend and asked how she could murder her grandchild. That's when she stopped speaking to me. The stress level remains the same, but at least it's quieter."

Neither of us saw Alex approach, and Leila jumped when he kissed the back of her neck. He wrapped his arms around her from behind and grinned at me. Leila set money on the bar and slid off the stool.

A few steps away, in the hotel lobby, Mrs. Chen, the long-time restaurant owner, greeted us. We selected a table in the corner, and Alex pulled out Leila's chair. He had an olive complexion and his straight black hair bounced slightly when he moved. He was good looking.

He sat down across from me. The waiter put small plates of nuts and carrots on the table. Leila requested tonic water, and Alex suggested he and I have a bottle of wine. From his questions to the waiter, he sounded like a connoisseur.

Alex turned his attention to me, and I began to piece together a portrait of him. He was a year older than Leila and from a lower-middle-class Christian Greek Orthodox family. While an engineering student at AUB, he became active with a pro-Soviet communist party. His conversation continuously gravitated to politics, and he went to great lengths to explain why secularism was Lebanon's only hope for the future. He tore apart the existing sectarian political system and saw no reason why a Soviet style government wouldn't work in Lebanon.

"The French screwed us," he said in perfect French. "People complain about suffering for four hundred years under Ottoman rule, but we got rid of them. But what the French did still poisons us today. Our problems began at the end of World War I when the French and British divided the Middle East like a game board. How did they justify keeping Lebanon as a French mandate for twenty-five years? And when we gained independence, they were behind the unwritten national pact. Have you ever heard of a modern country where the president has to be a Maronite—not any Christian, only a Maronite. And the prime minister has to be a Sunni Muslim—not any Muslim, only a ..."

"She knows." Leila sounded agitated.

"Don't forget our trash collectors have to represent the eighteen recognized religious sects." He mocked. "And if you claim no religion, that's fine. However, you will have no rights under the law unless you belong to one of the recognized religious groups."

"Enough, Alex," Leila snapped. "We're here for an enjoyable evening and not to discuss frustrating topics with no solutions."

"That's the problem; we need to discuss things in order to solve them. But okay, my love, you're right. Tonight isn't the time." His mouth tightened, and he forced a smile. "Maya, Leila loves you. If I listen to her, you should be put on a pedestal." His voice carried a sinister tone, and I felt uncomfortable.

Joe arrived twenty minutes late due to an emergency and apologized. His presence made the gathering more relaxed. I couldn't tell if Joe liked Alex. A couple of times they ganged up to tease Leila and me.

Alex offered to drive us home in his Mini Cooper and, although it felt like riding in a tin can, it beat walking through the dark, empty streets. He turned up the music on the radio, and in the back seat, I moved closer to Joe. He kissed my neck. Suddenly, armed men at a makeshift checkpoint appeared a few meters ahead. I sat up straight. Alex slowed down, muted the radio, stopped the car, turned on the interior light and rolled down his window. The warmth of the wine collided with icy fear in my stomach.

Joe leaned forward to the open window as if to take charge of the situation. It made me nervous, but before he could say anything, one of the armed men spoke.

"How are you, my brother?" he addressed Alex.

"Good, thanks be to God."

"God be with you." He motioned with his hand for us to leave.

It surprised me how easily they let us through. The armed man didn't ask any questions and didn't demand our identity cards. I could detect from his accent he was Lebanese, probably from Beirut. I couldn't tell if he knew Alex or if he just wasn't interested in two men with women. I'd ask Joe what he thought about it later.

* * *

At the pizzeria where Joe and I meet the following night, only a few tables were occupied. Over the years, hundreds of candles had perfumed the air as they melted down on empty

Chianti bottles. In anticipation of the pitcher of red-rose liquid, I pushed the candle on our table to one side. Sangria was the best drink to have at a time like this. It's happy, fanciful and full of surprises. The flavor is never monotonous and the effects of the liquor are pleasantly disguised. It's a mixture of uncertainty and hope, mirroring this city of passionate life lived on the brink of death and destruction.

The sangria arrived. I took a long drink and set my glass down on the tiled table. I reached for the candle, pried off a soft wad of multicolored wax and rolled it between my hands into a perfect ball. I presented it to Joe on my open palm. He took it and kissed my hand. A tingle of anticipation ran through me

"A vegetarian pizza for *mademoiselle*." The waiter placed the individual-sized pie in front of me. "For *monsieur*." He put down the second plate. "*Et pour vous deux*." We had ordered a salad to share.

With my knife and fork, I cut into the pizza. The aroma of roasted artichokes and peppers satisfied me before anything touched my tongue. *Unbelievable food in this crazy city. A pizza and a glass of sangria rival the best food and wine at Chasen's. Why did this LA restaurant come to mind? I know why—a woman across the room looked like Marlene Dietrich.*

And one night at Chasen's, the real Marlene stared at me for an entire evening from where she sat at the margins of an inattentive group who vied among themselves for attention. I pondered if, combined, their fame equaled hers, but in Hollywood, who cared—youth and ambition ruled, and at that point in her life, she had neither. I'd wondered what she thought about—the more than half-century between our ages, or maybe I reminded her of someone, or perhaps she felt amused by my attentive date. Probably, she watched me because her dining companions ignored her. I was too young to care—even when the waiter leaned down to whisper, "You have intrigued Miss Dietrich."

Now, in a dimly lit Beirut restaurant, I looked at the man facing me. I wanted to intrigue him. Like a child, with my fingers, I reached into my glass and pulled out a piece of pink-stained apple. I let it linger on my lips, slipped it into my mouth and washed it down with sangria. He watched silently, but I knew the look in his eyes. Fearful of where I might be leading him, I diverted his obvious thoughts. "Joe, out of the eighty-three students in my two classes, sixty-nine are premed. They're competitive, and I know the grades will be skewed."

I didn't think he heard, but he said, "What'd you say about sixty-nine?"

I didn't react.

He continued, "Seriously, why don't you run this by others in the department to see how they handle such situations?"

I had successfully lured him away from the sexual tensions of our body language and its implications in our discussion. Now I wondered if this was the type of evening I wanted and quickly decided it wasn't. I took another long sip of my drink and sucked in my lower lip. I knew I had to ask one more question before I let the fantasy of sangria take over the evening. "Joe, why do you think the militia men let us pass through their checkpoint so easily last night?"

"I'm not sure. Maybe because two women were with us and they wanted us to enjoy the evening."

"Be serious. Do you think they knew Alex?"

"They might have, but you can't read too much into that. After all, he's lived in the area for years. They've probably come across one another on numerous occasions."

His matter-of-fact explanation made sense. "Would you like to taste how good a meatless pizza is?" Before he could answer, I stabbed a piece with my fork and rubbed the dough along the outline of his mouth.

"Maybe next time I'll let you order for me." He refilled our glasses. His face relaxed and looked fuller.

I placed my hands under my chin. He reached over, cupped mine with his and lowered them to the table. "Even when you try to look serious, you're beautiful."

I smiled. The sangria was not going to work tonight. It was too soon. He would have to wait.

CHAPTER 15

Distorting memories is the privilege of having lived through the moments.

—SELMA

The man I was about to meet had almost singlehandedly kept the largest employer in the country flourishing due to his brilliant ideas and decisions. Middle East Airlines remained recognized and admired in the international aviation industry for its outstanding management, technical knowhow and customer service—despite the war.

Mr. Habib, an impeccably dressed man in his mid-fifties, stood to welcome me as I entered his office. A million questions ran through my mind, but I let him direct the conversation. After some polite inquiries about me, he outlined his vision for the company. He believed the large-scale fighting had subsided, and the future appeared optimistic. He intended to keep this well-respected company in the limelight as a leader.

I knew the company had remained solvent by leveraging assets and expertise. Planes with entire crews were leased to other carriers; customized training programs and instructors were marketed to other airlines; and employees became technical, financial, and human resource consultants in the industry. The management also made risky but profitable currency speculations.

Now, Mr. Habib planned to create an in-house consulting group to provide services to all departments within the company. The lead, an American-educated engineer named Nabil, had extensive management experience. The group included four specialists, of which I was one. Twelve analysts executed the projects. Departments were invited to submit requests for review by Mr. Habib, Nabil, and the specialists. Some were already pending—enhancing engineering maintenance schedules, flight attendant training, employee technical and language testing, customer satisfaction surveys, and a more efficient reservation system.

Mr. Habib made clear the importance of this new initiative. It aligned with his vision, and he was invested in its success. He asked for the three of us to meet again the following morning. He wanted me to select projects in my area of expertise and to get my take on this endeavor.

"You feel his passion," Nabil said as soon as we left. "He's amazing. He's a strategic and financial genius. He began at the company as an office clerk with little education. He studied at night for his degrees and is now in line to be the next chairman. He treats everyone with dignity. We're fortunate to work on his team."

A study in contrasts best described my new boss, Nabil and my old one, Jeff. On the way to my office, he stopped to greet everyone we passed in the hallways and poked his head into offices to introduce me to other employees.

As we exited one building and entered another, I asked Nabil about the cots I saw in most work spaces.

"Many employees lived here during the bad fighting," he said.

My hands began to sweat at the memory of Amo Fred driving us on our fear-filled trip to the airport, only minutes down the road from where we now stood. I remembered he planned to live in his office. I tried to brush my emotions aside. "How was it to live at work?"

"If the situation hadn't been dire, it would have been lots of fun. Almost like being back in boarding school. On the nights when we knew our families were home safe and the fighting wasn't heavy, we had good times."

"How about food?"

"The canteen staff prepared meals. Employees bought groceries and personal items at the onsite co-op. And the flight crews often brought us food from their trips—wines and cheese from France, olives and feta from Greece, fish from Spain, and bread from Germany."

Nabil told me he'd left IBM in Paris five years earlier. "My wife's a doctor and wanted to return so our children could grow up around family and in our culture."

"Was it hard for you to leave?"

"Yes, even though I agreed with my wife, it was difficult to leave a secure country and job. I'd been at IBM for ten years."

"*Think!*" I shouted out IBM's slogan, but before he could react, a woman approached and he introduced us. "Mona is director of reservations. We met at MIT over twenty years ago."

* * *

Days and nights were full, and I was astonished at how much I accomplished. Six days a week I took the company bus to the airport headquarters. Monday through Friday, I rushed out of my office to catch the 2:20 p.m. bus to the American University of Beirut. The students in my psychology classes kept me on my toes. I needed to be well-prepared.

On week days, I'd arrive home around six thirty—twelve hours after I'd boarded the morning bus. Evenings began with the challenge of taking a shower. Spending time with Joe and lesson planning were my next two priorities. Papa joked about needing an appointment to see me. Most nights he, Maman, and Rima munched mezza and watched TV.

* * *

Two weeks after I began the job, Mr. Habib asked to see me. It seemed unusual for him to schedule something at the last minute. I inquired if I could go immediately. I didn't want to spend time anticipating what he wanted.

"Maya, I appreciate you coming to see me with short notice." Mr. Habib stood and gestured for me to sit down. "I gave you first pick of analysts for your upcoming project from the group of forty-five new graduates we hired. Why did you choose four women?"

"Only five men were in the group."

"Didn't you find any of them qualified?

"Yes, but…"

"What's the percentage of men in your classes at the university?" he asked.

"At least sixty, maybe more."

"Do you see any difference in how they regard you as a female instructor verses their male professors?"

"No."

"Exactly my point. When young men come out of college, they are accustomed to women in leadership positions. They have no qualms about having a female boss. If someone like you doesn't select male subordinates, we are perpetuating the wrong attitude. Men, especially those in the Middle East, need to accept women in leadership roles. You must be part of this change."

I nodded, and he continued, "I believe only Nabil and I know this, so it isn't too late for you to reexamine your selection."

I thanked him for his foresight.

During my final meeting that day, the vice president of personnel reminded me to take advantage of the free or highly discounted airline tickets and travel perks offered. "And your family also receives your benefits—parents, spouse, and children. Siblings receive discounts."

"How about if someone has two wives?"

"You know this isn't common in Lebanon. But just in case, the employee handbook states only one wife is eligible."

"How about two husbands?"

"You got me. I can't stop you, but you'll need to move quickly before we update the rules." We both laughed.

* * *

Later in the afternoon, I entered our apartment and found Monique waiting for me. She immediately stated the purpose of her visit. "My niece is getting married in Greece in two weeks, and I'd like you to come."

"But I don't know her or anyone else."

"Yes, you do. You know my parents. We'll leave Friday. The wedding's on Saturday."

"Sounds good. A weekend in Athens to celebrate the wedding of people I don't know with people I've never met." I thought I sounded sarcastic, but Monique didn't seem to notice.

"It'll be fun. Remember, in Lebanon we do things on the spur of the moment and won't miss a celebration because we might not be alive tomorrow."

"I guess I lived in America too long." I remembered how shocked I'd been when people planned vacations a year in advance.

"Seems so," Monique said. "Will you come?"

"Sure. I'll reserve the hotel. I can get it half price."

"I'm excited. We'll finally spend time together."

"Actually, it's a good weekend for me to go. Joe's off, but he'll be visiting his mother."

"Joe? I can't believe I'm behind on your news. I didn't realize we have so much to catch up on." She leaned forward, as if expecting me to fill her in, but Rima burst into the room with two friends. They plopped into chairs, talking all at once about a horrible professor and his unfair exam, which they were sure they'd failed.

* * *

In Greece, I was welcomed like family. We danced, sang, broke plates, prayed, and rejoiced. Monique and I spent the whole time together.

"You've really fallen for this doctor," she repeated every time I spoke about Joe. "Do you think he's the one?"

"I know I'm in love, but everything seems too good to be true."

"What's his biggest flaw?"

"Is that how you respond to someone who tells you she's in love?"

"You know I'm a big romantic, but reality differs from poetry. Success in long-term relationships depends on deep analysis. This is not one of the things I endorse for everyday fun. I need to meet him before I approve. I'll throw a party for him next Saturday."

Back in Beirut the following week, she hosted an elegant French cuisine dinner attended by the best artists, diplomats, and reporters she knew. Joe, touched by the effort she made to welcome him, appeared fascinated by the variety of people gathered.

* * *

Three days later, I flew to Paris to observe the cabin crew conduct the inflight passenger satisfaction survey my team had designed. The following morning, on the way to the airport for the flight home, the aircrew bus stopped at the fish market. I bought sole and two kilos of mussels. The moment the plane landed, I rushed to my office to call and invite Joe for dinner.

In the evening, the two of us sat at the far end of our long dining room table. The remaining fourteen chairs stood empty. Maman and Maria worked in the kitchen, and I made trips back and forth with food. Neither one of them wanted to interrupt our evening, or let Joe know how much they assisted.

"I didn't know you could cook. I'm impressed," he innocently said.

"I guess there are lots of things you don't know about me. Joe, do you ever question your decision to return home?"

His face darkened. "I was very happy in Boston. I always planned to come back, but I was in no hurry. I thought things would wait for me."

"Why did you return?"

"Things didn't wait. My father didn't wait. He passed away suddenly, and I realized time is on nobody's side. I came back because this is where I belong. It's where I can make the most impact. And I wanted to spend some time with my mother before it was too late."

"I'm sorry." I put my fork down. "I didn't know."

"How could you?" He put his hand over mine. "So, how big is the Paris fish market?"

"I'll show you sometime. I didn't realize certain flight crews make it a regular stop."

"Looks like you flew with the right crew."

"That's for sure." I went to fetch the fish.

I exited the room, closed the door, and saw Maria in the hallway. She had the next course on the wheeled double decker dinner cart.

"Why are you here?" I whispered.

"Madame thought Dr. Joe will be more impressed if you're speedy."

"What are all these covered dishes?"

"Madame made orzo with pine nuts, roasted beets with spinach, spicy mixed vegetables and the fish."

"I'm supposed to be the one cooking. How could I do all of this?"

"Miss Maya, most men are not inquisitive about food preparation. They only like to eat it. If he asks, say you're the head chef and your assistants washed and chopped."

I opened the dining room door and wheeled in the cart.

"This orzo is wonderful." Joe put another serving on his plate. "Does it have feta cheese in it?"

"It's a family secret. It is only shared when someone officially joins the clan."

"A good reason to join." He didn't miss a bite.

When I cut into the lemon meringue pie, I told him it was exclusively Maman's masterpiece. He moved the angle of my hand to ensure a larger piece.

"This is delicious. You should add it to your repertoire," Joe continued. "A friend of mine invited me to a picnic in the Chouf Mountains on Sunday. Will you come?"

"Do I know him?"

"His name's Makram Izziddin."

"I don't."

"He's inviting a bunch of old high school classmates. I think you'll like him. He's unique but not as original as Monique."

Maybe Makram wasn't up to Monique's standards, but what happened at his picnic forever changed Joe and my relationship.

CHAPTER 16

———

In Lebanon, tragedy dances with dreams.

—*MAYA*

The drive through the Chouf Mountains southeast of Beirut was magnificent. The region, less developed than Teta's mountain, had an air of nostalgia. In the early nineteenth century, the emirs of Lebanon chose this area to build their palace. Small villages clustered along the mountain sides; mostly Druze and Christian but also some Muslim. And without asking, I knew from his name our host was a Druze. I found this religion with its secretive theology fascinating, including elements of Judaism, Christianity, Islam, Hinduism, and Greek philosophy. Reincarnation is a central belief, and as a child I intrinsically understood it, but could not articulate it once I reached my teens.

Together we loudly sang "Sweet Caroline," overpowering the sound of the radio. I put my hand on Joe's thigh. He raised it, kissed it, and put it back on his leg.

"I hear the Cedars of Barouk have more trees than the Cedars of Lebanon," I referred to a nature reserve in the area. "I've never been."

"It's beautiful. Let's plan to go soon. We can combine it with apple picking."

"Can we also visit *Deir al Qumar* Monastery of the Moon?"

"Sure." The mountain became steeper, and he shifted the car into a lower gear.

We stopped in front of an elegant old two-story home. A large arcade with an open door led into the building. Multiple arches graced the façade of the house, including the upstairs windows. The red-tiled roof completed the traditional Lebanese home. From the doorway, we looked into the living room and through the parallel back door to an outside courtyard where a group of people sat. The structure harmonized and opened up to the surrounding nature.

"Welcome! Welcome! You are most welcome!" Makram greeted us, his arms wide open. He grabbed Joe, kissed him on both checks, and hugged him. He stepped back, looked at me, and leaned forward to kiss me. "What a pleasure. What a pleasure. Come. Come. Everyone is in the garden."

His guests sat on sofas and chairs placed along the edges of the patio. The quadrangle of people stood to greet us, and Makram escorted me to make introductions. Joe followed. He knew most of the them.

"What can I get you to drink? I recommend arak. It's homemade by my grandfather."

Makram came back carrying two milky drinks. I smelled the anise and remembered stomping on Teta's grapes. After they fermented in barrels, she added aniseed in the second distillation.

"Okay, here's the plan," Makram announced. "We'll drive a few minutes, park and make a short walk up the mountain to our picnic."

When we arrived at the plateau, everything had been set up. I thought we'd find blankets and baskets of food, but instead, dozens of small mezza plates were placed on a table covered with a white cloth. Off to the left, two boys fanned skewered meats on low charcoal grills and three maids stood in attendance.

Makram walked to the head of the table, waved his arms and instructed everyone to find a seat. A dozen chairs were placed on either side of the table. I sat next to Joe's old classmate, Mike, whose wife, Yolla, sat across from me.

Food and drink kept coming. Clear arak poured in glasses became milky when water was added. Bottles of wine were opened, and a few *Bebsis* were served. We started with the cold mezza—tabbouleh, hummus, goat cheese, salads, lima beans, vegetarian stuffed grape leaves, baba ghanouj, nuts, and vegetables arranged in large platters. Raw meats were soon served—kibbi, liver, and filet—followed by sausages, pastries (cheese or spinach filled), fried kibbi (stuffed with meat, pine nuts and onions), and rolled grape leaves (with rice and meat). When the platters of grilled meats arrived, people declared themselves satiated but somehow managed to eat more. Finally, the maids cleared away the meal and replaced it with honey-drenched sweets and fresh fruit.

"Desserts help you digest." Yolla scooped spoonfuls of *ashta* and honey into my plate. My mouth watered in anticipation of the milk-based sweet pudding.

"Okay. Okay." Makram pushed his chair back and stood. "Siesta time. Those of you who are adventurous can climb further up the mountain and sleep like our ancestors but with some modern comfort. The first three caves have sleeping mats. The rest of us can find comfortable places here." He waved his arm to indicate where carpets, large cushions and blankets were spread out. Low couches and hookahs were placed nearby.

"I ate too much." I held Joe's hand. "Let's be the ones who go in search of a place to rest."

A couple began to venture up the mountain. We followed along with Mike and Yolla. The climb was relatively easy, but a few minutes into it, the woman wanted to return because her shoes hurt her feet. Her companion shrugged and followed her back down.

We zigzagged on what was probably a goat trail. Low shrubbery grew along the sides of the dirt path and out of cracks in the limestone mountain. Parts of the mountains were barren rock and other areas sprouted low trees and an occasional umbrella pine.

Mike and Yolla stopped at the first cave for a nap.

I tugged on Joe's hand. I wanted to continue. We soon came upon a slightly bigger grotto with an arch-like entryway.

"Let's look inside." We ducked to enter, but once inside, Joe could stand. As Makram had said, we found thick mats with neatly folded blankets and pillows.

We stood in semi-darkness peering out at the sparkling Mediterranean almost a thousand meters below. At the horizon, sky and sea became one.

Joe put his arm around me, and I turned to him. His hands slid down my back. I lifted my face, and he kissed me. I tried to slow my breathing to control the slight tremble in my body.

He pulled me closer, and I began to relax. He unexpectedly stepped away. "Maya, are you okay with this?"

I nodded.

"Are you covered? Is this safe? I don't have anything with me."

I couldn't hold back. Although I knew better, I probably would have taken the risk. "I should be. My period finished last night."

We kissed, and he unbuttoned my shirt to touch my breasts with gentle firmness.

Afterward we lay in each other's arms on the mats. We could only see the sky through the entrance of the cave. The bright blue soon become infused with red and orange slivers as the sun began its descent into the sea.

"I think we need to get back." Joe lightly scratched my back and kissed my ear.

"Do we have to?" Reality is a cruel interruption.

Joe rose to retrieve our clothes from next to the cave entrance. I knew he was fit but didn't realize how muscular. He turned my shirt and pants right side out and placed them next to me.

* * *

"There you are," Makram exclaimed as we approached the group.

"We were wondering what happened to you? I'll have the maid make you coffee. How do you like it? Medium sugar?"

It seemed as though two dozen pairs of eyes focused on us. From the looks on their faces, I pretty much sensed everyone knew what we'd been doing. I felt my face redden. I wanted to turn around and run. Joe seemed nonchalant. He took my hand and led me to a seat on one of the low couches. The man sitting next to him slapped him on the back, and the woman beside me gave me a wink. I wanted to disappear into the ground.

"Maya, relax. It's okay," Joe spoke in a low, reassuring voice.

We took small cups of Turkish coffee off the tray the maid presented. Joe sipped his, and I finished the thick semi-sweet liquid in two gulps. I couldn't wait to leave.

People began to say their goodbyes, and I nudged Joe. He looked at me, smiled, pulled me closer to him before kissing my forehead. Then he squeezed my hand and stood up.

"Makram, thanks for a wonderful day, as always," Joe said.

"It was a pleasure to meet you, Maya. I've never seen Joe this happy. Please come again soon." Makram kissed me on both cheeks.

Before starting the car, Joe leaned over to give me a long kiss.

"I have never felt so embarrassed in my life," I said.

"What's there to be embarrassed about?"

"Everyone knew what we were doing. Did you see the looks people were giving us?"

"I only saw *you*. Really, why do you care what people think?"

"I just… I don't know. Hey, at least we have one secret everybody doesn't know. I bet nobody guessed it was our first time." I tried to smile.

"Now you've got the right attitude."

This time I leaned over and kissed him.

"Why don't you come to my apartment for dinner before I take you home?"

I'd never been there, and when he opened the door, I was struck by how neat it looked. The living room, dining room, and kitchen were all one room. I could see the bedroom through the open door to the left.

Joe took out food from the refrigerator. I knew he hired a lady to clean and cook daily. Today she'd left pastries filled with vegetables and something in a second container. I approached to help him, and we never touched the food.

When he walked me home two hours later, I felt different. My body had a sense of fullness, every bit of it satisfied. It was happy, achy, yearning, and I craved more.

"I finish at the hospital around seven tomorrow. Are you available for dinner?"

"Are we going to eat like we did tonight?"

"If that's what you'd like." He kissed me once more before he ventured back out into the deserted streets.

I turned the key softly in our apartment door. I was in luck. Everyone seemed asleep. I walked to my parents' bedroom and shut the open door. If they woke, they'd know I had returned.

Since we had no electricity, I lit a candle in the bathroom. I rotated the sink tap. Nothing came out. Then I saw the bottle of water and glass Maria had left for me. I brushed my teeth and washed my face with the cool water.

Rima stirred slightly when I got in bed, but she only turned over. I held one of my pillows close to me. I missed him. I thought about Joe back in his apartment. It didn't seem right we slept in separate beds on this night.

CHAPTER 17

If you are going to live here, you must believe your destiny is written or this place will drive you insane.

—MAURICE

I tried to leave the bedroom quietly, but as I opened the door, Rima sat up in her bed. "Hey, where're you going?"

"To the French Embassy." I needed to pick up the report I'd requested on French nationals who visited Lebanon.

"Wait, I need to talk to you. I feel like you're ignoring me. You keep rushing off when I'm asleep, and you're always out in the evenings. Stay for a few minutes and let's at least have coffee together."

"I really need to get going. I've got a lot to do in the office, and I'm going to be late."

"I haven't talked with you since you went on the mysterious picnic over three weeks ago."

"How about catching up tonight? I'm not going out."

"But I am. Oh, come on, spend some time with me now. Life finishes and work doesn't. A few minutes won't make a difference. You keep forgetting this isn't America."

"Okay, okay, I'll tell Maria to make coffee, but get up now."

Rima wobbled into the kitchen in her bathrobe and Winnie the Pooh slippers I bought her in LA. They were intended as a joke, but I think she actually liked them. She sat sideways on a chair and leaned her back against the wall. "Joe," she said.

Maria put the demitasse cups of thick coffee in front of us and left to continue her morning chores.

"He's amazing. I can't believe I've met the perfect someone. I'm in love."

"Wait. You're going too fast. Let's backtrack. A few weeks ago you were just having fun. When did this change?"

"It's too much to tell you now. I promise I'll tell you everything very soon. Let's go out to lunch on Saturday."

"It's a date—can't wait."

I took the last swallow of coffee, grabbed my briefcase, and darted out of the apartment and the building. I walked past two pedestrians and made a right turn up the hill to the embassy. I never arrived.

* * *

I woke up in a small windowless room, shaking and disoriented. Four people were crowded in the space.

"My daughter, are you all right?"

I looked up at the elderly woman dressed in black. "What happened?"

"We're not sure. You were walking in front of our building when a large explosion from the direction of the French Embassy happened. You fell, and my son rushed out to carry you inside. Praise be to God, we're fine, but I know other people a few meters away are not."

Two men kneeling next to me rose. One said, "Since you seem okay, we need to go out to survey the situation."

The old woman begged them not to, but they ignored her.

She stood up and instructed me to follow her. Still unsettled, I did as told. We entered an apartment on the ground level of the building. She poured rose water syrup into a glass and added water. She bemoaned not having ice to make a proper drink. She hadn't had electricity for two days. Nevertheless, she believed the beverage, even at room temperature, would make me feel better. I drank it, thanked her, and left. My head pounded, and my right shoulder ached.

A small crowd stood about three hundred meters up the hilly road, and I walked to them, curious as to why they were so quiet. Most stared up into the treetops. I approached and looked. Above me blood dripped from a torso with a swinging arm. I turned my head and threw up. The man standing next to me jumped away, but it was too late.

He showed no reaction to his splattered pants and shoes. I glanced at him and down at the blood and human tissue on the street. I ran down the hill almost certain I had stepped on fingers blown off of a hand. Images of human body parts dangling from tree branches or rolling down the hill filled my mind.

Our concierge, whom I did not see rushing toward me, grabbed my arm. "Your mother, your sister, they're looking for you. Did you see them?" he shouted.

"No."

"Go into the building. I'll find them." He scurried away. I sat on the cold marble lobby steps. Tears poured down my face although I wasn't crying properly. At some point, Maman, Rima and the concierge raised me to a standing position, supported me, and walked me up to our apartment.

I barely heard Rima's words, "Thank God I insisted you have coffee with me. Maya, we need to go to church and light a candle. Our Lady is watching over us."

The remainder of the day I sat or curled up in a fetal position in the family room reclining chair. I wished Teta was with us. Maman checked on me frequently. Rima skipped her classes and rarely left the room. Maria rubbed my shoulders, arms, and neck multiple times. Neighbors tried to comfort me. Papa came home for lunch and a nap but skipped both to stay with me. I didn't listen to anyone's words. Rima tried hard to make me understand Joe was on the phone, but I ignored her.

The following morning, when Maria woke me up, she'd already selected a suit, shoes, and accessories. She helped me dress. I didn't ask any questions. The pill I'd been coaxed into taking the night before had knocked me out. Maman handed me a lunch bag, and Papa walked me to the bus stop.

I boarded and walked to a window seat in the back. A sales manager, Maurice, whom I often talked with on the ride, took the seat next to me. For a while, he said nothing, but then he spoke in a soft voice. "Maya, I heard about yesterday, and I'm sorry you had this experience. But thank God you're okay."

I stared ahead.

"Maya, if you are going to live here, you have to become a fatalist. You have to believe your destiny is written or this place will drive you insane. Remember the old Arabic saying, *his oil ran out*? Their time was up, but yours wasn't. That's the reason you were a few meters down the street when the bomb exploded."

I turned to face him. "Do you really believe that?"

"Of course, I do. Think of all the Lebanese who escaped the war to live abroad. Think of the strange circumstances in which some met untimely deaths—pneumonia in a London hospital, falling down steps in Rome, a plane crash in the Soviet Union, or a bicycle accident in New York. We all know someone who didn't escape their fate."

"You grew up in France. Do they believe such things?"

"This is a belief held by our forefathers. It's part of what makes us who we are. I don't care what the French think, because it'll make no difference to me. Once you accept this, your life will be simpler and you'll enjoy it more." He patted my hand. "I know you have family and friends to help you through this, but if you ever need anything, remember I'm here." He reached for his briefcase and retrieved a photo of his three young daughters. "I took this last week at Lana's fifth birthday party."

"They're adorable." Seeing their happy faces and bright eyes erased the tension in my shoulders.

"One day you'll have kids, and life will take on a whole different perspective. Life's too short. You have to make the most of each moment."

I looked out the window at the morning Mediterranean—pale blue and tranquil.

During the day, I forced myself to focus on work and avoided people. I frequently had to stop and intentionally refocus my mind to put it back on track. I thought of calling the hospital to page Joe, but I knew I'd cry when I heard his voice.

Employees crowded onto the early bus home. Many people who usually drove to work had opted for company transportation because of increased fear after the car bomb.

Twenty minutes later, I disembarked and bumped into a man who stepped directly in front of me on the sidewalk. Joe grabbed me around my waist and swung me away from the door.

"What are you doing here?"

"You thought you could get rid of me that easily?"

"No, seriously."

"I came to be at your service, my lady."

"How'd you know I'd be here now?"

"I have my sources."

I looked at the ground, and he put his arm around my shoulder. "How can I help you?" I turned to face him and began to cry. He held me and kissed the top of my head.

People getting off the bus walked around us, and Joe nudged me away from the curb.

"I have to go to St. Rita's." My voice wobbled. "I need to light a candle."

We walked a few blocks to the church. The concrete block structure was built in the space between two buildings. It shared an exterior wall from each. Single rows of pews ran down the center of the narrow interior. Burning and extinguished candles, planted in an elevated sand box table, represented prayers of thanks or cries for help. Joe stood at the entrance, and I moved toward the illumination. I placed money in the metal box, pulled a new candle out from under the table, touched it to a lit one, and stood it in the fine gravel. I gave both my prayers of thanks and cries for help for those who yesterday had not been as fortunate.

Back outside in the sunlight, I asked, "Do you believe in God?"

"Yes." Joe didn't hesitate.

"Are you sure you do? Suppose there's no God and life's a bad joke."

"And what if it is? What difference does it make? Do you have a choice? Can you create a god if one doesn't exist? Regardless, being alive is beautiful." He squeezed my hand, and I realized how much I'd missed him.

"Do you believe your destiny is written or do we have free will?" I wanted answers from this man who planned to enjoy life, regardless.

"Believing solely in a predetermined destiny is a cop out. Certainly, some things we can't change, but many we can. We were given brains to use them. You wouldn't send a kid to play in the street and blame destiny if he's hit by a car. But if a child played in the garden and an out-of-control car hit him, you might think it fate. It's probably a combination of free will and destiny."

"How do you rationalize everything happening around us?"

"You don't. You need to have faith in a power bigger than us and do the best you can. It's all we can do."

For the first time since I woke up in a room of strangers, I felt safe. My heart beat fast, but I wasn't frightened. I felt comforted—almost as though I had come back to life.

"I wish I had things figured out like you do. You make sense."

"I'm glad to hear that because sometimes I wonder." We laughed and stopped walking.

"I know something significant we can do—something we can totally control." I surprised myself with the excitement in my voice. "Let's go to Maroush and get chicken-and-garlic panini sandwiches. We'll order the good kind—the ones where we ask them to add a little chicken to the garlic."

We did just that. I held the warm sandwich in one hand and gripped Joe's hand with the other. We walked down the street eating. His rational belief in this world and maybe the next gave me comfort. I imagined my candle burning down and the flame emitting hope as it shrank.

In Lebanon, tragedy danced with dreams. But when Joe led, calamity stepped aside and watched.

CHAPTER 18

———

Prayer is like taking an extra loaf of bread with you when you venture into the forest. If you don't need it, you don't need it. And if you do, you're saved.

—TETA AS TOLD TO HER BY HER TETA IN 1901

Rima yelled at me, "Sleeping Beauty, it's two fifteen. Looks like you slept through one job. Don't you need to go to the other?"

I realized the pill I took before going to bed had worked too well. I rushed to get ready for my class. The minute it finished, I raced through the campus and to the hospital, anxious to see Joe.

Our meeting place, the hospital lobby coffee shop, had neat rows of tables and pink smocked ladies from the Women's Auxiliary who served patrons. An elderly woman behind the cash register watched the comings and goings from her perch on a tall stool. I went to her.

"Maya. When did you come home?" She popped off her seat and came around the high table to hug me.

"A couple months ago."

"Oh my gosh, it's wonderful to see you." She hugged me again.

"It's nice to see you, too, Mrs. Martin. How are you?"

"I'm wonderful. Busy here every day. Trying to make the little bit of difference an old lady can. But look at you. You've become a beautiful woman."

"Thank you. But do you mean I wasn't a beautiful eleven-year-old?"

I looked closer at Mrs. Martin. She seemed small now compared to the intimidating American RN who left her paid job over twenty years ago to manage hospital volunteers. For six years I'd reported to her every Saturday morning as a candy striper.

"Of course you were. Until you became a teenager and started to cause trouble."

"I really didn't mean to drop lab specimens in the hospital corridor two weeks in a row. I was petrified of your reaction."

"You mean you didn't like working in the laundry?" She smiled. "But in good conscience I couldn't leave you there. You were too smart. I figured serving coffee in the operating lounge would give you the opportunity to observe surgeries from the gallery and ask questions. I sort of hoped you'd become interested in medicine."

"Really?" I had no idea.

"Nicole did. She's a pediatrician in San Francisco."

"Wow. Aren't you tempted to live close to her or in the States?" Mrs. Martin only had one child.

"No, this is home. I've been here since 1943, the year Ralph and I married and came as missionaries. After all these years, everyone I knew in Maine is gone and Nicole is very busy. Enough about me. Let's talk about you."

Before I could respond, two men in scrubs approached the cash register, and she climbed up to her post to take their payment.

"I'm working at MEA and teaching at AUB in the afternoons. And, Mrs. Martin." I stepped closer. "I'm dating an amazing man."

Every wrinkle in her face seemed to smile. She reached over to squeeze my hand, "You're a good girl, Maya. You deserve the best."

"I didn't realize you know Mrs. Martin." Joe stood behind me.

I turned. "She was my boss."

"Isn't she everyone's boss?" he teased.

"Perhaps, but she's most fearsome when you're a candy striper."

"Enough of that," Mrs. Martin scolded. "A table in the corner just opened. Go grab it."

I followed Joe to the table but turned back to look at Mrs. Martin. She made a shooing gesture with her hand, but the smile on her face made my heart skip.

Joe pulled out the chair for me. A lady in a pink smock approached. "What can I get you?"

"I'll have a cup of American coffee, please. I ate at two thirty."

"A club sandwich for me, please," Joe said. "You mean you slept until two thirty this afternoon?"

"I took the pill you gave me, but I'm not complaining. I desperately needed sleep."

"I'm glad it worked."

"Will you give me another one for tonight?"

"I think I know a better way to relax you tonight." The message in his eyes was unmistakable.

I waited impatiently for him to finish eating. We bid Mrs. Martin a hasty farewell, and I promised to visit her soon. We walked hurriedly to Joe's apartment.

* * *

The security situation in the country continued to deteriorate. More armed men roamed the streets and local militias reinforced check points. Random bombs were placed in cars, and a woman even left an explosive device in a brown paper bag on a street vendor's vegetable cart. The poor man and his customers were killed.

Days and nights became increasingly tense and our life settled into a routine within the radius of the few miles of Ras Beirut. It was the most cosmopolitan area of the country, but like everywhere else, people were consumed with fear. I tried not to think of every parked car as a potential bomb but would often avoid walking past a specific one or run as fast as I could past another.

Our small section of the city was mostly self-contained. We had hospitals, schools, universities, foreign embassies, shops, restaurants, bars and beaches. Only three significant places were located outside our zone: the airline offices, Joe's mother's apartment, and Teta's village.

Teta discouraged us from visiting and promised to come for Christmas.

Joe, however, continued to cross the Green Line every other weekend to see his mother. On December 18, he asked if I would like to go with him to meet her. I decided not to tell my parents.

We drove up to a five-story apartment building, and as Joe parked, he waved to a lady seated on the first-floor veranda.

She stood, walked to the opening in the banister, and waited at the top of the three steps.

"Maya, it's a pleasure to finally meet you." The tall, slim woman with delicate facial features spoke in impeccable English as she extended her hand. Her blonde hair pulled into a bun accentuated the angles of her bone structure.

She took Joe by the shoulders and kissed him on each cheek. It seemed as odd a reception for a child as did her perfect English salutation until I remembered she was Dutch.

"Please make yourself at home." She stepped to the side and motioned to the porch swing on the wide terrace. "How are the roads? The radio news said random checkpoints are appearing because rumors of kidnappings are rampant."

"We saw nothing unusual." Joe sounded abrupt.

"And if there were, I doubt you'd tell me." She turned my way. "Joe takes too many chances. He thinks he's invincible. I have trouble persuading him he can't talk his way out of everything. Words are no match for bullets." She sighed and looked down at the floor.

Joe glanced at her, but she continued, "Maybe you can talk some sense into him. But if you can't, I won't be surprised. By now, you must know he's stubborn."

Did she want to frighten me off? Or was she worried about her son? Or stressed by the situation? I remembered how fondly George had spoken about her and concluded she had nothing against me.

"What's for dinner?" Joe sounded oblivious to her concerns.

"Your favorite." Her tone softened. "I found fresh herring and rookworst at Aziz's Market. Everything's ready. I thought we'd eat right away so you can drive back early."

I enjoyed the evening. She told me she came to Lebanon thirty-seven years earlier as a young bride. She had met Joe's father, a medical resident in Amsterdam, when she worked as a nurse in the same hospital. She had Joe in her mid-thirties and, in spite of trying, she never got pregnant again.

She asked me questions and seemed genuinely interested in me. I put the last bite of real Dutch *appeltaart* into my mouth. She smiled broadly when I said I had a new favorite dessert.

"We should leave before it's too late." Joe stood

"I'm glad you and Joe found each other. Please take care of him." She kissed us both and closed the door. *How European.* My parents would have stood outside waving, even after we were out of sight.

"I'm glad I met your mother."

"I could tell she liked you."

"I liked her, too. She's right. You need to take danger more seriously."

"I'll be fine. I only do what I have to do."

I didn't like his tone, but didn't want our first argument to be about this subject.

* * *

It became a struggle to keep homes warm with the weather getting colder. Radiators heated our whole apartment building. The high price of fuel made many of the tenants unwilling to pay for twenty-four-hour warmth. Everyone agreed the heat would be turned on from 6 a.m. to 8:30 a.m. and from 7 p.m. to 10:30 p.m. We needed to supplement with personal auxiliary systems.

Papa purchased wheeled gas heaters designed to hold a large canister. They were effective, but Maman, paranoid about a leak, instructed us to remain awake when the heater was in the room and to roll it to the kitchen before we slept at night. Maria placed hot water bottles in our beds. Although a big retrenchment from the way we'd lived before the war, we adjusted.

Joe, by contrast, resided in a furnished apartment with uninterrupted heat and hot water. Many of the occupants were foreigners with short-term leases. The owner and his staff scrambled around to ensure the tenants had everything they needed. I began to spend more evenings at his apartment. I always showered before going home.

Each morning I took the bus to work and, in the afternoon, returned to the confinement of Ras Beirut. With Christmas approaching, I made frequent trips to Hamra Street—once one of the world's finest shopping districts. The merchants tried hard to maintain past glories and holiday spirit. Faded tinsel decorations and rarely lit decorative lights, remnants of happier times, were stretched across the main street. These valiant efforts at normalcy made things more melancholy.

Regardless of religious beliefs, almost all took delight in the celebrations. Shopkeepers displayed fancy liquor bottles, tiny crystal glasses, and decorative bowls of Jordan almonds on silver trays. They graciously continued the tradition of offering drinks and sweets to store patrons.

The Tuesday before Christmas, Monique and I planned to meet at her favorite boutique. I arrived early, and as I browsed through the racks, I heard someone shout my name. Monique stood at the entrance of the shop. Her hair wet and her face red. She plopped into one of the large armchairs to the side of the doorway. I shoved the dresses on my arm at the store attendant and rushed to my friend.

"Oh my God. You won't believe what happened. I was at the hairdresser when armed men entered. They demanded everyone's money and jewelry."

"Oh my God. Did they hurt anyone?" Concern and anger mingled inside me.

"No. They were quick. Everyone was in shock, and the moment they left some of the women couldn't stop crying. The hairdresser and his two assistants tried to calm them, but they must have been scared, too. People from the neighborhood entered and tried to help comfort everyone."

The boutique owner handed Monique a glass of liquor. She finished it in one swig.

"I sat in the shampoo chair," Monique continued. "I slipped off my rings and necklace and dropped them into a bottle of conditioner. Fortunately, I was in the back of the place and had more time." She held up her empty glass for a refill. "I only had enough money for tips because I have an account at the salon. I had my checkbook, but they would never dare steal it."

I knew she didn't have credit cards, because they were rarely used. A forged check was a liability for thieves since banking transactions were scrutinized.

"Which group do they belong to?" the boutique owner asked.

"People were trying to figure it out when I left." Monique put her glass on the table.

"Animals," the boutique owner said. "Which hairdresser?"

"Tony's on Rue Makdissi," Monique answered.

"I know the militia who control the area. They'll catch them." The owner sounded confident.

For survival, business owners needed to know the armed groups in their area and maintain good relationships with them. These guys were territorial and resented anyone committing violent acts in their domain. They wanted the people to like them and count on them. In return, residents often provided them with food and monetary gifts.

Monique reached for her glass, but I stopped her.

"Mademoiselle, would you like to try on your selections?" The shop assistant looked at me.

"Come with me." I pulled Monique up by the hand and into the changing room.

We left an hour later, and I insisted I walk her home. She'd halfheartedly protested, and I knew she still didn't feel safe. A friend from Cyprus was visiting her for the week, and I confirmed the woman was in the apartment before I departed. I went to meet Joe in a restaurant a few meters away from Tony's Hair Salon.

The rumble of electric generators on balconies and the street dominated everything—the sights, smells, and ordinary noises. I fastened the top button on my coat and maneuvered between parked cars, bits of sidewalk, and pavement on my way to the café. Joe, already seated, saw me through the glass paneled wall and rose to meet me at the entrance. We'd planned to go to a movie but hadn't decided on one. He wanted to see *Reds,* and I preferred *On Golden Pond.*

We'd deferred the decision until we met for a drink before show time. Movies were one of the few predictable things left in the country. All theaters ran their projectors at 3:30, 6:30 and 9:30 p.m. Assigned seats fell into three categories: the cheap, the average (double the cheap), and the expensive (triple the cheap). Amazingly, new releases made it almost instantaneously to Beirut.

I wasn't in much of a *movie mood* given the dramatic afternoon experience, so I didn't mind seeing his choice. Joe promised we'd see my movie the following week.

On the walk home, we spoke about our holiday plans. Christmas was three days away, and Joe was going to spend it with his mother. New Year's Eve belonged to Joe and me. We could make of it whatever we desired.

* * *

The moment I kissed Joe goodbye and wished him a Merry Christmas, I felt lonely, hollow and anxious. The fearful situation in the country penetrated the pores of my body and the soft mesh of my brain. My soul struggled, searching for comfort and hope.

Christmas Eve wasn't for a few hours, and I decided to pay Leila an overdue visit before going home for the evening.

The maid opened the door at her parents' apartment. The sparkling lights on the Christmas tree made the blue and silver decorations appear like fine jewels.

"It looks beautiful. Doesn't it?" I turned to see Leila. Pregnancy made her even prettier. She wore a crochet top over silk pants, looking remarkably slim and elegant at eight months. "I love Christmas. Ever since I was a child, I designed our trees." Like many Muslim Lebanese families, hers put up a tree and celebrated the spirit of the season. "Now I feel I have more ownership, considering my baby will be baptized Greek Catholic." Children followed their father's religion.

"How are you feeling?"

"Great." She sat down on a golden satin chair, and I sat on an identical one. "I'm beyond excited. The renovations of our apartment are finished and the furniture will arrive next week. We'll be in our new home to start the New Year. We will have a new beginning in 1982: new home, new baby, and a new life for Alex and me."

"Just in time." I reached over to pat her hard belly.

"I want to have a party on New Year's Eve. Will you come?"

"I'd love to, but we already told Makram we'll go to the Chouf."

"Isn't it too cold to sleep in a cave?" She tilted her head. "I have a warm guest bedroom."

I had told her about the picnic. This "most romantic first-time story" enthralled her.

"I wish, but we already told him we'd come, and we're driving with another couple."

"I guess everyone is spending the night."

"Yes, he's preparing dorm rooms to accommodate us."

"Sounds like fun, but I think I made a much better offer to you and Joe."

"Next year. By the way, who are you inviting?"

"I haven't decided yet. I still haven't told Alex."

I walked home around five thirty. The streets were empty. I figured most people left work early and the students were on vacation. I fished my gloves out of my bag, pulled my coat tighter around me and ran home through the eerily vacant streets.

I entered the apartment to the sound of Christmas carols. Maman, Papa, Teta, and Rima were in the family room. Lights sparkled on the Christmas tree, and logs blazed in the fireplace. The aroma of chestnuts filled the air. I pulled off my boots, gloves, and coat and handed them to Maria before joining my singing family.

I thought about past Christmas Eves spent with close family friends—now impossible because they lived on the other side of the Green Line. We used to arrive at their home for dinner around nine o'clock. At eleven thirty, we'd all pile into cars and drive to midnight Mass in the Chouf. After the service, the parents went home. We continued to downtown Beirut for drinks and eventually breakfast. We only slept a few hours early Christmas morning.

Our choir got bigger when neighbors arrived. We sang, ate, and spoke about the birth of the Christ child a few miles south from where we huddled. We wished for a miracle to save our country.

On Christmas morning, armed guards stood outside the Catholic Church on Hamra Street. Most people ignored them, but they scrutinized everyone who entered and occasionally pulled a young man aside to frisk. The Italian priest prayed for the impossible—peace.

We started our walk home past closed shops and restaurants. Maria, who had sat with her Filipino friends during the mass, ran to catch up with us. Rima held her hand out for her, and I took Teta's hand. Maman linked arms with Papa. We sang and Papa whistled *Silent Night* all the way home.

* * *

At four thirty on the thirty-first, Joe rang the doorbell. A few minutes later, we were in a car with a couple we'd just met—Makram's friends.

Papa and Maman were not too pleased about this plan. They frowned on my spending the night outside the house, but due to the situation, they knew I couldn't come home. I told them a big group of people planned to sleep over and promised I'd try to call when we arrived.

Makram instructed a maid to dial my home phone number until it connected. Three hours later, I spoke briefly to Maman. Afterward, I felt relieved and ready for an exciting night.

Before I returned to join the partiers, I investigated the sleeping arrangements. Makram wasn't kidding. He'd placed wall to wall beds in four bedrooms. Two other rooms had mats and sleeping bags lined up. I staked out two beds, pushed them together in the corner of the room, and placed my belongings on them.

The lit disco ball spun from the living room ceiling. People danced, sat, or stood with drinks. The DJ had set up his equipment next to a large bar, and waiters served appetizers. I spotted Joe standing with two men. The moment I approached, he kissed me, slipped his arm around my waist and introduced me.

We danced, drank, ate, talked, laughed, toasted the New Year, and even snuck into the empty communal bedroom for a few romantic minutes. At 3 a.m. Makram rang a cowbell and herded his guests into the dining room for a breakfast buffet.

On our way to bed, Joe and I stopped and gazed out of a large window. Sparse lights dotted the mountains and the clustered city lights glittered like a vast fairyland below. For one magical moment, fantasy and reality were only separated by a fine line.

CHAPTER 19

———

A continuum of strangers march through our lives. Some will comfort and others will kill.

—*HAJJ AHMAD*

"It's a boy. He was born this morning at three—Sunday, January 17, 1982—the most important day of my life. I never imagined I could survive such pain. I wanted to tell you right away, but I didn't want to scare everyone in your house with an early morning phone call." The excitement in Leila's voice was unmistakable.

"I wish I'd been with you. Congratulations."

"Wish you'd been here, too. My mother and Alex stayed with me. The doctor tried to get Alex to leave, but he refused. He was very attentive, I think my mother might be starting to like him."

"Let me get dressed, and I'll come."

Within twenty minutes, I arrived in her room.

"Karim. We decided to name him Karim. It means generous."

"It's a beautiful name."

"And it's both a Muslim and a Christian name. Both families are pleased although I really don't care." Leila rolled her eyes.

When I saw Karim, I exclaimed he was adorable, but in all honesty, I thought he looked like a hairy rat. The nanny Amo Mohammad had hired rocked and cooed at him until Leila, annoyed, told her to return him to the nursery and go sit in the hallway.

"Joe came earlier," Leila said. "He asked me to tell you he's in surgery but should be done by mid-afternoon. He'll come here before he goes to his apartment. You can meet him at either place."

"I'll come back after lunch and spend some time with you. Do you need anything?"

"Why don't you eat here?"

"Maman and Papa are expecting me. My cousin, Selma, and Roger are coming with the kids. I'll be back soon."

"Are they still madly in love?"

"Yes. Isn't it amazing after all these years? They're one couple that's meant to be."

"That's for sure. I've never met anyone like them."

"Maybe you and Alex will be like them." I leaned over to kiss her.

She held me tightly. "Maybe. Today's a good omen. Oh, how I pray I'm right."

* * *

Trying to live a normal life in the increasing tension and chaos became progressively more difficult. We went about our daily tasks, pretending the horror around us would miraculously subside. We knew better, but this was our home, and in remaining we felt we were contributing in our own small way.

The Green Line became even more dangerous. Fearing snipers, people crossed from one side of the city to the other only during daylight hours. When I was approached to participate in a management seminar on the east side of the city, I discussed it with Papa and Joe. We decided if I left in the early afternoon and returned the following morning, I would be safe.

On a March afternoon, the concierge put my suitcase in the Fiat. I planned to drive the most direct route linking the two halves of the city—the ring. I was excited. I knew this experience would give me exposure to smaller companies and provide consulting opportunities. I hadn't thought much about how I would find the time.

I reached the short tunnel crossing and saw only one car ahead of me on the open stretch of road with no turnoff. I heard the first shot, followed by a barrage. A sniper with an automatic weapon was aiming at me. *Zigzag, zigzag.* I knew what I had to do. I shifted into a lower gear, floored the gas, switched into a higher gear and swerved wildly from side to side.

I made a sharp right turn onto the first side street. When I removed both feet from the pedals, the car stopped abruptly and jolted me. I shook violently and couldn't feel my legs; although, they must have been working because I leapt out and ran into a shop.

A woman looked up from the flower arrangement she was making. I trembled. My body had no substance, like a ghost filled with wind.

She ran to me and coaxed me into a chair. I cried, and she stroked my hair.

"We heard the sniper fire. Where are you going?"

I don't know how she understood me. I struggled with the words. "Sniper... aiming me... hit car." Tears streaked down my flush cheeks.

A young man handed her a small glass of water, and she held it to my lips as I choked it down.

She squatted in front of me, looked into my eyes, and said, "I need a few minutes to close the shop. Then we will help get you where you're going."

Her son drove me in my car to the seminar on side roads out of the sniper's reach. The shop owner followed to bring him home. When we arrived, he gave my car to the valet, and she stepped out of hers to hug me.

"I can't thank you enough for your kindness," I said.

"No, I must thank you. I'm grateful God put me in your path today. He gave me meaning."

A concerned company employee waited for me in the lobby. He heard my story and told me not to worry since I still had an hour before my presentation. He assured me a warm shower and a glass of wine would make me feel fine. He was right. Fear turned to determination, and survival became confidence. I left with three company contacts. Two wanted senior management training seminars, and one asked me about reviewing their employee wages and benefits.

The following day, I joined a convoy of cars to West Beirut. We took the museum crossing and fortunately had an uneventful trip.

I went straight to the hospital and paged Joe. He had just finished a surgery and met me in the hallway outside the operating room.

Papa, enraged when he heard the story, suddenly looked old and tired. For the first time in my life, I saw tears forming in his eyes. Maman, Rima, and Maria wept.

Other than going to work, I didn't leave the area for the next month.

* * *

Everything changed on a Saturday afternoon in mid-April when a snipper aimed at and hit Papa. He and Maman were on their way to visit Teta for the weekend. When Rima and I didn't hear from them after their anticipated arrival time, we tried to call. We gave up after three hours. We figured Teta would have found a way to send a message if they weren't there. Rima showed no reaction when I told her I wanted to spend the night at Joe's apartment. I could count on her not to tell anyone, including Maria.

Joe and I made dinner, opened a bottle of wine and basked in knowing we could enjoy a whole night together without the dreaded walk to my home.

I thought nothing of it when Joe leaned over me in bed to answer the phone the following morning. I pulled the sheet up to my chin and daydreamed about our plans for the day.

He covered the receiver with his hand and spoke in a calm voice, "Your father's okay, but he's in the hospital in East Beirut."

I grabbed the phone and heard Leila's voice. "He's okay. He got hit by a sniper crossing the Green Line at the port. Tante Mona called your house, but Maria said you and Rima were not home. So she called my mother who asked me to find you."

"How do you mean okay?"

"I only know he was hit in the chest and was in surgery most of the night. He's in intensive care at St. George Hospital."

My face felt swollen, and tears poured from my shrinking eyes. I handed the phone to Joe.

"I'll see how I can get her and Rima to the hospital." He hung up and turned to me. "Let's find Rima and get your things."

I quickly dressed.

Rima entered the building at the same time we did. Joe calmly told her about Papa.

"Maria, please pack an overnight bag for them in case they can't make it back tonight."

Rima, Maria and I cried uncontrollably, but Joe pushed forward. "I'm going to the hospital garage to see if Hajj Ahmad can drive you. Meet me as soon as you're packed."

Hajj Ahmad pulled the old Mercedes out of the garage. He instructed Rima and me to keep low on the back seat. "Don't worry. I'll soon get you to your father."

"Lie on the floor," Hajj Ahmad yelled at us moments later. He sped through the "ring crossing." We heard gunfire, but I didn't know if it was aimed at us. Our amazing driver risked his life daily to help others.

My mind raced. *Was Papa really alive, or were they telling us this until we arrived?*

The car came to an abrupt stop at the hospital entrance. Hajj Ahmad told us to go inside while he parked.

Maman stood at the entrance of the ICU.

"How is he?" Rima shouted.

"He's doing well, considering." She looked exhausted. "An M16 bullet hit him. Thank God it wasn't the exploding kind. Fortunately, he had his elbow on the armrest of the car door. The sniper aimed for his heart. The bullet went through the metal and padding before it entered his elbow and chest. This kept it from puncturing his lung."

I half-fell against the wall.

Maman continued, "Because of the heat, Papa didn't immediately feel the bullet and kept driving. We crossed to the east side and Lebanese army soldiers ran to the car. Blood was everywhere, and Papa was in great pain. I asked them to take us to AUB hospital, but they said it was too dangerous to cross back to west Beirut. They moved Papa over, and a soldier jumped in the car and drove us here. Papa collapsed upon our arrival."

"Can we see him?" My heart beat wildly.

I hardly recognized the dwarfed figure in the bed. Wires and tubes twisted around his body.

"Papa," I sobbed and held his hand. "I love you. We're all here." *Please, please, Papa, don't leave us. Dear Jesus, please don't take him.*

Rima cried too hard to say anything. I gave her his hand and gently touched his shoulder. *What would we do without Papa? How could we live? Beloved Virgin Mary, protect and heal him.*

Maman wasn't crying. I knew she acted strong for our sake. The nurse nodded at her and tilted her head to the exit.

Hajj Ahmad stood in the corridor. Maman spoke to him. Rima and I just cried.

"I think he's right." Maman looked straight at us. "You've seen Papa and now you should go back home." She turned to the driver. "Can you give them a few minutes to see their Teta and the relatives?"

"Half an hour is fine. I'll wait here." He pointed to a chair.

People packed the general waiting room. Teta sat with a rolled scroll in her lap. She let out a shout when she saw us.

Following tearful hugs and kisses, I asked her about the rolled paper she had handed to a woman next to her.

She retrieved and opened it up for us to see. "Our Lady of the Annunciation. She's your father's protector. As a small child, he wandered off in the forest. I frantically prayed to Our Lady of the Annunciation. When he was found two days later, I declared her his mother." Teta had told us the story many times.

"Yesterday, when word reached the village, we all rushed down to the hospital. We were waiting for him to come out of surgery when a young man, the son of a relative—I don't know the younger generation—came up to me and without a word handed me this scroll. When I saw the picture, I knew your father would recover."

Papa remained in ICU for three days and in the hospital for five weeks. Maman moved into his room. When the phone worked, she gave us updates. Every Sunday, Hajj Ahmad took Rima and me to visit.

Papa came home in May, determined to make as full a recovery as possible. A physical therapist came daily, and he followed a rigorous exercise schedule. Soon he began walking to his office for half a day.

On a beautiful spring evening, Papa gave one of his few predictions. "The situation is coming to a head, and I think something major is going to happen. The Palestinians are getting too strong and there's a lot of tension between them and the Israelis."

"There's a rumor Israel will invade Lebanon," Maman said. "The ladies in the grocery store were talking about this today."

On June 6, 1982, it happened.

CHAPTER 20

———

Why do you complicate your life? Use the brains God gave you,
make the sign of the cross, and go.

—TETA

I wandered into the kitchen Sunday morning, and Maman
greeted me. "There's fighting in the south."

"There's always fighting in the south."

"It's more serious this time. The Israeli army crossed the
border."

"Maybe we need a big war to end all of the small ones," I
said. "Maybe then we'll find a solution."

Maman snapped at me. "War isn't a solution. The innocent people suffer. If armed forces want to fight, and they're
truly brave, let them conduct their duels away from civilians."
She had become extremely tense since Papa was shot.

The coffee percolator on the counter thumped softly. I
watched the brown liquid appear and disappear.

The Palestinian Liberation Organization (PLO) had
become a state within a state in Lebanon. Our weak army
had fought them on numerous occasions before the civil war
began, but they were a more powerful military force. They

kept heavy arms in their refugee camps throughout West Beirut and on the southern border with Israel. Fighting there had caused civilian casualties on both sides, and their animosity extended beyond the two country demarcations and into other parts of the world.

The coffee pot stopped, and I poured a cup. "Where's Papa?"

In a crisis, the first step is to account for everyone. Rima was in bed, and Maria read a magazine on the balcony. On her day off, she usually went to church and spent time with her friends.

"He's listening to the news."

I sat at the table, no longer hungry. Papa entered, and a scratchy voice blasted on the transistor radio he carried. Maman glared at him, and he lowered the volume.

"It's not looking good. The Red Cross is reporting casualties on both sides," Papa said.

"Updated news report," the radio announcer shouted. Papa rushed out of the room with the transistor to his ear. We followed to the dining room for the best reception. The news indicated more deaths confirmed.

Papa looked at Maman and no doubt saw the weariness in her face. He turned off the radio and reached for the hand she had placed on the table. "Let's try to call Selma to see if they can join us for lunch today." My mother's niece, husband, and children invariably cheered her up. "We'll pick a restaurant that's close." Maman usually didn't cook on Sundays.

Later in the afternoon, Joe came to visit as did friends and neighbors. The group included Lebanese Maronite Catholics, Protestants, Sunnis, Shiites, Palestinians, and a French diplomat. The opinions were as varied as the visitors, and although quite impassioned, they listened politely to one another.

When Joe stood to leave, I walked to the stairwell with him. He wrapped his arms around me, but his pager buzzed. He gave me a quick kiss and hurried down the stairs.

Maria looked at me questioningly when I reentered the apartment. I walked past her to my room. I needed to grade final exam papers. Luckily, my class exams had been scheduled on the first two days of June. I wanted to turn in final grades as soon as possible.

The fighting intensified, and the Lebanese Christian militias sided with the Israelis. The PLO received support from some Lebanese Muslim militias and the Syrian army. These were not necessarily the divisions among the people. Many splits among the Lebanese were socioeconomic, but everyone had a common denominator—fear.

In the office on Monday, most people wanted to analyze the situation and persuade others of their insights and predictions. I found it hard to concentrate on work.

On the bus home I sat next to Maurice. "I don't know if you know this, but both sets of my grandparents were Palestinian. I usually don't tell people because they might perceive me differently."

"Are you telling me now because of what's happening?"

"Not really." He stroked his chin. "But it's something I've been thinking a lot about lately. In the days of my grandparents, there weren't borders. They moved between homes in Haifa and Beirut, but they were born in Palestine. My parents were born in Lebanon as was I."

"God, Maurice, why is it all so complicated?"

"I wish I knew. Don't most people want the same thing— to live peaceful lives with opportunities? My grandmother, God rest her soul, used to say she couldn't understand how people cut from the same cloth—the Jews and the Arabs—could cause one other so much pain."

I glanced out the window to the approaching checkpoint. The bus stopped, and three armed men climbed aboard. They ignored the driver's plea to let the company bus continue. They walked down the aisle and demanded passengers show their identity cards. A woman let out a scream, but her colleague immediately put her hand over her mouth and pulled the panicked woman's head to her lap. One of the gunmen stopped, but the other two shoved past him and he moved away.

We sat in fearful silence. The tension level rose when they examined some documents longer than others and asked questions. Finally, they walked back down the aisle. The last one turned around and said, "God be with you."

"And the devil be with you," Maurice muttered under his breath.

Unintelligible conversation filled the bus, but the curses were clear. I knew the armed men belonged to the PLO and might be looking for anyone they thought could be aiding their enemies.

"It makes me sick to think they control our country," Maurice said. "They've become too sophisticated and powerful."

"Do you think the Israelis will break them this time?"

"Hard to tell. They're well-armed and trained and they have the latest technology." Maurice shook his head.

"They do?"

"Have you heard of a facsimile machine?"

"No."

"It copies a document, and the printed copy is received in another location."

"You mean I could be in New York and send a copy of a letter to you in Beirut?"

"Exactly. A fax."

"Wow. Have you seen one?"

"I've read about it. Companies are beginning to use them. Only one exists in Lebanon, and it's owned by the PLO."

The bus stopped. "See you tomorrow." I grabbed my stuffed briefcase.

"Let's see what tomorrow brings." He sounded tired.

At the university, I turned in my semester class grades to the department secretary. I posted exam scores and final grades on the bulletin board by my office for students to check. I felt a sense of relief. From now, until October I only had one job to worry about.

The next two days were much the same at the airline offices. Distracted employees barely accomplished the essentials. Joe had a lot of work, and I saw him only once. We weren't comfortable going out late. More armed men and vehicles roamed the streets. Anticipating something bad was about to happen, most of the six hundred thousand residents of West Beirut stayed close to home. Papa, extremely concerned, made the radio an appendage. He listened to local broadcasts and to the BBC. I knew the station from the music played before newscasts.

A week after the invasion, the Israeli forces and their allies surrounded West Beirut. On June 22, nine days later, Papa proposed we leave for the mountains. "People are forming car convoys. I believe it's the best way to travel. If armed men detain someone, the others are immediately aware and can seek help."

Maman's clothes looked baggy on her, and her skin tone seemed more ashen. "Today I heard the Israelis are telling the residents to leave before the fighting intensifies. I talked to Mona and some other friends. Most want to stay. They're fearful squatters will occupy their homes."

Rima and I sat on the sofa holding hands. I remembered the fall morning almost seven years ago. At least this time Papa was with us and we planned to remain in the country.

"Squatters are a risk we have to take. Some of the residents will never leave. The concierge definitely won't. Hopefully, we'll be fortunate and once again find everything when we return." Papa had made up his mind.

"When are you thinking of leaving?" Maman held on to the back of a chair and guided herself to the seat.

"I spoke to people who want to arrange a convoy for Thursday morning. I wanted to discuss it with you before I answer them."

June was one of the hottest months in the city, but I felt cold. From Rima's quivering lips, I knew she felt the same.

"This doesn't give us much time." Maman looked around the room.

"Ideally, we'd leave tomorrow. But I knew you'd want more time."

Maman called for Maria. Papa sat down next to Rima and me. He placed his hand on top of ours and smiled weakly. "You'd better go get ready."

I told Papa I needed to tell Joe. The phone hadn't worked for days.

"Give me ten minutes, and I'll walk with you."

"I'll be fine. I promise I'll be back in half an hour. Please."

"Half an hour. Otherwise, I'll come after you."

I ran and within three minutes entered the hospital lobby. The female voice paged: *"Dr. Kassir, extension two four five* two. *Dr. Joe Kassir, extension two four five two.*" The wall phone on the wall rang. Joe said he'd meet me.

I watched perplexed and anxious people walk past me. Joe appeared from behind a group of women. I spilled out our evacuation plans.

"I'm relieved. I'll feel better knowing you're out of immediate danger. Things are getting worse."

"And you?"

"I'll be fine. I'll be in one of two places—either here or a few buildings away at my apartment. If the shelling or air strikes are bad, I'll stay here. No one will hit the hospital."

I knew he would stay exactly where he belonged, doing what he was trained for and loved.

"I need to go before Papa comes to look for me."

"I'll walk you back. Let me call the department receptionist to tell her I'm delayed."

It wasn't unusual to see doctors in their white coats walk with young women, but to see them hand in hand with one was not common, and people looked at us curiously.

"I'll try to take a couple of days off as soon as I can to come to see you. I haven't seen my mother for over three weeks, so I'll visit her at the same time."

We stood at the building entrance as I stoically looked up at him and tried to control my emotions. I wanted to scream, to cry, to hit something, but mostly I didn't want to leave him. He pulled me to him, gave me a deep, quick kiss on the lips, stepped back, looked at me, and hurried away.

Rima had piled her clothes and belongings on her bed.

"How much can we take?" I asked.

"A couple of cases each." She motioned to the four suitcases placed against the wall.

"You know, Tante Mona and Gibran are coming with us. She's on the verge of a nervous breakdown, and her husband wants her to leave the city. Since they don't have a place in the mountains, Maman insisted she stay with us. That's why we can take extra stuff. They have a big car and only the two of them. Her daughters are staying with their dad."

"Is Gibran staying with us, too?" I referred to her son.

"No. He'll be with his friend who lives nearby."

"Good." I didn't intend to sound mean, but neither of us liked Gibran. He was a year younger than Rima and extremely spoiled.

* * *

As she had done years before, the elderly widow came down to our apartment to bid us farewell. Once again, Maman locked the door and handed her the keys. This time, we'd only be a few miles away, and Maman left the house clean.

The old lady walked down to the street with us, sprinkled holy water on the car and made the sign of the cross over each of us. Maman promised to send her a message as soon as possible.

The convoy met at the entrance of the hospital garage. The six cars were stuffed with people and belongings. The drivers huddled to consult with Hajj Ahmad on the safest road.

Three car crossing points existed along the ten-mile stretch of the Green Line: the ring (where the sniper aimed at me), the port (where the sniper hit Papa), and the museum (where many kidnappings occurred). The designated lead passed out hand-written lists of all the drivers' names and their order in the convoy. Everyone rapidly scribbled down the passengers' names. If a car happened to be detained or its occupants removed, knowing their identities would aid in trying to locate and free them. The possibility a vehicle might be destroyed by a rocket or roadside bomb added to the danger.

We were assigned fourth place. The leader, a bank manager, hoped to get his family to safety and return the following day. A woman with five children—three of her own and two nephews followed. Tante Mona and Gibran drove ahead of us.

Papa had almost regained complete use of his left arm and insisted he drive. His severed ulnar nerve and the permanent bend in his reconstructed elbow didn't hinder his steering ability. Maman and Maria nervously moved their fingers across rosary beads.

Rima and I sat close together, our feet propped up on bags and small boxes of household valuables, among them, Maman's wedding silver, crystal glasses and porcelain figurines wrapped in clothing, photos and two small Persian carpets. I stroked the front pocket of my jeans to feel the outline of my glass cedar.

Traffic clogged the streets with people trying to escape West Beirut. Our drivers had a tough time staying together, but after passing the first checkpoint, manned by PLO fighters and their sympathizers, we managed to regroup.

At the next checkpoint, the first two cars were waved through, but Gibran was ordered to pull over. Papa slowly maneuvered our vehicle into the space Gibran's car vacated. Papa rolled down his window and asked the militia men why they stopped his sister's car, which he had to claim, or they would say it didn't concern him.

One of the armed men told him to move our car to the side of the road behind hers. We didn't know if we were suspects or the guy wanted to help by keeping us together. Travel with a young man was always a peril. They were frequently scrutinized and assumed suspicious. Men Gibran's age often remained in a dangerous area rather than take the risk.

"Allah, spare us." Maman crossed herself repeatedly with her rosary in hand. "Allah, have mercy."

The rest of us sat silently and watched the final two cars of our convoy get waved through the checkpoint.

Three heavily armed men approached Tante Mona's car. Superiors usually checked out suspicious or threatening individuals. Tante Mona leaned across Gibran's seat to talk to the hefty man at the driver's window.

Virgin Mary, Virgin Mary, help us, I silently repeated, fearing they would take Gibran and make the rest of us leave.

Finally, the man took a step back, put his right hand over his heart and bowed slightly. He approached our car. "Your sister's a good woman." He spoke with a Syrian accent. "For many years my brother worked as her driver. She was generous to him and gracious to me when I visited him." He smiled at Papa. A gold tooth sparkled against a mouthful of brown rotten ones.

"Thank you for your kind words. God bless you in your work." I heard Papa muttering curses under his breath. How had the people of his beloved country sunk to this level with armed Palestinians, Syrians, and now Israelis fighting their wars here?

The other cars waited for us around a bend in the road. The lead car started moving as we approached. Within minutes, another checkpoint appeared, manned by the enemies of those at the ones we'd just crossed.

Now, our concern turned to the woman with the five children although we were less worried than we'd been with Gibran. As a Sunni Muslim from West Beirut, they might question her reason for coming to the Christian east. Thankfully, they waved her through. We drove into the eastern half of the city along the sea road for about ten miles before turning onto a side street bordered by orange groves. Everyone got out of their cars to breathe deeply, stretch, and kiss and hug. Most of us began the short journey as strangers and ended it as comrades. Loud explosions came from the direction of West Beirut. We said hasty farewells and drove off in different directions.

Papa made a right turn, and soon we ascended the mountain. I imagined how surprised and happy Teta would be to see us. Over the past few weeks, she'd only received occasional news about us. People who left the city delivered messages to relatives on the other side.

Teta didn't run down the outdoor steps when we arrived, but her neighbor rushed to greet us. "Thank Allah for your safe arrival." She kissed us one by one.

"Is Teta home?"

"Yes, she's in her room," the old lady said.

"In her room?" Papa didn't wait for an answer. He bolted up the stairs.

"She has shingles. But she's much better now," the neighbor said.

"Why didn't someone tell us?" Maman still clutched her rosary beads.

"She made us promise not to tell you. You couldn't do anything except worry, and you had enough worries. Her sister's staying with her."

Maman let out a deep breath and headed up the steps. Rima and I followed. Maria and the neighbor began unloading the car.

If Teta had known we were coming, I'm sure she would have gotten out of bed and downplayed her suffering. She never wanted others to be concerned with her aches and pains. She was the ultimate giver. I had never seen her in bed sick.

Papa stood at Teta's bedside. The big smile on her face was out of proportion to her frail body. I bent down to kiss her, and she wrapped her arms around my neck. "Ta'aburnee," she softly muttered. Her endearing words literarily meant *may you bury me*—a way of expressing she couldn't live without me.

Her sister stood at the foot of the bed wearing an identical smile. She was ten years younger and worshiped Teta, who had kept the family alive during the great famine of 1915 to 1918. A drought, locusts, poor crop selection, and a cruel Ottoman blockade had caused over half of Lebanon's population to perish.

"The only firsthand news I received about you came last week when Selma arrived." Teta looked up at Papa.

He kissed her forehead and said, "Now we can enjoy some time together. But first, let's all help Maria empty the car."

Everyone left except me. Teta didn't want to talk about herself but rather the friends we'd left behind. "Are you still enjoying your time with Joe?" she asked.

"Teta, he makes so happy. I feel complete with him. He promised to come visit." I told Teta things I would never tell Maman.

I wondered if she suspected we slept together. From her stories, dating back to the time of her grandmother, I knew forbidden sex had always taken place.

"I've been worried about all of you." Teta changed the subject. "It isn't even completely safe here. A rocket hit the forest two days ago and caused a fire. Thank God nobody got hurt." Tears glossed her eyes.

"No secret lovers hiding in the forest?" She'd told me stories of people who met there over the centuries.

She smiled wryly. "I think people these days have better places to meet."

"I remember you told me the women were often married. If they got pregnant, they could pass the baby off as their husband's. Did you ever look at a child and think he resembled someone other than the father?" I surprised myself with this question, but Teta wasn't always willing to talk about this subject.

"All the time." I couldn't tell if she was serious.

"How about the unmarried women who got pregnant?"

"They had bleak choices. They often went to a lady who *cleaned them out*. Many died painfully from this procedure and others could never get pregnant again."

"You mean abortion?"

"That's what they call it now. Back then we didn't have a name or a complete understanding of what happened. The *cleaning lady* would insert a stick into the woman and mess around with her insides."

I wished I hadn't asked.

Teta continued, "Sometimes, the lover was forced to marry her. But if he was already married, the girl's parents often found a man from a poor family. They paid him to marry her. People figured out the truth but accepted it."

"How horrible."

"I'm glad it's different now. You can use products to help you not get pregnant. But if a girl does, she doesn't have to risk dying to end the pregnancy. Although, I know the decision still remains hard. And, I hear," she lowered her voice even though no one else remained in the room, "some women don't bother to get husbands at all. They have the baby alone."

"I might do that. But I'd leave for Europe or America."

"Let's pray you won't face such a situation," She continued. "Did you say Joe is coming to visit?"

She knew.

Around two o'clock, Rima entered with a tray of food for Teta, and I left to eat.

* * *

Over the following days, we sat on the balcony and watched from the mountain perch as our city was attacked by land, air, and sea. Flashes of light, smoke, dust, and loud booms were nonstop. Each day became worse. The news reported over five hundred buildings destroyed. It was all I could do not to think about the people. I prayed they were safe in shelters. To cope, I pretended to be watching a movie and not real life. I daydreamed. *The cable car went up the mountain to the restaurant. I waved at Frank Sinatra, and he smiled.*

In retaliation for the Israeli invasion, the militias and armies in the western part of the city shelled the eastern half. Not long after, artilleries were aimed at our mountains. They wanted to inflict damage and carnage on those who supported their enemies.

Our mountain home was a three-story building of independent apartments connected by external stairs. Maria stayed in a two-bedroom apartment with a garage on the street level, and Teta's three-bedroom home was above. We lived on the top floor. A large gate with a private entryway of steps led to the top two apartments on one side of the structure. A public path of stairways and landings on the opposite side provided Teta a place to work while socializing.

The street level apartment was the safest because the structure had been carved into the mountain, which protected three sides. Only the façade opened onto the winding village road. Workmen with axes had chiseled into the limestone mountain over a hundred years ago to create the foundation of the building. When the shelling became heavy, this floor served as a gathering place. People often stayed overnight listening to the radio, playing cards, talking, and trying to sleep. Each morning, everyone cleaned up the soot from candles and kerosene lanterns.

The shelling usually stopped at daylight. The reprieve allowed people to fetch water, get food, and see another day, but surprise rockets remained a possibility.

* * *

"Hello. Is anyone here?" I heard Joe's voice.

I lay on my bed and had not changed my position since I'd returned to my room at dawn. I'd had had no reason to get up. I bolted upright and wondered if I was dreaming, but I ran anyway to the direction of the voice. He stood by the kitchen door.

Tante Mona entered the room behind me. "What a wonderful surprise." She kissed him. "When did you leave? How is it?"

"I left yesterday and spent the night with my mother in Achrafieh."

"I didn't know your mother lives there." I knew she wanted him to tell her news of West Beirut.

"When I left the hospital, things weren't good. I haven't ventured out of the immediate area, but heard some parts of the city are unrecognizable. We're having trouble keeping up with the casualties, and supplies are running low."

"Did you hear any news of the Lions Building?" Her husband and daughters were in their apartment there.

"The area's fine. Don't worry. It's one of the safest places." He sounded confident.

"When are you going back?"

"Wednesday. I found it difficult to get away, but after five weeks without a break, I needed to see the people I love." He looked at me.

"Teta had shingles when we arrived," I addressed Joe.

"She's an amazing woman," Tante Mona said. "She was relieved to have her family here. She insisted she had no more pain and got out of bed the very next day."

"Happiness conquers pain," I said.

"I believe it," Tante Mona said. "Attitude is so important." She turned to leave. "I'll see you later. I have to make lunch."

"Where is everybody?" I asked.

"Your parents and Rima left a few minutes ago to visit Selma. You were asleep."

"And Maria?"

"Downstairs with Teta preparing the ingredients I need for the meal."

"What are you making?"

"It's a surprise." She giggled like a teenaged girl.

I had accounted for everyone. I quickly concluded Joe and I had at least half an hour alone. Even if Maria or Tante Mona came back upstairs, neither would enter my bedroom. I took his hand and locked the door behind us.

We sat in the living room sipping cold mulberry juice when my parents returned. They welcomed Joe and bombarded him with questions about the people and the city.

Tante Mona's surprise was a gourmet tower built of layers of miniature stuffed squash, eggplant and grape leaves topped with lamb cutlets. My mouth watered at the sight of the inverted layer-cake-like structure. For dessert, our guest chef made little butter cookies, *ghraybeh*. Maman only served seasonal fruit after meals.

"I think it best you stay here tonight. It's not safe on the roads this late in the afternoon," Papa said, out of the blue, to Joe.

"I should be fine. I'm only going to Achrafieh."

"Will your mother worry if you don't go home tonight?" Maman asked.

"No. She knows where I am, and I told her I might spend the night with a friend in this area."

"We have an extra room and a cot in the shelter," Papa said. "You can leave in the morning?"

"If it's no imposition, I'd be glad to stay."

I didn't look at him. I didn't want anyone to notice my delight. One night seemed like a lifetime to enjoy. *Isn't that how it was for Romeo and Juliet?*

Now, we had our night.

CHAPTER 21

———

Metal demons, launched in hatred, rule our nights.

—*MAMAN*

I knew it was a mistake, but I lifted the glass and took another sip of the cool liquid. The vodka and orange juice slid down my throat and hit the fluid already churning in my stomach. For an instant, the nausea subsided. It would be worse in the morning. Perhaps I wouldn't see morning. Why worry about something we might never live to see?

I blew on the dice in my hand, tossed them onto the mosaic game board, and grinned at the double sixes. The backgammon pieces clicked loudly when I moved them. Like a mischievous elf, I smirked and waved my hands to jinx Joe's dice. With an even score and twelve more games to go before declaring a champion, I wanted to get ahead—even though I knew we wouldn't finish for a couple of hours.

Suddenly, whistling noises flew over, chased by loud booms. Night became a blinding flash.

My heart banged in my chest, and my body shook. "No, no, I can't take it anymore." I placed my hands over my ears and dove to the ground. *So far removed from a Romeo and Juliet night.*

The rockets came in record numbers. Earlier in the evening, despite my parents' pleas, I refused to go to the shelter. I wanted to enjoy Joe—not spend the night with crying babies, women chanting prayers, and men talking politics.

I persuaded a cousin and his wife to remain in the house with Joe and me. No shells had been sent our way since early the previous night. We wrongly assumed we would get a break. Before dark we arranged comfortable chairs around low tables laden with backgammon sets. End tables were filled with plates of nuts, cheese, vegetables, fruits, scotch, vodka, orange juice, candles, and a kerosene lantern. Our prized possession, the few remaining pieces of ice, would be taken out of the freezer at the last minute. We'd had no electricity since the day before.

The evening started off well. Before dinner, Teta lit some extra candles so we could see our food and said a prayer for the less fortunate. My cousin and his wife arrived as we finished eating. Papa hadn't objected to me staying with Joe in the house because he knew the visitors planned to stay for our all-night backgammon tournament. Joe assured Papa we'd make a dash for the shelter if shelling began.

Now lumpy sour liquid burned a path from my stomach to my mouth. The rockets were not hitting our area anymore, but we could hear them landing nearby. Joe patiently held a bucket for me. I straightened up from what I hoped was the last bout of retching and saw the sun rising over the mountain. I believed we'd have a few calm hours. Once again, we'd defied the demons of the night.

Joe returned to the city later in the morning, and we lost contact. I prayed he arrived safely. The phonelines were completely dead. I kept reminding myself bad news traveled fast.

* * *

"Is Miss Maya here? I have something for her." I heard a man's voice and rushed out of my room. Maria stood at the half-opened front door.

"Hi, Hadi. How are you?" I really wanted to ask my cousin what he had for me.

"I've been living at the hospital for two weeks and left this morning to come home for a few nights. Joe asked me to bring this to you." He handed me a white business-sized envelope.

"Please come in." I moved to the side of the door.

"No, I need to get home. I came here on my way because I promised Joe I would." He turned to leave, but stopped. "You know, Joe's a really nice guy. Those of us trapped in the hospital ate dinner together. The hospital pharmacy is in the basement. Every night we scrubbed the long table used to mix drugs and everyone brought whatever food they had. We turned it into a feast." He stepped inside.

Although anxious to open the envelope, I wanted to hear first-hand information about Joe.

"Sometimes we ate canned tuna, boiled eggs, and random pieces of fruit. Other times we got lucky, and someone's mother or wife managed to send something delicious."

"It's the camaraderie…" I began to say, but he cut me off.

"That's what keeps us sane. These relationships sustain us, and we get to know one another really well." He stepped back over the threshold.

"How good are the jokes?" I knew humor played a big part in wartime survival.

"Joe told some of the best. Ask him to tell you the one about the Lebanese, Syrian, and Israeli businessmen. I'm going back on Wednesday. Let me know if you want to send anything."

I felt sure I held my first love letter from Joe and snuck into the bathroom to read it privately.

My Dearest Maya,

I can't believe how much I miss you—your smile, the way you wave your arms when you talk, the words you say, your view of the world and its people. I miss being with you. And believe it or not, I even miss holding the bucket while you throw up. You are always beautiful, even then.

The hospital is chaotic, but I am glad I am here and able to help. I saw Mrs. Martin today. She lives close by and is constantly here doing whatever she can to assist. She's working as a nurse because many can't get here. She brought me a pound cake and a note thanking me for "doing God's work." Such a nice lady. Maybe we should invite her to dinner when the situation gets back to normal—whatever that means. It has been three weeks and nothing lasts forever—except the good things we believe in.

I will try to send messages whenever I can, but please promise me one thing—you will keep smiling your amazing smile. It makes everyone around you feel better. I am sure I'll feel it here, and I'll smile, too.

I love you,

Joe

P.S. I think the situation might be better here than where you are. We've had no shelling since I returned.

I don't know how many times I read the note, but when Maria knocked on the bathroom door to check on me, I realized it had been half an hour. I folded the paper and pushed it into the pocket of my jeans. I didn't want anyone to see it.

The following day, August 4, the city was shelled for twenty continuous hours by land, air, and sea. The hospital received a direct hit. A blockade made food and fuel scarce, and the water supply was cut off. The Israeli military forces bombarded the city and, in retaliation, those fighting them heavily shelled the Christian areas.

Papa didn't remove the radio from his ear. When he spoke to us, he tried to sound optimistic, but I overheard him tell Maman the hospital sent out an urgent appeal for fuel to keep their generators running.

The shelling resumed over the following days and, like wicked spirits, the missiles no longer operated only under the cover of darkness. The shrill whistling sounds seemed to come out of nowhere and destroy everything. It happened on dark depressing nights and on bright, beautiful days. The sound got louder as the weapons drew nearer. With each occurrence, my ears became more sensitive, and I reacted faster. My hair follicles became pins in my body, my neck stiffened, my jaw locked, and my legs moved faster than realistically possible. It only took a fraction of a second for me to get to another location or fall to the ground, prepared for impact. The land always shook as if regurgitating the evil. It, too, was a victim.

From the dust, debris, cries, and sounds of human suffering, we could estimate the location of a hit. I would stand, numb and stiff, take a few seconds to regain my composure, make the sign of the cross and run to assist others who were less fortunate. Instinct, skill, and luck dictated survival. I hated the rockets. I hated the war. I hated the evil in the hearts of man.

CHAPTER 22

Never confuse your goal with the means.

—*T E T A*

"Change will come whether you want it or not." Teta and I sat on the open-air terrace in front of her apartment door. She held a smooth, flat stone above walnuts. "Those who do best are the ones who accept change. You may like it or you may not, but you need to recognize reality and adjust." She leaned over on her low stool and systematically broke open the nuts on the ground before her. She moved them to a tray, took another bunch out of the burlap bag and spread them out to repeat the process.

Rima sat on the makeshift outdoor couch across from Teta. She selected a bunch of hair and picked off the split ends. I couldn't tell if she listened or daydreamed.

I lifted the tray from the ground, replaced it with an empty one, and resumed shelling walnuts. "Does World War I seem like a long time ago, or more like yesterday?"

"Like yesterday. I was seventeen when it ended sixty-four years ago and remember everything. I pray no human will ever experience what we endured—especially the starvation.

Mothers howled in the night when they awakened to find their dead babies." Her face tightened.

"Imagine if you hadn't married into a family with money."

"We wouldn't be sitting here." She gazed at the city below. "My mother sent my youngest brother to visit me every day. I'd pin pieces of meat fat inside his clothes. She used it for a broth made with weeds. If people knew he carried a morsel of food, he would be in danger."

"How old was Amo Fred when you breastfed him?" His father, Teta's cousin, died of starvation before Fred's birth, and shortly afterward, his mother passed away.

"One month. Your father was two months old." Teta didn't take her eyes off the city. I'd rarely seen her stop working. "I breastfed both of them for three years." Almost as an after-thought, she added, "Death and separation defined the times. The famine raged and emigration to America, Brazil, Australia, Africa, Europe, and everywhere took loved ones away."

We sat quietly, fixated on the metropolis sprawling below. I remembered our harrowing journey to catch the final Pan Am flight and how the man seated next to me questioned why they were asked to wait for a family. I never told him the Station Manager, Amo Fred, owed his life to Teta.

Teta broke the silence when she stood and walked through the open door of her apartment. She returned with ice-frosted glasses of her homemade mulberry juice. The tradition began before the famine when Lebanon had a thriving silk industry. Silkworms eat mulberry leaves.

I took a sip of the sweet cold drink and relished the present. Teta sat back down and cracked more nuts.

"Teta, tell me about Miss Wolf." I never tired of hearing about the young British nurse who lived in the village during the war. I knew Teta liked to tell this story of intrigue.

Spies had been an integral part of Lebanon for generations. Some served occupying forces and others major masters, like the US and the USSR. A renowned Arabic language school established by the British, commonly known as the Spy School, had trained both Western diplomats and intelligence agents. Spies intermingled in Lebanese society. Kim Philby had lived in the same Beirut neighborhood as my parents and belonged to their social circle until he disappeared in 1963. Although he became world-famous, I preferred Teta's stories of lesser-known spies.

Teta smiled and shelled nuts. "Miss Wolf came with British missionaries to work in the hospital affiliated with the Quaker high school in the next village. But in 1914, at the beginning of the war, the Ottomans took over the hospital and the school. A nurse from our village invited Miss Wolf to live with her until she could return safely to England. But since Miss Wolf was a British spy, she planned to stay and probably arranged this invitation without Nurse Rita realizing it."

"How did you know she was a spy?"

"She'd disappear for many hours and nobody knew where she went. Abou Tannous, my cousin, swore he saw her in Beirut with European-looking men."

"Didn't it take about three hours to get to Beirut on horseback? How could she leave without Nurse Rita noticing?"

"Rita had small children and worked. She barely had time to think."

"Or," I interrupted, "maybe British Intelligence also recruited Rita. Isn't this possible?"

"My child, anything is possible, but these things were beyond us. We worried about survival, and Miss Wolf helped us. She tended to the sick, distributed medicines, delivered babies, and built a special box for a premature baby. For the first time, such a baby lived. It was…"

"…a miracle." I finished Teta's sentence. "Teta, you've seen many miracles. Wasn't the first car a miracle? The first airplane? The first telephone?"

"This world keeps getting better. I wish people would enjoy it and focus on making more miracles and stop senseless war. If only people realized miracles are the enlightened future and wars the primitive past."

We looked at the city and the sea beyond. Dark smoke from bombs blocked the urban area, but the bright blue sea sparkled under dazzling sunshine.

"Those poor people." Teta shook her head. "Every evening in church, we pray for them—the people with nowhere to go. We are blessed to have our mountain."

I thought about Joe and others who stayed to help. The night the hospital was bombed, I went to church with Teta.

I shelled the last nut, stood, dusted off, stretched my arms above my head and carried the tray to the kitchen. Teta would sun-dry them later.

"Why don't you and Rima go visit someone while I finish preparing dinner?" Teta now chopped parsley.

"Good idea. Maybe I should go see cousin Lana. I haven't seen her for a long time. Rima, want to come?"

Rima looked up. From her blank expression, I knew she hadn't heard anything.

"Do you want to come to Lana's?"

"Sure." She let go of the strand of hair she held.

I headed down the steps to the narrow street. Rima flicked her hair back with both hands and followed. Not a single car drove by.

"Maya, Rima!" Lana, waved from her balcony. "Did you hear the news? It's over! The war is over!"

We sprinted to her house and dashed up the stairs to the front veranda. A group of people surrounded a radio placed on a low table.

"They agreed on a ceasefire negotiated by the Americans. The war is over!" Lana shouted.

My skin chilled and my eyesight blurred. People gradually moved away from the radio and positioned themselves in a circle of chairs. Some lit fresh cigarettes and extinguished stubs they'd left in ashtrays.

"The Americans finally got it right. They gave the task to a man of Lebanese origin—Philip Habib. He understands the people of the Middle East."

Visitors nodded enthusiastically to Lana's father.

"Do you think Ambassador Habib's family left under the Ottoman occupation?" I asked.

"Probably," a woman responded. "They're Maronite Catholic—the largest group to emigrate. He was born in Brooklyn in 1920. It would make sense."

I thought about the irony. *The cruelty of Ottoman occupiers led to the birth of a diplomat. Had his family not been forced to flee, would he have returned as a peacemaker? Was it destiny or chance?*

"The news reports the truce calls for the Israelis to withdraw, the PLO to be expelled from Lebanon, and the Syrians to pull out their armed forces. Unfathomable," Lana's father spoke in a loud voice.

"And Western nations are sending troops to make sure they all go," Lana's uncle added. "It's a new beginning."

"Maya," Rima whispered. "We should go home."

We ran all the way to Teta's. The smell of spinach stuffed pastries and Maria greeted us at the open kitchen door. A smile wreathed her face.

"Isn't it wonderful news, Maria?"

"Yes, for sure, Miss Maya. Sir and Madam are very happy."

"Maria, I keep telling you to call me Maya—no Miss."

"Yes, miss."

"No Miss." I smiled and shrugged.

We walked into the medley of higher-than-normal pitched voices on the terrace. Maman hugged us, and Papa beamed.

Papa, however quickly turned somber. "As happy as we are, we can't forget those who suffered. And we must keep things in perspective; there are many moving parts to this ceasefire deal. But it is good news."

I lay in bed and thought about Joe. Was he in the operating room? Was he asleep? It had been a week since I'd heard any news of him. My body ached imagining things that could be wrong, but I willed my mind away and focused on my breath.

* * *

Events happened at an incredible pace over the next three weeks. Multinational troops landed to oversee the foreign armed forces evacuation. Surreal scenes on TV showed PLO fighters and their leader board ships for Greece on their way to Tunis. A president was elected. The Green Line was cleared. The Lebanese army entered West Beirut for the first time in over ten years.

The morning of September 6, Maria knocked on my bedroom door. "Madame says to pack. We're returning to the city today."

"Can we eat first?" I knew the answer. Food came foremost in our house.

Teta washed fruits and vegetables at the kitchen sink. "My soul. My eyes." I loved her greetings. I kissed her soft cheek and sat down.

She dried her hands on her apron. "I picked all the fruits and vegetables for breakfast this morning, including your favorite—figs."

She placed tomatoes, cucumbers, mint, green thyme, homemade yogurt cheese, white cheeses, olives, pita bread, and olive oil on the table. I rolled everything up in one large pita sandwich. In between bites, I sipped herbal tea made from Teta's plants.

"Are you coming to the city with us?"

"Not now. I have too much to do here." She opened the door for the cleaning lady who came every Monday to assist with heavy housework.

I inhaled the bittersweet medicinal steam from my tea. "I'll miss you."

"I'll miss all of you. Although you came for a sad reason, it was sweet to have you here. Maybe this time true peace will return."

"And work will return." I had been off for almost three months. "You know, Teta, it's strange how priorities change and we return to our basic instincts. Work seems important until overshadowed by survival."

"That's the world, my daughter."

"If someone doesn't need to work, should they?"

"Work is good for you. But don't confuse the means with the goal. Work provides the means to get to your goal—your passion. I've noticed those who are happiest focus on *people* as their passion. They find the right person to love, they take pride in their children, they focus on helping less fortunate people—things of this type."

Teta arranged tiny cups and saucers on a tray. The cleaning lady filled each halfway from the pot of steaming thick black coffee. She made a second round to top off each. This ensured the last cup didn't have an excess of mucky fine-ground coffee.

Teta called Maria to take the coffee tray and serve the morning visitors. She looked back at me. "No matter the path you choose, always find a way to be you—to do something for yourself. Develop a talent or pursue an interest you enjoy."

* * *

Maman, Papa, and Maria rode in the Buick. Rima and I followed in the Fiat that my cousin Hadi had driven up to the mountains for us a few days earlier. I never imagined Beirut as it looked. Whole buildings had collapsed into piles of rubble. *Are bodies lying under them? Had they screamed or was it too sudden? Did babies cry for their mothers? Don't think. Don't think.* No way to make sense of evil's cruelty.

The concierge rushed to the car as we pulled up. "Thanks be to God for your safe arrival." I watched him kiss Papa's hands and cry. Papa gently patted the old man on his shoulder. We unloaded the cars, and Papa and I drove around the block until we found parking spots.

"Papa, I'm going to see Joe."

"Do you want me to walk with you?"

"No, I'll be fine." I saw his disappointed look and added, "But if you feel like walking, it would be nice to have company."

We silently navigated the familiar neighborhood. A misty layer of dust covered everything—cars, trees, buildings and streets. Fortunately, this part of the city was not totally devastated.

We reached the hospital, and Papa said he needed to go home because Maman would worry it had taken too long to park. I knew this wasn't the reason. He often ran into friends on the street and spent a considerable amount of time talking with them. Maman always gave him an hour's slack.

Papa gently kissed my forehead and left. He understood my homecoming wouldn't be complete until I found Joe.

People filled the hospital foyer. Most displayed pathetic expressions, wore shabby clothes, and looked like they didn't belong. The well-dressed didn't linger and hurried through with an air of purpose.

I took the elevator to the surgical floor and stepped off into another mass of humanity. The staff made their way around people, whom I assumed were visitors or refugees with nowhere else to go. I craned my neck but didn't see a familiar face. I decided to go to the hospital café where one of the volunteers might have news of Joe.

"Maya. Welcome back." Mrs. Martin rose from her stool to kiss me. "Joe had a late lunch and left about ten minutes ago. He's been on call for three days, covering for doctors unable to get here. He went home to sleep."

"Thank you." I rushed to the door and called over my shoulder. "It's good to see you." I doubt she heard.

My mind flew ahead of my legs. I didn't bother to check if the elevator had electricity. I ran up twelve flights of stairs and banged on his door with both hands, afraid he might already be asleep.

He opened. His shirt was unbuttoned, and his belt unbuckled. I didn't expect the surprised look on his face, and for a split second he didn't move. Then he put his arms around my waist, pulled me into the apartment, and kicked the door shut.

My body molded in his tight embrace. For the first time in months, I allowed myself to relish a moment. Horror, fear, and uncertainty all evaporated into warm anticipation. His hold lessened, and he put his hands on my shoulders and stood back to look at me before he pulled me to him once again. He stroked my hair, and I slipped my hand under his shirt.

"My God. I've missed you, Maya."

I didn't say anything, fearful I'd break the spell. My heart beat against his chest. If I had one wish, it would be to melt into him and not be separated again. Eyes closed, I imagined it possible.

Joe led me to the sofa. "All these weeks, the thought of holding you again gave me strength. I'm thankful you weren't in the city." Tears formed in the corners of his eyes, and I leaned over to softly kiss them away.

"I worried so much about you. We kept praying the hospital remained safe. Then we heard it was hit… oh my God." I knew my words tumbled out, but I couldn't stop. "It took a whole day before we found out none of the staff was hurt. We were frightened—everyone but Teta. She had faith and lit a candle for you every night."

He squeezed my hand, and for the first time he smiled. "I knew a special angel watched over me."

I beamed, and he leaned toward me, but I pulled away. I had one more question. "How's your mother?"

"She's okay. She stayed with my uncle and his family."

We both fell silent. He reached down and gathered my hands into his, and I kissed his neck. He bent his head slightly to kiss me. My whole being lightened. I hadn't realized the extent of the burdens of the past weeks.

I fumbled with the zipper on his pants while his mouth moved down my neck. I wished our lovemaking could last for at least as long as the suffering had.

Lying in bed, an hour later, I examined his profile silhouetted against the glass balcony doors behind him. Outside, the sky darkened, and I traced his features with my fingers. "I need to leave. It's getting late."

He pulled me to him. "I love you, Maya."

"I love you, too," I surprised myself with the words, but I looked at him and realized I had spoken the truth. "I wish I could stay, but everyone is going to worry if I'm not home soon."

He kissed me and loosened his grip as I reluctantly pulled away. He entered the living room as I bent down to look under the coffee table for my clothes. He retrieved them before I did and teased me by holding them behind his back until I gave him a kiss.

He reached for his pants, but I stopped him. "No need for you to walk me home. It's not very dark, and I run fast."

"Please. I'll feel better."

"And I'll feel better if you stay here and get some sleep."

He remained quiet for a moment before he said, "When are you going back to work? I'm off the day after tomorrow."

"Are you going to last until then? Don't you need to make up for lost time?" I smiled.

"Tomorrow, after my early morning surgery, I'm going to see my mother. I should be back around five. I can pick you up."

"Great. By the way, I go back to work on Wednesday. Tomorrow's my last day off."

* * *

On September 8, I boarded the airline's employee bus and took mental inventory of the people, terrified someone would be missing. I counted one tired and drained face after another and became thankful everyone seemed present.

Maurice had embarked before me. He gave me a weary grin and nodded at the empty place next to him. I carried a stack of files from my office that I'd planned to work on at home but hadn't. I stumbled, and they fell into my intended seat. Maurice reached over and collected the papers on his lap. I bent down to put my large briefcase on the floor and stood up as the bus began to move. I lost my balance; my purse fell off my shoulder and I landed, with the grace of an elephant, next to Maurice.

He shook his head and laughed. "Maya, I love you. Nobody can brighten up a day like you."

For the next half-hour we shared the fearful experiences we had endured. He'd taken his family to their mountain village in the Chouf. I spent the rest of the day in much the same fashion, sharing stories, hopes, and fears with fellow employees.

On Thursday conversations centered on positive apprehension. A new president-elect, new alliances, new foreign armies and old armed forces expelled. Political bedfellows shifted.

By Friday, work became the focus, and many of us stayed late into the afternoon to catch up. For the first time since 1975 peace became a serious possibility—at least for a few days.

* * *

Less than a week later, on the day Princess Grace of Monaco died, everything spun back into fear and uncertainty for Lebanon. The news spread quickly. I found out when Maurice burst into my office. "Grab your things. A massive explosion ripped apart the building where the president-elect was holding a meeting."

We squeezed into the standing-room-only bus. At each bus stop, people exited quickly—as if they were spat out.

I disembarked onto an empty street and ran the half-block home.

"Madame, sir, Miss Maya's here," Maria shouted.

My parents and Rima rushed to me.

"Maria," Papa said. "Bolt the protective door."

She opened the wooden front door, stepped out into the landing, and pulled closed the iron door which had been installed in hopes of keeping armed men out. She pushed the long slat into the ground and bolted it. She then closed and secured the four locks on the wooden one. We were in for the remainder of the day and night and maybe more. With everyone accounted for, I felt secure for a fleeting moment.

"Papa, did he die? Some people on the bus insisted he did and others swore he escaped."

"The news on the radio is reporting the same thing. I guess we won't know for a while."

Our generator hummed loudly on the balcony. I walked into my room, threw my things on a chair, and flopped on the bed.

"How'd you get here so fast?" Rima, already sprawled out on her bed, asked.

"Maurice came to get me from my office. The bus driver drove like a madman. I can't believe this is happening. God, Rima, don't we ever get a break?"

"You're the optimist. You can't give up now. Maybe he's alive. Who knows." She stood. "Let's go watch TV with Maman and Papa."

In the morning, the prime minister confirmed the assassination. No one left our building all day. Neighbors visited back and forth. The news headlines were about two people who had nothing in common, except the day they died. The beautiful American-born Princess Grace and the president-elect of a war-torn country left the earth together; beauty and hope vanished in an instant.

* * *

Israeli troops entered West Beirut. Armed militias overran refugee camps, and horrifying massacres transpired. Fear, gloom, and darkness resumed.

Somehow Joe managed to call for a few seconds, and we confirmed the safety of everyone close to us. Hardly anyone left the building for a week. Neighbors drank coffee together, shared somber meals, and discussed the uncertain near future.

Despite the terrible tragedies, hope resurfaced within days. The parliament unanimously elected a new president. The multinational forces, which had overseen the peaceful withdrawal of the PLO, planned to return to show support for the government. An unexpected dawn broke over the country.

"It's neat to be stopped at the new checkpoints." Rima grinned. "I think the Italians are the best looking, the Americans are the politest, and the French wear the best uniforms."

"And none of them will kidnap or kill you," I added.

"I think I'm going to finish my master thesis. I've procrastinated too long. If Beirut's making a comeback, I want to enjoy it."

"Good idea." I hardly paid attention. I focused on getting ready for dinner with Joe.

That evening we walked down the street and, for the first time ever, passed a Lebanese army tank. The soldiers waved and smiled. They had decorated their vehicle with the flowers people handed them throughout the day. They had woven some into chains—delicate and alive. The armed militias had disappeared like cockroaches into the cracks of the broken city.

The sorrow of lives lost hung heavily in the air, but hope for a future of peace blew like a lace curtain in a soft breeze.

CHAPTER 23

Immortal, Beirut will rise again.

—PAPA

The poets say Beirut has been destroyed and resurrected hundreds of times. They say survivors rise from ashes like the magnificent phoenix and build a more splendid city. Historians count seven major reconstructions of the ancient city. Today people were simply thankful for an end to the terrors and eager to return to a normal, peaceful existence.

In places where the only sign of life was weeds and wildflowers growing out of sidewalks by destroyed buildings, people returned to resurrect the deserted pockets of the once cosmopolitan metropolis. City dwellers, like moles, emerged from underground shelters to bless the warm sunlight touching their skin. Ecstatic the unbelievable had become reality, people returned from remote parts of the country or overseas to their homes and businesses. Rebirth and vitality created intoxicating amnesia.

The Green Line vanished. Debris and garbage were replaced with construction and flowers. For the first time in over seven years, people could drive freely around the city and the country. Energy shifted from avoiding death to breathing life.

Looking back, if I could preserve any time of my life, it would be the nine months to come. Fortunately, I savored the days. Joe and I worked hard and didn't waste a minute. Like birds released from captivity, we reveled in the freedom to explore the beauty and history around us—ancient Phoenician sea ports, Roman temples and ruins, crusader fortresses and castles, the Cedars of Lebanon, the caves of mystical saints, and the homes of world-celebrated poets. We picnicked on river banks and by splendid waterfalls. We visited restaurants where trout was caught and cooked. We planned for the ski season and decided we'd do something we'd never done—ski in the morning and swim in the afternoon.

Endorphins replaced valium. People tirelessly rebuilt their lives and country. We'd climbed out into the light at the end of the dark, gloomy tunnel where we once appeased ourselves, pretending we thrived. Finally, a basic human right was restored—the chance to live fear-free.

One afternoon I waved airline tickets in Joe's face. "I found seats on the London flight tomorrow. I got mine for free, and I bought a cheap one for you. If you come with me, I'll invite you to the theatre and to dinner in Covent Garden."

"London for a night. It's a deal, but dinner's my treat."

"Okay, but I have to confess I also reserved seats for Athens in two weeks, and I know exactly where I'll take you to dinner."

"Maya, slow down. We don't have to do everything now."

"We have to make up for lost time."

Days and nights were full. My jobs required much work, and I wanted to enjoy experiences with Joe. Late one afternoon as I packed up my text books and notes, I realized I hadn't seen Leila for more than two weeks. I decided to pay her a visit.

Leila and Alex lived in one of Beirut's finest new buildings. I always marveled at the desert-rose marble floors and walls in the foyer. This sanctuary did not allow a speck of dust or dirt. A well-dressed concierge questioned everyone who entered.

On the tenth floor, a uniformed maid opened the door, "Madame Leila's not here."

"Do you know where she is?"

"No, miss."

"Please tell her I came."

Joe was working late, and since I had no plans, I decided to see if I could find her at her parents' home.

Amo Mohammad opened the door. "Where have you been, my daughter?" He answered his own question. "With your doctor. You don't know how happy this makes me. Two wonderful people."

"Thank you, Amo." I caught myself before gushing about how fortunate I was to love someone everyone liked.

"I dream of dancing at your wedding."

"But he hasn't asked me to marry him."

Amo's eyes sparkled. "He will."

"You think so?"

"I know so. I've seen a lot in my life—a man in love is unmistakable."

"How about a woman in love?"

"You both deserve the best, and I'm as happy as a parent can be for their child."

"Thank you." I kissed him on the cheek.

"I don't think you came to visit me." He stepped aside and gestured for me to enter.

"Actually, I'm always glad to see you. You're a blessing, Amo. But you're right."

"Leila came home from the office and went straight to her old bedroom. She usually rushes to the nursery to see Baby Karim, but for the past few days she seems preoccupied." I could tell he was worried and wanted to talk.

"What do you think is bothering her?"

"I wish I knew. I have a couple of suspicions, all disconcerting. Maybe she'll confide in you."

"I hope so." I wondered how I would handle Leila confiding in me and Amo Mohammad's expectation.

I knocked on her bedroom door and entered. Leila propped up on her bed, stared straight ahead and didn't acknowledge my presence. I took a step, and she turned. She extinguished her cigarette in an ashtray placed on her bed cover. She stood and kissed my cheeks. "I've missed you. Many times, I wanted to visit you, but I figured you wouldn't be home." She held me tightly.

"I might have been."

"It doesn't matter anymore because now you're here. Have you eaten?"

"Yes, thanks." I sat on the pink sofa. "I thought you gave up smoking?"

"I did, but sometimes I need comforting habits. It's temporary. I'll quit." She grinned and looked away at the wall.

"Where's Karim?"

"In the nursery—a guest room my parents converted. They insist I bring him here when I go to work. They've hired someone to help Old Nanny take care of him."

"Nice. You don't have to worry about him."

"It works well, especially these days."

"Why, especially these days?"

It took her a few minutes to answer. "Things aren't going well between me and Alex. He's changed. He's hardly home. When I ask him where he's been, he gets agitated. I know he's getting more involved in politics and attends communist party meetings. I'm not quite sure of his role, but I'm guessing he's moved up." She shifted and looked down at the carpet.

"How do you know where he's going?"

"I hired someone to follow him. At first, I thought he was seeing another woman because he's been cold to me. We haven't had sex in over a month," she shouted out the last sentence.

"Wow, and this is the guy who couldn't keep his hands off you."

"Weird how things change. Isn't it? I used to joke about having to fight him off, but it was the best part of our relationship. I loved his mind, but his body won me over." A mischievous glint came over her face and she hugged a satin pillow. "Imagine, almost every time we made love, he had to come twice. Sometimes he never pulled out, but he always made sure I enjoyed it, too." She stood and walked to the window. On the way, she picked up the cigarette pack but then threw it back on the bed.

Leila had rarely spoken this explicitly about her sex life. She'd merely alluded to it being wonderful.

"I don't know what to do. How can I lure him from his mistress—politics? It's harder than another woman."

"I'm surprised he's becoming more engrossed. The country's getting back on its feet with the government gaining control. Why would anyone increase their involvement in a fringe political party?"

"Oh, Maya, don't kid yourself. Lebanon's a small strategically located country with a weak government and millions of fault lines. Think merely about the big powers: the Soviet Union and the US and how they want to dominate the area. Then think about the countries desiring to control Lebanon—Syria, Iran and Saudi Arabia. And remember the Palestinian refugees. Some want to wage war from our shores and others want to become naturalized. Now, throw the Israelis into the pot. And for the sauce, remember the Lebanese themselves—exploited by entitled political dynasties and the leaders of eighteen religions."

"Talk about pessimism." I stood.

"The Lebanese are optimists. This keeps us going. Look at my father and yours. But you can't build a country on hope alone."

I didn't want to talk about politics. "Have you considered talking to your father about Alex?"

"You know how much my father hates divided politics and politicians. What can he tell me? And I can't talk to him about sex."

"Maybe you don't need to bring up politics or sex. You could tell him Alex is acting cold and you don't know why." An idea came to me. "Why don't you and Alex go on a vacation? You could go to Europe for a few days."

She perked up. "That's a great suggestion. My birthday's in two weeks. He can't refuse to go, especially if I tell him Baba bought the tickets and will pay for the hotel as my birthday gift."

I felt proud although I'd probably heard this recommendation from some American TV marriage counselor.

"Let's go see Karim." I opened the door. "I bet he's grown."

"You're going to be surprised. He's amazing. But sometimes it pains me to see him. I watch the beauty of his development contrasted with Alex and my wilting relationship."

"Hey, this is the man you were madly in love with. You're going to get away and rediscover each other." I definitely learned this stuff from some show.

On my way home, I considered going to the hospital to look for Joe, but I knew he'd be busy. Only a few weeks ago, I wouldn't have been out alone this late. Tonight, I felt safe with the Lebanese army and security forces deployed. Suddenly, I remembered Leila's words and imagined the militias had not gone away but lay in wait to jump out of the fault lines and terrorize the country again. My vertebrae felt like a chunk of ice. *Dear God, please no.*

Maria quickly answered the front door, and the smell of spices filled my nostrils. "Sir and madame are having a dinner party. Lisa, the cook, has been here all day."

"What's she making?"

"Everything, but don't go into the kitchen. Lisa won't let you taste anything and doesn't like company."

I saw Maman in the living room and went to talk with her.

"I thought I told you people are coming for dinner." She put a flower arrangement down.

"Maybe. I don't remember."

"Do you have plans?"

"No, Joe's working. Who's coming?" It really didn't matter.

"Your father's old classmates—Dr. Hagopian, Dr. Najjar, the Haddads—about twenty people." Maria handed her another flower arrangement, and she placed it on a corner table.

"I'll shower and join you."

I stood for a few seconds under lukewarm water. I lathered Teta's homemade olive oil soap on her hand-picked loofah and washed quickly before the water flow dried up.

I heard the doorbell ring and the sound of laughter. I wondered if the voices in Leila's home this night were loud or hushed.

CHAPTER 24

———

Like cockroaches, they hide in broken places to plot their return.

—*LEILA*

It only took a few months for Leila's dire predictions to materialize. Evil suffocated the laughter and rebirth and touched everyone's lives.

The deafening explosion, the shaking building, the shattering glass, and Rima's scream seemed simultaneous. I ran toward her cry. Barefoot amid broken glass, my bloodied sister stood at the kitchen sink with her hands cupped under her chin and blood dripping through them. The wooden patio door framed her, its blown-out glass, like spiked clouds at the feet of a saint.

I grabbed a dishtowel to wipe the blood streaming from her face. "Her shoes," I shouted to Maria. I supported Rima while Maria lifted one foot at a time to brush off the glass and put on a shoe. The three of us crunched across the debris.

"We need to go to the hospital, but first let's find out what's happening." I picked up a radio and guided Rima to a chair in the foyer. Before she sat, we heard a key in the front door. Papa and Maman rushed in.

Maman removed the dishtowel and put her arm around her trembling daughter. "Let's wash this with soap and water to see how bad it is."

"We heard a bomb exploded at the American Embassy." Papa turned on the radio. Mama's in-control and calm behavior made me feel comfortable leaving Rima. I followed Papa out of the room to listen to the latest news.

I returned to find Rima's wound bandaged. "Once we cleaned it up, it didn't look bad," Maman said.

"Aren't you worried about glass being in the cut?"

"No. It bled a lot. I'll keep an eye on it. The hospital must be chaotic. Besides, I don't think we need to go."

Rima looked calmer, and we went to the family room to listen to the news. Despite the loud volume, Papa's ear almost touched the radio. I heard a pungent male voice. "... at the American Embassy... the Red Cross and emergency personnel... removing the dead and injured... rumors are high-ranking CIA directors were meeting... anti-American group is claiming responsibility..."

Maman and Rima began to cry. Papa moved between them on the sofa and placed an arm around each. I inched closer to Maman and put my head on her shoulder. Months of hopeful expectation shattered in an instance. Did this tragic event mark the end of hope or was it a horrific speed-bump on the rough road to restoring a country?

The radio blared. "*Today, Monday, April 18, 1983, at 1:03 p.m., a suicide bomber drove a van packed with two thousand pounds of explosives into the American Embassy in Beirut. Sixty-three people are reported killed and 120 injured...*"

CHAPTER 25

———

The people of Lebanon must be given the chance to resume their efforts to lead a normal life, free from violence, without the presence of unauthorized foreign forces on their soil. And to this noble end, I rededicate the efforts of the United States.

—PRESIDENT RONALD REAGAN

In nauseated horror, we watched the removal of bodies from the rubble. Feeble logic attempted to rationalize why years of war could not cease without atrocities. The world swiftly reacted and President Reagan declared criminal acts would not deter the US from the goal of establishing peace. Terror would not win. The US Congress approved 251 million dollars to support the Lebanese government and military.

The world appeared to come to its senses. A chaotic Lebanon had the potential to destabilize the entire region. Terrorism could not be contained within the borders of the Middle East, and its venom would poison other countries, including Europe and America.

An air of sadness and extra caution described the demeanor of the country. Joe and I attempted to live a normal life. We met every evening at a restaurant, pub or one of our apartments. On weekends, we continued to roam the country. We camped overnight on the banks of rivers, hiked the highest mountain—10,128 feet above sea level—and picnicked in Baalbek among the well-preserved Roman temples.

We lived on a razor's edge without acknowledging the possibility we could be slashed at any moment. Politicians and radical groups increased their rabid rhetoric and threats. The noose around the country and its people tightened, but we raised our hands and, in our minds, loosened it. The bright window of opportunity slowly closed, and nothing within our power could stop it. We existed on hope and in denial.

People spoke about emigration. Many sought foreign passports or permanent residencies in other countries as an insurance policy. Visa applicants crowded embassies. A disproportionate number of the educated left. The wealthy came and went. They had the privilege of departing to safer pastures at any time. The poor and the die-hard patriots continued to plow through their lives.

* * *

We knew we belonged in our homeland, but questioned the wisdom of remaining. The rocks overlooking the sea in the port city of Byblos provided a place of peace. Joe and I often sat on them, drank wine, and discussed our thoughts.

One afternoon while overlooking the waves, I asked Joe the question neither of us had verbalized. "Do you think about returning to Boston?"

He watched a fisherman cast a net off his boat. "Imagine, two thousand years ago, Christ and his disciples cast their nets on these waters."

I nodded. "So much happened here—events that shaped our world." *The name Bible comes from this city. You'd think it would be a place of peace.*

Although I realized he hadn't answered my original question, I pursued the new topic. "Have you been to Cana?"

"No. Have you?" Joe looked away from the ocean and in the direction of a church constructed by the Crusaders over eight hundred years earlier.

"No, but I've always wanted to see where Christ performed his first miracle."

"Not all scholars agree. A village in Galilee makes the same claim." He turned to face me.

"As long as no one knows for sure, I can believe whatever I want."

Joe pulled me closer to him. "I think I love you more each day."

We visited the cave in Cana the following Saturday. Local tradition says Jesus reflected in it before he attended the wedding. We took pictures in front of the stone carvings of the apostles. A local Muslim man volunteered to be our guide, and we marveled at his pride in recounting Biblical stories. "Go to *Sur* (Tyre) for lunch. It's only ten kilometers away, and we know for sure it is the place Jesus healed a Syrian woman's daughter."

Joe tried to give him a tip, but he refused. "It's my duty to show you around. Making others closer to God makes me closer to him."

"But you're not Christian, Hassan." I spoke without thinking.

"How many gods are there, miss? We travel different paths to the same Allah."

"You're right, of course." His wisdom could have spared the world much tragedy.

We continued to Tyre. Babylonians, Persians, Egyptians, Greeks, Romans, Crusaders, and Ottomans had all laid siege or conquered the city throughout history. It was the birthplace of the Greek goddess Europa—the Phoenician woman after whom the continent of Europe is named.

From here, the ancient Phoenicians exported their famous purple dye. St. Paul walked the streets to preach the Gospel, and the Romans built a stone twenty-thousand-person hippodrome, a bathhouse, and an aqueduct—abundant history in an almost forgotten place.

We entered the outskirts of Beirut as the sky began to darken. From a distance, I saw Papa and the concierge standing on the street in front of our apartment building. We pulled up, and Papa bent down and looked into the car window. "You mustn't be out this late. The situation is very tense."

"You are right, Amo." Joe got out to greet Papa and open my door. I mouthed, "I love you." He winked at me, and I had to restrain my urge to kiss him. How I ached to go home with him.

Maman waited at the apartment door. "You had us worried."

"Didn't mean to. We went to Cana and Tyre and didn't realize the time. It took us two hours to get back."

"I went to *Sur* a few weeks ago," Rima said. "Where did you eat?"

"A fish shack by the sea. They placed the table where the waves hit the shore. We removed our shoes, and the water washed our feet while we ate."

"Sounds nice," Rima said.

"Was it clean?" Maman asked. "Did you check the bathroom?"

"Oh, Maman. It's a shack with the most delicious grilled fish and vegetables. An old lady sat at the entrance cutting up potatoes for fries. Everything tasted amazing."

Before she could say more, I left to my room.

The oppressive July heat bothered Maman, but Papa needed to remain in Beirut for his work. He suggested we go to the mountains without him, but Maman refused, despite the fact she always looked forward to spending summer there. Both Rima and I wanted to stay in the city. I had taken a summer break from teaching, and my commute to the airlines, although longer, remained convenient. However, proximity to Joe was my reason. Rima wanted to remain because of her research. This rendered Maman the frustrated one.

Over the next month, Joe and I didn't leave the city, except for a three-day trip to Rome. We spent our free time in his apartment. The increased tension in the country allowed us more opportunity to explore each other.

In August, Papa decided we should go to the mountains. Maman needed no coaxing, and protests from Rima and me were overridden.

Joe had a few days off and planned to stay with his mother. At least he could easily visit the mountains. This gave me something to look forward to.

The night we arrived at Teta's, our mountain was shelled. The following morning, Joe casually strolled up to the veranda where we sat with neighbors.

"How did you get here?" I asked.

"I drove." He realized I wasn't looking for humor and continued, "The roads are fine. Shelling seems confined to nighttime. As long as I leave before dark..." A shell whistled overhead. We only had time to throw ourselves to the ground.

"It hit the forest," someone yelled.

We ran inside, and Papa told Joe he should stay with us for the remainder of the day and night. I lifted the phone—no dial tone.

"Go to one of the neighbors' homes," Papa ordered. "Soon none of the phones will be working."

We attempted to call his mother, uncle, or neighbor to let them know Joe's plans. After an hour, his uncle's phone connected.

The remainder of the day and night were quiet. No one felt the need to stay in the shelter. We opened a bottle of Teta's wine to drink with our mezza.

The following day, Joe returned to the city early on a calm morning. It was impossible to fathom the night of terror awaiting.

CHAPTER 26

———

I am forever locked in the cage of sorrow.

—SELMA

Incoming rockets suddenly spiked through the sunlight of our late afternoon. Papa's voice boomed through the house bouncing between the sound of explosions, "Quickly—get to the shelter."

I sat in a corner too anxious to doze off and too tired to talk. My body involuntarily jolted with each irregular impact.

Around five in the morning, we heard yelling in the street outside. Papa immediately opened the shelter door and about a dozen people quickly entered. A woman clutched the hands of two children—Selma's children. Maman rushed to them.

My cousin, Hadi, addressed Papa in a panting voice. "During a lull, Roger went up to his apartment to get food for us. Almost immediately there was an explosion. When he didn't return, I ran up to check on him."

He stopped talking and looked down at the ground. "Amo, he was hit by shrapnel in his head. He lay dead on the kitchen floor."

"Where's Selma?" Papa looked frantically at the small group of people.

I didn't need an answer. I bolted out. I felt electrified as though small wires pierced my body. Surreal horror propelled me. I ran. I burst into the small room used as a shelter for the residents of Selma's building. I raised my head and saw her. Pain penetrated every cell of my body. She sat like a mime with a white powdered face and eyes sunken into their sockets. It seemed as if all her bodily fluid had been drained, leaving stained paths on parched white skin, vibrating lips the only sign of life.

I stepped forward and touched her hair. She wrapped her arms around me and encircled my body in misery. Salty water crawled down my shoulder. Its path burned my skin. I held her close. A sickening sensation formed in my stomach. It seeped into my organs and bones, and it oozed from the pores of my skin.

"Why didn't you leave with everyone else?"

"I couldn't. They tried hard to take me. But I want to meet my fate where he met his."

I realized I was her only hope. I mustered the words, "You have to come with me."

"He was the only man I ever loved."

"I know." I tried to keep my voice level and ignore the shrill whistle followed by the dull thud. It was a matter of time before the screeches would become louder and the earth beneath us would be torn apart. Multiple rockets were usually sent to the same coordinates.

Does the thinking brain command strength or is it survival instinct? Somehow, I picked up a body heavier than mine and ran. I needed to save my widowed cousin.

* * *

Two days later, I leaned forward to fill my lungs with the smell of incense. It mixed in my brain with the ancient Aramaic funeral chants. Joe stood next to me. His body seemed to curve from pain. His skin, pulled tightly over his face, emphasized the pitiful helplessness in his being. Sadness and powerlessness defined us all. Together we prayed for the soul of the only man Selma ever loved. The land soaked up the blood of another innocent.

Selma insisted she host the mourners in her home, not far from Teta's. People came and went for days. They made feeble human efforts to lessen the pain. Most recounted their belief in a loving God. Others said no one is taken before their time. Some said a person is never given a cross too heavy to bear. A few told stories about people who fled the war only to meet their fate in safe havens. Everyone agreed we are all travelers on the same road to death. People, people, people—they served a purpose—those who loved and lost had no time to marinate in solitary pain.

CHAPTER 27

———

Show me the value of worry and I will join you.

—JOE

A ceasefire was negotiated. We had lost count of the truces. Summer drew to an end, and in late August we returned to the city. In September, Joe planned to spend his three-day break with his mother. I didn't mind, because I wanted and needed time alone. My period was late, and although worried, I decided not to tell him straightaway. His mother invited me for lunch on the final day of his visit. I would wait until then to share my concern.

On my drive to their home, I coached myself on how to act nonchalant. The three of us sat in the living room for a few minutes and I thought I had succeeded. However, the moment his mother stepped into the kitchen, Joe asked, "Maya, are you okay?"

"I have… well, I have some bad news. I'm two weeks late—my period."

He smiled and reached for my hand. "So what's the bad news?"

I spat out my reply. "What do you mean *what's the bad news*?"

"Look, you didn't get into this alone, and you're not in it alone. We'll work it out."

"What's there to work out?"

"If you're pregnant—you might be and you might not be— we'll deal with it together."

"What do you mean deal with it?"

"Maya, let's not make assumptions and worry about things that might not be. Let's relish today together. Come to the hospital tomorrow afternoon, and we'll do a test."

"And if it's positive?"

"Then maybe I've finally found a way to get you to marry me." He leaned over and kissed me just as his mother appeared with a tray of fresh lemonade.

I tried hard to enjoy the afternoon, but I couldn't shake the fear of pregnancy. This is not the scenario I envisioned for me and Joe. Wasn't living with the terror of everyday life enough?

CHAPTER 28

———

In my heart I know my destiny is set, so why does my mind keep playing games of chance?

—MAYA

"Maya, are you all right?" Maurice's voice sounded loud. "I've been talking, and you seem somewhere else. It's not like you. What's wrong?"

"I'm thinking about a project," I lied.

"Can I help?"

"I don't think so." I racked my brain for something to say if he asked more, but he didn't. He gave me a slight grin and turned to look out the window. I liked this quality about Maurice. He was available when I needed him, and he knew when to back off. We had become good bus buddies. Every once in a while, I'd get off at his stop and walk home with him for lunch. His wife invited me the first time, but then it became impromptu. Despite his protests, I always stopped on the way to buy a cake, flowers, chocolate, or some treat they probably wouldn't buy for themselves.

Okay, Maurice, I think I'm pregnant. I imagined his reaction. He'd probably take it in stride. I gazed at the dirty brown bus floor and then back up at the coiffure of the woman in front of me. I wondered how long it took her to tease her hair every morning. I tried to think of anything except my fear.

I had a busy day. Meetings allowed me little time alone until I boarded the 2:30 bus.

Twenty-five minutes later I walked into the hospital coffee shop to meet Joe. I greeted the volunteer at the entrance, glad it wasn't Mrs. Martin, and walked to a table in the back of the room where I sat facing the wall. My body language must have communicated my desire for solitude to the waitress because she didn't approach me.

Despite the noise in the room, I could hear the ticking of the wall clock above me. I looked up—3:20. I checked my watch to confirm. Joe was often late, but by now he usually sent a resident to find me. "Miss Coury," the young doctor would hesitantly say. "Dr. Kassir asked me to tell you he's delayed…"

The silent emptiness hurt my head. I stood and walked to the lobby wall phone. "Please page Dr. Joe Kassir."

"Dr. Kassir, extension seven one four, Dr. Joe Kassir, extension seven one four." The hospital PA system blasted. I stared at the phone in anticipation, wishing it to ring, ordering it to ring, but silence. I leaned on the wall.

"Maya."

I jumped, slamming my back against the concrete block.

Sammy pushed his wire rimmed glasses up his nose. "What are you doing here?"

"I came to meet Joe. Do you know where he is?"

"No, I haven't seen him today. I've been at a conference and came back to see patients."

"We were supposed to meet around three."

He looked at his watch. "It's only 3:45. He's probably delayed in surgery. Come to my office, and we'll page him."

"I paged him, and he hasn't answered."

"Maya, how can he if he's in surgery?"

"But he always sends someone to tell me."

"Maybe he didn't have anyone to send. Let's go." He walked past me.

I stepped away from the wall and followed him to the elevator.

"Please page Dr. Joe Kassir." His receptionist nodded. "Come wait in my office. I have to see two patients, and then I'll join you."

I sat on a hard-stuffed leather chair and examined the diplomas on the wall and the shelf of doctor figurines. I recognized the Lladro collectable of the obstetrician holding the newborn baby upside down. I wondered who gave it to him.

Sammy returned and sat behind his large desk in time to answer the phone. I watched the expression on his face change and tried to figure out the other end of the conversation. "How do you know? Are you sure? Who spoke with her?"

Paging Dr. Rhodes. Paging Dr. Rhodes. Paging Dr. Rhodes. The voice in my head repeated the hospital's secret emergency page.

He hung up and didn't look at me. I imagined he'd received news about a patient. *Should I ask him to order a pregnancy test?*

He stood and came to sit on the chair next to mine. "Joe left his mother's home early this morning and never arrived at the hospital. The hospital administration called his mother to confirm. No one has seen or heard anything since, but the hospital is using all of their contacts to locate him."

He took his glasses off and placed them on the table between us. My body stiffened, and my head spun. Sammy reached over and held my hand. "Maya, the hospital has excellent contacts with all of the political parties. Don't forget, we treat their wounded, and they need us. They'll put pressure on everyone to find Joe."

Hammers banged inside my skull. "You mean he was kidnapped?" My eyes blurred, and I could barely focus on him.

"Most likely. This has been going on for some time now, especially along the Green Line. Someone is in the wrong place at the wrong time and…"

"Oh my God. Oh my God." My body turned cold. He rubbed my hands between his. The noise in my head grew louder. I had to strain to hear his words.

"The good news is there were no explosions, no snipers, and no casualties. He's most likely somewhere with someone. We should be able to locate him quickly and negotiate his release."

Sammy handed me a tissue box. When I made no attempt to take one, he moved closer and wiped my face. Then he wrapped his arms around me and let me cry.

"I'll walk you home."

We passed the worried-looking receptionist, entered an elevator of anonymous people, and walked out to the street.

"Will you walk with me to Manara?" I referred to the old lighthouse district.

"Don't you want to go home?"

"I need to see someone. Someone who can help find Joe." I struggled to breathe. I didn't wait for his answer. I turned and walked quickly in the opposite direction.

The maid opened the door, and I rushed past her shouting, "Amo Mohammad! Amo Mohammad!"

"What's wrong, my daughter? What's wrong?" He met me halfway through the second living room.

"Joe's missing. He never made it to work this morning. He left his house in Achrafieh and never arrived at the hospital. No one knows where he is."

Amo Mohammad held me tightly against his shoulder. Sammy stood behind me, and in a calm voice, he provided the details. Amo Mohammad asked questions and then said, "I'll make contacts immediately."

"Habibti" Amo Mohammad looked down at me. "I know this is hard, but please try not to worry. You can't do anything at this moment. We'll find him. Now, let Ali drive you and Dr. Sammy home."

Sammy had never met my family. Maria opened the door, and he asked for my parents. I didn't say anything. Maria rushed off and returned with them. I vaguely remember him introducing himself and recounting the events. Maman stood with her arm around my waist. Sammy stepped closer to Papa, and I heard something about Xanax.

"Please excuse us. I'm going to help Maya get ready for bed," Maman said.

Sammy looked at me but addressed Maman. "Can I help with anything before I leave?"

"No need to leave. Please feel free to stay with Amo. Rima should be home soon. You know Rima?"

"No, I've never met her, but I need to go. The driver's waiting. I'll come to see you tomorrow."

Maman and Maria gave me a sponge bath, helped me brush my teeth, and put on a cotton nightgown on me. Maman sat on the side of my bed and handed me a white pill. Maria stepped forward with a glass of water. I lay back on the pillow.

* * *

"Maman, it's noon. Why didn't someone wake me?" Barefoot and still in my nightgown, I walked into the hallway where she stood talking on the phone.

She put her hand over the receiver and mouthed, "Just a minute."

I went to the kitchen and opened the medicine cabinet in search of Panadol for my splitting headache. I saw Maria in the back garden hanging laundry. The light coming through the glass doors hurt my eyes, and I turned away.

Maman entered. "Everyone is working on it. There isn't a single political party or group not involved in finding Joe."

I fiddled with the bottle of painkillers in my hand.

"Maya, they'll find him. All you can do is pray and remain hopeful. I didn't wake you up because yesterday was a draining day. You have to teach this afternoon and you can go back to your office tomorrow. This is what Joe would want."

I opened the bottle, tossed two pills into my mouth and swallowed.

"You shouldn't take pills without water," Maman scolded. She poured some from a bottle into a glass. I took a sip and sat down on a wicker chair.

Maman placed her hands on my shoulders. "Maya, you have to stay strong. This is not the time to fall apart. If you want to help, be strong."

I rested my head on the table.

"Leila came over early this morning. She didn't want to wake you. She said she'll return around noon. Why don't you wash your face and get dressed before she comes? Would you like help?"

I shook my head.

"Come." Maman nudged me from behind. I followed her to my bedroom.

Moments later, Leila rushed in wailing. "Oh my God. Oh my God. I can't believe this happened. Don't worry. Baba's all over the place. He's meeting with political leaders, religious leaders, everyone. We'll find him. Where's Rima?"

I looked at her like she'd asked a bizarre question I could not answer.

"I asked you where Rima is."

I forced myself to focus. "She's at the university. Remember, she's a graduate assistant."

"Oh, yes. By the way, don't you teach this afternoon?"

"At three."

"Don't you need to get ready? I have an idea. Why don't I attend your class? You can impress me."

"With theories of motivation?"

Leila sat in the back of the classroom. Her presence made me feel more secure, and I often caught myself looking in her direction. From my students' mannerisms and facial expressions, I gathered they knew about Joe. Word traveled fast in the university community and beyond.

This class foretold the events I experienced the next day. It began with the people I saw on my way to the bus stop, continuing on the bus and then in the office. I needed to get used to it, remain strong and ask for help from everyone. Most would try to console me, as I had recently done after a coworker's husband was kidnapped. Together, we would attempt to make sense of the pain and horror human beings inflicted on one another.

During the first quiet moment I had at the office the following morning, I realized I'd forgotten about my potential pregnancy. I smiled sadly at myself. Frightening events, like everything else, are ranked by urgency.

I opened my desk drawer and took out the picture of Saint Maron (the patron saint of Lebanon). Teta had given it to me for my office. I visualized him roaming the mountains of Syria and Lebanon to convert pagans to Christianity. I gazed deeply into the picture, focused on the black specks of his eyes, and begged him to bring Joe back. "Don't worry. Have faith." I chanted out loud. My shoulders dropped, and my breathing slowed. A knock on the door jolted me out of my trance.

Maurice entered. "Have a few thoughts I'd like to share with you—provided I'm not interrupting."

I dropped the picture in the open drawer and quickly closed it. "No, come in. I'm glad you're here. I'm finding it hard to focus on work."

"Only normal, given the circumstances." He pulled a chair closer to my desk. "I think you should personally approach some of the executives here to ask for their help. It's one thing for others to ask on your behalf, and it's another for you to ask. None of them know Joe and considering how well liked you are, it can only help."

He had a point. The company leadership ran the gamut of political and religious organizations in the country.

"I made a list of seven I think have the best connections. I've included their phone extension and the names of their assistants."

"Thanks. I'll make appointments."

"Theories are beginning to circulate about who took Joe and why. Try to avoid listening or engaging. It will only upset you. I suggest you focus on the tangible." He reached for the cigarette pack in his pocket, removed one, and tapped the filter side on my desk, but he didn't retrieve his lighter. "I know you have lots of family and friends, but don't forget Mary and I are always here for you. She asked me to invite you to lunch today."

"I appreciate it, but let's save it for another time."

"I understand." He stood. "Stay strong and remember how many people want to help. I pray this will be over soon."

* * *

Had it only been three days not three years? Everybody and anybody made efforts to find Joe. Political leaders, religious leaders, or anyone deemed to have influence. Each produced a story, a theory, and different information.

Amo Mohammad visited most afternoons to give Papa updates. Sammy came over several times a week. He suggested we visit Joe's mother. At first I was reluctant. I didn't think I could handle seeing her, but he told me I would find her optimism comforting. Her friends and family never left her alone. When she saw me, she hugged me tightly. "I smell him in you." This old expression unnerved me. Did she sense my pregnancy?

On the way home, I debated asking Sammy about a pregnancy test but decided I couldn't deal with a potential positive. If it remained unknown, I could attempt to put it out of my mind.

My nonworking hours were spent at home with numerous visitors who came to console and counsel. I rarely heard anything they said. I didn't even hear Leila invite me to Sunday lunch and only realized it when Maman accepted for me—happy I had a place to go because she knew I wouldn't go with her and Papa to their lunch invitation.

I then heard Leila extend an invitation to Rima and Sammy.

"Thanks," Sammy replied, "but I'm having lunch with friends on Sunday. Rima, would you like to come with me?"

Rima's face turned red. "Okay," she answered in a small voice.

"Looks like everyone's set." Leila stood to leave. "Just one missing piece."

Resounding silence filled the room, and Leila froze in place.

"God willing," Papa said. "Joe will be with us soon."

* * *

The moment we sat down to lunch, I asked. "What do you think, Amo Mohammad? When do you think you'll find Joe?" I knew he couldn't answer.

He took a long breath. "With time, he'll be located."

"But why did they take him? Who took him?"

"If I could answer such questions, I would be God and not a man. I can only presume. Two Muslim men were kidnapped the day before and Joe could have been taken in revenge because he's Christian. Or he could have been taken for an exchange with another kidnapped person. Or maybe some fanatic group is holding him. Or he could have been targeted as a doctor. No one knows. Our job is to work on and pray for his return."

He probably had the best connections out of all the people helping.

Tante Samia dished more stuffed squash onto my plate. I picked at it. My ears rang against the backdrop of silence. Leila said Alex couldn't come for lunch because he had a meeting. By the tone of her voice, I knew it wasn't the whole story. However, I didn't have the energy to ask. I couldn't handle things I didn't know on top of things I did.

"Amo Mohammad, do you really believe in God?"

"Maya. What kind of question is that?" Tante Samia dropped her fork and glared at me. "Who doesn't believe in God? You should never question."

Amo Mohammad addressed his wife in a soft voice. "The girl has every right to question. Look what she's going through." He paused. "Yes, I believe in God but it was not always so. For me, it was a long and difficult search before I came to grips with what I accept as truth. It can be much harder to believe than not to believe."

"Why would God let this happen to Joe?"

"You can't let sorrow define or destroy your beliefs. I'm not a Christian, but the mother of Christ suffered the ultimate sorrow, and we know God loved her."

"I feel I can no longer pray."

"Be gentle with yourself. Doubt is part of the journey. Why don't you go to church this afternoon and spend some time reflecting? Perhaps Leila can go with you." He looked at his daughter.

"Of course. We can go to Saint Rita's." Strange Leila should pick the church I had visited with Joe.

Tante Samia opened her mouth and then closed it. She looked straight ahead. "It will be good for both of you," she said in a flat voice.

When I woke up the following morning, I recognized the wet sticky fluid between my thighs. Rima slept with her back to me. To confirm, I pulled up my nightgown and looked into my panties at the bright red spot. I felt stomach cramps and slipped out of bed. I hurried to the cold shower to quickly wash.

I dried off, put on clean underwear, fresh pajamas and climbed back into bed. Relief turned to sorrow. No part of him lived inside of me. I curled into a fetal position and cried.

CHAPTER 29

—

Comfort and love the hopeless; together you will find strength.
—JANICE'S MAMA

"Maya, can you hear me?" Christina's voice faded in and out.

I shouted into the receiver and silently cursed the phone system. "Kind of."

"Omar's father's making contacts… Syria. As … we heard the news… called him…friends in the government… help … personal favor. Omar … talk to you."

Omar got on the line. "Don't worry… We'll find him … Everybody… father knows. We love… be strong." His voice died out.

"Hello." Static. "Omar."

I flopped into the chair next to the telephone table and gazed at the family portraits on the wall. The faces seemed as distant as Christina and Omar in California. Nothing felt real anymore.

I don't know how long I sat there before Rima gently took the phone receiver out of my hand and returned it to the cradle. "The Egyptian woman is coming to do our sugar depilation and manicures."

I blinked at the emptiness.

"Let's change into our bathrobes. My legs are very hairy. I can't wait for her to remove everything." Rima examined her lower legs.

"I don't feel like doing anything."

She ignored me. "Remember when you did a total bikini depilation? With the first pull you screamed. We got scared Maman would come into the room. Remember, the esthetician only agreed to do it for us if we didn't tell Maman." She chuckled. "After we witnessed your pain, Leila and I chickened out. But it looked really cool. 'Just like a bride prepared for her wedding night in Cairo,' the woman kept saying."

I remembered Joe's shock when I surprised him with my new look. He liked it. For the first time in days, I smiled.

Two hours later I stood under a barely warm shower and scrubbed with a loofah to remove the tiny pieces of sugar stuck on my body. I dried off and rubbed my hands along the silky skin on my legs and underarms. The woman didn't have time to do a manicure, pedicure, and massage for me, but she promised to return the following evening. She rarely had availability on two consecutive nights for the same family, but I noticed Papa paid her more than usual.

I climbed into bed and took a white pill from a prescription bottle. I fell asleep as I begged for Joe's safe return in a pitiful prayer.

* * *

At work, I made every effort to keep myself occupied. My mind raced through progressively terrifying scenarios about Joe when I wasn't busy. The good memories of the time we'd spent together were becoming less frequent, overcome by waves of anxiety.

Several days after Joe had gone missing, I absent-mindedly stepped off the company bus. Two people grabbed me from both sides. My captors laughed, and with my startled reaction, they cackled louder.

"Thought I'd drop in from LA to check up on you," Chrissy chirped.

"What are you doing here?"

"She told you," Leila responded.

I burst into tears. They stepped closer and hugged me.

"We love you." Chrissy rubbed her hand up and down my back and cried.

Leila put a hand on each of our shoulders. "Let's go. We're blocking people getting off the bus." She took my hand and reached for Christina's. We walked, nursery school style, along the narrow city sidewalk.

We entered our favorite juice store. "Three large glasses—apple, carrot, sugarcane, and mango—equal amounts of each," Leila ordered our special high school concoction.

A young guy fed the fresh ingredients into the juicer. Suddenly, a short, toothless old man stepped out from behind the high counter. "Is this possible?" His low voice cracked. "Am I seeing reality?"

"Yes, Abu Samir, the three of us are really here," Christina said.

"Thanks be to God. I can't believe it. Oh, my wife will be so happy to know you've all returned."

"How is she?"

"She's getting old. A tired body but still a sharp mind."

"I hope to see her while I'm visiting." Christina smiled at him.

"She'll probably come every day to wait for you."

As if on cue, we loudly slurped the last drops of the sweet juice through our straws. The final step of our ritual.

Chrissy said, "I arrived last night and had dinner with my family. This morning, I spent time with my mother. Now, I'm yours for the next two weeks."

"I've arranged dinner tonight," Leila announced. "Ali will pick you up at nine. We're going to a cute new restaurant, *A la Mouff*."

"Who gets picked up at nine?" Chrissy asked.

"This isn't LA. He'll get one of you around nine and then the other one. You need to relax. This is Lebanon."

* * *

The following morning, I woke to see Chrissy poking her head into my bedroom. "Finally. I've checked on you at least five times. I know Sunday's the only day you can sleep in, but I think you've overdone it."

"What time is it?" I lifted my head, then let it fall back onto the pillow.

"That's not important. Get up. I want to see you."

Rima turned over in her bed. It couldn't be too late because she never slept past ten.

I shoved my feet into slippers, stepped out into the corridor, and closed the bedroom door. Christina walked ahead of me. "Your parents left to visit Teta. I've been sitting with Maria."

"Did you eat?" I asked.

"Yes, Maria made me an omelet. Should I ask her to make you one?"

"No. I just want coffee." I felt nauseated. I had a restless night. I headed to the family room, and Chrissy went to find Maria.

"Being back feels strange. Nothing has changed, yet everything's changed. Does this make sense?" Chrissy positioned herself at one end of the sofa, removed her shoes and tucked her feet up under her.

I nodded, and she continued, "I know parts of the city have suffered massive destruction, but here in Ras Beirut, there's not so much physical damage."

Tears clustered in my eyes.

"Oh, I'm sorry... I didn't mean it like that."

"It's okay." I wiped my eyes with the sleeve of my nightgown.

"Think about the good things—like me being here." Her voice sounded artificially upbeat. "It's only a matter of time before we find Joe. Everyone's working on it. Omar's father has many contacts in Syria, and he's using them all. I'm sure whoever has him knows he's a doctor and they're treating him well. Maybe that's why it's been difficult to find him. They need a doctor."

Maria entered, placed the tray of coffee down and retrieved a box of tissues. She handed it to me, hesitated a moment, and left. She wore her church clothes.

"How's LA? Who have you been seeing?" I needed to change the subject.

"It isn't the same without you. None of the old group of friends get together anymore. I called Donna, Janice and Laura before I left. They all said they wished they could be with you. Janice said to tell you both she and her mother pray daily for Joe."

"That's comforting because I'm too scared to truly pray. I want to get on my knees and beg, but what will happen if my prayers aren't answered?"

"It shouldn't stop you. You need faith."

"This time, it's too high risk. If Joe doesn't return, will I stop believing?"

"Don't think like that. Joe will return. By the way, Dan called me. One of his Lebanese friends told him about Joe. He asked if he should come to Beirut, but I told him I didn't think he could do anything to help. Although I didn't say it to him, I also thought it might be a liability having an American roaming around. He'd be a prime target for kidnappers. He said he'd called and left several messages for you." With an uncharacteristically loud gulp, she finished her coffee and put the demitasse on the table.

"I know. I can't bring myself to talk on the phone." I stared at the dark liquid in my cup. "I'd love to have Dan here— like our college days. But you're right, he shouldn't come." I looked up at Chrissy. "And Mark? Any news of him?"

"Nothing. It's like he disappeared into thin air. He really loved you. When you left, I think he felt the best way to deal with it was to cut off all contact."

"Sweet Mark. He's such a nice person—maybe too nice for me. But I wouldn't have survived the comfortable, predictable life. When I told him goodbye, I felt I'd never see him again. I hope he's found someone."

"He's a great guy. I'm sure lots of girls would love being with him."

I tightened my grip around the small porcelain cup. I envisioned the Getty. Mark's and my laughter echoed in my head. I placed my coffee cup down, untouched. "What's happening with Omar?"

"He's finally going to graduate in January. But he told his parents he'll finish in May. He wants to buy more time in LA."

"I can't believe his parents let him stay this many years."

"They don't care. They have lots of money. He's their only child, and they want to keep him happy. Eventually, he'll take over the family business." She leaned forward, put her head between her legs and shook out her hair. She removed an elastic band from her wrist and tied a ponytail. She flipped her hair back and straightened up.

"What'll you do when he leaves?"

"Get married and go back with him." She twisted her hair into a bun and reached into her purse for a hairpin.

"You will?" I knew it was the most likely scenario, but I dreaded the ramifications.

"I don't have a choice. You know that. I want to be with him, and he has no options."

"And your career? Your independence? You're the girl who swore she wouldn't live in the Middle East?" I realized I was shouting.

"When push came to shove, I realized how much I love him. I told him I'll convert to Islam to please his parents." She raised both hands and pulled the hairpin out. Her ponytail swung.

"Would you really?" I enunciated each word.

"You think I'd joke about something like this?" She sounded annoyed.

"Okay. What did he say?"

"That his parents wouldn't care if I convert because it isn't a religious requirement. A Muslim man can marry a Christian wife."

"And?"

"Well, he told me he loves me, but there's no rush to get married. He's right. We'll get married right before he returns."

"Are you going to tell your parents?"

"Not now. What good would it do? I'm here for a few days, and I don't want a showdown. Besides, I came for you."

"Okay. I guess you might as well wait before you devastate them?"

"I'm being realistic." She seemed to ignore my sarcasm. "Why don't you get dressed and come to my house for lunch? My parents keep asking about you."

"I don't feel like getting dressed or going out. Let's do it another time."

"When? I'm only here for two Sundays and who knows what'll happen next week. My mother's family from Aleppo might all decide to converge on us." I didn't answer, and she continued, "It's only my parents and us. You don't need to dress up. Do you want me to help you get ready?"

"No, it's okay. I'll get dressed." I knew she couldn't stay, and Rima always had Sunday plans. I didn't want to be alone.

Rima stood in front of the wardrobe mirror admiring herself from different angles. She smiled and asked how she looked.

"Like Audrey Hepburn—you look great. Where are you going?"

"To lunch with Sammy." The excitement in her voice evident.

"Chrissy's here. I'm having lunch at her house."

"I'll go keep her company while you get dressed." Rima ran out of the room. I got the impression she didn't want to talk about her plans. I wondered where she and Sammy were really going.

* * *

Half an hour later we were in Chrissy's parents' living room. The four of us sat in awkward silence. In the past, her father always engaged me in conversation about school or work.

"Isn't it wonderful to have Christina home?" My voice seemed to echo.

Amo Levon shifted his weight in the chair and his wife answered, "Yes, it is. Would you like a drink before lunch?"

"No thanks."

"Are you sure?" I waited for this usually talkative woman to continue, but she didn't.

"Yes, I'm sure." I twisted the gold bangles on my wrist.

Amo Levon slouched deeper into his chair. Chrissy moved to the edge of hers and straightened her posture. I felt I should say something, but I couldn't think of anything. I wished I'd stayed home.

"Okay," Chrissy finally shouted. "Just ask me? Ask me if I'm still with Omar? And tell me how much you hate him and all Muslims, and tell me again how I'm ruining my life."

"Christina," her mother began, "you know…"

For a split second I thought her father would explode. His face and eyes reddened. He pushed his clenched fists down on either side of him, stood up, walked to the door but turned around once he reached it.

"Christina." He spoke in a controlled voice. "You're wrong. I don't hate Omar and I don't hate Muslims. But maybe it's time to tell you something I haven't shared with you. I didn't want to burden you with the past. We're proud Armenians, and you know this, but you know nothing about my life before I met your mother. It is something I've never talked about."

Chrissy's shoulders slumped, and she raised her head slightly to look at his face.

"You know my parents died before you were born. You probably assumed I was born in Syria. I wasn't. I was born in Turkey into a wealthy, successful, and well-respected Armenian family."

From the way Chrissy cringed, I guessed she thought something bad had happened. We had studied in school about the Armenians in Turkey at the beginning of the century.

"Toward the end of World War I, everything changed when the Ottomans turned on the Armenians." Amo Levon paused. "My father was killed. My mother, my brother, my two sisters, and I were sent on the death march into the Syrian Desert. I was three years old. Only two members of my family survived—my father's sister and I. Kind Syrians provided us with food and shelter. Eventually, we made it to Aleppo. There, the large Armenian community welcomed us. They understood our suffering."

I kept my eyes fixed on Amo Levon. Many Armenians lived in Lebanon, but I had never heard a firsthand account of the Armenian Genocide.

"In spite of the reassurances of the community, my aunt didn't feel safe in Syria. Older and wiser people told her nothing had ever happened or would ever happen to the Armenians living there. She still didn't feel secure and wanted to live in a country where Christians were the majority—a place where she didn't have to live in fear of being massacred because of her religion. With the help of the church, we immigrated to Lebanon when I was seven."

He took a monogrammed handkerchief out of his jacket pocket and wiped his face. He seemed vulnerable. I felt the urge to comfort him, but at the same time, I wanted to bolt out the door and run down the street screaming. I remained motionless.

"I lost my family because of religion. I don't hold individuals responsible. Some of my best friends and your best friends are Muslims. That's the way it should be. But for me, after all we suffered, I cannot accept my only daughter will marry and have children who do not carry on our ways and traditions."

Chrissy walked to her father. They wrapped their arms around each other and wept.

CHAPTER 30

——

Lebanon—once an exquisite wine, now an empty bottle.

—*MAYA*

The twenty-two-year-old tea party tradition called for us to arrive at Leila's parents' apartment in our finest dress-up clothes and fancy hats. Sometimes I wore a sparkling dress with a pink feather boa. Chrissy often wore a tight lace suit and always carried a Mary Poppins umbrella. We acted oblivious to the looks people gave us as we walked on the city streets. Leila would welcome us with her finest British accent and escort us to the wide balcony overlooking both the sea and the mountains.

"Oh, isn't this lovely," Chrissy habitually said as she took her place at the table. She admired the perfectly arranged porcelain tea cups on the satin table cloth.

"Delightful," my line.

"Glad you could come, my dears." Leila's words were the signal for us to all burst into laughter.

Now, we recited our customary lines and then fell silent. Eight years since our last tea party, but this time, none of us dressed up for the occasion. Where three little girls once gathered in eccentric dresses now sat three twenty-seven-year-old women in jeans. Instead of talk, laughter, and dreams of the future, tight faces questioned how much control we had over our lives.

I looked at the emerald-green Mediterranean, dotted with ships, and then veered right to the blue-grey mountains. I imagined Joe escaping on a ship.

Cook caught my eye and smiled—not a happy one, but rather an expression of kindness and sympathy. He poured our tea, and a maid rolled out a black and gold cart filled with plates of tiny sandwiches and cakes.

"Let's not think." Leila's voice could probably be heard by the people on the balcony below. "Let's enjoy the here and now for a little while."

"I give us permission not to worry for fifteen minutes." Chrissy looked at her watch. "I'm the official timekeeper. Deal?"

Leila and I nodded.

My gaze moved back to the water. "I can't believe how many beautiful colors the Mediterranean takes on—from deep blue to light green. It's never ugly. I wonder why?"

"Well, at least something remains consistently beautiful." Chrissy popped a tiny cucumber sandwich into her mouth. "Besides us."

We laughed, and I felt my shoulders drop. I inhaled a deep breath of the moist, salty sea breeze and released it slowly.

"Try the scones with clotted cream." Chrissy finished her second one.

It felt heavy in my mouth, and I couldn't taste the thick raspberry jam I'd smeared on it. I reached for my teacup, and my friends grabbed theirs. We recited our standard toast. "Here's to tea parties forever."

Leila grinned. "It's like no time has passed—like we've been alive and together forever."

"I'm happy I came," Chrissy said. "If it hadn't been for your situation I wouldn't be here. I hope we'll always have each other until we're really old and ready to die."

"Speak for yourself," Leila said. "I'll never get old, and I'll never be ready to die."

"To never getting old." I raised my tea cup. "And to happy endings."

* * *

I dreamt of Joe that night. In my dream, he stared calmly into the eyes of a man about to shoot him. Virtue over scum. I screamed and sat up. Sweat dripped from my cold face. The pounding in my chest hurt my ears. I looked at Rima. Her expression serene, she hugged her pillow and turned over.

I crossed myself and whispered, "Dear Mary, dear Jesus, please don't let it be so." *Did God know I could muster up more of a prayer?* I wanted to wash my face and get a drink of water, but it was too cold to move through the warm night. I lay back, clenched the sheet, and looked at the dark ceiling.

In the morning, Sunday, October 23, we woke to the news. Suicide bombers had driven two trucks of explosives into the US Marine barracks in Beirut. Terrorists robbed hundreds of young American and French men of their futures and tossed their families into a valley of endless sorrow and pain.

The carnage happened on the airport road just across the street from my office on the only day I didn't work.

We stayed home. Visitors came. The radio news blasted.

"I don't like the Americans or the French foreign policy. They should not be here, but this is criminal—barbarian.

Each of those boys is a mother's son. My heart aches." Our elderly Palestinian neighbor reached for a tissue.

In the afternoon, Chrissy came to say she'd decided to return to LA the following day. "There's no telling what's going to happen. I can't risk not getting back to work."

Emotionally overwhelmed, I felt too numb to cry.

"I came to help you, but this trip ended up being more for me. It's the first time I understand my father and where he's coming from. He always seemed like a man who couldn't get beyond old-fashioned prejudices. But, God, when I think of the pain he and his family endured, it puts everything in a different perspective."

"So, what are you going to do?"

"I don't know. I feel different because I understand his suffering, but it takes the fire out of my rebellion. It complicates everything. I love Omar but now realize the choice is extremely painful for my family. Maya, what should I do?"

"I wish I knew. I only suggest you wait. Don't marry before he returns to Syria. Once you're separated, maybe you'll realize you can't live without him, or you'll decide to make your time together a memory. That's what you need to do—wait."

Chrissy sighed. "You're right."

"Time goes fast. Think of it this way, by this time next year, it will be settled." As I spoke, I couldn't help but wonder where I would be in a year. *Would I be celebrating or in despair?*

"I miss you in LA. When Joe's found, do you think he'll stay here or go to the US?"

"I don't know. He returned here because he knew he could make a difference, but now, I don't know. Oh God, I just pray he's safe and they haven't harmed him."

"Look, Maya, it's the one thing everyone agrees on. They think there's some group holding him as a bargaining chip. He'll be back. You have to keep your faith."

"It's so hard. I had a terrifying nightmare last night about him."

"You know dreams don't necessarily mean anything. And if your dream meant something, maybe it foreshadowed the tragedy early this morning."

Tears streamed down our cheeks. The pitiful attempted to comfort the pathetic—both in search of meaning where there was none.

* * *

The country returned to a paralyzed limbo. I didn't go to work for several days. The day I did, I came home in time for Chrissy's hysterical phone call. "Stop crying. I can't understand anything you're saying."

She sniffled. "The first days back were wonderful. I was still on vacation, and we drove to San Diego." Static filled the line. "And… married."

"You got married?" A popping noise singled a dead connection.

I tried to get a dial tone, but it might as well have been a toy phone. Occasionally it emitted a jingle but nothing more. Frustrated, I gave up and walked to Leila's.

"Is she crazy? I can't believe she'd be this stupid." Leila waived her hands in the air.

"I know. I thought she'd agreed to wait."

"I wonder how he convinced her. What do you think?"

"What is there to think? Stupid, stupid, stupid."

"Let's try to call her. You use this phone, and I'll use the one in the bedroom."

Amo Mohammad had insisted she install two separate phone lines.

On my first attempt, the operator answered, and on her third try, it connected. "Why'd you get married?' I shouted.

"I didn't get married. He got married. Omar's married."

"What?" Despite the fact she'd repeated it twice, I didn't understand.

"I told you. He's married."

"To you?"

"No. Not to me. I found a letter from his pregnant wife in Damascus."

"What?"

"I was looking for an old bill and found a letter stuffed in the back of a drawer. I couldn't believe it. I read it over and over. I confronted him when he got home. He didn't deny it. When he visited Syria last year, his mother selected a cousin as his bride. They'd wanted to surprise him with her. The original plan was for his father to stand in for him at the wedding and they would send her to LA as a gift."

"You're kidding. I thought they stopped doing these things ages ago."

"They obviously haven't. Can you believe it?"

"Why didn't she go back to LA with him?" My head hurt.

"Because the bastard was having fun with me. He told her she'd be lonely and homesick. She'd be happier waiting for him, and he'd return in a year or two."

"Do you think she knew about you?"

"What difference does it make? The stupid woman would have no choice in the matter. He's allowed four wives."

"Wow." I knew Chrissy suffered, but I felt relieved. Her dilemma was solved.

"I told him to get out of the apartment. He's staying with a friend."

"Look at the bright side. You don't have to make a decision."

I wondered if Omar's father would continue to search for Joe. I wanted to ask, but she probably didn't know.

"Bastard. I was willing to give up everything for him."

"I'm sorry. You know Leila and I are here for you. She's trying to call you from the other phone. I worried we'd be disconnected if I left to get her."

"I love you both—wish we were together."

"Me, too. Are you okay?"

"Yeah, I'm fine. Don't worry."

"Please take care of yourself. We'll talk soon." I didn't want to run up the phone bill and needed to tell Leila the news.

It was the first time I saw the bedroom she shared with Alex. The heavy curtains were drawn, and Leila sat on a brown and beige bed cover.

"You're not going to believe this. She didn't get married. Omar did."

"What?" She stood.

"Some cousin in Syria." I kept my voice controlled. "His mother arranged it, and he didn't tell Chrissy. She found a letter from her."

"I never liked him." Leila seemed to spit her words onto the floor. "Such an ass. Thank God she didn't marry him. I can't believe it." She stood and paced back and forth in the semi-dark room. "You think she's okay?"

"She seemed to be. At least she had the sense to throw him out."

Leila stopped pacing. "We need to call and make sure she's changed the locks."

"Tomorrow."

"Good idea. I guess it's been enough for today. Let's go sit on the balcony."

"You know, this is the first time I've been in your bedroom."

"Alex chose the furniture. It's too dark for my taste, but he wanted it this way—especially the drapes. He stays up late at night and sleeps during the day—the opposite of me. Anyway, that's how it was when he lived here."

"What do you mean when he lived here?"

"Things have gone from bad to worse. But let's not talk about it now. Chrissy's situation is much more interesting."

CHAPTER 31

———

War changed me, greedy, corrupt politicians changed me, and
ignorant religious leaders changed me. May God curse them all.

—*TANTE SAMIA*

The maid blocked the space between the frame and the edge
of the open door. "No one's here, Miss Maya. They're at the
hospital with mister."

"What do you mean they're at the hospital with mister? He
called me last night and asked me to come here after work."
Amo Mohammad always kept appointments. I pushed on the
door, she stepped back, and I entered the eerily quiet house.

"We were all awakened around four this morning by
madame's screams. I arrived first at the bedroom." She wiped
the corner of her right eye with a small cloth. "Mister lay in
the bed with his eyes wide open."

I leaned against the wall for support, too anxious
to breathe.

"His left arm was raised, and he kept turning his wrist in
front of his face as if trying to read his watch." She sped up
her words. "Madame shouted, 'What's wrong with him?' I
only thought to get him a glass of water. I rushed back, and

cook passed me in the hallway carrying mister. Madame had the car keys in her hand."

"What was wrong?" I wiped my damp hands on my straight-cut black skirt.

"I don't know. They told me to rush to Miss Leila's apartment and tell her to meet them at the hospital. The phones weren't working."

"Then what happened?" I breathed rapidly.

"I came back home, miss."

I ran out of the apartment, back down the stairs and seven blocks in my high heels to the American University Hospital where, I assumed, they took him.

The lady at the desk flipped through pages of patient names and gave me his room number.

I raced to the elevator and sighed aloud when the door shut before I reached it. I banged the call button multiple times and shifted my weight from foot to foot. I half expected Joe to grab me from behind.

The moment the door opened on the fifth floor, I saw Leila at the end of the corridor. As always, she was the focal point. Her hair pulled into a ponytail highlighted her perfect features. People clustered around her in a visitor waiting area. She met my eye.

"What's wrong? What happened?" I mouthed the words, raised my hands and twisted my wrists. She reached me, and we wrapped our arms around each other.

"They say it's a stroke." Emotion shook her as a sob escaped.

"Can I see him?"

"The rules allow one person in his room, but I was there with my mother and no one said anything. I tried to get her to take a break, but she refused. Besides she doesn't want to sit with the visitors. I wish my brothers weren't traveling."

Tante Samia stood up when I entered the room where Amo Mohammad lay in the hospital bed. "Maya. Oh Maya. Look what's happened to us." Her pale skin exposed fine lines across her unmade-up face framed by disheveled hair. Her normally spry body slouched. For the first time, she appeared frail to me.

"God is generous, Tante Samia. God willing, he'll recover," I surprised myself parroting the phrases I'd heard thousands of times from the lips of old women.

"It's true. God is generous, but all I see is blackness in front of me. God willing, I'm wrong."

I reached for Amo Mohammad's listless hand and bent over to kiss his forehead, where his hair had receded. I whispered, "Amo, we love you. We need you with us. Please get better. I know if it's in your hands, you will. We're patient; we can wait. Just please get well." He squeezed my fingers weakly. I don't think it was my imagination.

I wiped the moisture from my face and turned to Tante Samia. "Maya, he loves you like his own daughter. To him, you are the perfect child: smart, kind, hardworking, loving, loyal, and a pleasure to be around. Sometimes I think he loves you more than our own children. You are his child by choice."

"I love him, too." I looked back at the pale, serene, once-grand man who now looked tiny and helpless in the bed. I ached with sadness.

"Sit with me." She patted the seat beside her on the under-sized couch.

Silently, we focused on the man lying before us. I longed for Joe. His competence and reassuring manner would have made things seem better. I hit the sofa with my fist. Tante Samia didn't seem to notice.

The door opened, and a nurse entered. We both sat up straighter. She ignored us, walked to the IV stand, and timed the drip by her watch. She placed a blood pressure cuff on his arm, pumped it up, and listened with her stethoscope. She found his pulse and looked back at her watch. While she shook the mercury down on the thermometer, Tante Samia broke the silence. "How is he?"

"Stable, madame," she answered in English. "This is good for now, madame." She gave us a tight smile. I wondered if she and other Filipino nurses regretted signing contracts to work in Lebanon.

"Tante Samia, it's seven. Why don't you go home? Leila and I will stay with Amo tonight. I'll go tell my parents and get clothes."

She didn't move. I put my arm around her shoulders. "Please go. You have to save your strength because Amo needs you." I gave her a gentle push, and we stood up together. We exited into the crowd of people seated in the visitor waiting area.

"Samia, my darling." A woman with a small face and a pointed nose rose from a chair and took a step in our direction, but Tante Samia kept her eyes focused on the ground, and the woman stepped back to let us pass. No one else moved except Leila and Ali who followed us to the elevator. The buzz of whispering voices filled the air—*haram*, poor woman.

"Ali will drive you home and return for you after he takes my mother home."

"It's easier if I walk. It'll only take me a few minutes. Do you need anything?"

By the time I returned, only Leila remained. We put on slippers and picked at the food I'd brought. We sat on the couch facing Amo Mohammad's bed, propped our feet up on chairs and covered them with blankets. I drifted off to sleep longing for Joe. I woke abruptly when a monitor beeped. A nurse rushed in, made adjustments, and left. Through the ajar door, we heard her speak with someone in a low voice. I wandered out. Both she and a doctor greeted me. I asked about new developments and both ladies shook their heads. I continued down the hallway to fetch hot tea.

At five, we realized neither of us would get any sleep. Leila went to buy *manakish*—hot pita bread topped with thyme, sesame seeds and olive oil. I ate and left to catch the bus to work.

In the afternoon, the situation remained much the same, except Leila's brothers had arrived and taken charge of the visitor situation. They filled the role of family crisis hosts. People spoke in hushed voices. "*Inshallah*," God willing, rode periodically above the low chatter. Chocolates and sweets were offered to the entire group every time a new visitor arrived.

I greeted each person and sat with the group for a few minutes before I slipped into Amo Mohammad's room. Leila and her mother stood on the far side of the bed looking out of the window. They turned to face me, and I stepped back, intending to leave, but Leila waved me over.

"I'll come back later."

"No, we need your opinion now." I felt unnerved by Tante Samia treating me as Amo Mohammad did, instead of in her usual aloof manner. "Alex has disappeared. Any decent man would be with his family at a time like this. We know he's aware of what's happened. One of Leila's friends told him." Her black eyes were glossed in anger.

Leila glanced out the window.

"I say we should send him an ultimatum. This is an embarrassment for the family. Leila disagrees. She says we shouldn't force him to come." She looked at Leila, but I knew I was the one expected to reply.

"I agree with Leila. Leave him be." I worried about his attitude or what he might say or do if a demand was made.

"Fine. But he brings shame on our family."

"Maya will you walk home with me? I want to see Karim before the nanny puts him to sleep." Leila turned and left.

"Do you need anything, Tante Samia?"

"Will you ask my sister Maha to come in?" Her voice faltered.

We exited the building, and Leila burst out. "I needed to get away. I don't know how much more I can take. My father's barely hanging on to life, my stupid mother's worried about what people will say, and my bastard husband is an ass. God, I wish I knew what he's doing. How did everything get so screwed up?"

I focused on avoiding the cracks in the sidewalk. It was difficult. Time had worn many into it, but it freed me from thinking of something to say.

Leila didn't appear to notice my silence, because she talked and I watched out for sidewalk cracks until we reached her building.

"Enjoy Karim."

"Don't you want to see him?"

"I'd love to, but I'm too tired. I had a rough day at work, and I still have tests to correct."

"Thanks, Maya. Thanks for everything."

I turned away, engrossed with the task at hand. *If you step on a crack, you break your back.*

Papa greeted me. "Your mother and I visited Mohammad today. Samia insisted we spend time in his room. I didn't like what I saw. He was awake but didn't seem to comprehend anything."

"You think it's very bad?"

"I'm guessing he has serious brain damage, but God willing, I'm wrong. Why don't you take a shower before we have drinks and a bite? Rima's helping Maria prepare a surprise."

I wanted to climb into bed, but I knew I would become more depressed.

Onion tart was not the treat I hoped for, but after my third glass of wine, the world receded and it tasted delicious. Sorrow subsided, and I basked in the comfort of family. My students would have to wait for their grades.

* * *

I arrived at the hospital the following evening around seven o'clock. I rushed through the empty visitors' area and into Amo Mohammad's room. Tante Samia sat alone.

"Maya, what are you doing here? The situation's bad. Didn't you hear there were two explosions?"

I shook my head. "No, where? I was in class and then I met with students."

"Next to the British Bank."

"Are there casualties?" I felt weighed down.

"So far, one person dead and many injured. They were brought here. I insisted our visitors leave. Ali drove some home, and he's coming back for me. We'll take you home."

"How's Amo?"

"He was agitated and making grunting noises. They gave him something to help him sleep. He had another scan this afternoon, and they had a difficult time because he wouldn't stay still. By the time they finished, the radiologist had left. God willing, we'll know the results tomorrow."

"You must be tired."

"Fatigue is nothing if the end result is good. Do you know tomorrow we will have been married for thirty-five years? December 5, 1948."

"Wow. I hope you'll be together another thirty-five."

"How everything's changed. It used to be simple. We were better people. We liked someone for who they were. Small things made us happy."

"If the war ends, maybe things can return to how they were." I wanted to believe my words.

"No, it will never be the same. The people we've lost won't come back, and I don't mean the dead. I'm speaking about all of the Lebanese who left. The majority won't return—like my best friend. Did I ever tell you about Sara?"

"No." *When did you ever tell me anything?* Only Leila and Amo Mohammad made me feel part of the family. Until lately, she always seemed indifferent to me.

"Sara was the rabbi's daughter, and we grew up in the same apartment building. Born within two days of each other, we were inseparable. We played together, shared secrets, and celebrated both Jewish and Muslim holidays with equal joy. Her father always said to mine, 'If we switched Samia and Sara, we wouldn't know a different child was in the house.'" She smiled at the last sentence. "When I married Mohammad, Sara was more excited than my own sisters. We had arranged marriages in those days, but she told me I couldn't have found a better man if I'd searched the whole world." She looked fondly at her sleeping husband.

I followed her gaze. "This I know."

"As close as you and Leila are, it's nothing compared to Sara and me. She stayed in the room with me for the births of all my children. It wasn't common, like it is now, to have someone with you, but she insisted and the medical staff gave up. She was a free spirit and no matter how hard her parents tried, she refused to marry. She became a reporter, but her passion was poetry. She wrote mostly in French and published several books."

"Did she write under her own name?"

"Strange you should ask because oftentimes she didn't. She used her name for her poetry but wrote political essays and novels under a pseudonym. I think people knew, though. She held poetry reading cocktail parties at the Phoenicia and Le Vendome hotels."

"It must have been nice." I remembered the LA dinner conversation with Jeff about the Phoenicia's pool-bar. It could have taken place in another lifetime.

Tante Samia looked wistful. "In the early sixties, Beirut was a shining pearl—the Paris of the Middle East. Cultural events, intellectual politics, espionage, business deals, banking, celebrities, writers, artists—you name it. Beirut had it." She shook her head. "And then on June 5, 1967, the Six-Day War took my best friend away."

"She died?"

"No, no. God forbid. It marked the turning point. Her family and many other Jewish people felt they no longer had a future in their own homeland because of their religion. Her father arranged for one of her sisters to marry a distant cousin in New York. Soon after her parents got green cards and in turn, all their children did. Sara and her father were the last to leave. She didn't want to go, but he wouldn't leave without her."

"Didn't she come back to visit? Didn't you go to visit?"

"No. Life was busy, and we kept saying, next year. We wrote long detailed letters, but they became fewer and fewer until no more."

Her voice trailed off, and I couldn't think of anything to say. I looked at the floor tiles, counted them in each direction and multiplied the numbers in my head.

"You're probably wondering how I changed this much. War changed me. Greedy, corrupt politicians changed me, and ignorant religious leaders changed me. I listened to them and because of the environment we live in—one of uncertainty and fear—they made sense. May God curse them all. The blood of innocents is on their hands and…"

A knock on the door stopped her mid-sentence. Ali peered in. "I'm back, madame."

"We're ready to go. How are the streets?"

"Empty—except for armed men."

Tante Samia kissed her husband, and I noticed a tear on his forehead as we left into the empty, fear-filled night.

CHAPTER 32

Once reason conquers passion, the mind rules the heart.

—*MAYA*

"Do you think he knows where Joe is?" I tried to keep up with Papa's pace on the narrow city sidewalk.

"*Inshallah*. God willing. This man has good connections and comes highly recommended. I'm somewhat hopeful. But only God knows." The path widened, and he stopped. I took his hand and, for a brief moment, my world felt a little brighter.

We climbed the stairs in the rickety, dusty building. One of the two doors on the third-floor landing stood open, and a receptionist, who looked about my age, banged on the keys of an Arabic typewriter. She returned the carriage with her left hand, flipped back her long black hair, and looked up at us.

"Is Sayad Tariq available?" Papa inquired.

"Welcome and take a rest. I'll tell him you're here."

She knocked on the door behind her desk and entered. We sat down on chairs lining the wall.

She emerged. "He'll be with you shortly. How do you like your coffee?"

"Medium." Papa answered for both of us about the amount of sugar we preferred in Turkish coffee.

She walked to the entrance, and I noticed how stylish she looked in her tight skirt, fitted shirt, and high heels. *Knock-offs—the women in her type of job earned very low salaries.* "Two coffees, medium," she yelled into the stairwell.

She sat and typed. I watched the right to left motion of the typewriter. *Why is Arabic written backward—or is English written backward? Why is there no letter p in Arabic? Did I learn why in school or are there no answers?*

A teenage boy entered carrying a tray. He placed a glass of water and a demitasse in front of each of us and left as the receptionist's phone buzzed. "Kindly go in." She motioned to the closed door behind her while she walked to the open entrance to yell for the boy. He returned, put everything back on the tray, and followed us.

"You are most welcome." Tariq stood to greet us. We sat in the two chairs facing his desk. The boy put the coffee and water on a low table between us.

"How is your health?" Papa began with a traditional greeting.

"Good. Thanks be to God. And you, Amo?" Tariq leaned into his black leather chair. His belly protruded.

He had nodded to me when we entered, but now focused entirely on Papa. Although we had come for a specific purpose, he continued the customary small talk. I shifted in my chair, anxious to find out what this pudgy man might know.

Ten minutes later, he finally said, "Amo, the doctor you are looking for is alive and well. I know people who have seen him."

My heart pounded. I formed fists and dug my nails into my palms. *Thank you, dear God, thank you.* My brain churned and my eyes blurred. I tried to focus on his words.

"It's a complicated situation." He lit a cigarette and took a long puff. "Those holding him are doing it for political reasons. I've inquired about buying his freedom, but they aren't interested. However, you understand, money is needed to keep the channels open."

"Naturally."

"Also, they don't want a hostage swap. Although I think we might be able to leverage this." He stopped talking and looked directly at Papa. "Amo, perhaps this is best discussed between men and the young lady would be more comfortable with Aida."

I wanted to jump across the desk, grab his stubby neck, hit his punching-bag belly and call him choice names. Instead, I stood, and to conceal my desires, I avoided looking at him. I didn't want to put Papa in an awkward situation.

Aida filed a broken nail. "Stupid typewriter." She spoke to no one. "A man must have designed it. Men think they're smart. They don't know how stupid they really are."

She raised her hand in front of her face to check her nail. On her desk, a bottle of bright red nail polish sat next to one of *Wite-Out*.

"Would you like something to drink?" She didn't look at me.

"No, thanks."

"What did he tell you? He has man talk?" she mocked. "Men are idiots. They think they run everything, but they don't. We do, and they're not smart enough to realize it."

I sat further back in the chair. This was the first time I heard anyone say they knew someone who'd seen Joe. I wondered if I could find this person, trail him and locate Joe. Hope pulsated through my body.

Aida, like a ditzy butterfly, fluttered in my peripheral vision.

"Two 7-Ub," she yelled into the corridor. "7-Ub makes you feel better." She stood facing me. "You need one and I need one."

The boy appeared and placed an empty glass on the table next to me and one on Aida's desk. He produced a bottle opener from his pocket. Americans would have put ice in the glass, but here soft drinks were chilled because ice dilutes the flavor.

Aida began typing, and I got lost in the rhythmic hammer noises of type bars striking the platen. I imagined my reunion with Joe. *Would he be the same? Had they tortured him? Had they played mind games with him?* The pathways in my brain felt clogged.

Twenty minutes later, Papa emerged and bent down to kiss my forehead.

"I'm sorry, miss," Tariq said. "But I didn't want to burden you with man talk."

I looked up at him and nodded. He was the closest I'd come to Joe. As much as I wanted to hate him, I couldn't.

"I'll be in contact with you soon, Amo." He walked us to the door.

We passed Aida's desk and Papa thanked her. I turned back to wave goodbye just in time to see her stick her tongue out at Tariq's back. She smiled and winked at me. I liked her.

* * *

Days and nights became increasingly tense. Fear crept into every aspect of life, like thick syrup filling cracked surfaces. Attacks on US reconnaissance flights elicited gunfire on December 14 and 15 from the *USS New Jersey*, a once-mothballed World War II and Vietnam War battleship brought back to life in the Mediterranean. Destruction erupted from the earth, rained from the sky and crashed in from the sea.

Teta arrived on the twenty-fourth, and we attended an afternoon Christmas mass with security guards both inside and around the church. Meanwhile, Bob Hope performed on the *USS New Jersey* and attended mass at sea. On land and water, people prayed for peace and grasped at dismal rays of promise.

On the walk home, I gazed to the left, in the direction of Cana. *Dear Jesus, you performed your first miracle down the road. Won't you please work another one?* The Mediterranean looked black.

Selma and her children joined us for a mellow evening. We sang carols, drank mulled wine, ate delicacies and gave our still-grieving cousins many gifts. Later, we headed to bed to dream of brighter Christmases.

Santa left presents for Rima and me. Teta gave us each five hundred dollars. Maman set the brunch table with china, crystal, silver and surprise gag gifts. Then Christmas finished.

* * *

Rima and Sammy begged me to attend an overnight New Year's Eve party with them, but I refused. Papa and Maman insisted I spend the evening with them at our neighbors'.

After dinner, around eleven, I descended the steps, guided by the rays of my flashlight. Maria had stayed at her friend's apartment. I sat alone in our cold, dark house. The thoughts I'd silenced throughout the evening now shouted at me. I slumped into the chair in the foyer and cried.

Does Joe know it was New Year's Eve? Is he being held in an apartment, a house, or an underground prison? Is he hungry, cold, or frightened? If only I could hold him one more time, I'd never let go.

The realization Maman and Papa would soon be home made me get up and go to bed.

The following day, Maman greeted the New Year with defiance. "They won't defeat us." She arranged platters on the dining room table in preparation for her annual open house. "I refuse to cancel. We've hosted this event every year since we married in 1952."

Tante Mona took in a long breath and let it out slowly. She continued to roll forks and knives in cloth napkins and tie them up with silvery ultramarine ribbon. They complemented the intricate embroidered traditional Syrian *aghabani* tablecloth—deep blue cotton cloth filigreed with silver threads.

I watched Maman, Maria, a hired waiter, and a cook scurry around. Maman paid attention to the details. We didn't have the most extravagant parties, and people could never pinpoint why they were among the best. But Maman knew her meticulous planning ensured success. She left nothing to chance, especially the lighting. It made the difference, like a secret ingredient in a recipe.

Tante Mona tied the last bow and sat down at the table. "I'm afraid it's going to be a hard year. I can't get rid of the bad feeling in my bones."

"Oh, Mona. Why are you pessimistic?" Maman lit the candles on the table.

"I think I'm realistic. Everyone else seems delusional. But maybe that's the only way we can live here." She stood and pushed the chair to the wall to allow the guests unimpeded access to the buffet table.

"Lebanon survives on optimism and hope. It's New Year's Day. Let's celebrate and, of course, pray for better days." Maman adjusted the dinner on the light switch.

"You're right." Tante Mona looked at me. "Today, let's forget all our worries and enjoy ourselves."

I smiled weakly and helped move the remaining chairs away from the table.

Soon two small clusters of people stood in the room. I joined the group where Papa stood in time to hear Tante Mona's horrified question. "She was murdered?"

A man stepped aside to make room for me to join the circle. I leaned forward to hear about this latest tragedy. The man I didn't know spoke. "I heard a couple of old people with her were also killed. I don't know the details."

"She was the midwife who delivered me. She's probably in her eighties now." Tante Mona's voice sounded weak.

"She delivered me, too. It seemed like she was the midwife for every woman in the Chouf. Everyone loved her. I don't know who would commit such a crime." The man shook his head and looked down at the rug.

"A Christian shouldn't have stayed in a Druze area. People are only safe living with their own kind." The woman in a red dress slid caviar toast into her mouth.

"What are you talking about?" The man, who had just spoken, looked at her. "I'm Druze, and I loved her like a mother. We all loved her. Whoever committed this crime is not Lebanese. It's someone who wants to set us against one another, and we're too stupid to realize it."

He walked away and sat alone on the end of a sofa in the living room. He placed his head in his hands. Tante Mona followed and sat beside him—a Christian and a Druze who had both begun their lives aided by the same woman.

Tante Lina, Maman's eccentric friend, must have been in the room all along, but when I noticed her, she stood by the open French doors separating the living and dining rooms. The sight of her all decked out, hair swept up in a *My Fair Lady* hairdo, heavy Cleopatra eye makeup, and a sequined ballroom gown fitted tightly to her tall, lean frame made me smile. Her cigarette rested in a golden holder whose length competed with her brightly polished nails.

"Maya, darling." Her voice sultry like a Hollywood starlet. "Please ask the waiter to bring me champagne and smoked salmon." She walked to where Tante Mona sat by the man and situated herself on the other end of the sofa. He glued his eyes on her, his mouth slightly agape.

"We're all on the same road," she spoke as if addressing the entire room. "Maybe those who die sooner are the lucky ones. But since we're still here, let's make the best of it and refrain from sad thoughts." She took two glasses of champagne from the waiter's tray and handed them to Tante Mona and the man. "Drink to the moment, and I guess in some perverse way, let's drink to the new year." She drained her glass in one gulp and grabbed another.

I reached for a glass. An unknown number of drinks later, with the house still full of guests, I crept into my room and fell into a warm dreamless sleep.

* * *

"Malcom Kerr is dead—assassinated." Mama greeted me with slow, heavy words. She and Tante Mona sat in the plush leather chairs of the family room.

Tante Mona spoke in a throaty low voice. "He was born here, grew up here, met the woman he loved here, and died here—an American, but truly a Lebanese. I told you, I felt it in my bones. 1984 is not a good year, and it's only January 18."

Hours earlier, Malcom Kerr, the president of the American University of Beirut, was murdered in his campus office building. My thoughts drifted to the bright spring day a few years earlier when I'd met him as a professor at UCLA. His eyes had lit up at the mention of Beirut and now they had been extinguished forever in the city he loved. I sat, pulled a blanket tightly around my shoulders, crossed my arms, and rocked back and forth.

"Poor Ann." Mama had known Malcom's wife since the mid-1950s when she came as an American student to AUB.

"And their children. What a tragedy. Are they here or in America?"

Maman didn't seem to hear Tante Mona.

Maria entered with a tea tray. She set it on a table, poured a cup, and sat next to me on the sofa. She pressed her body against mine in a gesture of comfort. I stopped rocking. She handed me a cup of tea and watched me take a sip. She stood, served the two ladies, put another log in the fireplace, and left.

Maybe I should have been, but I wasn't prepared for Papa's suggestion a few days later. "I think it would be a good idea for you to return to America until things improve here." I didn't answer and he continued, "The situation is rapidly deteriorating. I know you want to find Joe, but there's little you can do now. We have people working on his case. Maman and I would feel better knowing you're safe."

"What are you talking about?" I shook my head. "You're all here. Why shouldn't I be?"

"Things are especially rough. A break of a few months will do you good."

I didn't realize I'd clenched my fists and jaw until I felt the pain.

"Think about it," he continued. "You're only teaching one class next semester. Maybe another instructor can add it to their schedule. And the airline is offering unpaid leave to employees. When things improve, you can return. Just consider it. Okay?"

I felt like a cartoon character flattened by a fast-moving car. "All right, Papa, I'll think about it."

"That's my girl." He leaned over and kissed my forehead. "I'm going to visit Leila. I'll be back for lunch."

The bright sun disguised the chilly Sunday morning. I walked, head down, and collided with a man coming from the opposite direction.

"Maya, where're you going in such a hurry?"

"Oh, I'm sorry… Mounir." I looked up at the handsome face I'd spent many high school hours dreaming about. "I haven't seen you in ages. You must also be in a hurry, or you wouldn't have run into me."

"Or maybe I did it on purpose. Seriously, Maya, you should pay more attention to your surroundings when you're walking on a street."

"I guess I let my mind wander."

"Would you like to come over?" He gestured to his house.

This tall, lean man, although twelve years older than me, didn't look his age. He'd always treated Rima and me like younger cousins. Growing up, every first Sunday of March, we celebrated our *Annual Greatest Neighbor Event* at his house. His mother served fancy treats, and he told funny stories about silly people or animals. We all enjoyed a memorable afternoon.

"Sure, but I can't stay long."

"A cup of coffee, a bit of catching up, and you can be on your way."

He unlocked a solid metal gate in a long stone wall bordering the sidewalk to reveal a lush garden and a villa perched on a small hill. We climbed wide steps to the elegant structure. The entire complex, the only single-family house remaining on a street of apartment buildings, was hidden from view. Mounir rang the doorbell and a butler opened. We entered a high-ceilinged living room where arched windows and glass doors framed a landscaped yard. A home built for a wealthy family during the Ottoman rule.

Mounir asked the servant to bring coffee to his living room. Although he and his mother lived in the same house, he maintained separate, smaller quarters.

"You've changed the furniture." I sat on a low settee built along three of the walls.

"When were you last here, Miss Maya?"

"Probably when I thought a lollipop was the best treat in the world."

"Hard to believe you're all grown up. I wish you had a better world to live in. I'm sorry about Joe. I know my cousin Mohammad was very involved in locating him. I don't have political connections, but several family members who do continue to work on this. If not for you, for Mohammad who is well-respected and loved."

"Yes, I know. Everyone is very kind."

The butler returned with coffee. The small sugar bowl on the tray indicated it was made without. I preferred sweetener dissolved in the boiling water with the powdered coffee grounds. It tasted smoother.

Without thinking, I blurted. "This morning Papa said I should return to America." I immediately wished I could grab back the words.

"He's right. You should leave."

"What do you mean I should leave? I need to be here for Joe."

Mounir remained quiet for a few seconds before he answered. "I wish you remaining would help find Joe, but you can't do anything at this time. If there was, I'd be the first to insist you stay."

"But..."

"Actually, we should all leave. Look around you. Everything has changed. This isn't our country anymore. We thought we had a real chance when the multinational forces came in, but they, too, suffered and gave up. I think the Americans will pull their troops out soon."

"How can we give up?"

"No one's more patriotic than me. For generations my family has lived here. We're the Sunni Muslims of West Beirut. I never thought I'd say this, but let me put it to you this way. Imagine this room filling up with water. Although it might be uncomfortable, at first you can manage. Soon you realize if you're not a fish, you'd better get out, and if you don't, you'll drown."

One of Lebanon's most eligible bachelors looked me straight in the eye. "You know I've always loved you like a little sister and I only want the best for you. It's time for you to go."

I stood to leave. He hugged me tightly then walked me to the gate.

Unless you're a fish, you'd better get out. Unless you're a fish, you'd better get out. My mind chanted all the way to Leila's.

Tante Samia met me at the door. "He just sits." She motioned to her husband in the adjacent room. "He grunts but can't say a word. Sometimes I swear he understands everything, and at other times I don't think he comprehends anything."

I went to Amo Mohammad, kissed him, held his hand, and sat on the satin chair beside his wheelchair.

Leila moved close to me. "Does he look better?"

I gave the answer she wanted to hear, but in truth, I didn't notice any change from a few days earlier. "What do the doctors say?"

"What do they know?" She spoke with a trace of contempt. "They say there's no hope. He has severe left hemisphere damage. But I think he's improving. We have an amazing therapist who comes every day. She's noticed he responds to music. When he hears a familiar song, he smiles and moves his head to the beat. It's like he's back to his old self."

"God willing." I looked at the helpless man next to me. "This morning Papa told me I should go back to the US."

"Yes, I know."

"How do you *know*?" I emphasized the last word.

"I saw him a couple of days ago on the street. He's worried about you. He thinks it would be good for you to take a break from all the tragedy here. As much as I don't want you to go, I agree with him. It would do you good to leave for a while."

My head hurt, and I suddenly felt cold.

"Are you okay?" I nodded and she continued, "Baba believed, in times like this, the Lebanese who leave are the most valuable to our country."

"What?"

"Think about it. If everyone stayed, we'd all be victims, but those who leave provide support. They carry our voices and our predicament to the world. They get good jobs in hospitals, in government, in industry, and they assist those who remain. They send money to their families, fund students and universities, and help medical graduates locate positions for residencies abroad. This is critical for Lebanon's survival."

I looked at Amo Mohammad and wished he could personally tell me. Suddenly, I realized his wisdom and kindness had begun to blossom in both his daughter and wife.

* * *

A week later, I stood on the sidewalk with my family, friends, and neighbors. Mounir, a few feet away, leaned on the stone wall that hid his villa and watched Ali load my suitcases into the car. The long farewell began with kisses and blessings. I'd insisted no one accompany me on the risky trip to the airport.

The car pulled away from the small crowd. Maman and Papa stood close together and waved. Leila had her arm around a crying Rima.

* * *

"Why are you weeping, miss?" The immigration officer held my passport. I didn't answer and he continued, "Thank God you can leave. We can't."

"Maybe you're luckier because you have no choice."

"No, miss, people with choices are the blessed ones." His words sounded kind. "May Allah protect you."

I opened my mouth, but my voice caught. Instead, I nodded at him and squeezed his hand in thanks when he handed me my documents.

The wheels of the plane lifted. I turned my face away from the window and shut my eyes. This time I didn't bid farewell to my ancient land and its sparkling sea.

PART III

LOS ANGELES, FEBRUARY, 1984

PARIS, MAY, 1984

NEW YORK, JANUARY, 1985

CHAPTER 33

————

LOS ANGELES, FEBRUARY, 1984

Are people randomly born somewhere or is there a great plan?

—*MAYA*

"Girl, don't you got no umbrella?" I spun toward the familiar voice.

"Janice. What are you doing here?"

"You think I'd miss the chance to greet you?" She hugged me tightly. "I'm glad you're here and safe and sound. C'mon, Chrissy's in the car."

Had it been raining when the plane landed? I never looked out. *You failed to greet the mighty Pacific, so perhaps it sent water to welcome you.* This whimsical notion brought a faint smile—the first one in days. An airport with no armed men and no nervous people felt strange.

Straining, Janice picked up a suitcase, and I lifted the second one. Despite the weight, she maneuvered expertly around people on the crowded sidewalk. I wasn't as skilled and apologized multiple times.

A group of Japanese tourists walked past trailing their guide with her oversized umbrella. I marveled at their identical upright wheeled suitcases—four small wheels on the bottom and a handle perched on the top. Each person pushed a vertical case alongside themselves, as if parading in twos. I hadn't imagined such a thing. *What kind of ergonomist was I not to have thought of wheels on luggage?* I'd bought my large blue suitcases because of the TV advertisement with a gorilla throwing one around, unable to break it.

I looked down at the cracks and dents in my American Tourister, and in my head I composed a letter to the company. *Enclosed are three pictures—one of your damaged suitcases and one of me. I want to show you what this gorilla did to your luggage. Alleged strength has lost to innovation. Check out the Japanese…the third picture.*

Chrissy jumped out of her Toyota, ignoring the downpour. She embraced me firmly, and I reciprocated. For the first time in a long time, I felt less vulnerable in a safe place.

The two girls lifted the suitcases into the trunk as I watched. Janice held the front passenger door open for me, but I didn't notice. Chrissy put her arm around my waist and gently directed me.

I looked out the window. *How can two places in the same world be this different?*

"How's the empire?" Chrissy referred to the transit night I'd spent in London.

"It's still there." *Are people randomly born somewhere or is there a great plan? How simple it would've been if I had been born here.*

"And Her Majesty?"

"She's well, but I didn't have time to visit her." It used to be fun when we pretended like this, but it wasn't anymore.

"Remember, my dear," Chrissy spoke in a British accent. "In the end only five queens will remain. The four in the deck of cards and the queen of England."

"What?" Janice asked.

"It's an old joke."

"Are you hungry?" Chrissy moved to the right lane.

"Not really."

"I don't have food in the fridge. I thought we'd stop to eat, but Janice left her car at my place and needs to get home. I figured we'd pick up something. Any preference?'

"No. I'm not hungry." I gazed out the front windshield, suddenly feeling very tired but strangely enervated not having to be alert to my surroundings.

"Well, we're going to get something." I recognized Chrissy's determination.

"Anything's fine."

"I know, we'll get comfort food from Marie Callender's— chicken pot pie and apple pie. The food you love. It'll make you feel better."

She pulled up to the restaurant and ran through the rain as Janice and I watched.

"Girl." Janice leaned forward. Her face almost touched the back of my head, and her breath stirred the hair on my neck. "I'm sorry you lost your man. My friend Marcy's man was shot dead last week, and she's got two kids. She's the second friend this has happened to in the past month. But Chrissy says maybe your man's still alive somewhere. Mama's praying for him."

"Thanks." I looked at the light smudging on the wet car windows and wished she hadn't said anything. She placed her hand on my left shoulder, and I cried.

"You gotta pray. It's all we got."

I opened my mouth but only nodded.

"John called a department meeting last week. He told everyone you're coming back to work on the joint Boeing/FAA project. People are happy. You know they all like you. You're nice to everyone."

Again, I didn't answer. She patted my shoulder, sat back, and left me alone in my hollow of melancholy. My eyes burned, and I felt nauseated. The flight left Beirut Wednesday morning, and I'd spent a restless night at a London airport hotel. No same-day connection existed, and the airline paid for the stay, but I'd skipped the meals. During the eleven-hour flight to LA, I didn't even try to crane my neck to see the inflight movie on the small aisle screen. I probably should've made myself watch the *Curse of the Pink Panther*. Maybe I would have smiled. I used to enjoy entertainment.

Janice coughed. I remembered where I was and felt bad for ignoring her. I turned around to ask about her daughter.

Chrissy returned with two bags. "Small one's for you, Janice."

"You didn't need to get me nothing." Janice sounded touched. "How much I owe you?"

"My treat."

"Aw, thanks."

A few minutes later, Chrissy steered through a lush land-scaped area. "You're really going to like my new apartment. I'm moving up in the world and have two large bedrooms. I'm glad we'll be roommates again."

"I still haven't grasped what's happening. Everything seems strange. I'm not even sure I should be here or where I belong."

"Girl, you belong here with us—at least for now." Janice opened the car door. "I gotta go."

She clutched her purse and the paper bag close to her chest and hurried through the drizzle.

Chrissy and I carried the suitcases into the apartment. I opened one. I wanted a long, hot shower.

"Red or white?" Chrissy held two wine bottles in front of me the moment I came out.

"Red." I knew if I didn't choose, she'd open both.

"Let's dedicate tonight to relaxing and being thankful for our friendship."

We clinked glasses, and I gladly took a big swallow.

"I've taken the day off tomorrow. We can spend a long weekend together before you start work."

Pot pie comforted my palate, and wine calmed my mind. I sat deeper in the brown corduroy chair and steadied my plate. The room's brown, silver, and orange colors blurred together. Two shiny frames ran around abstract paintings and screamed for attention. I felt the urge to rip them off the strangled artwork.

"Maya. You've stopped eating."

The frames receded, beaten back by Billy Joel's blaring song on the radio. I rested my head on the back of the chair.

* * *

"Are you feeling okay?" Chrissy stood at the door of my bedroom.

I looked at my watch, closed my eyes, and opened them again 10:30 a.m.

"I don't remember coming to bed."

"You kind of passed out. I helped you stand, and you were awake enough to brush your teeth—sort of. I'm surprised you don't remember anything."

"That's my goal these days."

"To pass out?"

"No, to forget."

Chrissy bit her bottom lip with a sad look in her eyes. Her mouth opened as if to say something, but she didn't.

I pulled myself up and sat on the side of the bed. I wondered if my slippers were under it or still in my suitcase.

"I made oatmeal. I know it's one of your favorites. Come eat before it gets cold."

After breakfast Chrissy said, "Let's go to the Mormon Temple on Santa Monica Boulevard. We can sit in the gardens and talk. Dan asked if he could meet us. Are you okay with this?"

"Sure."

It's serene, spiritual and comforts those in turmoil. The words of the Mormon on my first flight into LA echoed in my head.

On the way, Chrissy tried to start numerous conversations, but I hardly spoke. In Westwood, before we entered the temple grounds, she said, "Look, you don't have to talk if you don't want to. We've both been through a lot although my experience is nothing compared to yours. I guess you could say I had bad taste and worse judgment. You had good taste and bad luck."

A chihuahua, dragging its leash, ran straight to Chrissy. A thin lady, holding on to the tether of another one, rushed to us. Chrissy laughed, bent down, patted the little dog, picked up the leather strap, and handed it to the owner. She mumbled some words of thanks and continued walking.

Chrissy looked into my eyes. "In a way, we're back where we started. Thank God we have each other."

I leaned against a wall. "I feel guilty being here. Is this where I should be? Did I abandoned him?"

I hit the wall behind me with my fist and only felt pain when I saw Chrissy look horrified at my scraped hand. She reached forward and held my wrists. I tried to pull loose, but she tightened her grip.

"I can't answer, but there's hope he could be found. Think of the positive. This ordeal will bring you closer. Maybe there's a reason."

"How can a reason exist?" *She's trying to help me, but how can she possibly understand?*

"We have to believe there's a purpose. Look around you. Imagine the faith it took to build this beautiful place. Faith in a God who is good." She released her grip on my wrists.

I turned to face the emerald green lawn. Like a necklace of prized jewels, it surrounded and protected the magnificent temple and the slender trumpet-blowing angel perched on the top.

Dan walked across the grass to us. He hugged me tightly. "Maya, I believe there's a reason for everything. I'm here for you all the way—be it here or back in Lebanon."

"I should have stayed and continued to look for him." My gaze rested on the palm trees that appeared to brush the building like the ones on the Beirut corniche. *Maybe they are an omen.*

"Maya, get real. What could you have done? People more influential and connected than you are working to secure his release. From what I know about Joe, I'm sure he'd want you out of harm's way." Dan's voice remained calm but firm.

"Still, it doesn't seem right." I held back tears.

"It might not feel right, but it *is* right. You made the best choice for now. And you're fortunate to have a life and job to come back to."

"Suppose he's not found? Suppose they've killed him?" I lowered my head and watched my tears splatter on the sidewalk.

"You can choose to think positively or negatively, but nothing will change. I suggest the positive, but it's your choice. No one can force you," Chrissy answered.

"I promise, you will never be alone in your search." Dan squeezed my shoulder.

"I'm beyond grateful for you guys." I looked up at the golden angel with the palm trees swaying below her feet and silently begged for help.

CHAPTER 34

———

America nourishes my potential, but Lebanon nurtures my soul.

— *MAYA*

"Welcome back," John greeted me at the building entrance. He offered me a stiff, awkward hug. When I wrapped my arms around him in return, he sprang back. "Let's get you a badge. The whole department is waiting, and I promised I'd get you there quickly."

He looked thinner, but maybe his new glasses made his face appear longer. As we'd done on the first day we met, we walked down the long corridors. Two people we passed nodded at us. I half smiled at them and wished for a time machine. I could begin all over again with Joe waiting in the future for us to meet. *Could I change the latest chapter? Is our destiny written or can it be changed?*

John made a comment I barely heard. At the same moment, Laura appeared. She ran down the corridor and spared me from asking him to repeat his words.

She grabbed me tightly. "I'm so glad you're back."

The commotion alerted department members who came out of their offices. Laura let go of me but stood very close. I didn't know if it was my imagination, but the mood appeared melancholy. John interrupted the kind pleasantries to announce I needed to get to work. "Consultants are expensive. She's more valuable this time." No one laughed at his attempted humor.

The amount of work I agreed to take on probably made me a cheap, although unenthusiastic, consultant. The wondrous young woman was now a toughened lady. Passionate eagerness replaced with the well-prepared matter-of-fact. However, it helped achieve my goal of less time to worry about Joe. I felt an eeriness. Was Lebanon with Joe a dream, or was California the dream?

Chrissy and I spent most of our free time together and planned weekend trips. We worked a lot—even in the Las Vegas MGM lobby. Men sometimes interpreted two girls working on calculators with papers spread on tables as a unique pick-up technique—until Chrissy's death stare would stop them mid-sentence.

Maman and Papa, trying to sound cheerful, called most Sunday mornings. Rima, rarely home, didn't participate. The conversations seldom lasted more than five minutes, and we generally didn't talk about politics and war unless it directly impacted the family, but I knew they were upset about the late-February pull-out of the US Marines. It was inevitable, and now Iran plotted to strengthen its foothold in Lebanon.

Rima joined a late March call to tell me she and Sammy were getting engaged at Christmastime.

"Hopefully, the situation will be better by then, and you can come home for good," Papa chimed in. He always finished with updates on the search for Joe. He tried to put a positive spin on things, despite the lack of new developments.

Unless you're a fish, you'd better get out. Despite my determination, I woke up every morning to wrestle sadness, trying to keep its snaky head under my foot.

Chrissy only occasionally commented on my demeanor until the evening she came out of the shower and confronted me. "Why do you look more upset than usual?"

"Two guys in the flight simulator control tower recording are talking about me. It isn't uncommon for them to chat when they're not communicating with the cockpit, but listen to this." I pushed the play button.

"She's changed. She used to be delightful to be around. I feel sorry for her, but I don't know what to say to her."

"Yeah. I know what you mean. She's gone from someone you sought out to someone you kind of want to avoid."

I punched the stop button.

"You shouldn't be surprised." Chrissy tilted her head to towel-dry her hair. "I mean, c'mon, you've lost your spark. You're not a bubbly, happy person anymore." She bent forward and vigorously rubbed the back of her head. "I told you, Maya, your attitude is your choice." She spoke in an unsympathetic tone. "It's time for you to start living again. Do you honestly think Joe would want you miserable? He truly loved you, and I think he'd be heartbroken to see how you've become."

"Am I really despondent?" I looked up at her from my position on the floor.

"Yes. I hope to God I never experience what you have, but you owe it to yourself and to Joe to make the *choice* to be happy."

"How?"

"How? Look around at everything you have. You're a smart, beautiful woman with an amazing personality. People liked being around you. You made them feel good. Your smile captivated."

As she pulled the brush through her long hair. I wondered how different my life would be if I hadn't returned home.

"You should start dating. Come with me to Janet's party on Saturday."

"But I'm not invited."

"You don't need an invitation. She doesn't know half the people who show up. It's part of her job." Janet owned an art gallery.

The following day, Chrissy brought dresses and accessories home for me to select. She refused to let me pay for my *rejoining-the-living outfit*. "You look stunning, Maya. I know you're going to turn heads tonight." A couple of years earlier I would have taken it literally.

* * *

On the way home, Chrissy spoke about the doctor we'd met. "I'm glad you gave him your phone number. I worried you wouldn't."

"I couldn't be rude, especially in front of his friend. But Chrissy, he's a doctor. I can't date a doctor. It doesn't feel right." I looked at the cars rushing on the freeway.

"At first, nothing's going to feel right."

"I hope you're right."

"Right, right, right." Chrissy chanted and we both giggled.

"You know, for the few moments I scraped memories from my mind, it felt refreshing. I've missed myself and who I used to be."

* * *

Early the following morning, the ringing phone woke us up. "Leila, is everything okay?" My heart pounded in anticipation.

"Yes, everything's okay."

I collapsed into my pillows and let out a trapped breath.

"Things are the same. Baba's a little improved, but he's still aphasic and incontinent. My mother's handling it better. My brothers are managing Baba's business. Karim's growing fast."

"And Joe? Any news?"

"Every day we hear a new rumor. Sometimes we think one will lead to something, but nothing yet."

I stared at the crumpled bed sheets. "Do you think we'll find him?"

"My brothers are doing everything they can. They've hired a man to help." She sounded tired.

"Are you okay?"

"I'm fine. Life's difficult but we're luckier than most."

"Why don't you take a break and come visit?"

"I tried to get a US visa, but they're making it impossible for Lebanese. I guess they're afraid we won't return home."

"It's not fair how they categorize people. I can't imagine not letting you visit."

"That's not important. I really don't care to go to America. I only want to see you. Can you meet me in Paris?"

"Meet you in Paris? Are you serious?"

"I want to see you."

"It's not easy to leave. I've only been on the job a few weeks, and I have deadlines approaching. How about September when my contract ends?"

"Maya." She sounded exasperated. "I must see you now."

"What's so urgent?"

"Please. Don't ask questions. Just trust me."

"Is it something to do with Joe?"

"It has nothing to do with his well-being, but I need to see you."

"Okay, I'll check my schedule and call you back. When are you going to Paris?"

"I'm calling from Paris. You have to come next weekend. You can leave Friday night and fly back Monday."

"I'll see what I can do."

"Can I speak to Chrissy?"

Chrissy had entered my room when I answered the phone and stood by my bed. I passed the receiver to her and half listened to their conversation, trying to figure out Leila's motive. I knew she could be impulsive, and when she wanted something, she wanted it immediately, but this didn't make sense.

Chrissy spoke, hung up, fetched the phone book, dialed Air France reservations, got put on hold and handed the receiver to me.

"What's this about?"

"Don't really know. She just needs to see you badly. I think you should go."

"It's a long way and a lot of money. It doesn't make sense."

"Leila insisted she pay for your ticket. She's wiring the money to my account. She said it's what her father would want."

"I'm scared she has bad news and wants to tell me in person."

"Or good news. Remember attitude's a choice. Think positive until you hear what she has to say."

"*Bonjour,* I need to make a reservation to Pairs."

Chrissy sat next to me and the moment I finished, she suggested we walk to the beach.

CHAPTER 35

———

*I'll wait for you under the spitting gargoyle of Notre Dame,
every Saturday and Wednesday morning at six. And I will
continue to go and wait until you come.*

—JOE

Nobody stood in the airport taxi line at five fifteen on Saturday morning.

"*Notre Dame de Paris,*" I said.

The driver nodded, and for the next half hour, neither of us spoke. I appreciated the silence. I'd taken a sleeping pill upon departing Los Angeles and felt groggy. I barely remembered the wheels of the airplane touching down and the comforting sound of the thrust reverser.

Almost at our destination, I asked the driver if he knew the location of the spitting gargoyle on the cathedral.

"*Oui, mademoiselle,* he faces *tour Eiffel.*"

"Will you show me, *s'il vous plaît?*"

"*Bien sûr, mademoiselle.* I will tell you where he is, but you must look up very high to see him."

Paris was barely awake as I made my way toward his perch. I knew exactly what he looked like and had imagined this moment before. I repeated in my head the question I had asked Joe many months ago. "*What if something happens and we lose contact with each other? Maybe we have to flee the country separately and have no way to get in touch. What'll we do?*"

"*We'll do what you used to do with your friends at Disneyland. We'll decide on a meeting place.*" His voice was strong in my ear.

"*Where will this place be?*"

"*Pick a city.*"

"*Paris.*"

"*Paris, it is. I'll be waiting for you under the spitting gargoyle on the side of Notre Dame, every Saturday and Wednesday morning at six. And I will continue to go and wait until you come.*"

The cathedral bells began to ring. I rushed to find the gargoyle. I stood under him, tilted my head back and strained my eyes to get a better look at the stone creature. I heard footsteps and spun around. Then I whirled in the opposite direction. Strangers walked by, and each step I heard made my heart race faster. I turned around in circles, slowly at first, looking wildly at everyone. Faster and faster I twirled, looking at nothing until I collapsed onto the ground, spotting the stones with tears.

I saw someone's feet. I gazed up at an elderly gentleman. "*Puis-je vous aider?*" He spun with the cathedral.

Bracing my hands on the moving ground, I hunched and stood. "*Non, merci.*" I stumbled to the church. The world still twirling around me, I tried to enter the cathedral, but the doors were locked. I gazed up at the sculpted tympanum, above the doorway, the Portal of the Last Judgement. I focused on the figure of Jesus and begged for the impossible, crossed myself, and quickly turned away and walked briskly to the café across the street.

I sat by the window and watched the people walk past the empty tables and chairs on the sidewalk outside. I ordered *chocolat chaud* and a croissant but touched neither. In an hour, I would take the metro to meet Leila.

The last time I'd been at Leila's apartment in the 8th Arrondissement was the summer we graduated high school. Her parents suggested the three of us go to Paris for two weeks. Chrissy and I were especially thrilled because we wouldn't have to pay for a hotel. We'd packed a suitcase full of food from the pantries at home because we wanted to spend our money on clothes for college. The surprised look on the face of the French customs inspector when he singled out and opened our food suitcase is still etched in my memory.

He put bags of pita bread, cans of soup, boxes of pasta, and a container of homemade grape leaves on the long table. His supervisor approached. "Don't you think we have food in France?"

He addressed Chrissy, slightly overweight at the time. Leila and I stood next to her and tried not to laugh. She'd get upset when we told her she'd gained weight.

"I want to save my money for shopping," Chrissy said.

The agent shook a box of spaghetti, opened a container to check the contents, and folded a bag of pita bread back and forth. The supervisor nodded at him.

"*Bienvenue en France.* But save some money to try our food. They say it's the best in the world." The men smiled kindly while the three of us threw everything back into the suitcase and hurried away.

Today, I rushed up the familiar steps I'd climbed many happy times before but now with dreaded anticipation. When Leila opened the door, I barely recognized her, and when I hugged her, she felt half the size I remembered. Her puffy eyes looked out of proportion with her thin face, and her normally glossy black hair looked stringy. *Is she sick? Could this be the reason she insisted I come?*

"It's wonderful to see you. Is Karim here?" I stepped into the entrance, trying not to show my dismay at her gauntness.

"No, I'm here for a few days. I can't manage him without his nanny."

"Is he a terrible two?"

I didn't think she heard me. I followed her into the living room. The deep blue velvet curtains were closed, but a slit allowed in a weak shaft of sunlight. The furniture looked dusty. Had the light in the room been stronger, I wouldn't have been surprised to see cobwebs. I wondered how long it had been since her mother was here. She would have brought cleaning ladies and ordered all the windows open to let in sunshine and air while they scrubbed.

I coughed when I sat on the long prickly sofa. I didn't know velvet could become stiff.

"Would you like water?"

"No, thanks." I coughed again.

She ignored my response and brought a glass of water. She handed it to me, stood for a moment, and then sat in a chair to my right with her back to the window.

"How's everyone?" I couldn't think of anything else to say.

"We're all managing despite the miserable situation in the country. We have to stay optimistic, but each day it gets harder and harder. How's LA?"

"It's okay. Sometimes it doesn't seem real. Reality has become a blur. Thank God I have Chrissy. Otherwise I don't think I could cope."

"And your other friends?"

"They're around. Mark's getting married next month. He moved to Santa Clara and works for a company called Intel. He loves computers and technology. It sounds like a great fit for him."

"Haven't heard of it. Is it a good company?"

"I guess. He's a smart guy. I'm sure he checked it out."

"Have you met his fiancée?"

"No. I've only spoken with him twice since I've been back. He mentioned the wedding date but didn't invite me." I looked beyond her and noticed the light trickling in from outside appeared diffused by fog.

She turned around and followed my glance, staring at the nothingness filtering in through the curtain slit.

"Leila. Are you okay?"

She rose, walked to the antique desk in a corner of the room, and retrieved a large manila envelope from the hutch. The tear at the top looked as if it had been opened in haste. "I found this among Baba's papers."

I emptied out the contents onto the coffee table and from the corner of my eye saw Leila slump in the chair and close her eyes. Leafing through several sheets of paper, I pulled out what appeared to be a report. Scanning it quickly, I saw a name I never expected. The apartment fell away. The fog fell away. Leila fell away. Shock and grief surged.

"No!"

"I'm sorry, Maya. I'm so sorry. It's my fault. I was stupid."
She wept uncontrollably.

I buried my face in my hands, braced my elbows on my knees, and sobbed. I didn't know I had this abundance of tears left in me.

Leila moved to sit on the arm of the sofa. "Baba received these papers two days before his stroke. When I found them a few days ago, I couldn't believe it. I showed the report to my brothers. They checked it out, and it appears true."

"But why? Why would Alex do this?" I wept loudly, my words choked by saliva.

"Maya, Alex had Joe kidnapped to prove his commitment to the cause. Don't forget he was the lone—or one of a few—Christians in the group. They probably doubted his loyalty and suspected he might be an infiltrator. What better way to prove his allegiance than to deliver a person like him—one of his own, a friend and a Christian?"

"I thought he was our friend." I spat out wet words.

"And I thought he was my husband. He was the man I loved and defied everyone to marry. These political ideologues play with people's minds, making them believe they have a noble cause. They begin to see lost lives as mere collateral damage."

"How low can someone go?" I started to shake and dug my elbows deeper into my thighs.

"Lower than we'd ever imagine." She stroked my hair with her clammy hand.

"Do you have any news about Joe?" I struggled to make my voice heard.

"No, but my brothers are doing everything possible. They care deeply and know this is Baba's wishes."

"Is there hope?" I needed to ask, despite being filled with dread.

"There's always hope. People are found all the time."

"Alive?" I sobbed.

"Yes." Her voice cracked. "Alive. You don't know how horrible I feel. I wish I'd never met him. How could I have been such a fool and not seen what he was doing?"

"Bastard." I stopped crying uncontrollably and my throat felt desert dry. "I wish I could confront him." I hit my right hand on the sofa, coughing from the dust I'd released.

"Scum. He's not even a human being. Where is he, Leila? Where is he?" I cried.

"If I knew, I would've wrung his throat myself. It's all my fault."

"It's not your fault. It's the fault of our corrupt, narcissistic politicians who manipulate people. They've allowed bastards from other countries to enter ours, and they've created monsters out of morons. Alex being the biggest one." My ears and the back of my neck burned. "No one will ever win. We've all lost, and the rest of the world doesn't care. But like cancer, it will spread and one day reach their shores."

Leila stopped stroking my hair. "I'm sorry you traveled here for this news, but I had to tell you in person."

My throat felt as if it were lined with dusty velvet, and I fought for breath. The walls seemed to close in. Shaking and sweating, I stood up. Emotions collided inside me—anger, confusion, fear, sadness—all wrapped in despair. I felt nauseated. I opened the apartment door and stumbled down the steps.

Leila called after me, but I kept going. I walked, I ran, I slowed down, but I didn't stop. Leila sometimes ran beside me but mostly she tried to keep up. We never spoke a word. Hours later, she coaxed me into a taxi and helped me up the stairs and back into the gloomy apartment.

CHAPTER 36

———

NEW YORK, JANUARY 1985

Some of us have to leave in order to help those who stay; one group works from the outside and the other from within. Only together can we achieve the Lebanon of our dreams.

—AMO MOHAMMAD

As we approached the hotel on Park Avenue, my nervous trepidation intensified. I had not seen Leila since Paris and was thankful to have Chrissy with me this time. Leila had reassured us she didn't have any shocking news, but this provided little comfort.

Chrissy, partly trying to distract me, went off on another of her fanciful tangents. "I wish I'd lived in New York when ladies wore their finest and promenaded down the alleyway between the two hotels. Oh, I would've loved strolling between the Waldorf and the Astoria. I would've been the talk of Peacock Alley."

"Well, now you have to settle for being the talk of the Peacock Bar and Lounge. In reality, that's probably a lot more liberating." I looked up at the skyscrapers.

"I still think I was born in the wrong era. I can easily be the talk of the bar. But being the talk of the Alley would require much more creativity, and I would have been famous." She stopped and posed as if waiting for a photo.

I continued walking, and she took a few skips to catch up. She gave the doorman a half smile and a small nod as he stood at attention, holding the door open.

"In those days, he would have greeted me by name."

We walked up the wide flight of stairs to the level of the lobbies and stopped when we reached the landing to take a slow twirl in appreciation of the spectacular beauty around us. I paused, facing the colored glass windows overlooking Park Avenue. I remembered the stained glass at Notre-Dame. *Would I ever stand here or there with Joe? What news would I hear today?*

Chrissy gently nudged me, I turned around and let out a deep breath.

"Do you think they have tours of the hotel? Let's find out. I'd love to hear the history and see everything. Maybe tomorrow," she said.

We walked in the direction of the central lobby and, on the way, entered the bar. I immediately spotted Leila at the back of the room. She saw us and jumped up from the leather chair by the low cocktail table.

"I can't believe they gave you a visa." I kissed both her cheeks. I stepped aside but she reached for my hand and held on to it while she kissed Chrissy.

"I think they finally realized I wasn't going to give up. After Baba's death, I really felt I needed to get away for a while. One of his friends pulled some strings for me."

"It's hard to believe he's gone," I said. "I truly wanted to come to his funeral."

"I know you did. We all know. But it wasn't the right time for you to come. As much as I miss him, he's better off. He was a smart, proud man and would've been mortified if he'd understood his situation." She let go of my hand, and we sat down.

"My parents said your mother is doing remarkably well."

"She expected it. That was no way for him to live. I know Baba would be very disappointed in us if we wasted our time together being sad."

Chrissy gestured to the waiter, "I'll have a B-52."

"Vodka and grapefruit juice, please." I couldn't think of anything except the potential news about Joe.

"Same for me, but hold the vodka," Leila turned to me as if to say something, but Chrissy interrupted the moment.

"Boring." Chrissy reached for the nut mix. "But I guess that's what happens when you're a responsible mother." She put a handful of the snack in her mouth, and almost as an afterthought asked, "How's Karim?"

"He's doing great. He's really smart—much smarter than I ever was. You should hear how well he speaks English. In our days they made us learn one language before introducing others, but Karim's mastering three at once."

"No bias here," Chrissy said. "It's funny how things turn out. Of the three of us, you were the one who didn't particularly care to have children and look at you now. Whereas Maya, here," she waved her hand in my direction, "used to say she wanted a dozen."

"Did I tell you, I got a divorce in Cyprus?" Leila ignored Chrissy's comments.

"No, when?" I asked, absentmindedly.

"A week before Baba passed away. I also changed Karim's surname to mine. He shouldn't have any connection to his bastard father."

"Do you know anything about him?" Chrissy asked. A cold draft raised the fine hairs on my arms and on the back of my neck. I rubbed my forearms with icy hands. I pressed my legs together and my feet into the ground to steady them. I felt nauseated. I wished they hadn't mentioned him. Neither of them seemed to notice me.

"No, he's totally disappeared. Rumor has it he's in Syria. I hope he's in jail being tortured."

Chrissy snorted. "I doubt it. His kind rarely pays the price. Maybe he can hook up with Omar. Filth begets filth."

The waiter brought the drinks and Leila and Chrissy raised their glasses for a toast before realizing I wasn't holding mine.

"Are you okay?" they asked in unison.

"I'm fine." I didn't want to spoil our time together.

We clinked glasses while they muttered some happy phrases and wishes. I took a long drink and hoped the alcohol would warm me. I noticed two men at the table next to us. When they saw me looking in their direction, one raised his glass and smiled. I looked away, but Leila noticed. "I wonder when I'll have the confidence to be with another man."

Chrissy shrugged. "Life's ironic. Not too long ago we each thought we'd found our soulmates, and here we are, all three of us, alone."

"At least there was one winner. Now we have to find him." Leila glanced at me.

I began to sweat. I wondered if she had news. Anxiety kept me silent.

"Leila, did I tell you I'm dating a wonderful guy?" Chrissy gushed.

"I hope you chose a good one this time."

"He's different from anyone I've ever known. He's an up-and-coming basketball player and…"

Leila interrupted. "What's your opinion, Maya?"

"He seems nice enough. But I told Chrissy I don't see it going anywhere. He's immature and self-centered." *If she had good news, she would have said by now.*

"Hey, I had my shot at true love. and we all know how it turned out. In this phase of my love life, I only want pleasure." Chrissy raised her glass.

"Sounds like you're subscribing to West Coast philosophy. If it feels good and you're not hurting anybody, do it. Wish I could buy into it." Leila shrugged.

"Maybe you should try. I've been pushing Maya to try. She's been on dates with three different guys over the past few weeks. She never wanted a second date with any of them, but I'm proud of her. I know it's not easy, but at least she's smiling more."

Leila shifted in the chair, clearly uncomfortable.

"I'm just trying not to think," I said. "I still dream about Joe. But Chrissy's right. Whether I spend each day in misery or try to make the best of things, it's not going to make him come back any sooner."

The waiter approached. "The gentleman at the next table would like to buy you a round of drinks."

I turned and looked at the man who earlier raised his glass to me. He smiled and nodded. I smiled back and shook my head.

"Please thank him, but we won't accept."

Chrissy turned to Leila. "Wouldn't you like to meet someone special?"

"I don't think I'm interested. I want to fall in love, but the way things are going now, it's going to take a miracle. But for Maya, maybe a miracle is possible."

I glared at her. My face heated and my heart pounded. *Could this be the news I'd prayed for?*

"What do you mean?" My voice sounded feeble.

"You have to come back to Lebanon. There's credible evidence of many Lebanese prisoners in Syrian jails. Those who were deemed of value weren't killed after they were kidnapped. There's reason to believe Joe is among them."

"How do you know?" Chrissy asked.

My head hurt trying to process too many cues at once—the words, Leila's demeanor, her facial expression, hidden meaning…

"My brothers have been working on this for months, but they've reached the point where they need help. They need someone capable of dealing with all sides without being seen as a threat—a person who can keep track of all the information and who will make hardcore men soften by reminding them of their mothers and sisters."

"And you're thinking Maya can do that?" Chrissy asked.

"We believe she's the only one who can. Look, Chrissy, Joe's an only child. His mother is too old and so are his aunts and uncles. All his cousins live abroad. Unless Maya returns, there's no hope for him."

They both looked at me. I focused on the ice cubes melting in my drink. One of them had jagged edges, like my glass cedar.

PART IV

BEIRUT, LEBANON
JUNE 1988

CHAPTER 37

---

*More happiness is derived from the memory of an occasion
than from the actual event.*

— DAN

"I think it's time." Dan squeezed my shoulder.

My eyes lingered on the Mediterranean Sea and its admirable personality. It was mostly calm with its different moods reflected in the changing color of its water. The tragic history it had witnessed was never shared with those standing on its shores. Onlookers saw unwavering beauty. Royal blue, rich indigo, intriguing emerald, soothing turquoise, and misty ultramarine were my favorite shades.

I lowered my gaze from the horizon to the rocks beneath us and watched the water lap at the shore. I felt numb.

Again, he spoke gently. "All life eventually gets reduced to memories, Maya. And short happy ones are more valuable than long painful ones."

In my cupped right hand, I held the necklace of flowers I'd strung together. I raised it to inhale the sweet, soothing smell of jasmine. *Is this how life ends?*

I knew Dan was right. Three and a half years was a long time. Shortly after I returned to Lebanon, he came to visit a friend. Within days he told me he decided to keep the promise he made to me in LA. He planned to stay and help in the search for Joe. He transferred from the graduate program at UCLA to the American University of Beirut. He claimed I'd given him the opportunity to escape a mundane existence and embark on a noble goal. He said I'd done him a favor.

He stayed with me every step of the way. He followed up on leads to Joe's whereabouts. He spent endless days and nights analyzing information with the band of friends and international agencies searching for the missing. He'd risked his own safety to go to shady places and meet sleazy people who claimed to have news of Joe. Most significantly, he provided comfort and hope for Joe's mother. She called him her angel. On the day she died, he held her hand and promised her we'd never give up.

Somewhere along the way he asked me to make him a promise. In return for his help, after he finished his PhD, if Joe hadn't been found, I'd leave Lebanon to build my future in the US. He didn't say we would end the search, rather it would enter another phase. I agreed.

Now he'd accepted an assistant professorship in New York. He and Leila arranged to spend a month in India before he began his job. They'd been dating for almost two years, but beyond their upcoming vacation, they had no plans. They wanted to clear their heads in Deli and plot their future. Her family had come to love and accept the gentle giant who made Leila the happiest they'd ever seen her.

I rubbed the side of my foot against the rough edge of a rock and focused on the soft sound of the waves.

"Maya, you're only saying *until we meet again*. As you say, *hope is forever alive.*" He removed his hand from my shoulder.

I stepped closer to the shore, kissed the chain of white flowers, and tossed them into the azure water.

EPILOGUE

The Lebanese Civil War began in 1975 and lasted fifteen years. The population of the country was approximately 3.5 million. Although the number of casualties is debated, the most established numbers are: 150,000 killed, one million displaced, one million left the country, and 17,000 disappeared.

The war officially ended with the signing of the Taif Agreement, which disbanded the militias, except for one. It allowed the Syrian army to control the majority of the country, and left the Israeli army in southern Lebanon along the border.

The warring factions were not required to provide information on the missing. Both foreign armies have since departed, but the country has never regained stability, dealing with corrupt, vying politicians, an armed organization representing Iran, and regional conflicts. Over forty years later, families still search for information about those who vanished. Hope fades. Loved ones pass away. The basic plea of the need-to-know is still denied.

ACKNOWLEDGMENTS

———

This book was made possible by family and friends. It began in an authors' workshop with Dorothy (D.A. Spruzen) and a group of dedicated writers. Over the years her guidance and generosity of time brought me to the point of publication. In investigating of my options, I was fortunate to be introduced to Georgetown Professor Eric Koester and New Degree Press. My manuscript was accepted by Venus Bradley and I became part of a professional and invigorating community. I would like to thank those I personally worked with: Brian Bies, Michelle Pollack, John Saunders, Kyra Ann Dawkins,, Carol McKibben—my remarkable revisions editor, and Amanda Brown for her astute copy editing.

My children are my tireless supporters. I thank: Tanya for her unlimited coaching and marketing advice, Paul for being my number one salesperson and technical advisor, Karla for her videography and professional skills, Anthony for his fact checking, Mira for her encouragement, Matt for being the first to purchase my book, and Amir for always positively assisting wherever needed.

I appreciate my beta readers, Kip–the lead, Charles, Laura, Lauren, Hania, Paul and Marianne.

I had the opportunity to presale *Glass Cedars* before it was published and I am beyond grateful to the people listed below—both new and old friends, for their support.

You have all made my dream come true.

Kathryn Abdul-Baki

Christine Abi Najm

Julie Aboumoussa

John Abraham

Magid Abraham

Hala Adra

Amir Afkhami

Sadaf Afkhami

John Akkara

Laura Aldrich

Maryam Alexander

Maha Alhassen

Enrique Alvarez

Samuel An

Leonardo Antunano

Elizabeth Armitage

Suha Atassi

Marcia Atsaves

Mari Baker

Amal Barakat

Kate Baroni

Mones Bazzy

Charlene Beaman

Jackie Bechara

Mary Beers

Laila Beidas

April Bellas

Jim Bellas

Nir Benlavi

Joshua Bernstein

Brien Biondi

Andrew Bluestone

Eva Boal

Connor Bolen

Kimberly Bolin

Tripp Bolin

Jeanette Bolton

Georges Bou Saleh

Hillary Brady

Gennady Bratslavsky

Maria Eugenia Brizuela De Ávila

Taylor Brockman

Nancy Brough

Suzette Brynn

Warren Burnam

Salim and Danielle Butrus

Kathy Canzoniero

Laura Capaldini

Stephen Carattini

Jose Carrion

Grace Cater

Maryann Cater
Paul Centenari
Ammar Charani
Grace Chehade
Claudine Chetrit
Dawn Clarke
Christopher Cole
Wayne Cooper
Susan Cosper
Ursula Cuneo
Makenna Curry
Alia Dajani
Madison Danoff
Cathy Davenport
Corey Davison
Ricardo De La Fuente
Abdoulaye Diallo
Carla Dibbs
Tamara Dierman
Alexander Duffy
Thomas Dunn
Patrick Dunne
Anne Eason
Charles Edson
Adam Eiseman
Jaime Ellis
Mayte Escudero
Elizabeth Etoll
Pierre Fares
Mo Fathelbab
Maria Fay
Anthony and Mira Feghali

Gaelle Feghali
Karla Feghali
Lori Feghali
Paul Feghali
Tanya Feghali
Pete Feinberg
Kip Fenton
Penny Firth
Drew Fitzmorris
James and Lauren Foote
Carol and George Frangieh
Ab Freig
Lisa Fulmer
Oula Ghanem
Robert Giaimo
Anthony Ginsberg
Vinod Goel
Katherine Gordon
Mark Gordon
Tyler Grim
Lawrence Gross
Steve Gross
Clay Grubb
Christine Gurland
Fouad Haddad
Tony Haddad
Aida Hafez
Karen Hajj
Karen Hammond
Masu Haque
Sue Harpole
Dorothy Hassan

Stephen Hecht
Gladys Henrikson
Martin Hertz
Richard Hibey
Christiane Huff
Leslie Hughes
Zachary Hughes
Khalil and Blanche Ibrahim
Jessica Ingraham
Catherine Irvin
Zachary Israel
Maha Jabr
Bushra Jabre
Salim Jarawan
Joe Joseph
Leigh Joseph
Talal Kabbani
Raja Kamal
Leila Kamareddine
Shirin Karsan
Myrna Kassis
Amale Katbe
Antoine Katbe
Steve and Francine Katz
Greg Kaufman
Susan Kawmy
Katherine Kelley
Roseanne Khalaf
Meher Khan
Moise Khayrallah
Samir Khleif
Michael Khoury

Stephie Kim
Terry Abdoo King
Michael Kissinger
Harvey Knowles
Eric Koester
Paul Korkemaz
Christine Daya Korkor
Joshua Krandell
Rosalie Learned
Lili Leonard
Megan Lucks
Natalia Luis
Kathy Maalouf
Judy Mackay
Kurt Maggio
Hania Mahmassani
Jamal Malaeb
Mohannad Malas
Diana Mann
Kathleen Manning
Michael Mansy
Maggie Marmo
Kiran Masson
Joseph Matar
Allison McKeever
Brandy Lee McNamee
Beri Meric
Troy Merigliano
Tamara Mezo
Lynne Miller
Brian Miloski
Roget Mo

Amal Mohamed
Elizabeth Moore
Karen Moore
Lauren Morton
Nour Moukarzel
Marianne Moyer
Imad and Tania Mufarrij
Malika Mukhamedkhanova
Nadim Muzayyin
Julia Nasr
Lawrence Neal
Matthew Nellor
Sue Nellor
Marcelle Nemr
Julia Nickles-Bryan
Jessica Nolan
Rosalie Norair
Glenn Nye
Donna O'Reilly
Leslie Parker
Clara Paye
Catherine Paykin
Jeanne Peck
Debra Pielack
Karen Princiotto Irvin
Joe Punaro
Maria Raggambi
Paulette Rainie
Sady Ramirez
Robert Reaves
Denise Reilly
M'Liz Riechers

Ramzi Rihani
Ashley Roberts
Regina Roman
German Rosales Jr
Eric Roudi
Leslie Routhier
Jess, Carolyn and Don Royan
Anthony Rueda
Sonia Runde
Patricia Ruppert
Assad and Rana Saad
Michael Saad
Kongit Sack
Robert Sager
Carolina Santarelli
Mona Sarkis
Karen Schaufeld
Jean Schiro-Zavela
Christopher Schroeder
Susan Scotti
Mitesh Shah
Joy Shanaberger
Matthew Shapiro
Zaynab Shatila
Baria Sibay
Catherine Siddique
Dick Simon
Neal Simon
Gihan Smalls
Stephen B H Smith
Anthony Socci

Gregory Soghikian

Dustin Stahl

Nikki Steltenkamp

Julie and Carl Sterzing

Benjamin Stievater

Kyle Stievater

Jam Sulahry

Greg Sullivan

Nicolas Tabbal

Janet Taborn

George Tannous

Oliver Tannous

Anne Tidwell

Joe Tidwell

Riva Trivedi

Holly Tsourides

David Tucker

Joy Us

Christoph Von Toggenburg

Aline Vorndick

Rany Wahba

Gerrold Walker III

Safiya Walker

Bryant Warmate

George Weckel

Ferris Wehbe

Janeann Welsh

Alyssa Joseph West

Matthew West

Melissa Williams

Kimberly Wilson

Angelina Yager

Karen Yankosky

Sam Zaccack

George and Vivian Zalzal

Karen Zughaib

Printed in the USA
CPSIA information can be obtained
at www.ICGtesting.com
LVHW010551231124
797327LV00063B/990